George Gresley Perry

The life of St. Hugh of Avalon, Bishop of Lincoln

George Gresley Perry

The life of St. Hugh of Avalon, Bishop of Lincoln

ISBN/EAN: 9783337414559

Printed in Europe, USA, Canada, Australia, Japan

Cover: Foto ©Raphael Reischuk / pixelio.de

More available books at **www.hansebooks.com**

THE LIFE

OF

ST. HUGH OF AVALON

BISHOP OF LINCOLN

With some Account of his Predecessors in the
See of Lincoln

By GEORGE G. PERRY, M.A.

CANON OF LINCOLN

AUTHOR OF 'LIFE AND TIMES OF BISHOP GROSSETESTE,' ETC.

To drawen folk to heven with fairenesse,
By good ensample was his besinesse:
But it were any person obstinat,
What so he were of highe, or low estat,
Him wolde he snibben sharply for the nones.
CHAUCER.

WITH A PORTRAIT

LONDON
JOHN MURRAY, ALBEMARLE STREET
1879

TO

THE RIGHT REVEREND

CHRISTOPHER WORDSWORTH, D.D.

BISHOP OF LINCOLN

THE SUCCESSOR OF

St. Hugh

ALIKE IN HIS VIRTUES AS IN

HIS SEE

THIS LITTLE WORK IS DEDICATED

BY ONE OF HIS CLERGY

PREFACE.

———

SOME time ago, after the publication of the *Metrical Life* and the *Great Life* of St. Hugh, Bishop of Lincoln, both edited by Mr. Dimock, I determined to endeavour to give to the English reader this interesting biography, as I had previously done that of Bishop Grosseteste. Learning, however, that another volume relating to St. Hugh was to be expected from the same able editor, I naturally deferred the completion of my work till this appeared. The unfortunate illness and death of Mr. Dimock, which deprived historical students of a most valuable guide, retarded the publication of the expected volume (vol. vii. of the Works of Giraldus Cambrensis) for several years. At length it has appeared, the able editorship of Mr. Freeman supplying what was unfinished by Mr. Dimock. It contains, in addition to the Legend of Remigius printed by H. Wharton, a Life of St. Hugh by Giraldus, previously inedited ; the Legend of St. Hugh, adapted for reading in church

on his festival; the Lives of the Bishops of Lincoln
by John de Schalby, a canon of Lincoln of the fourteenth century; and the account of the canonisation
of St. Hugh.   But very little new matter (if we except
the miracles) in addition to what was already known
of St. Hugh from the *Magna Vita*, is to be gleaned
from these sources.   A few additional facts are, however, recorded, of which the most important, perhaps,
is Hugh's great fondness for birds and squirrels, and
his power of taming and domesticating them, which
was shown both at the Grande Chartreuse and at
Witham.   This illustrates, and to a certain extent
explains, the singular story of the swan.   With regard
to the lives of St. Hugh's predecessors but little new
matter is obtained from the *Chronicles of John de
Schalby*, with which, indeed, I was previously acquainted in Dr. Hutton's *Extracts*.   The biography
of St. Hugh which I now present to the reader may,
therefore, be considered as a compilation from all the
various Lives of the Saint edited by Mr. Dimock,
but drawn, to by far the largest extent, from the
Magna Vita.   With regard to the lives of St. Hugh's
predecessors, no such rich and abundant mine of information as the *Magna Vita* is accessible.   The
notices of these are drawn from the chroniclers of
the general history of the country, with such help as
could be obtained from the local knowledge of Gi-

raldus and John de Schalby. Giraldus, the talented Welshman, was the Scholar of William de Monte, Chancellor of Lincoln during the last years of the twelfth century, and he was also probably again resident in Lincoln some years later. John de Schalby, a canon of Lincoln, can be proved by various documents to have written about 1330; but as he had access to all the local memoranda, his work has almost the same value as a contemporary history. It is unfortunate that both these writers, who might have supplied to us such vivid and authentic sketches of the bishops of whom they wrote, should have given only such jejune and concise notices as, in fact, they did. This, however, makes us value all the more the rich, full, and varied details of the *Magna Vita* of St. Hugh.

WADDINGTON, *January* 1879.

CORRIGENDA.

Page 56. Bottom line, *For* " brother " *read* " father."

,, 57. Note 1, *For* a " fuller account " of Herebert, *see* the admirable Life by the Dean of Norwich.

,, 96. Note, line 2, *After* " the " *read* " fourteenth.":

CONTENTS.

CHAPTER VII.

CHAPTER VIII.

CHAPTER IX.

CHAPTER X.

APPENDIX.

CHAPTER I.

THE PREDECESSORS OF ST. HUGH.

THE see of Lincoln, to which Hugh of Avalon succeeded in the twelfth century, was not known from its beginning by this name, nor had it always for the site of its Cathedral Church the grand position which the taste and judgment of Remi the Norman selected for it. Its earlier history is chequered and obscure; nevertheless, sufficient facts are ascertainable to enable us to trace the succession of its bishops from the Scotch Diuma, the disciple of St. Finan, down to the Monk of Fescamp, the last bishop of Dorchester and the first of Lincoln. What amount of Christianity may have existed in Lindsey during the Roman period, it may be impossible now to discover. Some, however, there doubtless was in a city so important in . Roman days as Lindum-Colonia. The first historical notice of the faith of Christ in that which was afterwards the see of St. Hugh, is connected with the preaching of Paulinus and the zeal of the Bretwalda Eadwin. The man "tall of stature, with stooping gait and black hair, of meagre

$\mathcal{SL}$ B

visage and aquiline nose, venerable and majestic aspect,"[1] who baptized in Trent, near to "the city called in the English tongue Tiovulfingacestir," vast numbers of the people, in the presence of King Eadwin ; who built a stone church in Lincoln of beauteous workmanship, and therein consecrated Honorius, Archbishop of Canterbury, was the real founder of the Church of Lincoln (633). But the labours of Paulinus were well-nigh effaced by the ferocious heathenism of Penda, King of the Mercians, who slew in battle, first Edwin, the disciple of Paulinus, and then Oswald, the pupil of St. Aidan. Whether before his death Penda relaxed in his heathen fierceness (as one passage in Bede indicates), or continued a heathen persecutor to the end (as another passage seems to imply),[2] it is certain that the cause of Christianity in Lindsey gained by his overthrow and death at the hands of King Oswiu, on the field of Wingfield (655). For Peada, the son of Penda, had been won to Christianity by his desire to obtain in marriage the Northumbrian Princess Ethfleda, the daughter of Oswiu, and together with his Christian bride, he had brought with him from Northumbria four of the disciples of St. Finan,— Diuma, Betti, Cedda, and Adda. These priests preached the gospel among the Mid-Angles,[3] and on the death of Penda, when the authority of Oswiu and his son-in-law extended throughout Mercia, Diuma was·

---

[1] *Bede*, ii. 16.   [2] Compare *Bede*, iii. 21 and 24.
[3] *Anglo-Saxon Chronicle.*

consecrated by St. Finan "bishop of the Mid-Angles, Lindisfaras, and Mercians."[1] His position was that of a missionary bishop, and he is said by Bede to have died at Reppington, in Derbyshire. To him succeeded Ceolla, a Scotchman, who returned soon after his consecration to Iona, and to Ceolla succeeded Trumhere, an English abbot. The next bishop of the Mercians was Jaruman ; after him came Ceadda or Chad. In him we come to one who holds a more distinct place in Church History, and who was one of a family which did much for the planting of the Church in this land. Chad was one of four brothers [2] who were all in holy orders and all eminent for their missionary work. Cedda, probably the eldest of these, had been one of the priests who came with Diuma, and after preaching among the Mid-Angles, had gone southward, and became eventually the second bishop of London. Chad had been consecrated by Wini, Bishop of Winchester, to fill the see of York in Wilfrid's absence, and had then given way to Wilfrid, and had been made bishop of the Mercians, being (on account of some canonical irregularities) reconsecrated by Archbishop Theodore, in 669, and located at Lichfield. Thus Lindsey would seem to have somewhat lost ground, but it was soon to have a bishop of its own. In the time of Saxulf, next bishop but one to Chad, the Northumbrian Prince Ecfrith conquered Lindsey from the Mercian King

---

[1] *Bede*, iii. 21, 24.
[2] Cedda, Cynibil, Caelin, and Ceadda or Chad.—*Bale.*

Wulfere, and appointed Eathed, his chaplain, Bishop of Lindsey. He was the first bishop who had that province by itself,[1] but in the following year he was expelled, on the reconquest of Lindsey by Ethelred, and Saxulf's authority restored. Nevertheless Lindsey was not to remain long uncared for. In 680 Archbishop Theodore, after consultation with other bishops at the Council of Hatfield, and by the consent of Ethelred, divided the large province of Mercia into five sees, the northernmost of which was that of Lindsey.[2] What, then, was the place of this see? Florence of Worcester says that it was "in the town which is called Siddena," and from various indications we may gather that this Siddena or Sidnacester was the modern Stow. For, when the Lindsey bishopric, after two centuries of existence, was overthrown in the Danish wars, and like another of the Mercian sees, Leicester, was transferred to Dorchester, the bishops of Dorchester, often also described as bishops of Lincoln,[3] had a peculiar care for Stow. Thus " Eadnothus II., Bishop of Lincoln, built in the famous place which is called in English the *Stou* of St. Mary, but in Latin the place of St. Mary, a church which Leofric and Godiva enriched

---

[1] *Bede*, iv. 13.

[2] The others were Lichfield, Leicester, Worcester, Hereford. It is doubtful whether the see of Dorchester existed at this time. It had been founded by Birinus (635), but was removed to Winchester. *Bede* (v. 23) makes no mention of Dorchester. Dorchester became part of the Mercian kingdom (778). During the Danish troubles it became a convenient place for the Mercian see.

[3] *Simeon Dunelm.*, 169, 175. *Rad. de Diceto*, 475 (Ed. Twysden).

with ornaments of great price,"[1] and Wulfwig, the last of the Dorchester bishops, executed a charter of grants to the church there. The *Anglo-Saxon Chronicle* speaks of the death of a bishop of Dorchester in the year 897, who is said to have been consecrated 886, and this marks about the time when the Northern Mercian sees were transferred to this more secure locality. But as both Lincoln and Leicester grew again into great importance under the Danish sway, being two of the "five burghs," it is evident that the episcopal superintendence of this part of Mercia could not long have remained at Dorchester, even if the Norman invasion had not occurred. Had, however, the return of the see to the north taken place before this, it might have been a question between Stow and Lincoln. The one could plead ancient prescription, the other a rising and constantly increasing weight in the land. The stimulus which had been given to Lincoln under the Danes continued under the sway of the English family. Coleswegen had founded the lower town of Wigford, and had built therein churches in honour of St. Mary and St. Peter.[2] There was also, besides a St. Mary in Wigford, another St. Mary's on the hill, which had its endowment of land, an All Saints' Church,[3] and the old Church of St. Paul, or, it may

---

[1] *Simeon Dunelm.*, p. 189 (Ed. Twysden).

[2] See Mr. Freeman's Preface to *Girald. Camb.*, vol. vii. p. lxxv.

[3] Both these are mentioned in the Survey. St. Mary Magdalen was incorporated into the Cathedral, and afterwards removed out of it.

be, of Paulinus.   Lincoln was already on the way to
be described as "one of the most populous cities in
England,"[1] and the same policy which marked it out
as the site of a strong castle would also mark it as
the site of a cathedral church.   For the policy of
the Conquest was not one of sentiment but of power.
The great talent of the Normans was that of organisation.   The less systematic English might tolerate
the existence of cathedral churches in villages, but
this arrangement could not commend itself to the
Normans.   With them the cathedral was to exist not
for itself, but for the diocese.   It was not merely to
pray and teach, but to govern.   Thus, with them the
ancient traditions and ecclesiastical claims of Stow
would avail but little against the rising importance
of Lincoln.   There, after four hundred years of
chequered and struggling life, the great Mercian see
was to reach its final home ; and in Hugh of Avalon
it was at length to find a saint, whose life and work
should cast a glory round the new site, and enshrine
it in the affections of the people.   In reviewing
somewhat more in detail the lives of the predecessors
of St. Hugh in the new home of the see, it may be
well to say a few words first of the immediate effect
produced on the Church of England by the Norman
Conquest.   The most important effect was its introduction into it of new vigour and life.   William of
Malmesbury, claiming to be impartial, as drawing
his origin from either race (*utriusque gentis sanguinem*

---

[1] *Will. Malmesb., de Gest. Pontif., s. v. Remigius.*

trako), says : " Is it not the case that the whole island is
resplendent with such great relics of native saints that
you can scarce pass a village of any note without hearing the name of some new saint ?   And of how many
has the memory perished for want of writers !   Nevertheless, the pursuits of literature and of religion
became obsolete as time went on ; and for many years
before the coming of the Normans the clergy were
contented with a mere haphazard instruction, so that
they could scarcely stammer out the words of the
sacraments.   Any one who should chance to know
grammar was an object of astonishment and a standing miracle to the rest.   The monks, using elaborate
dress and a diet in no way differing from other
people, cast ridicule upon the notion of a rule.   The
great men, given up to gluttony and lustfulness, were
not in the habit of repairing to church early in the
morning, as Christians should, but in bed with their
wives, carelessly listened to the solemnities of matins
and mass, which the priest hurriedly recited."[1]   Of
the Normans he says : " They raised up, by their
coming, the practice of religion, which was all but
utterly dead in England before their arrival.   You
might see everywhere, in cities, towns, and villages,
churches and monasteries rising in that new style of

---

[1] *Willelm. Malmesb., De Gest. Reg. Ang.*, iii. § 245.   See also
Roger de Wendover, ii. 3 (E.H.S.), who adds :—" Clerici quoque et
ordinati adeo literaturâ carebant ut ceteris esset stupori qui grammaticam
didicisset ; potabatur ab omnibus in commune qui tam dies quam noctes
in hoc studio produxerunt.   In cibis urgebant crapulam, in potibus
vomicam irritantes."

architecture which they had adopted."[1]   That this increased efficiency of the Church was reached by the
way of great injustice and harshness towards the
native clergy is not to be doubted.   A wholesale
expulsion of English bishops and ecclesiastics followed
the Conquest, and in their place were appointed men,
often, no doubt, more able administrators, but not so
acceptable to the people, nor so competent to instruct
them in their own tongue.

If the Church became more vigorous, it became
less national.   That peculiar feature of the Early
English Church which consisted in the union of
the spiritual and civil jurisdictions, was sacrificed.
William made a complete separation as regards
the administration of justice between temporal and
spiritual things.   But while reserving the latter
absolutely to spiritual judges, he at the same time
asserted a supremacy over the Church similar to that
afterwards claimed by Henry VIII.   He enacted
that the English Church assembled in council might
pass no laws or canons but such as he had recommended or approved.   He also ordained that no
chief tenant of the Crown might hereafter be excommunicated, except by his special precept.[2]   Scarcely
less important was the extension now made of the
feudal tenure to the lands of the Church.   All
ecclesiastical lands were made liable to knights'
service, and entered in a roll which Matthew Paris

[1] *Willelm. Malmesb.*, *De Gest. Reg. Ang.*, iii. § 246.
[2] *Eadmer*, p. 6 (Ed. Selden).

designates as the roll of ecclesiastical servitude.[1] In
these changes Lanfranc and the Pope, if they had
not heartily gone with the king, had nevertheless not
opposed him, but in another great change which he
attempted their Church feeling was excited to opposition. He had mercilessly plundered the monasteries, holding, as the chronicler who assumes the
name of Ingulphus states, that monks of English
race could only bear him ill will.[2] But his policy
was to go farther than this. He wished altogether
to break the power of the monastic body by introducing at the great centres of Church influence—the
cathedral cities—bodies of secular canons in place of
monasteries. It was argued that monks, who were
for the most part laymen, could not properly be a
council to the bishop, such as he ought to have in
his cathedral ; that the proper office of a monk was
not to govern, but to pray. In these views William
was strongly supported by his bishops, who
dreaded the independent spirit of the monasteries,
and thus the Norman Bishop of Lichfield proceeded
to take violent measures for expelling the monks, and
Walkelin, Bishop of Winchester, prepared a body of
forty canons to supplant the monks of St. Swithun's.
The same policy was projected for Canterbury, and
was successfully accomplished at Lincoln.[3] " The
monastic cathedral," says Mr. Stubbs, " was an in-

---

[1] *Matt. Par., Hist. Maj.*, p. 7 (Ed. Watt). *Roger de Wendover,*
ii. 7. [2] *Ingulphus*, p. 86 (*Anglia Sacra*).
[3] *Eadmer, Hist.*, p. 10 (Ed. Selden). See Inett's *History of
English Church*, ii. 60.

stitution almost peculiar to England.   The missionary bishop, himself a monk, accompanied by a staff of priests who were also monks, settled in the chief city of a kingdom or province.   He built his church ; his staff of missionary monks became the clergy of that church ; the church itself was called a monastery."[1] But as the dioceses were subdivided, the new sees had not the same character.   They were founded in the principal places of the district, and the bishop was surrounded by a staff of secular clergy, who after a time took the name of canons.   The distinction between the two classes of cathedrals had not perhaps been of much moment in earlier times, but, as the papacy advanced in power and pretensions, and it was seen more clearly by the popes that the regulars were the great prop of their power and claims, it became much more important.   Thus it was by no means a trifling matter for the improvement of the Church that the Conqueror should, in pursuance of his policy for checking the English, declare so decidedly for secular establishments of canons rather than for monks.[2]   But here the archbishop, a monk, and possessed by the spirit of his order, and the Pope, who saw the strength to be gained from the isolated communities of monachism, refused to go with him.[3]

---

[1] Preface to *Epp. Cant.*, p. 21.

[2] At the time of the Conquest York, London, Hereford, Selsey, Wells, Exeter, Rochester, Lichfield, Dorchester, and Thetford were secular—Winchester, Worcester, Sherborn, Durham, and Canterbury were monastic.—Stubbs' Pref. to *Epp. Cant.*, p. 23.

[3] *Eadmer, Hist.*, p. 10.

A letter from the Pope forbade the contemplated change at Winchester, and that designed for Canterbury had also to be abandoned.   But, at any rate, if the monastic foundations could not be at once got rid of they would not be extended and increased.[1] The monk, dedicated in early youth, not in any way selected for capacity, growing up in a routine of duties which narrowed and dwarfed the mind, without any opportunity of seeing the world and studying the manners and minds of men, could not, except by a happy accident, be a valuable adviser to the bishop. But the secular canon, selected by the bishop for his high qualities, engaged in active life, with a reputation for learning, or sanctity, or administrative power, would equally of necessity be a valuable aid.   Hence, to take the case of Lincoln alone, both St. Hugh and Bishop Grosseteste in the twelfth and thirteenth centuries, acknowledge the greatest obligations to their canons, and it is certain that the canons of Lincoln of that era included some of the foremost Churchmen of the day.

Another great element of strength brought to the Church of England by the Conquest was the wonder-

---

[1] It appears, however, that Rochester, which was composed of secular canons at the time of the Conquest, was changed into a monastery by Gundulfus.   In his life, by a *Monachus Roffensis*, we are told that the possessions of the church of Rochester were placed in his hands under the condition that monks should be established.   Of the five clerical canons who were found there some joined the monastery, and the number of monks was increased to sixty.   *Vita Gundulfi, Anglia Sacra*, ii. 280.

ful taste and skill in architecture possessed by the
Norman prelates. In almost every see in England,
new and splendid cathedrals sprang up under their
hands, elevating the thoughts and deepening the
devotion of the faithful. Nor did they fail, in
the midst, indeed, of many grievous oppressions,
to work substantial improvements in the social condition of the people. It is an eternal disgrace to
the Anglo-Saxon Church, which enjoyed such considerable power, that it should have tolerated the
open practice of the selling by their proprietors of
their serfs as slaves to the Irish. Remigius, the
first Norman bishop of Lincoln, vigorously opposed
this horrible practice, and St. Wulfstan, an Englishman indeed, but under Norman rule, and by
the aid of Norman laws, was able to put it down.[1]
Nor was this the only social improvement wrought
by the Normans : "never had the king's peace been
so good, never were murder, robbery, and violence
so unsparingly punished as under the Conqueror."[2]
It was not alone by their stately churches, their
superior skill, their higher learning and polish, that
the Norman prelates worked a reformation, or at any
rate an improvement, in the English Church. They
boldly met, and to a certain extent abated, the crying evils of their time. They were peremptory and
domineering, often, doubtless, tyrannical, for the

---

[1] A graphic description of the Anglo-Saxon slave-trade, as carried
on at the port of Bristol, is given by William of Malmesbury in his *Life
of St. Wulfstan*.   [2] Pearson, *Early and Middle Age*, i. 291.

laissez-faire carelessness of the Anglo-Saxon was not of their nature. But they showed many examples of indomitable energy devoted to the highest ends ; of great designs carried out, sometimes with a deficient scrupulousness as regards the means, but always with the utmost vigour. The leading race in every country of Europe in the eleventh and twelfth centuries, they maintained also their character in England. Alien though they were in language and birth, yet the force of character often availed to overcome the disadvantages belonging to their foreign origin, and to attract to them the affectionate regard of the people. Thus Hugh of Avalon, a more complete stranger to the English than any Norman, soon, by the influence of the beauty of his character, became the most popular man in England. Of his foreign predecessors in the see of Lincoln the first was Remi, a monk of Fescamp in Normandy.

REMIGIUS, FIRST BISHOP OF LINCOLN—
1067-1094.

The work done by this prelate in first building the splendid church dedicated to St. Mary, which crowns the hill of Lincoln—the liberality and great-heartedness which were apparent in his work, and which are freely ascribed to him by all chroniclers, —these, as well as other traits which we can gather of him from the scanty notices which remain, naturally dispose English Churchmen to regard Remigius

with reverent affection.   It is, however, not to be
forgotten that there is something to be put on the
other side—that the way in which he reached his
dignity—perhaps, also, the nature of the employments in which he was previously engaged, are by
no means free from scandal.   All we can say is that
the irregularities of his episcopal commencement were
eclipsed by the splendour and excellence of the administration of the office which he reached, and though
he can never stand on the same eminence as Hugh
of Avalon and Robert Grosseteste, yet that in many
ways he challenges our admiration and gratitude.

The chroniclers assert [1] that Remigius, a Norman monk of Fescamp, bought (*emerit*) an English
see prospectively of Duke William, for certain
assistance furnished to him in fitting out his expedition against England ; that after his consecration
he made a journey to Rome, to seek for absolution,
and by his voluntary cession of his episcopal staff
into the hands of the Pope, distinctly confessed the
simoniacal act.   The exact valuable consideration
paid for the episcopal appointment is variously told.
In the roll of the assistants of the Conqueror, he is
set down as providing a ship and twenty fully armed
knights ;[2] Giraldus Cambrensis says, a ship and
ten men at arms.[3]

---

[1] William of Malmesbury says : "Willielmo Comiti Normannorum
in Angliam venienti auxilium in multis præbuit, episcopatum si vin-
ceret pactus."—*De Gest. Pontif., s. v.* Eadmer says *emerit*, in which he
is followed by Radulph de Diceto, Brompton, Knyghton, etc.

[2] *Palgrave*, iii. 607.   [3] *Op.* vii. 14.

Eadmer, Radulph de Diceto, and others, say that the work which Remigius had done for the Norman duke was of many and various sorts, and that the expenses which he had incurred were manifold.[1] And here arises a somewhat curious question. Remigius was a monk of the monastery of Fescamp, and the treasurer of that establishment. Were the monies which he dispensed " in manifold ways," and especially in hiring a ship and armed men, the monies of the monastery, and if so, were they expended with the consent of the house? or were they, being in the power of the treasurer, perverted to these uses, which were to benefit himself alone, while the brethren were unable to find redress, because the judge to whom they would appeal was deeply committed against them?[2] Probably the house of Fescamp, inspired with a patriotic ardour for the success of the Norman arms, and hoping probably for some marks of favour for itself if .the expedition should succeed, may have authorised this disposal of its funds. Of the life of Remigius previously to his being brought into notoriety by the Norman expedition, it is not to be expected that much should be recorded. There is one circumstance of it, however, mentioned by Henry

---

[1] *Eadmer*, p. 10 (Ed. Selden). *Radulph de Diceto*, p. 483 (Ed. Twysden).

[2] It seems to be pretty certain that whatever was done by Remigius was done by consent of the whole body, from the fact of the great honour done to Fescamp when the Conqueror went to keep Easter there after his return from England in 1067.

of Huntingdon, which is important as illustrating his eager and ambitious character. He evidently had been a person long well known to and in favour with Duke William, but suspicions had arisen as to his fidelity to his lord. He had even been formally accused of treason, and the accusation had been so far supported or believed that he had been called upon to clear himself from it. It was probably a mark of favour from the Duke that he was allowed to make this purgation by ordeal, and an ordeal in which the test was to be applied not to himself but to one of his servants. The test applied was the walking over or grasping in the hand heated iron, and the servant was able to do this so successfully that the charge against his master was held to be disproved, and he was again reinstated in the royal favour.[1] Duke William, with his secret plans and long covert preparations against England, needed active and intelligent agents, especially among Churchmen. Lanfranc served him well at Rome, and doubtless Remigius did in Normandy. "In many things he gave useful aid," is the expression of Brompton and Knyghton, and the zeal (contentio) which is ascribed to him by Eadmer, Radulph, and other chroniclers[2] was extremely valuable when so many held back, and so much unwillingness was

---

[1] *Henry of Huntingdon. Brompton*, p. 983 (Ed. Twysden). "De regia proditione fuerat impetitus, sed famulus ejus judicio ferri igniti dominum purgans regio amori restituit et maculam pontificis detersit."

[2] *Radulph de Diceto*, p. 483. *Brompton*, p. 983. *Knyghton*, p. 2348 (Ed. Twysden). "In multis opitulatus."

manifested among Duke William's men to undertake
what must have seemed to most of them a hopeless
enterprise.   Of this energetic and intelligent monk
the most distinct information which remains is that
which describes his personal appearance.   He was
far below the ordinary height, so much so as to be
fairly described as a dwarf.   Nor does it appear that
he had anything to compensate in width of limb for
his deficient height.   He was as slight as he was
short, and so small that he seemed to men to be
almost a strange and monstrous creation.[1]   Nor was
this all.   His complexion was not of the ordinary
colour of the Western European, but tawny or
brown.[2]   But the mention of his appearance only
gives to the chroniclers the opportunity of adding by
way of antithesis, "though little in stature he was
great in heart," "though dark in complexion he was
brightly beautiful in works," for all, without exception, sing his praises for the work which he did for
the Church in England.   The monk of Fescamp,
who had long been so useful to Duke William in
arranging the preliminaries of his great expedition
against England, embarked with his master on that
perilous venture.   It was William's policy to give as
much of a religious character as possible to the
expedition.   He carried with him the papal bulls
and the sanction of the Church.   He denounced
Harold as one who had perjured himself after swear-

[1] Præ corporis exiguitate pæne portentum videbatur." *Willelm.*
Malmesb., De Gest. Pontif.   [2] "Colore fuscus."

ing over holy relics, and a large number of priests
and monks accompanied him on his voyage. Among
these the little energetic monk of Fescamp soon distinguished himself. He, in all probability, was " the
monk of Fescamp" who acted as a messenger
between the two armies, carrying William's reply to
Harold's message, when he loftily upbraided him
with his treachery and offered to decide the quarrel
by single combat.[1] And it is probable that he did
not limit his aid to such ministrations, but, though so
small in stature, was, with Odo of Bayeux, the war-
like bishop who said mass with his armour under his
rochet, in the thick of the fight at Senlac.[2] The
Norman cause triumphed, and Remigius soon saw
himself within reach of his high aspirations. In the
very next year after the landing of Duke William,
Wulfwig, Bishop of Dorchester, died,[3] and Remigius
was at once promoted to the vacant see. He was
consecrated by Stigand, Archbishop of Canterbury,
and made his formal promise of canonical obedience
to him,[4] in all probability before the journey of
William into Normandy, when he carried with him
Stigand, Edwin, and Morcar, and all those likely
to be dangerous to him if left behind in England.

[1] *Guill. Pictav. Guizot, Memoires*, 29, 397. William of Poitiers
solemnly declares that he relates the exact words of the message as it
was delivered, and invented nothing.

[2] Henry of Huntingdon says " Bello interfuit."—*De Cont. Mundi.*

[3] He died at Winchester, but was buried at Dorchester. *Hoveden*,
p. 278 (Savile). *Simeon Dunelm.*, p. 197 (Ed. Twysden).

[4] See the Instrument given, p. 23.

For Stigand, although doubtless already marked
out for the ruin which. afterwards overtook him,
could not as yet be assailed with impunity, as it
was William's desire to lull the English to security.
So long, then, as he remained as metropolitan he
must needs do the acts pertaining to his office.
When he should be afterwards declared to be uncan-
onically bishop it would be easy to remedy, by the
Pope's intervention, any informality which might
attach to those on whom he had laid hands. Great
must have been the joy and triumph with which the
new Bishop of Dorchester returned with his conquer-
ing master to the home which he had left a simple
monk. The Conqueror proceeded with every circumstance of pomp and triumph throughout his
Norman dominions. At Rouen orations were pro-
nounced in his praise likening him to the most
famous conquerors of Rome, and declaring his glory
to have exceeded that of Cæsar. But Remigius was
destined to witness and share in the greatest glory
of the triumph at his own abbey of Fescamp. " It
was during the Paschal feast at Fescamp that the
great display was made. Here were exhibited the
choicest treasures of the English kings ; the results
of foreign commerce and national industry which
had rendered England so flourishing amidst every
calamity. William had invited to this feast a host
of the nobles of France, who, mingled with Normans
and Britons and Flemings, were the spectators of his
honour and glory. The guests raised with wonder,

as they quaffed from them, the huge buffalo horns, tipped with gold and silver, often emptied before at the carouses at Westminster and Winchester. Lamps and coronals which Bagdad and Byzantium might have prized, bespoke the skill of the craftsmen of London and Canterbury ; curtains and tapestries which had decked the halls of the Confessor, or the bower of his Queen ; robes and garments heavy with embroidery, worked by those who were now weeping for the husband or the son. 'More wealth has the Duke brought over from England,' was the general exclamation, 'than could be found in thrice the extent of Gaul ;' and the learned priest declared how England might be called another Araby for gold, and the very granary of Ceres for fertility. But the wealth of England scarcely excited so much interest as the aspect of the more youthful among the strangers ; their race still retaining that personal beauty, the long tresses of flowing auburn hair which first led the great Gregory to seek their conversion."[1] Of course, in putting into the hands of Remigius this huge see, extending over a great part of England, William knew that he was entrusting power to one in whom he could thoroughly confide for carrying out his policy and supporting his cause. No one saw more clearly than this acute chief that the principal strength of the English resistance would be in the Church, in the great sanctuaries of the monasteries, and in the secret correspondence which might so

[1] Palgrave, *Hist. of Normandy and England*, iii. 413.

easily be kept up by Churchmen one with another. Hence his carefully chosen appointments of Norman prelates, and hence the wholesale deposition of Saxon bishops and abbots which took place soon after in the Council of Winchester. "The king took especial care," says the chronicler, "that as many as possible of the English stock should be deprived of their honour, that he might put in their place persons of his own nation to strengthen his newly acquired kingdom. Thus some bishops and abbots, without any cause, or any condemnation either by Church or State law were condemned, deprived of their honours, and kept in prison for the rest of their lives."[1]   In place of these suspected persons a careful selection was made of those who would without scruple or hesitation support the Norman regime. "The Duke," says Eadmer, "desirous to preserve in England the customs and laws which he himself and his fathers had been wont to support in Normandy, took care to make bishops and abbots of persons of such sort as would scorn the notion of not obeying what he commanded, whatever other consideration might intervene ; and none of whom would dream of standing out against him in any matter whatever. They were all well aware from whence they came and for what purpose they were brought there ; all things therefore, both divine and human, were waiting for his nod."[2]

---

[1] *Simeon Dunelm.*, p. 201 (Ed. Twysden).
[2] *Eadmer, Hist. Nov.*, p. 6 (Ed. Selden).

. The promulgation and announcement of this ecclesiastical policy of the Conqueror was made at a council held at Winchester in 1070. At this synod, probably, Remigius was not present. Its object was to depose Stigand and some other of the Saxon bishops. The fact of his having been consecrated by Stigand, and thus having been made partaker of whatever canonical irregularity attached to him, would prevent him from sitting in judgment in such a matter. Indeed he may be regarded rather as one being tried than as in a position to act as judge at Winchester. The judgment of the council, and the deposition of Stigand, touched him nearly, inasmuch as he himself had been consecrated by these uncanonical hands.[1] Hence, after the consecration of Lanfranc, and the visit to Rome presently to be mentioned, before professing canonical obedience to him, Remigius made a " profession" as follows :—
" At the time when I, Remigius, was chosen Bishop of Dorchester and Leicester, and of the province of Lincoln, and the rest of the provinces over which my predecessors presided, Stigand was presiding over the holy church of Canterbury. For, despising the smallness of the church of Elmham,[2] he had been translated to the see of Winchester, and, his ambition stimulating him still farther, after a few years, partly by force partly by craft, he drove out Robert, the

[1] Giraldus Cambrensis, in the account he gives of Remigius, says he was consecrated by Lanfranc, but this is an error.

[2] The original of Norwich, Elmham, is only a small village in Norfolk.

archbishop, intruded himself into the metropolitan see, and feared not to usurp the pall which Robert had brought from Rome, carrying this off with the other things. When this audacity was heard of at Rome, he was frequently summoned by the Roman pontiffs [but paying no heed to them], he was at length condemned and excommunicated. Yet for nineteen years, in the obstinacy of his heart, he remained in the see, during which time Leo, Victor, Stephen, Nicholas, Alexander, were Popes, and each sent their legates in their own time into England, and prohibited by their apostolical authority any one going to Stigand for ordination. I, however, not being altogether informed about the matter, though I was not entirely ignorant,[1] came for ordination to him, made profession of obedience to him and his successors, and received the episcopal charge from his hand who consecrated me. After a short time the before mentioned lord Alexander sent his legates into England and ordered him to be deposed, and all those who had been ordained by him either to be cast out or to be suspended from their offices. But I, when you, O Lanfranc, the prelate of the same metropolitan see, went to Rome, approached the aforesaid Pope, and by your mediation asked for and obtained indulgence. Knowing, therefore, by the authority of the said Pope, that he never was your

---

[1] There is a naïveté about this confession. Of course Remigius must have known all about so notorious a matter as Stigand's feud with the Pope. It consorted, however, with William's policy that he should be consecrated by him, and *some* excuse must be made.

predecessor, and that you are not his successor, I here offer to thee my written profession of obedience, and promise that I will obey thy commands and those of thy successors."[1] By the end of the year 1070 all the great posts in the English Church were in the hands of foreigners. Lanfranc was Archbishop of Canterbury; Thomas, a canon of Bayeux in Normandy, Archbishop of York; Walkelin, Bishop of Winchester, and Walkerine, Bishop of Durham. The sees of Norwich and Chichester were filled by Herefast and Stigand, Lichfield by Peter, Salisbury by Herman, and Lincoln by Remigius, all Normans. And those bishops who were allowed to remain in their places were chiefly such as had been advanced by the Norman faction under King Edward, being foreigners, and for the most part Normans. Of this number was William, Bishop of London, a Norman; Leofrick, Bishop of Exeter, born in Burgundy or Lorraine; and Giso, Bishop of Wells, a Frenchman —so that except Wulfstan and Siward, Bishops of Worcester and Rochester, there was not one bishop in England by the end of the year 1070 who was not in the Norman interest. Lanfranc was consecrated on the 26th August 1070, and among the eight consecrating bishops we find the name of Remigius, Bishop of Dorchester and Lincoln.[2] After his consecration Lanfranc consecrated Thomas, Arch-

---

[1] *Professio Remigii*, printed in *Girald. Camb. Op.* vii. 151. See also Dr. Inett, *Ch. Hist.*, i. 479.

[2] *Willelm Malmes.*, *De Gest. Pontif.*, f. 117 (Ed. Savile).

bishop of York, having been careful to exact from him professions of subjection and canonical obedience, which Thomas at the first convenient opportunity endeavoured to set aside.   Soon after, having been thus raised to the highest dignity of the English Church, Lanfranc, as a dutiful son of the Pope, prepared to go to Rome, taking with him Archbishop Thomas and Bishop Remigius, both of whom, as well as himself, needed a friendly exercise of the supreme power which was supposed to reside in the Romish see in order to the removal of certain difficulties and scandals attaching to them.   The chroniclers all agree as to this journey to Rome having been made by the bishops, but as to what took place there some have much stronger and more damaging statements than others.   If we are to follow William of Malmesbury, a writer living within fifty years of the events, and one of the most accurate and trustworthy of our annalists ; Eadmer, a monk of Canterbury, who wrote in the earlier part of the twelfth century ; Radulph de Diceto, Dean of St. Paul's in the latter half of the twelfth century; Brompton and Knyghton, whose date was somewhat later, but who are yet held to be trustworthy writers, that which took place at the interview of Lanfranc and his attendant bishops was as follows :—At the entry of Lanfranc into his presence, with Thomas and Remigius attending him, Pope Alexander, preventing by a gesture his advance to make the customary prostration, rose up and advanced to meet him.   " This honour," he said, "we pay you, not on account of your office of Archbishop, but because we would do reverence to the master from whose teaching we have learned all that we know. You may now perform that which becomes you out of reverence to the blessed Peter." The Pope then retired to his seat, and Lanfranc prostrated himself at his feet, but was immediately raised up and saluted with the kiss of peace. The Pope then presented Lanfranc with two palls, one the usual pall given to an archbishop, taken from the altar, the other that in which he himself was wont to say mass, which was designed as a special mark of his love. Having been thus conspicuously honoured, Lanfranc could with the greater confidence present himself before Alexander again on the following day to transact the business of Remigius and Thomas. He went through the form of himself making a charge against each of them. Against Thomas, that being the son of a priest, he was by the canons prohibited from any advance to an ecclesiastical dignity ; against Remigius, that "he had made an agreement, and so bought his bishopric of William, who had afterwards become king, for the price of the service which he had done in helping him when about to make his expedition into England, by zealous aid of many sorts, and manifold outlay of money." Neither of these, said Lanfranc, desired to defend themselves or had any excuse to offer. They resign their pastoral staves into the hands of the Pope that he might do with them as he pleased. Yet, said the archbishop, if I may be allowed to plead for those who have been guilty of these irregularities, I would urge upon your Holiness that "both of them are men of great and varied learning and knowledge, and both especially necessary to the new king in the new arrangements of his kingdom which he is carrying out."[1] The little comedy had doubtless been all rehearsed before, and it was played out to the.end with becoming gravity. Moved by the appeal of Lanfranc, the Pope, holding the pastoral staves in his hand, turned to him with a bland smile. "Look you now," said he, "you are the father of that country to which these men belong, let your wisdom and prudence consider and judge that which is fitting. Here are the pastoral staves which they have returned, take them, and make use of them as shall seem to you most advisable for the support of the Christian religion in that land." Upon this, Lanfranc taking the emblems of the episcopal office from the Pope, restored them to Thomas and Remigius.[2] After having been thus skilfully extricated by the Archbishop of Canterbury from the dilemma of his birth, it might have been thought that Archbishop Thomas would show a becoming gratitude, and not

[1] Multarum rerum scientiâ fultos, novo Regi in novis regni dispositionibus pernecessarios."—*Eadmer*.

[2] *Eadmer, Hist. Nov.*, p. 6 (Ed. Selden). *Willelm. Malmesb.; De Gestis Pontif. Angl.*, p. 122 (Ed. Savile). *Radulph de Diceto*, 483 (Ed. Twysden). Immediately after this it is probable that Remigius made his profession (given above), renouncing Stigand and promising allegiance to Lanfranc.

bring before the Pope anything likely to vex and annoy his patron. Such, however, was not the case. The opportunity was too important to be lost. The conflicting claims of the metropolitical sees of Canterbury and York had never been thoroughly settled, and the new occupant of the northern primacy now made a bold attempt to effect the equalisation of his power with that of his southern brother. "He acted in this matter," says William of Malmesbury, "more from ignorance than from ambition and obstinacy. For he was a man new to the country, and altogether ignorant of the customs of England, and more than was fitting was disposed to believe the words of flatterers." Thomas grounded his claim on a supposed constitution of St. Gregory, which decreed that the two archbishops should be equal, but that the right of precedence should belong to the seniority of consecration. But it was not only this equality which Thomas claimed. He claimed the subjection to him as metropolitan of the three sees of Lincoln, Worcester, and Lichfield, saying that these three bishops had always been suffragans of his predecessors. Remigius was then directly interested in this matter, and that had come to pass already which he had been told would happen when first he began to prepare for his church at Lincoln. The Archbishop of York had already claimed him as one of his suffragans. But the rights of Canterbury could not be in better hands than those of Lanfranc. He, says William of Malmesbury, was greatly annoyed by the claim which Thomas made before the Pope, but he contented himself with simply denying the truth of the Archbishop of York's assertions, and pointing out that the constitution of St. Gregory did not refer at all to the relations of York and Canterbury, but to those of York and London.   The Pope immediately and very wisely declared that this was a matter to be judged in England by a solemn council of all the chief ecclesiastics of the land, and could not be satisfactorily disposed of on *ex parte* statements at Rome.   Accordingly, soon after the return of the three bishops from Rome, a council was held at Windsor (1072), and after much and long debate the primacy was clearly assigned to the see of Canterbury, while the limits of its metropolitical jurisdiction were declared to be marked by the river Humber towards the north, all northward of this being under the jurisdiction of the Archbishop of York.[1]   At the council Remigius was present, and signed the acts of it as Episcopus Dorcacensis.   It would no doubt be a relief to him to have the question settled, and to find himself still under the headship of his friend and patron Lanfranc, and he would proceed with his great work at Lincoln with renewed vigour.   The question, however, was destined to emerge again, and at a time when it could not be so well met by him as now.

A man of so active a spirit as Remigius was

[1] *Willelm. Malmesb., De Gest. Pontif.,* f. 121 (Ed. Savile). *Wilkins,* ii. 325.

no doubt not long absent from his diocese, and the work which he had projected, perhaps already commenced, at Lincoln.   If we are to believe Giraldus,[1] his devotion to his episcopal work was intense and his success marvellous.   He found the flock which had been committed to his charge stained with the most grievous sins, ready, according to the chronicles, to sell the sons which they had begotten into slavery, and their daughters for prostitution,[2] thinking perjury, adultery, and incest but trifling crimes, and holding the promiscuous intercourse of the sexes as nothing.   Therefore, with preaching and instruction, this vigorous pastor and untiring eradicator of vice began to apply his earnest zeal.   He brought his influence to bear on his whole diocese from one end to the other, and, arranging all things with tender care, he ceased not to go all round it, and to penetrate into every part, until, as far as might be, he had rooted out these grievous enormities,

---

[1] The account of Remigius by Giraldus was written professedly to obtain canonisation for him, which would have been an immense profit to his church, and is no doubt full of exaggerations (see Mr. Dimock's Preface to Giraldus, vol. vii.), but yet may contain some elements of truth.

[2] *Willelm. Malmesb., Vita St. Wulfstani.*   Sir F. Palgrave says : "Slavery was exceedingly extended.   Hard as the situation of the Theowe was in earlier periods, it had now become infinitely worse. The provision, merciful to a certain extent, which prohibited the sale of the slave out of his native country, was entirely violated, and it was the common practice to sell these miserable creatures to the pagan Danes in Ireland ; so that Bristol was the regular slave-market, and the English connected their slave-dealings with disgusting profligacy." —*Hist. of Normandy and England*, iii. 336.

and like a good shepherd and not a hireling, had planted virtues in their place. And when these things were excellently well done, this magnanimous man of God then gave his whole care to the finishing of his church and the final preparations for its dedication.[1] In the year 1075 was held the council of London under one of the Pope's legates. In this council it was solemnly decreed that all episcopal sees should be transferred from *villæ*, small towns or villages, to *civitates*, larger towns or cities. The particular sees mentioned are Sherborne, which was to be transferred to Salisbury, Selsey to Chichester, and Lichfield to Coventry. But *no mention is made* of the transfer of Dorchester to Lincoln—a clear proof that this transfer had been formally effectuated before this date. Remigius was present at this council, and signed the acts of it as Episcopus *Lincolniensis*, without any addition of Dorchester. The grounds of the change from Dorchester to Lincoln are thus given by the chronicler, Henry of Huntingdon :—" The bishopric of Dorchester on the Thames was by far greater than any in England, extending from the Thames to the Humber, and Remigius, its bishop, who had been a monk at Fescamp, thought it altogether inconvenient and troublesome that, at the very extreme limit of his diocese, and at a town which he disliked on account of its smallness, the episcopal see should remain, when there was in that see the

[1] *Vita Remigii, Girald. Camb., Op.* vii. 20.

very famous city of Lincoln,[1] which seemed to him far more worthy of the episcopal residence. Therefore, on the very highest point of that city, near to the castle, soaring aloft with its strong towers, he bought certain lands and erected a church—strong as the place was strong, and fair as the place was fair— dedicated to the Virgin of virgins, which should be a delight of all servants of God, and, as befitted the time, unconquerable by enemies."[2] The charter in which William confirms the change of see, issued after the council of London 1075, treats the change as having already taken place, and the church at Lincoln as having already made some progress towards establishment. The charter, directed to all' sheriffs within the diocese of Remigius, bids them know that it was by the advice and authority of Alexander the Pope[3] and his legates, and Lanfranc the archbishop, and the other bishops, that transferred the see from Dorchester to Lincoln, and sufficiently

---

[1] Lincoln was at this time almost purely Danish. It was the chief of the five Danish burghs, and was governed by twelve hereditary *Lawmen*. This government subsisted during the whole time of the Conqueror. In spite of the Conquest the inhabitants of Lincoln continued in alliance with the Danish kings ; so that a treasure belonging to the Scandinavian monarch was permanently deposited there, either concealed from the Norman or too well guarded for him to attack it.— *Palgrave*, iii. 346. William of Malmesbury says of Lincoln that it is "one of the most populous cities of England, and a great mart for men coming to it both by land and *Sea*."—*De Gest. Pontif. s. v. Remigius.*

[2] *Henricus Huntindon*, p. 213 (Ed. Savile), followed almost verbatim by *Brompton*, p. 983 (Ed. Twysden) and others. Giraldus says that the place where the church was built had been marked out long before by abundant miracles, prophecies, and visions.—*Anglia Sacra*, ii. 415.

[3] Alexander died at the beginning of 1073.

endowed it[1] there with lands free and quit of all claims, with a view to the construction of the mother church of the whole diocese and the buildings required therewith. " Desiring, however, for the good of my soul, to give this church some benefit, I first grant to it two manors, viz., Welton and Sleaford, with their belongings, and next, the churches of three of my manors with their lands and tithes, namely Kirton, Caistor, and Wellingore. I add, also, all the tithe of the whole rent of the same manors, and two churches in Lincoln, namely Saint Laurence's and Saint Martin's. Besides, at the special request of Remigius the bishop, I grant to the same church a certain manor called Leicester, and which Earl Waltheof had already given to the said bishop by my hand,[2] and a certain other called Woburn,[3] which I had formerly granted him with the episcopal staff. Four churches also, namely, Bedford, Leicester, Buckingham, and Aylesbury, which his predecessors had held, and which I had given to him for perpetual possession with his consent and the consent of the said church, with all their appendages, I grant in perpetuity, and by my royal authority confirm."[4] Thus, under

[1] Compare this with Henry of Huntingdon's words that it was Remigius who bought the required lands.

[2] That is, Earl Waltheof had given it to the king to give to the bishop, but the king had retained it for a short time until Remigius had been obliged to ask for it.

[3] The manor of Woburn was alienated by Remigius from the see for the benefit of his kinsman Deincourt or Deyncourt, in which family it long remained.—Churton's *Life of Smyth*, note, p. 95.

[4] Dugdale, vi. 1270.

D

royal favour, and amidst a shower of royal gifts, did the energetic bishop commence and carry on the building of his grand church. The astonished people of Lincoln beheld designs, dimensions, and richly elaborate details of carving and grouping of which they had before no conception. The Norman builders, with new and strange powers, and mechanical appliances, rapidly advanced in their work. The "famous church" of St. Mary of Stow, built by Eadnothus, was now thrown into insignificance, by the new and larger building.

It was probably soon after this that the king issued the important charter which follows :[1]—

"William, by the grace of God, King of the English, to the Earls, Sheriffs, and all persons whether French born or English who have lands in the bishopric of Remigius. Know all of you and all other my subjects who abide in England that we judge it right to amend the Episcopal laws which have hitherto been in England, inasmuch as they are not good nor according to the precepts of the sacred canons. Wherefore, having taken counsel with and by the advice of the archbishops, bishops, and abbots, and all the chief men of my kingdom, I command, and by my royal authority direct, that no bishop or archdeacon should any longer hold pleas on the Episcopal laws in the Court of the Hundred, nor allow any

---

[1] There is another copy of this charter, being a direction from the king to the people of Essex, Hertfordshire, and Middlesex.—*Inett*, ii. 101. It is a very remarkable and important document, as it is, in fact, the instrument which established the separation between the civil and ecclesiastical jurisdictions in England.

cause which relates to the cure of souls to be submitted to the judgment of secular men, and that
whosoever shall be indicted under the Episcopal
laws for any cause or fault, must come to the place
which the bishop shall choose and appoint for this
purpose, and there answer in his cause, and not
according to the laws of the Hundred, but according
to the canons and Episcopal laws must do right to
God and his bishop.   But if any one, elated by pride,
shall be unwilling to come to the bishop's court, let
him be summoned once, twice, thrice, and if then he
will not come let him be excommunicated ; and if
there be need that this be enforced, let the power
and justice of the king or the sheriff be made use of.
But he who having been summoned to the bishop's
court has refused to come, for each summons shall pay
a fine according to the Episcopal law.   But this I
forbid, and by my authority interdict, that any sheriff,
or king's officer, or any layman whatsoever should
interfere with the administration of the laws which belong to the bishop, or that any layman should try and
sentence another layman (in such matters) without
the judgment of the bishop, and trial is to be held
in no other place save the Episcopal see, or that
place which the bishop shall appoint for the purpose."[1]

This fundamental change in the administration
of the law, the distinct separation between secular

---

[1] *Dugdale's Monasticon*, vi. 1270, quoted from an *Inspeximus* of
Henry VI., *Rot. Lit. Pat.*, 8.   *Rymer, Fœdera*, i. 3 Henry VI., p. 2,
m. 10.

and ecclesiastical, the introduction of the entire body of the canon law as part of the law of the land, had effects of almost incalculable importance on the future history of England. It doubtless gave efficiency and vigour to the Church, and may have been needed for the present necessity, but it erected a dangerous *imperium in imperio* which, in the unscrupulous hands of popes and legates and bishops, became an intolerable burden and galling slavery. Half our history is henceforth occupied with the disputes between the civil and ecclesiastical powers, and with the attempts, more or less successful, made by outraged kings and parliaments to control the abuses and pretensions of their rivals. One immediate effect of this change was its necessitating the appointment, with a definite local jurisdiction, of archdeacons and rural deans as disciplinary officers of the bishop. These officers had existed in Saxon times, but it does not appear that they had any special work to do in the diocese, but now they were assigned districts with special courts and powers, the archdeaconry generally following the limits of the county, the rural deanery that of the Hundred.[1] In the treatise written by Henry, Archdeacon of Huntingdon, in the next generation, we have the names and some characteristics of the first occupants of the seven archdeaconries into which Remigius divided his vast diocese. Richard was the first archdeacon of Lincoln, "the most wealthy

---

[1] See *Inett*, ii. 103, 104, who quotes Bishop Stillingfleet *On the Duties and Rights of the Parochial Clergy.*

archdeaconry," says the chronicler, "of all that are in England." Nicholas presided over the counties of Cambridge, Huntingdon, and Hertford. "Than him there was none more beautiful in body, and the beauty of his life almost equalled his bodily comeliness, and when about the time of his death the county of Cambridge had been separated from our bishopric and had received a new bishop,[1] I myself succeeded as archdeacon to the two other counties." Nigel was made archdeacon of Northampton, Ralph of Leicester, Alfred of Oxford. Buckingham was given to a clerk known as "Alfred the little." The seventh archdeaconry, that of Bedford, was entrusted to Osbert. "All were most honourable clerks and venerable persons."[2]   Remigius thus provided for the supervision and discipline of his diocese, while at the new headquarters of the see he hastened forward with all zeal the building of his grand cathedral church, and of the houses destined to accommodate the twenty-one canons who were to minister in it. Fortunate we must believe it to have been for the efficiency of his work, and salutary in its influence on the future of his church, that he did not set himself to reproduce at Lincoln an establishment similar to that in which his early life had been spent, but adopted an arrangement of far greater power and capacity. The monastery of Fescamp, tracing back its origin to the Mero-

---

[1] Diocese of Ely separated from the diocese of Lincoln 1109. Its first bishop was Harvey.

[2] *Henric. Huntingdon, De Contemptu Mundi, Anglia Sacra,* ii. 695.

vingian kings, honoured by the favours and visits of dukes and princes, distinguished by rules and customs of its own, which were admired and imitated by others,[1] must have seemed to him who had been one of its chief officers worthy of all honour, and the temptation to him to reproduce the abbey of his youth in a daughter house worthy of its glory must have been strong to Remigius. But what Lanfranc, the learned and politic archbishop, could not bring himself to do at Canterbury, though he must have seen as clearly as any man its importance, Remigius did at Lincoln. He rejected the monastic system and chose that of secular canons, following the customs of the church of Rouen[2] rather than striving to reproduce the monasticism of Fescamp. At what precise period the cathedral church was finished is not easy to determine. It probably was completed in all essential parts some considerable time before that which was ultimately fixed for its consecration. Remigius, says Simeon of Durham, feeling his health failing, was anxious to dedicate his cathedral church, but Thomas, Archbishop of York, continually resisted him,[3] declar-

---

[1] Roger de Hoveden tells us of a terrible disturbance in the Abbey of Glastonbury, when Thurstan of Caen, appointed abbot by William the Conqueror, endeavoured to supersede the old Gregorian method of chanting, and to introduce the use of "a certain William of Fescamp." The abbot brought soldiers to coerce the monks, who were repulsed, and several persons were slain and wounded.—*Roger de Hoveden*, p. 263 (Ed. Savile). *Simeon Dunelm.* (Ed. Twysden), p. 212.

[2] *Giraldus, Opera*, vii. 19.

[3] The imperfect tense is used, from which a repetition of the resistance may be inferred.—*Simeon Dunelm.*, p. 217 (Ed. Twysden).

ing that it was built in his diocese.   The claims of
the Archbishop of York to have Lincoln as his
suffragan, decided against him by the Council of
Windsor, had, it seems, now been changed into a claim
that Lindsey was actually part of his *parochia* or
diocese, and an exchange had to be negotiated with
the archbishop before he would give up his claim to
the district north of the Witham.   Giraldus says
that the church was finished in a short time ;[1] but
whatever was the exact time taken in completing it,
it is not probable that Remigius waited for its absolute completion before appointing the dean and
canons who were to officiate therein.   We have
the testimony of Giraldus that he did actually
appoint twenty-one canons, assigning them the prebends which were to be their support, and the altars
at which they were to officiate, and the oblations
of which they were to receive.

Having thus prepared the building and those who
were to minister in it, Remigius was earnestly desirous
to put the finishing touch to his work by procuring
the consecration of his church.   But difficulties stood
in the way so as to hinder this end being reached.
While the Bishop was distinctly conscious that his
own death was drawing near,[2] the Archbishop of York

---

[1] *Op.* vii. 19.   Henry of Huntingdon says,. "non segniter opus
inceptum peregit peractumque clericis doctrinâ et moribus approbatis-
simis decoravit."—Ed. Savile, p. 213.   It is evident, therefore, that
Remigius did appoint the first canons, though he did not live to see
the consecration of the church.

[2] *Roger de Hoveden*, f. 265 (Ed. Savile).

still doggedly and unreasonably opposed the consecration of the church on the ground that parts of
the district of Lindsey, and specially the towns of
Lincoln, Stow, Louth, and Newark, were legally
within the diocese of York, and had been wrongfully
purloined from his predecessors.[1] Such a claim
would not have mattered much had Lanfranc been
at hand to refute it and advise the king how to act,
or if the king had been a wise and resolute prince
as the first William was. But the Conqueror and
the Archbishop were both gone,[2] and the young king,
absorbed in his quarrels with his brothers, was not
inclined to pay much attention to Church affairs,
save to rob and spoil wherever he could find an
opportunity. The province of Canterbury was without a head, the king was unrighteous, misapplying
its revenues ; how then was Remigius to obtain that
which his soul desired, the authority for the consecration of his church as a suffragan church of the see of
Canterbury ? There was but one way of influencing
William Rufus, a prince who " feared not God, neither
regarded man," and that was by offering him a bribe
large enough to make him bestir himself in the matter.
The bishop doubtless grieved that the great and pious
act of the dedication of a church to Almighty God
should have to be procured in this way, but there
was no help for it ; neither could the charge of
simony be fairly made against him for this, as it had

---

[1] *Act. Pontif. Ebor.*, Stubbs. Twysden, p. 170d.
[2] Lanfranc died 1089.

probably often been made for the way in which he procured his appointment to the see. Accordingly he gave a large sum of money to the king to induce him to forward the work,[1] and, influenced by this, William sent forth a general mandate to all the bishops and abbots of England to assemble at Lincoln, in readiness to consecrate the cathedral church on Sunday, May 9, being the Sunday after Ascension Day. For the Archbishop of York and his claim over Lincoln, Louth, Stow, and Newark, an exchange was promised,[2] and though this prelate was still unsatisfied, yet the decided action of the king, and the general consent of the prelates who hastened to obey the royal orders, were too strong for him openly to resist. To second the king's edict, and to procure as general an obedience to it as possible, Remigius added, on his own part, pressing invitations to the bishops and abbots.[3] His mind was set on having as large and splendid an assembly as possible, and as he was probably persuaded that this would be almost his last ecclesiastical act on earth, he desired to make it a worthy one. There was a universal readiness to come. The fame of the splendid building, the reputation which Remigius enjoyed

---

[1] *Henry of Huntingdon, Roger de Hoveden.*

. [2] *Giraldus, Anglia Sacra*, ii., 415. The exchange probably was the same which afterwards was given when the matter of the consecration of Bloet was settled, namely, the abbey of St. German in Saleby, and the church of St. Oswald in Gloucester. This by no means satisfied the archbishop, but he was obliged to accept it. See *Inett*, ii., 118.   [3] " Magnanimi viri hortatu."—*Willelm. Malmesb.*

for munificence, attracted all.   Long and great had
been the preparations which Remigius had made to
receive his brethren with an hospitality worthy of
the occasion,[1] and before Ascension Day, May 6, 1092,
all the clerical magnates of England, with one
notable exception, had either arrived at the cathedral
city, or were on their way thither.   The exception
of which William of Malmesbury tells us was, if his
account be true, a very strange one.   " Robert, Bishop
of Hereford," he says, " had refused to come because
by inspection of the stars he had certainly convinced
himself that the dedication would never take place
in the lifetime of Remigius, and this he had said to
many."[2]   The Bishop of Hereford proved a true
prophet.   When all difficulties had been surmounted,
all preparations made, and nothing remained but for
the heart of Remigius to be rejoiced by seeing his
great work consummated, and the noble building made
the House of God for ever, suddenly, on Ascension
Day, which was also the feast of St. John before the
Latin Gate (May 6), the bishop was cut off, and the
frail and feeble body which had enshrined a great
spirit lay still and lifeless.[3]   A more tragical and
remarkable incident it is hardly possible to conceive,
nor one more likely to strike awe into the hearts of

[1] *Giraldus, Op.* vii. 21.

[2] *Willelm. Malm., De Gest. Pontif.,* f. 165 (Ed. Savile).

[3] Most of the chroniclers say Remigius died two days before the
day fixed for the consecration ; Giraldus says the fourth day.   There
is no contradiction, as the interval between Ascension Day and the
Sunday might be described either way.

the great ecclesiastics, not all of them men of God, who were preparing to assist in the ceremonial. The service of dedication was changed into that of a funeral, and the builder of the stately fabric, the dwarfish Norman monk, clever, vigorous, energetic, generous, perhaps unscrupulous, took lasting possession of his church by being interred within its walls in front of the altar of the Holy Cross. The stone that marked his tomb may still be seen, though it has long ceased to occupy its original position. According to Giraldus, in a great fire which took place in the cathedral thirty-two years after Remigius's burial, part of the roof fell, and broke in two the stone which covered the grave. The canons then determined to transfer the body to a more retired part of the building. The tomb was opened with due reverence. The body was found fresh and intact, and it was re-interred on the northern side of the altar of the Holy Cross. The sudden death of the bishop naturally put an end to the projected consecration, and some years were to elapse before the new cathedral was finally dedicated to God.

The church built by Remigius ended towards the east in the favourite Norman form of an apse, its termination being just a little within the present choir. The apse was not formed merely by internal arrangement, but was structural. On each side of it were apsidal chapels, and farther west was the ritual choir, over which was raised on arches a lofty tower nearly in the same position that the present central tower occupies. North and south of the ritual choir were narrow transepts which are supposed by some to have been furnished with upper chambers. Then stretching westward from the central tower to the extent of eight fine arches, was built the long nave with its aisles on either side of it, the whole forming a span of some seventy feet. The roof was formed of wooden panelling highly ornamented. At the west end were three great recessed entrances, and a tower rose on either side as the termination of the aisles. The very small portions of the work of Remigius which remain will not allow us to judge much as to the amount of ornament expended upon it. There was no doubt an imitation of the church of Rouen in the structure as well as in the other arrangements of the church. But the church of Rouen has also perished, so that the actual appearance of the first Lincoln cathedral must be left a good deal to the imagination. "The three arches of entrance, with their great height and cavernous depth, must have had a very good effect, and the western façade with its north and south gables, would not only form an excellent screen to the whole church, but would give great variety and a new circumstance of light and shadow to the sides of the nave."[1] We may gather from the chroniclers that as the church of Remigius was one of the first of the great Norman churches finished in England, so it was one of the

[1] *Architectural History of Lincoln Minster*, by Rev. G. A. Poole. Proceedings of Lincoln Archæological Society for 1857.

finest.   Like the second cathedral church of Alexander, and still more the church of St. Hugh as it
stands at present, the notable fabric on the hill at
Lincoln was not easily to be surpassed.

ROBERT BLOET, SECOND BISHOP—1094-1123.

From the history of the first Norman bishop of
Lincoln, whose character and doings were in many
ways remarkable, we pass on to one less distinguished
indeed, but who, nevertheless, did not fail to leave
some mark in the history of the see, afterwards made
so famous by the virtues of St. Hugh.

When William, the great duke, lay slowly dying
at the monastery outside Rouen, his sons[1] were
impatiently waiting by his bed-side to hear his will
about the succession.   He declared that he could
not leave the kingdom of England to any one, as he
had not inherited it, but acquired it by force—that
he replaced it in the hands of God, but that he
desired his son William to inherit it.   Being requested
to express this wish in writing, he indited a letter to
Archbishop Lanfranc to signify his pleasure.   This
letter was entrusted to one of his chaplains named
Robert Bloet.[2]   Immediately on receiving it Bloet
hastened away, accompanied by William.   Eager to
anticipate all opposition, they did not wait for the
king's death, but yet, fearing probably impediments
which might be put in their way, they did not embark

[1] " The English-born Henry was not at hand."—*Freeman*, v. 75.
[2] Sir F. Palgrave calls him the " Conqueror's confidential chancery
clerk."—*Normandy and England*, iv. pp. 14, 55.

at one of the ports which lay directly in their route,
but took a considerable détour to Touques, from
whence they sailed to England.[1]   Before, however,
they had left France they heard the news of the death
of the king, and William, still, doubtless, accompanied by the chaplain, hastened to Winchester to
take possession of the royal treasure.   Archbishop
Lanfranc readily yielded to his dying patron's wishes,
and William II. was crowned by him September 26,
1087.   Some of the ill-gotten treasure of the Conqueror was directed by his successor to be distributed
to the churches of England, and in this work Robert
Bloet would doubtless be useful to the new king.
Each principal cathedral and monastery received ten
marks of gold, besides many other rich presents of
crosses, candlesticks, and ornaments for the altar ; the
parochial churches received 5s. apiece, and the poor
of each county one hundred pounds.   It must have
been sorely against the grain of his covetous and
grasping nature, that William Rufus made these
largesses, supposed to be " for the good of the soul "
of his father, and if any Churchman, deceived by these
gifts, expected to find in the new king a liberal
patron, their hallucinations were soon dispelled.
From the very beginning of his reign William Rufus
set himself steadily to extract everything that was
possible out of the Church.[2]   He refused to fill up

---

[1] *Ordericus Vitalis*, b. x. ch. 11.

[2] William of Malmesbury says : " Vivente Lanfranco archiepiscopo
ab omni crimine abhorrebat."   But Lanfranc soon followed the Conqueror to the grave.

vacant sees and abbeys, and without a shadow of right appropriated their revenues. Ordericus Vitalis says : " For the sake of the revenues which the king's avarice gathered into his treasury, the churches were suffered to remain vacant, and deprived of their proper pastors, the Lord's flock were exposed to the ravages of the wolves. Of the reverend prelates that died the rents and property were for a long time in the hands of Flambard and his brother Fulcher. On the death of any abbots the king's officers seized the monasteries through the whole of England, with all that belonged to them, supplying the monks with a very moderate allowance of food and clothing, and paying the surplus of the revenues into the royal treasury. At last, after a considerable time, the king conferred these ecclesiastical dignities on clergy and monks who were about his court, as if they were stipendiaries, promoted not for their religion, but for the obsequiousness of their services in secular affairs. Thus Robert Bloet, who had been chaplain to William the elder, was, after the death of Remi, promoted to the see of Lincoln."[1]

But it was not until struck by a sudden pang of remorse and fear that this appointment was made by the wicked king. After the death of Remigius the see of Lincoln was at once handed over to the tender mercies of Randolph Flambard or Passeflambard, a man of such notorious and extraordinary wickedness that even in those evil

[1] *Ordericus Vitalis*, b. x. ch. 2.

days he obtained a bad pre-eminence. "There was none," says the chronicler, "more astute and subtle in doing ill than this man. The churches which were given him he spoiled of all their goods; rich and poor alike were reduced by him to so great need that they would rather die than live under his power."[1] William of Malmesbury has left us a powerful sketch of this miscreant, who was afterwards actually raised to the dignity of Bishop of Durham, which, as also giving a picture of the times, is worth reproducing. "The mind of the king, inclined to unjust gains, was farther excited in its covetousness by one Ralph, a clerk, who by power of speaking and by cunning had raised himself from the very lowest class to the highest. This man, whenever the king had ordered the land to pay a specified tribute, straightway doubled it,—a pillager of the rich, an exterminator of the poor, a confiscator of the heritages of others. With a power of arguing a cause which could not be surpassed, overflowing with words as he was eager and bold in action, he was equally disposed to rage against those who were suppliant to him as against those who openly opposed him. It was under his advice that the sacred honours of the churches, when the pastors died, were put up to sale; and that when the death of a bishop or abbot was heard of, straightway a clerk of the king's was despatched, who took an inventory of all that he found, and carried all the

[1] *Annal. de Winton, s. a.* 1092.

revenues which arose after into the royal treasury. In the meantime an inquiry was made for some one to be put in the place of the dead, not on the ground of who was the best fitted for the post, but on the ground of who would pay the most money ; and the honour was at length given, so to speak, merely naked, though it had been bought at a great price. This seemed the harder as in the time of William I. all the rents were carefully kept to be given up to the new incumbent, and fitting persons were selected ; but in a few years all was changed. Now there was no rich man that was not an usurer, no clerk that was not a lawyer, no priest that was not a profit-monger.[1]   Let a wretch be even of the lowest condition, let him be guilty of any crime you please, if only he could appeal so as to insinuate a way of gain for the king, he was straightway listened to.   The rope would be taken off the very neck of the robber if he had promised any advantage to the royal exchequer.   Military discipline was at end, the courtiers ate up the substance of the country people, consumed their fortunes, and tore away the food from the mouths of starving wretches.   With long and flowing hair, luxurious garments, boots with curved points ; with studied effeminacy, mincing gate, debauched manner and dress, did the young men love to appear.   Without energy, with a listless

---

[1] *Fermarius* (ut verbo parum Latino utar)—*Will. M.*   It applies to *farming* any revenues, *i.e.* giving a fixed rent for them to the owner, and making as much out of them as possible.   The livings of incumbents who possessed great pluralities were thus ordinarily treated.

E

indolence they seemed to endure with difficulty their existence; sworn foes to anything like modesty in another, and having none of their own. The Court was followed about by a crowd of prostitutes and odious wretches."[1]   Such was the society in which he who was to be the new Bishop of Lincoln was, by his connection with the court, constrained to live, and such was the king he served.   He had been raised to the post of chancellor,[2] and as such, he must needs have been mixed up more or less in the iniquitous proceedings of Randolph Flambard, and in the perversion of all justice, which is sketched for us by the historian.   However virtuous and just in himself, he could not have remained in this foul atmosphere in the enjoyment of influence and power without being to some extent contaminated by that pitch which he was forced to handle.[3]

The see of Lincoln remained for a year without any one being nominated to it, and writhing in the

---

[1] *Willelm. Malmesb., De Gestis Regum*, iv. 314.

[2] The Chancellor of England at this time had no distinct Court of Judicature in which he presided, but he acted together with the justiciary and other great officers in matters of revenue at the exchequer, and sometimes in the counties upon circuits.   The great seal being in his custody, he supervised and sealed the writs and precepts that issued in proceedings pending in the King's Court and in the exchequer. He also supervised all charters that were to be sealed with that seal. He was usually a bishop or a prelate, because he was looked upon as chief of the king's chapel, which was under his special care.— Hardy, *Preface to Close Rolls*, p. xxviii.

[3] Sir F. Palgrave describes him as "an able and efficient man, with no peculiar vice, but who did not possess any principle inducing him to become disagreeable to the king."—*Normandy and England*, iv. 55.

deadly grasp of Randolph Flambard.   We may well
believe that all the costly preparations made by
Remigius in anticipation of the dedication of his
church were now seized as a prey, and that the dean
and canons, being without a protector and without
help from the law, were forced to submit to the
most atrocious exactions.   At length, however, a ray
of hope shone upon them.   Early in the year 1093
William Rufus, who was at one of his palaces at
Alvestone, near Gloucester, leading the wild and
dissipated life which was his wont, was struck with
a violent malady.   He was conveyed to Gloucester,
where he lay through the whole of Lent in a critical
and dangerous state.   Believing that his end was
approaching, and touched with some sort of compunction for his misdeeds, he listened to the voice of
some of his lords who pressed upon him the necessity
of restitution and reformation.   He had held the
Archbishopric of Canterbury in his grasp for more
than four years ; now he consented to make an
appointment nominating to it the illustrious Anselm,
Abbot of Bec.[1]   To the church of Lincoln he also
nominated a head in the person of his chancellor
and friend, Robert, " a man," says his friend,
Henry of Huntingdon, " whom no one excelled in
beauty of form, serenity of mind, and sweetness

---

[1] Anselm was at the time staying in the neighbourhood of Gloucester, and was sent for to minister to the king in his illness. He was
very unwilling to accept the archbishopric, but yielded to the entreaties
of the barons.   Before he did so, however, he obtained a promise from
the king to make restitution of all church lands.—*Eadmer*, p. 17.

of manner."[1] These excellent courtier-like qualities were not perhaps any very special qualification for the episcopate, but matters might have been much worse. Lincoln might have had the profligate spoiler who afterwards was inflicted upon Durham, and who had already preyed upon her for a year, but happily the king's partial repentance did not allow him for the moment to promote Randolph Flambard. Bloet, though he had perhaps lived a somewhat irregular life,[2] proved a generous benefactor to his church, and probably a fair administrator of his diocese. The character given him by William of Malmesbury agrees upon the whole with that of Henry of Huntingdon, which, we may be sure, was as favourable as might be. The former says of him : " He was kind and merry with his people, and little inclined to be severe ; a man second to none in his knowledge of secular affairs, but not so well skilled in ecclesiastical matters ; he enriched the church over which he presided with most precious ornaments."[3] And the latter, after having spoken of him in his history as quoted above, in the book *De contemptu mundi* speaks of his magnificence, " His splendidly equipped knights, the noble youths who attended him,

----

[1] *Henric. Hunting. Hist.* (Ed. Savile), f. 213 ; *Roger de Hoveden* (Ed. Savile), p. 255.

[2] He is described by many of the chroniclers as *libidinosus*. His son Simon became Dean of the Cathedral (Brompton, 1022, Ed. Twysden). Mr. Dimock, whose authority for this period is very great, earnestly defends Robert Bloet.—*Preface to Girald. Camb.*, vol. vii.

[3] *Willelm. Malmesb., De Gestis Pontif.*, f. 165 (Ed. Savile).

his costly horses, his golden and gilded vessels, the number of his dishes, the splendour of his attendants, his garments of purple and fine linen. He was esteemed the father and lord of all, yet he greatly cherished and loved the world. . . . He was mild and humble, one who raised up many and oppressed none, the father of orphans and the delight of his people."[1] It is clear that Bloet was a magnificent prelate, of gentle and amiable disposition, but much more of the man of the world than the bishop.[2] It may be considered to have been an advantage for the see of Lincoln at such a time, and under such circumstances, to have obtained a head with even these qualifications. Obstacles, however, were still to be interposed to his succession. The appointment was made by Rufus on the first Sunday in Lent, the 6th of March[3] (1093) and the king continuing ill throughout Lent, no further steps were immediately taken in the matter."[4] But when, as the year advanced, the king recovered his health, his views as to the epis- copal appointments entirely changed. He could not well prevent the consecration of Anselm, but he made demands upon him for the payment of a large sum, which he pretended to be still due to himself from the revenues of the see when vacant, and this became

---

[1] *Anglia Sacra*, ii. 694.

[2] " None more able than Bloet in matters of State, but miserably qualified for such a dignity and charge."—*Palgrave*.

[3] *Radulph de Diceto*, p. 491 (Ed. Twysden).

[4] " Bloet appears to have at once entered into the episcopal endow- ments and jurisdiction."—*Palgrave*, iv. 138.

the subject of their future quarrels. But over Bloet
he had a more direct power, and he did not scruple
to use it, though in order to do so he resorted to the
meanest and most discreditable practices. It has
been already said that Remigius for a large sum of
money had procured for his cathedral the formal
recognition of its being part of the province of
Canterbury, and that the Archbishop of York had
assented, though unwillingly, to the arrangement.
It is probable that the promises of compensation
then made to the York prelate had not in any way
been fulfilled, and now William Rufus, taking advantage of this which was his own wrong, secretly excited
the archbishop to make a formal protest against the
consecration of Bloet.[1] Thus when Thomas, Archbishop of York, had, after considerable difficulties,
consecrated Anselm at Canterbury, and the elect of
Lincoln was present there, expecting to be consecrated by Anselm, Thomas made his protest, and
interdicted the ceremony, and Bloet was obliged to
return unconsecrated. Bloet, who knew his master
well, at once perceived that there was but one way
to overcome this difficulty. He must either make
up his mind to give a large sum to procure his consecration, and thus become guilty of simony, or else
he must abandon all hope of promotion, and leave
the see of Lincoln still exposed to the rapacious
exactions of Ralph Flambard and his crew. If, under

---

[1] Cum archiepiscopo Eboracensi dictum Robertum Bloet calum-
niatus est rex, etc.—*Brompton*, p. 988 (Ed. Twysden).

any circumstances, it could be justifiable to pay money
for the advancement to an ecclesiastical office, surely
this was a case in point.[1]   Robert Bloet, who probably
was not troubled with many scruples as to this offence,
then almost universal, at once decided to offer the
king a bribe, and for the consideration of a sum
which is variously stated by the chroniclers as one
thousand pounds, three thousand marks, and five
thousand pounds,[2] the king withdrew his opposition
and compelled the Archbishop of York to yield, upon
receiving, in lieu of his claims over Lindsey, the
abbey of St. German's at Saleby, and the church of
St. Oswald in Gloucester.[3]   This discreditable transaction is made to assume in the formal document which
announces the arrangement an act of liberality on
the part of the king.   " I, William, by the grace of
God King of the English, the son of William, the
king who succeeded to King Edward by hereditary
right, seeing the Church of the English divided and
discordant, and desirous to bring together that which
had been evilly divided, and to recall to the unity of
love that which had long remained in discord, have
redeemed out of my own private possessions the

---

[1] Henry of Huntingdon says : " Quod regi quidem simoniæ, præsuli
vero justitie deputatum est," f. 213 (Ed. Savile).

[2] Stubbs (*Act. Pontif. Ebor.*, p. 1708, Ed. Twysden) says 1000
pounds ; Ann. de Winton (*Ann. Monast.* ii. 37) 3000 marks ; Henry
of Huntingdon (the best authority for this), 5000 pounds (f. 213, Ed.
Savile), in which he is followed by Brompton and Knyghton.   Roger
de Wendover makes it only 500 pounds, *Flor. Hist.* ii., 42. pp. 968,
2364 (Ed. Twysden).   [3] " Neither of them his to give."—*Palgrave.*

claim which the church of York and Thomas, the archbishop thereof, made over Lincoln and Lindsey, and the houses of Stow and Louth, and I have given instead of them to the church of St. Peter at York, as perpetual possessions the abbey of St. German at Saleby and the Church of St. Oswald at Gloucester, with all things that pertain unto them ; and I have given to Archbishop Thomas and his successors the abbey of Saleby in the same way as the archbishopric of Canterbury has the bishopric of Rochester."[1] The opposition to the consecration of Robert Bloet was thus overcome. In the spring of 1094 King William was at Hastings preparing to pass over into Normandy to carry on war with his brother Robert. The winds, however, were contrary, and he was delayed more than a month. A large number of nobles and " almost all the bishops" were in attendance upon him. Various pieces of ecclesiastical business were transacted. The church of Battle Abbey was dedicated to the honour of St. Martin. Herebert, Bishop of Thetford, was deprived of the pastoral staff. It seems that he had bought the bishopric of the king for himself and the abbey for his brother, and then had secretly applied to Pope

---

[1] *Dugdale, Monastic.*, vi. 1271, from the instrument said to be in the Register of the Dean and Chapter of Lincoln. "For about one hundred and fifty years from the time of Archbishop Lanfranc and Bishop Gundulf, the Bishops of Rochester seem to have acted as coadjutors or vicars to the Archbishops of Canterbury, and during all that time and long afterwards the archbishops exercised the same privileges as regards the temporalities of Rochester which the king enjoyed in respect to all other sees."—Note by Mr. Griffiths to Inett, ii. 118. See *Vita Gundulfi* in *Anglia Sacra.*

Urban for absolution.   Whether it was that the king
was angry at the scandal thus divulged, or that the
bishop had applied to the wrong pope, does not appear.[1]   And here at Hastings in February 1094 Robert
Bloet was consecrated by Anselm and seven of his
suffragans to be Bishop of Lincoln, "in the church
of St. Mary, which is within the castle itself."   An
attempt was made by the king to cause Anselm to consecrate Bloet *absolutè*, *i.e.* without any oath or engage-
ment of canonical obedience to himself.   But this he
would not do ; and the due oaths of submission and
obedience to the see of Canterbury were first taken.[2]

It is charged against Robert Bloet by some of
the chroniclers that after his consecration he was but
slack in completing the dedication of the Cathedral
Church of Lincoln,[3] but this charge seems to be unfounded.   Not only did Bloet procure the consecration of the church,[4] but he enriched it out of his
great wealth with magnificent gifts.   Giraldus says :

---

[1] *Roger de Hoveden, Annal.* f. 266 (Ed. Savile).   For a fuller
account of Herebert, see William of Malmesbury, *De Gest. Pontif. Ang.*
i.   He received back his pastoral staff afterwards, and became a great
opposer of simony in his latter days.   He removed the see to
Norwich, and built the cathedral.

[2] *Eadmer, Hist..Nov.*, p. 23 (Ed. Selden).

[3] Prædictam ecclesiæ dedicationem Lincolniensis postea segniter
implevit.—*Brompton*, p. 988 ; *Knyghton*, p. 2364 (Ed. Twysden).

[4] I have not been able to discover the date of the year of the consecration of the church, but incidentally the *day* of the consecration
may be inferred.   In a MS. left by the late Mr. Ross, it is stated that
in A.D. 1397 the feast of the dedication of St. Margaret's, in the close
of Lincoln, previously kept on the morrow of the nativity of the
Blessed Virgin Mary (Sept. 9), was changed, on account of its falling

" He furnished it in the most praiseworthy manner, with palls, all of silk, with copes embroidered with gold, with reliquaries, chalices, and copies of the sacred text bound in gold and silver, and wonderfully fashioned by the skill of the artificer." And to this magnificent furniture he added still more substantial gifts. He doubled the number of prebends, thus increasing the twenty-one canons of the first founder to forty-two, and providing amply for their endowment.[1] He was thus a very great benefactor to the Church, and, so far as gifts and endowments went, Lincoln could hardly have been more fortunate. Probably, however, the new bishop did not contribute much to the evangelising of the degraded and ignorant people in his diocese. He had been habituated to a courtier's life, and to this, as we may gather from Henry of Huntingdon's account, he still clung after his elevation. Like Thomas Becket in his commencement, he was not like him in the succeeding part of his career. We don't find the name of the Bishop of Lincoln as standing by Anselm in his

in harvest-time, to the day of the dedication of the cathedral church, *i.e.* the third day after the feast of the Relics, which was the second Sunday after the feast of SS. Peter and Paul (June 29). I am indebted to the kindness of the Rev. Precentor Venables for this information. I am also informed by my friend Canon Simmons of York that in a MS. copy of the *Horæ Eboracenses*, date about 1420, the *Festum Reliquiarum cathedralis Lincoln* is put down in the calendar under July 14, so that on that year the feast of the dedication would be July 17. *Probably* the year was 1095. Mr. Dimock says, "At the very least close upon two years after the death of Remigius."—*Pref. to Girald. Camb.*, vol. vii. p. 25.   [1] *Giraldus* in *Anglia Sacra*, ii. 416.

long-continued struggle against the Crown.   In this struggle, indeed, neither side was free from blame, and we should not be inclined to censure Bloet for supporting the national party against the arrogant pretensions of Rome, had it been done upon principle, and not simply as the courtier-helper of the king, whatever overbearing course he pleased to pursue.   On one occasion only do we find Bloet joining with his brethren to support the views of the great Primate. A second archbishop Thomas of York, had conceived the same bold views of independence of, and equality with, Canterbury, as the Archbishop Thomas, promoted by the Conqueror, had contended for.   Elected at a time when Anselm's life was evidently drawing to an end, Thomas craftily put off his consecration, hoping that the Primate being gone, in the vacancy of the see no claim would be made on him for the oath of canonical obedience to Canterbury.   Anselm, anticipating this craft addressed a solemn letter to each of the bishops of England, calling upon each of them before consecrating Thomas, to take care that he made the proper submission to the chief metropolitical see.   King Henry who was disposed to take the side of Thomas, was by the general consent of the bishops obliged to yield, and Thomas made the due profession before he was consecrated.[1]   In this matter we find the Bishop of Lincoln joining with his brethren against the king, but this was a rare, perhaps a solitary, instance of independent spirit.

Eadmer, p. 103 (Ed. p. Selden).

About six years after Bloet's accession to the see,
William Rufus ended his ill-spent life, and the arrow
sent by chance or design opened the way for the
advancement of his brother.   The elder brother was
absent in the Holy Land, and Henry the younger,
by a mixture of daring and conciliatory measures,
gained the throne.   But Robert, on his return, was
induced to make an attempt upon England, being
supported by some of the barons, and especially by
Robert de Belesme, Earl of Shrewsbury, a man in-
famous even in those days for his abominable
wickedness.   The weak-minded Robert was bought
off, and then King Henry determined to take vengeance on those who had supported him.   The Earl
of Shrewsbury was pursued to his castles of Arundel
and Bridgnorth, while Robert, Bishop of Lincoln, with
a part of the king's army was despatched to lay siege
to his castle of Tychill.[1]   The rapid and complete
success of the king, the banishment of the Earl of
Shrewsbury, and the humiliation of the other un-
friendly barons, probably soon released the bishop
from his military duties, and left him in a position,
had he been so disposed, to give himself to the
administration of his diocese.   The dispute between
the king and Archbishop Anselm on the subject of
investitures now ran high, and many of the bishops,[2]
and among them the Bishop of Lincoln, took the
national view of upholding the king's prerogative

---

[1] *Simeon Dunelm.*, p. 227 (Ed. Twysden).
[2] *Collier, Ch. Hist.*, ii. 110.

against the encroachments of the Pope. The real difficulty was that the upholding of the royal prerogative in the case of such kings as Rufus and his brother, was in fact the establishment of a gigantic system of simony. No considerable appointment was made without a price being paid for it, and if the king was free to nominate bishops and order their consecration, the whole of the Episcopal body would soon be tainted with simony. There was, therefore, some sound religious basis for this contest about investitures as regards Anselm, though, inasmuch as it advanced the extravagant ambition of the Pope, his part in it is usually regarded with disfavour.[1] A lull in the dispute enabled Anselm to summon a synod at Westminster to endeavour to correct some of the most crying scandals of the time (1102). At this synod Robert, Bishop of Lincoln, was present. It was now the time when, for the advancement of the ambitious views of the Roman Pontiff, a fierce war was being waged against the married clergy throughout the whole of Europe. Anselm, with his disciplinary and ascetic views, threw himself eagerly into this struggle. It was now enacted that no archdeacon, priest, deacon, or canon should

---

[1] "The real question at issue," says Sir F. Palgrave, "was whether there should or should not be one law and gospel permitting sin to kings, princes, and great people, and another law and gospel prohibiting sin to the mean, poor, and small?"—*Normandy and England,* iv. 87. "Anselm throughout strives," says Mr. Freeman, "not for forms and ceremonies, but for righteousness."—*Norman Conquest* v. 221.

marry, and those who were already married were enjoined to quit their wives. On this Henry, the Archdeacon of Huntingdon, who was himself the son of a priest, wisely remarks : " This seemed to some to be taking a great step towards purity, but others thought it full of danger, lest by exacting a purity too great for human strength, they should cause men to fall into horrible filthiness to the disgrace of the Christian name."[1]   That the Bishop of Lincoln was a father we know ; whether or not he was married we do not know ;[2] but in any case this canon must have gone much against the grain to him, and the disturbances which followed it—many priests shutting up their churches and refusing to perform divine service—must have seemed to him recklessly and wantonly provoked.   There were other canons enacted at this synod which are not open to objection, but which were a wholesome attempt to abate crying evils. Such were those which strongly forbade simony, and the deprivation of several abbots who had notoriously purchased their places[3] showed that this was not to be a dead letter.   It was also forbidden to let archdeaconries out to farm, that sons of priests should succeed to their fathers' churches by way of inheritance,

---

[1] *Henric. Huntingd., Histor.* p. 217 (Ed. Savile).

[2] Mr. Dimock says, " Of this there is no reason to doubt."—*Pref. to Girald. Camb.*, vol. vii. p. xxvi.

[3] The abbots of Pershore, Tavistock, and Ramsey, Peterborough, Cirnell, and Middleton, were deposed for simony, and the abbots of Ely and St. Edmunds on some other accounts.—See *Roger de Wendover, Flor. Hist.* ii. 171.

that clergymen should act as lawyers or judges, and in especial that "the wicked merchandise" by which men were sold as cattle should no longer be tolerated.

The important matters which had been so long contested between the king and the Church came to something like a happy solution in the year 1107, when the king surrendered his claim to nominate bishops and abbots and to give them investiture, on the understanding that before their consecration he was to have the right of approbation, and that they were to do homage to him for their temporalties.[1] There seems to have been a general jubilation and congratulation on all hands: the new archbishop of York renews the promise of canonical obedience to the Archbishop of Canterbury which he had made when consecrated Bishop of Hereford, and no less than five bishops who had been waiting for their consecration till these disputes were settled, were consecrated by Anselm, assisted by the Archbishop of York and five of his own suffragans, of whom Robert, Bishop of Lincoln, was one.[2] The next ecclesiastical matter of importance in which Robert Bloet took a part has brought on him some obloquy, and perhaps somewhat unjustly. The transaction may not have been perfect in its disinterestedness, but it was useful in itself, and it set a good precedent for further use.

---

[1] See *Freeman's Norman Conquest*, v. 227.

[2] *Roger de Hoveden*, p. 270 (Ed. Savile). No one, it is said, could remember one occasion of so many bishops being consecrated in one day since the times of Edward the Elder, when Archbishop Plegmund ordained seven at once.

After the death of Richard, Abbot of Ely, in 1107,
Hervey, Bishop of Bangor, was sent down by the
king to reside in the abbey and to be a sort of acting abbot without formal appointment.   Hervey
represented himself as having been driven out of his
see in North Wales by the outrages of the Welsh,
but William of Malmesbury says of him, somewhat
unkindly, that "he had forsaken it in order to get
more wealth, and that it was only a pretence that he
and the Welsh could not agree."[1]   However that
may have been, he continued to recommend himself
to the monks of Ely, and they represented to him how
well contented they should be to have him as their
abbot for a continuance.   To this Hervey did not
object, but he had also higher views.   He represented
to the monks that their abbey might well be turned
into a bishop's see, that it was a fair place, well endowed, and ought not to remain in the condition of
an ordinary monastery.   The monks' ambition was
fired, they gave their consent to the proposed change.
Hervey next addressed himself to the king, perhaps
bringing forward reasons more weighty than words
why a new see should be erected and Ely thus
dignified.   The king took up the project heartily.
There was yet another person whose interests were
more directly concerned, and who must needs be consulted—Robert, Bishop of Lincoln—the diocese out
of which the new diocese of Ely was to be carved.
That the bishop might not be called upon to make

---

[1] *Willelm. Malmes., De Gestis Pontif.,* p. 167 (Ed. Savile).

a personal sacrifice of the revenue arising from the district proposed to be taken from him, he was offered in exchange for this the manor of Spaldwick, in Huntingdonshire, with its belongings, which appertained to the monastery of Ely, to be given to him and his successors for ever. To this Bishop Bloet agreed, and if the exchange was a fair one we cannot see how he rightly incurs the castigation of Giraldus, who speaks of this as one of "his mad errors"[1] and as an "enormous diminution of his church." If, on the contrary, the bishop sacrificed revenues by this transaction, as is probable, it is so much the more credit to him not to have stood in the way of a useful arrangement for the Church. The huge diocese over which he presided might have lost many such portions and still have remained inconveniently large for the supervision of one man. Bishop Hervey now repaired to Rome, and having obtained the Pope's approval of the arrangement, and being personally designated by the Pope as the first bishop of Ely on account of his conspicuous merits, was consecrated to the new see in 1109.[2] Had there been no spoliation of the see of Lincoln worse than this, Giraldus might well have spared his lamentations. It was probably soon after this transaction, which gave birth to the see of Ely, that the bishop's son, Simon de Bloet, was advanced to the dignity of Dean of the Cathedral Church[3] in succession to Ralph, the dean

---

[1] *Deliramenta*, Girald. Camb., vii. 33.

[2] *Hist. Eliensis*, *Anglia Sacra*, i.   [3] Le Neve puts it 1110.

F

appointed by Remigius. He, like his father, was a courtier priest, but not an entirely successful one, if the account given of him in Brompton and Knyghton may be relied upon. These chroniclers say : " In the time of Henry I. there was a certain Simon, son of Robert, Bishop of Lincoln, and dean in that church, who had been remarkable for his acuteness, renowned for eloquence, beauteous in person, of striking grace, a young man in years but an old one in wisdom. He was, however, tainted with the great fault of pride, which brought on him envy, which grew into hatred, and involved him in many quarrels, slanderings, and evil-speakings. Once he openly boasted about himself saying, ' I am among the courtiers like salt among eels,' looking only to one point of the simile and not observing the other. For as salt tortures the eels, so did he torture the courtiers by gibing at them. The salt, however, is at length destroyed by the moisture which comes from the eels, and so was he destroyed by the constant bitter attacks of the whole body of courtiers ; for at length he fell into disgrace with the king, was shut up in prison, and only escaped through a sewer, to die an exile."[1]

That the bishop took no slight pains and was at no little expense to stand well with the king is evident. Not only did he act complacently in the matter of the see of Ely, which, according to Giraldus, was an enormous diminution of his revenues,

[1] *Brompton, Chronicon*, p. 1021 (Ed. Twysden).

but he also began the custom of offering a magnificent present yearly from the see of Lincoln to the king, a tribute which afterwards fell with excessive severity upon St. Hugh.[1] Giraldus, knowing this, felt not unnaturally somewhat of indignation against the prelate who first began the custom. " Forasmuch," says he, " as riches are apt to produce folly, and the prosperity of fools shall destroy them, among other silly freaks of his, although his church was surrounded with many dangers, he gave to King Henry I. a cloak of the value of one hundred pounds, made of foreign skins of ermines, wherein the deepest black was interspersed with white, and lined with most exquisite cloth. And not only did he himself heedlessly give this, but he also bound his successors to similar gifts."[2] Yet, after all these acts of submission and devotion, the king did not scruple to inflict upon the bishop three very vexatious suits and heavy fines, which caused him such disquietude that he is represented by Henry of Huntingdon as bewailing in most miserable fashion his unhappy fate, and as furnishing a striking example of the vain nature of the riches and honours of this world.[3] It is probable that Bloet, as a secular priest and court chaplain was no great lover of monks, yet he, in common with almost all the leading men of his

[1] St. Hugh was called upon to make good a long arrear of this tribute, and not only did so at a great cost, but also redeemed and abolished the tribute for a large sum.

[2] *Anglia Sacra*, ii. 417.

[3] *Henric. Hunt., De Contemptu Mundi.*

day, made donations to monasteries. The *Annals of Bermondsey* tell us that he gave Charlton Manor to that house,[1] and the Abbey of Eynsham, near Oxford, which had been founded in 1105 by Ailmer, Earl of Cornwall, was enriched by him with many gifts and manors. To this house he transferred the monks of St. Mary of Stow, which had been resuscitated by his predecessor, Remigius,[2] and converted their monastery into an episcopal residence. In the year 1116 the Abbey of St. Albans was dedicated by Bishop Bloet, in conjunction with the Archbishop of Rouen, in the presence of King Henry, with high and stately ceremonial.[3] In the year 1121 Robert Bloet was one of the bishops who consecrated Richard, the keeper of the king's seal, to be Bishop of Hereford,[4] and soon after, on the death of Ralph, Archbishop of Canterbury (October 19, 1122), he took a prominent part in the opposition made by the bishops to the attempt of the monks of Canterbury, to impose one of their order on the primacy. "Monks," said the Canterbury deputation who came

---

[1] *Ann. Monast.*, iii. 428.

[2] *Willelm. Malmesb.*, *De Gestis Pontif.*, f. 165 (Ed. Savile).

[3] Radulph de Diceto says, Dedicatum est a Roberto (p. 491, Ed. Twysd.) *Ann. de Waverleia:* Robertus dedicavit per Ricardum Abbatem (*Ann. Monast.* ii. 215). Matthew Paris, who, as afterwards a monk of the House, would have the best information, says it was dedicated by the Archbishop of Rouen, but on account of the greatness of the work, the Bishop of Lincoln took part of the service at the request of the Abbot Richard.—*Matt. Paris*, p. 66 (Ed. Watts). See *Roger de Wendover*, ii. 193.

[4] *Contin. Flor. Wigorn.*, p. 75, E. H. S.

to the king at Gloucester, "from the time of St. Augustine had ever been primates of England.   It would be a monstrous thing if a secular ecclesiastic should be allowed to usurp this prize which was the crown and glory of the higher order."   "But," says the chronicler, "the bishops of the whole of England, who all were of the clerical order, cried out against this, and declared that they were not willing to have a monk as primate when there were clerks equally honest and equally fit for the government of the Church."   The king was on the side of the bishops, and the monks of Canterbury, much to their chagrin, were obliged to select one of four clerks whose names were put before them to make a selection.[1] They ultimately chose William of Corbeil, prior of the canons of Chiche in Essex, who was consecrated at Canterbury, February 16, 1123.   But before this had taken place one of the chief actors in the proceedings which had led to his consecration had ceased to exist.

Towards the end of his life Bishop Bloet would seem to have quite recovered the royal favour, and in the last scene of it he is found riding in friendly guise by the side of Henry, apparently in full possession of all that he could desire.   Then by a sudden and startling stroke he is cut off.   Henry had been keeping his Christmas at his favourite manor of Woodstock, where he had had a great hunting party,[2] and in the month of January (1123)

---

[1] *Simeon Dunelm.*, p. 247 (Ed. Twysden).

[2] Conventum hominum et ferarum statuerat.—*Henric. Hunting.*

was riding in some of the beautiful glades of the
Chace, accompanied by his trusty minister, the
Bishop of Salisbury, who rode on one side of him,
and by the Bishop of Lincoln on the other.[1]   The
king and the two prelates were engaged in pleasant
converse, when suddenly the Bishop of Lincoln was
seen to fall forward on his horse,[2] and would have
speedily reached the ground had not the king seized
him with a strong hand.[3]   Being laid down, it was
found that his power of speech was gone, and that
he was smitten with a violent stroke of apoplexy.
It was evident that the seizure was mortal.   He
was conveyed into the nearest shelter, still alive but
unable to speak,[4] and then he quickly breathed his
last in the presence of the king.   Having died at a
long distance from his cathedral church, to which it
was thought right that his body should be conveyed,
it was necessary that it should be disembowelled.
The entrails were reverently buried at the monastery
of Eynsham, to which Bloet had been so great a
benefactor, and the body was conveyed to Lincoln.
It is not necessary to give credence to the assertions
of later chroniclers, who regarded Bloet's memory
with no affection, when they tell us that "the place
of his sepulture was haunted by nocturnal spectres
which appalled those who were set to guard it, until

---

[1] *Willelm. Malmesb.—Henric. Hunting.*
[2] Decidere cœpit. —*Flor.. Wigorn.*
[3] Quem cadentem dum rex exciperet.—*Simeon Dunelm.*
[4] Vivus sed elinguis.—*Hen. Hunt.*

it was purified by masses and alms."[1]   His epitaph,
written by the friendly pen of Henry of Huntingdon,
may also perhaps require somewhat of abatement in
our acceptation of it : " Robert, honour of pontiffs,
whom fame will immortalise, dies, yet will not die.
Humble though rich, pious though powerful, merciful
in taking vengeance, mild when provoked.   To his
flock he was rather a father than a master, ever their
protector and defender in adversity.   On the tenth
of January he left the dreams of this deceitful world
and awoke to the true and everlasting verities."[2]

ALEXANDER, THIRD BISHOP—1123-1148.

When Robert Bloet was struck by the sudden
fit of apoplexy as he was riding by the king's side
at Woodstock, there was riding on the other side of
the king a prelate who then occupied by far the
most prominent position of any man in England.
This was Roger, Bishop of Salisbury, justiciary of
the whole realm, and as such the second man in
the land.   This magnificent prelate, highly spoken
of by his contemporaries,[3] had, we are assured, refused to take upon himself this great secular office
without express permission from the Pope and three

---

[1] *Brompton* and *Knyghton*, pp. 988, 2364 (Ed. Twysden).

[2] *Henric. Hunt.*, *Hist.*, f. 218 (Ed. Savile).

[3] See the high character given him by William of Malmesbury in
Gesta regum Angl., v. 408.   This, however, is a good deal modified
in the account of him in the *Historia Novella*.

succeeding archbishops of Canterbury. He stood
very high in the king's favour, and any word from
him as to the fit person to be selected for the
vacant see of Lincoln, would certainly meet with
ready attention from King Henry.[1]   That word
was eagerly spoken in favour of his nephew Alexander, and at the Easter following Bloet's death,
Henry, being at Winchester, nominated Alexander
to be Bishop of Lincoln, and on July 22 the new
Archbishop, William de Corbeil, having returned
from Rome with the pall, Alexander was consecrated at Canterbury by him.[2]   Alexander was by
birth a Norman,[3] and his after-life proved him to
have many of the special characteristics of that
famous race.   He had been Archdeacon of Salisbury, so that he was not altogether inexperienced
in the administration of a diocese.   But in the
turbulent times in which his lot was cast, amidst the
constant din and clash of arms, when prelates aspired
to imitate the lay barons in every martial feat, there
was but small thought or care for the true work of
a bishop.   Among the prelates of the first century

[1] Henry is represented to have said, "By the birth of God I
would give him the half of the kingdom if he should ask it.   He shall
tire of asking before I tire of granting."—*Wil. Malmesb., Hist. Nov.*,
p. 729, E. H. S.

[2] *Contin. Flor. Wigorn.*, p. 78 (E. H. S.)   His brother Nigel
became Bishop of Ely in 1133.

[3] *Giraldus*, vii. 33.   The Chronicon Thomæ Wykes says he was
brought by his *brother* from France (an error for his uncle) and that he
was "fraternæ superbiæ non tepidus æmulator."—*Ann. Monas.* iv.
17.

after the Conquest, there were some good and holy men, such as were St. Wulfstan of Worcester and St. Osmund of Salisbury. But the majority of the prelates were bent on mundane affairs, seeking to strengthen themselves by court influence or large bodies of retainers, or strong castles and fortresses, against the various turns of secular fortune.[1] Such a prelate was Alexander, the third Bishop of Lincoln, a courtier, not like his predecessor Bloet of a timid and cautious character, but bold, open and undisguised in his pursuit of power and in the magnificence and martial efficiency of his surroundings. An anonymous but contemporary chronicler thus describes him : " He was called a bishop, but he was a man of vast pomp and of great boldness and audacity ; neglecting the pure and simple way of life belonging to the Christian religion, he gave himself up to military affairs and secular pomp, showing whenever he appeared at Court so vast a band of followers that all men marvelled."[2] But Alexander had the virtues as well as the faults of this magnificent nature. His wealth was spent, not merely in the aggrandisement of his own power and state, but also in pious and useful works. If he built castles, he also built and endowed abbeys, and specially he was almost the second builder of the cathedral church over which he presided, and was

---

[1] The author of *Gesta Regis Stephani* pronounces the strongest condemnation on the bishops of his day, but excepts one prelate, Robert, Bishop of Hereford.   [2] *Gesta Regis Stephani* (E. H. S.), p. 47.

the first, according to some authorities, to introduce
the admirable feature of a stone-groined roof, thus
making his church in his day the comeliest in England.[1]   The chronicler, William of Newbury, thus
describes his building projects and their causes :
" He was a man of a most free and liberal spirit,
and, desirous to imitate his uncle, he too erected,
with most profuse expenditure, two noble castles.
But seeing that this sort of building did not seem
altogether agreeable to the episcopal character, in
order to take away all ill opinion which might arise
from it, and, as it were, to expiate the fault, he
built as many monasteries as he had castles, and
filled them with religious men."[2]   The number both
of castles and monasteries built by the bishop was
greater than the chronicler here credits him with.
The strong places of Newark, Sleaford, and Banbury, had an equivalent provided for them in the
Cistercian houses of Thame, Haverholme, and Louth
Park,[3] and the scale was turned in favour of the
monasteries by the erection of the house for Austin

[1] In deference to Mr. Dimock's authority, than whom there is no
better judge of the chronicles of the period, I have put Bishop Alexander's work in Lincoln Cathedral towards the end of his episcopate
instead of at the beginning, as some do.   The year before Alexander's
consecration there had been a terrible fire at Lincoln, in which one
hundred and forty men perished, but it is expressly said that the
" Episcopium et monasterium " escaped.—See *Chronicles of Margan,
Ann. Monast.*, iv. 11.

[2] *Guil. Neubrig.* cap. VI.

[3] Haverholme was built originally for the Cistercians, but when
they were removed to Louth Park it was given by Alexander to the
Gilbertine order of monks and nuns.

canons at Dorchester. There was indeed a complete mania for building in the time of Alexander.
His uncle Roger had erected four most beautiful castles
at Sherborne, Salisbury, Malmesbury, and Devizes ;
and the sudden outburst of zeal which the arrival of
the Cistercian order in England in the year 1128
evoked was covering the whole land with magnificent abbeys. Waverley, Rievaulx, Fountains, Gar-
rendon, Ford, Meaux, Thame, Kingswood, Kirksted,
Louth Park, Boxley, Woburn, Bruerne, Combe, all
date within the first ten years after the appearance of the White Monks in England, and these
are only a small part of those which were built.
The sees had all now been provided with cathedral
churches, and the zealous magnificence of the Norman prelates and barons could devote itself to the
erection of castles and abbeys ; the one to strengthen
the baron's power and give him security against his
enemies, the other to testify his zeal for Holy
Church and the good of his soul. Alexander's
castle-building was no doubt due to the wish to
strengthen the power of his family, a power which
rapidly became enormous during the last years of
Henry I.[1] His building of religious houses we may
fairly set down to a pious sentiment, which sought
to dedicate wealth to the glory of God, and the

---

[1] *Willelm. Malmesb., Hist. Nov.,* p. 728 (E. H. S.) With the
Bishop of Salisbury as chief justiciary, his son by Maude of Ramsbury
acting as his deputy or successor, his nephew Alexander holding the
huge province of Lincoln, and his other nephew Nigel that of Ely, the
power of this family must have been very great,

strengthening and upholding of his Church. Yet
even a chronicler most favourable to him[1] cannot
deny that to meet the profuse expenditure which all
these buildings required Alexander was often guilty
of much grasping and injustice. " He was brought
up," says Henry of Huntingdon, "in the greatest
luxury by Roger his uncle, the Bishop of Salisbury,
and hence he acquired a spirit too high to be good
for his people. Desirous to excel other nobles in
his magnificent gifts and the splendour of his works,
when his own resources did not suffice for this, he
was in the habit of plucking most eagerly the goods
of his people, to make his own smaller resources
equal to their greater ones. But yet he could not
succeed in this, inasmuch as he was ever squander-
ing more and more. Yet a wise man he was, and
liberal to such a degree that by the Court of Rome
he was called the Magnificent."[2]

Giraldus has the same complaint against the
bishop for robbing the see for these building purposes. He does not indeed complain of his castles,
all of which remained on the episcopal land, but with
regard to the abbeys he says that it was "robbing
one altar to clothe another."[3] Alexander was consecrated in 1123, and in 1125 we find him at
Rome, together with William, Archbishop of Canter-

---

[1] Henry of Huntingdon wrote his history at the suggestion of
Bishop Alexander, and addresses him in his dedication as "pater
patriæ, princeps a rege secundus."

[2] *Henric. Huntingd., Histor.*, p. 226 (Ed. Savile).

[3] *Opera*, vii. 33.

bury.[1]   Doubtless he then received investiture in his bishopric from the Pope, and he may have encouraged and counselled the archbishop to take the step which he then took, and which, perhaps, more even than the concession about investiture, was detrimental to the liberties of the English Church.   It was now first that an Archbishop of Canterbury, *alterius orbis papa*, as he had shortly before been described by a Pope, consented to receive legatine authority from the Pope, and to exercise his office in England as the delegate of a foreign bishop.[2]   This legatine authority also was liable at any time to be superseded by the arrival of a special legate, *a latere*, so that it was not only degrading to the archbishop's dignity but practically useless to him as a source of power.   "The Archbishops of Canterbury," says Dr. Inett, "were by this means stripped of their rights, and clothed with the shadow of them.   It is here that we are to date the vassalage of the English Church."[3]   Soon after the return of the prelates from Rome a council was actually convened at Westminster by the archbishop by virtue of his legatine authority,—"by the authority of Peter, prince of the apostles, and our own."[4]   In

[1] *Ann. de Waverleia, Ann. Monast.* ii. 219 ; *Henric. Huntingdon*, f. 219 (Ed. Savile).

[2] Mr. Freeman says this was the only remedy for the degradation of the primate being compelled to yield place to a legate (v. 236). But was it a remedy?   Even when the archbishop became ordinary legate of the pope—legatus natus—he was always liable to be superseded by a legatus a latere.   Thus afterwards Warham was obliged to yield the first place to Wolsey.   [3] *Inett, Ch. Hist.*, ii. 221.

[4] Cui Concilio præsedit ipse sicut archiepiscopus Cantuarensis et

this council the same canons which were passed in all the frequent councils of that day against simony, marriage of the clergy,[1] etc., were carried, but after it King Henry, now despairing of a male heir, caused all the barons and bishops to swear fealty, and promise support to his daughter, the Empress Matilda. "William of Canterbury and all the rest of the bishops swore," so that hereby Bishop Alexander was strictly and solemnly pledged to that which afterwards he so lightly cast off. It is possible, indeed, that Alexander, the nephew, deluded himself with the same sophistry with which Roger, the uncle, seems to have been satisfied in this matter of allegiance. "Often have I heard Roger, Bishop of Salisbury, say," writes William of Malmesbury, "that he considered himself released from the oath which he had taken to the empress, for that he had sworn on the express understanding that the king should not give his daughter in marriage to any foreigner without the advice of him and the other nobles of the kingdom." But if the marriage of Eleanor to Geoffrey

legatus apostolicæ sedis, considentibus secum Willelmo episcopo Wintoniensi, Rogerio Sarisberyensi, Willelmo Execestrensi, Herveo Eliensi, Alexandro Lincolniensi, etc.—*Contin. Flor. Wigorn.*, p. 85 (E. H. S.)

[1] This council distinguished itself by the iniquitous provision that the *concubinæ sacerdotum*, as they were called, might be sold into slavery.—*Cont. Flor. Wig.*, p. 88. Another council was held in 1129, as the provisions of this had proved inoperative. The married clergy were now handed over to the justice of the king to enforce the decrees of the Synod. The only effect of this was that the king, for a money payment, allowed them to live peaceably with their wives.—*Henric. Hunt., Histor.*, f. 220 (Ed. Savile).

Plantagenet released the bishops from their oaths of 1127, how was it with regard to the renewal of those oaths solemnly made by them long after the marriage in the year 1133?[1]

It was indeed a sad and troublous time in England when Alexander presided over the see of Lincoln. The most solemn obligations, the most sacred oaths, were disregarded in that universal eagerness of every one to provide for his own safety when the strong, vigorous, and wise rule of King Henry was brought to an end. The king having died in Normandy, and his daughter also being beyond seas, the realm of England lay ready as a prize for the first comer, and Stephen, the king's nephew, having lost no time in coming to grasp at the throne, he was received with universal acclamation even by those who were most strongly pledged to uphold the legitimate claim of the absent princess. Yet some sort of sophistry was necessary to be presented to the bishops before they could consent to act so distinctly and openly against their plighted faith, and this has been preserved in the pages of a chronicler who gives us the history of these times with great vigour and spirit from the point of view of a partisan of King Stephen. "William, Archbishop of Canterbury, came to him," he says, "a man with the aspect of a dove, and in outward appearance truly religious, but a greedy lover of money. Being earnestly pressed to crown the king,

[1] *Willelm. Malmesb., Hist. Nov.*, p. 698.

he said that he could not do it suddenly, but it was
a matter for grave consideration.   Henry had bound
all the chief men of the kingdom with a most stringent
oath that after his death they would receive no one
as their ruler but his daughter.   To this the king's
party answered, ' That it was true Henry had done
this by way of holding together the Normans and
Angevese, who were ever quarrelling.   By his violent
and imperious will he had compelled rather than
enjoined men to take this oath.   But he had done
this for purposes which related to his life-time, and
had not intended that it should remain fixed after
his death ; in fact, on his death-bed, among his other
sins, he had confessed this sin of compelling the
barons to take this oath.   An oath extorted by violence was not binding.   Stephen had been received
with acclamations by the citizens of London, and was
just the man needed to enforce order in the troubled
state of the land.'   Induced," says the chronicler, " by
such reasons, *and by some others which I pass over*,
the archbishop, and the bishops, and a vast body of
the clergy who were met together, consecrated and
anointed Stephen to be king."[1]   It was not long
before the Bishop of Salisbury, with his two nephews
of Lincoln and Ely, learned bitterly to regret having
thus forgotten their pledge to Matilda, and having
assisted the cause of the usurper.[2]   They had thought

[1] *Gesta Regis Stephani*, pp. 6-8 (E. H. S.)

[2] Henry of Huntingdon says : '' Rogerus magnus Salesburiensis
Episcopus qui secundus sacramentum illud prædictum fecerat et omnibus aliis prædicaverat, justo Dei judicio ab eodem quem creavit in regem

thus to preserve their power and wealth, but their calculations proved unfounded. Stephen was of course ready enough to make high-sounding grants to the Church in return for the substantial aid which it afforded him at this critical time. He published a charter, in which he declared that he would neither do nor permit anything to be done in the Church or Church affairs simoniacally, that he would confirm that all right of judging ecclesiastical persons or clerks, and all power over them and their goods, and all the distribution of the goods of the Church, should be in the hand of the bishops. All dignities of churches, with their privileges and ancient customs, should be inviolably preserved. All the possessions which Churchmen had in the time of William, his grandfather, should be fully guaranteed to them. Any claims which may be set up by the Church to property held in the king's life-time, but since lost, should be carefully considered. Any gifts made since his death should be confirmed. The forests which William, his grandfather, and William, his uncle, had, he reserved, the others which Henry, the king, added, he gave to the churches free of charge. Bishops and abbots who make fitting distributions of their goods before death should be protected in doing so : if a Churchman die suddenly the Church should make distribution for the good of his soul. Vacant sees should be committed, as to the guardianship of their

captus et excruciatus miserandum sortitus est exterminium."—*Histor.*, f. 221 (Ed. Savile).

G

goods, to honest clerks of the Church until the
canonical election of a pastor. All exactions of
sheriffs or others should be abolished. The good
laws, and the ancient and just customs in the
matter of murders, pleas, and other causes, should
be observed."[1] This was the magnificent profession
of Stephen towards the Church.

"Quid dignum tanto feret hic promissor hiatu ?"
After giving the charter as above, William of Malmesbury says he does not think it worth while to subjoin
the names of the witnesses, inasmuch as the whole
thing was a mere farce, "and it would seem as if he
had only taken this oath in order to exhibit himself
to the whole kingdom as a perjurer."[2] Henry of
Huntingdon says simply—"He kept none of these
things."[3] Yet Stephen is highly praised for his
devotion to the Church by some chroniclers.[4] He
was a builder of abbeys and a liberal endower, and
it may be that had it not been for the overweening
magnificence and state of the Bishop of Salisbury
and his nephews, which excited his cupidity and
tempted him to an act of grievous violence, his name
would have been handed down to posterity as one
of the most pious of kings. Alexander, having sworn
allegiance to the new king and exhibited his mag-

---

[1] *Willelm. Malmesb., Hist. Nov.* p. 709 (E. H. S.) See Roger de
Wendover. *Flor. Hist.,* i. 217. In the *Gesta Regis Stephani* the
"orations" of those who represented to the king the oppressed state of
the Church in the time of Henry I. are given, and the substance of the
charter subjoined, p. 16.

[2] *Ib.*   [3] *Histor.* f. 221.   [4] See *Gesta Regis Stephani,* p. 1.

nificent state and retinue as one of his supporters, eagerly embraced every opportunity of keeping up his influence with him. Thus in the year 1137, when Stephen went into Normandy and carried on a successful war with the King of France, Bishop Alexander was with him. In the grand pomps and shows that were then exhibited (the king, says Henry of Huntingdon—"egregie inter summos enituit,"[1]) the magnificent English prelate was no doubt conspicuous, and rejoiced in the favour of the monarch whose cause he had adopted. When Stephen returned to England in the winter of 1137 he took up his abode within the diocese of Alexander, and kept his Christmas at Dunstable, in Bedfordshire.[2] In the spring, with indefatigable activity, he was in Scotland carrying on the war with David, and then again in England besieging Ludlow Castle. The ceaseless wars in which Stephen was engaged, the sieges of one castle after another, which he was compelled to make, the difficulty he had in satisfying his friends, the constant machinations which he had to meet from his enemies, may well have served to sour and embitter a temper naturally generous and trustful, and to dispose him to acts of violence from which naturally he would have been averse. "Many persons," says William of Malmesbury, "induced by their high birth to despise law, demanded of the king farms, castles, and what not, and if he made a

---

[1] *Henric. Hunting., Hist.*, f. 222 (Ed. Savile).
[2] *Contin. Florent. Wigorn.*, p. 101 (E. H. S.)

difficulty about giving them to avoid the mutilation of the kingdom, straightway, in a passion, they fortified their castles against him and ravaged his lands for booty.   All this he bore with spirit, coming suddenly now upon one, now upon another, but never bringing matters to a settlement, more to his own hurt than to that of those who opposed him.   Many and mighty labours did he spend in vain.   He gave honours and castles, but all only served to purchase a hollow and temporary peace."[1]   In a temper, therefore, not very favourable either towards his pretended supporters or his open enemies, King Stephen came to Oxford in June 1139, to hold a great council with the barons and bishops favourable to his cause. Here he was greeted with the news that the strong castle of Devizes, built by Roger, Bishop of Salisbury, and garrisoned by his men, was closed to the king's people.   Enraged at this, he straightway sent off a pressing message for the attendance of Bishop Roger at Oxford.   Very unwilling was that prelate to obey the summons.   "I heard him say," says William of Malmesbury, who knew him well,[2] "By our Lady, my mind is strangely opposed to this journey.   I shall certainly be of no more use in the court than a young foal would be in a battle.   As he was to go, however, he determined to make the best show possible.   He took with him his two nephews, the

---

[1] *Willelm. Malmesb.*, *Hist. Nov.*, p. 712 (E. H. S.)

[2] The bishop when summoned was at Malmesbury.—*Flor. Wig. Cont.*

Bishops of Lincoln and Ely, with a very large following of soldiers splendidly furnished and equipped."[1]   The king suspected treachery, and gave orders for his men to be on their guard.   Among those who were with him was a fierce and savage noble, Alan, Count of Brittany, whose followers were probably of the same stamp as their master.   A quarrel soon arose between them and the bishops' men as to their quarters.   A fierce fight ensued, the Britons were put to flight, the Count's nephew dangerously wounded, and the bishops' men, though with heavy losses, remained triumphant.[2]   The king, seeing that instant action was necessary, despatched an armed band to the bishops' quarters to summon them before him to give satisfaction for the outrage. Bishop Roger of Salisbury and Bishop Alexander of Lincoln appeared before him ; Bishop Nigel of Ely, more wary than his relatives, escaped.   To the Bishops of Salisbury and Lincoln the king spoke sternly, commanding them at once to give up the keys of all their castles.   The bishops naturally hesitated to obey so startling a command.   The two prelates were then ordered into custody, and Roger, the son of the Bishop of Salisbury, and the Chancellor

---

[1] *Flor. Wig. Cont.*

[2] There are four contemporary accounts of these doings at Oxford —those, namely, of the author of *Gesta Regis Stephani*, Henry of Huntingdon, the Worcester monk, who continued the *Chronicle of Florence*, and William of Malmesbury.   They differ considerably as to details, but as William of Malmesbury, from his vicinity to the scene of the events and his acquaintance with the bishops, is most likely to be well informed, I have mostly followed him.

of England, was ignominiously bound in chains. Presently news is brought to King Stephen that Bishop Nigel had reached the castle of Devizes, and was holding it against the king. Stephen, full of fury, marched away to the place, carrying with him the unfortunate bishops and the chancellor, of whom he swore that he would make a terrible example if the castle was not at once surrendered to him. Bishop Roger was confined in an ox-shed, Bishop Alexander in a vile hut, with strict · orders that none but the meanest of food was to be supplied to them, while preparations were made for hanging publicly on a gallows before the castle, Roger the Chancellor, the son of the bishop. The heart of Bishop Roger quailed. He sent word to his nephew Nigel that he would neither eat nor drink until he had surrendered the castle to the king. Three days had he to keep his fast before the Bishop of Ely would yield. At length,· however, he had compassion on the miserable state of his uncle and brother, and surrendered the castle. Thus the magnificent castle of Devizes, which all the chroniclers combine to extol, that of Sherborne, which was scarcely inferior, Salisbury, and Malmesbury, all built at immense cost, "professedly as an ornament of the Church, but really a mischief and loss to it,"[1] had to be surrendered with the vast treasures which they contained. Nor did Alexander, Bishop of Lincoln, fare better. He too had to surrender his fair castle of Newark "built upon the

[1] *Will. Malmesb.*

river Trent in a most fair and pleasant situation, and adorned in a most showy style."[1]   Sleaford also, "not second to the other either in shape or situation," and Banbury had to be absolutely given up as the price of their builders' liberty.   And now men sagely deliberated on the right and the wrong of this affair. "Some," says William of Malmesbury, " said that the bishops were rightly deprived of their castles, inasmuch as it was against the canons for them to build castles, that they ought to be evangelists of peace, not architects of buildings to shield the doers of wrong."   Others, however, were greatly and terribly scandalised by this open violence shown to fathers of the Church.   The chronicler of the *Gesta Stephani*, a strong adherent of the king, cannot contain his indignation at this act of his.   It was nothing less than madness and the grossest wickedness thus to lay hands upon the "Lord's anointed."   This no doubt was almost the universal feeling among Churchmen. The king's brother, Henry, Bishop of Winchester, and legate of the Pope, strongly shared in it, and so general was the excitement produced that it became needful to hold a council at Winchester, to consider the whole business.[2]

The Bishop of Winchester held the office of Papal Legate, which had been enjoyed till his death by William, the late Archbishop of Canterbury.

---

[1] *Henric. Hunting.*

[2] *Willelm. Malmesb., Hist. Nov.*, 715-719.   *Gesta Regis Stephani,* 47-51.   *Henric. Huntingdon, Histor.,* f. 223.   *Contin. Flor. Wigorn.,* 107.

He had aspired to the primacy, but Stephen, not wishing his brother to be too powerful, had favoured the claims of Theobald, Abbot of Bec, who had accordingly been appointed to that place. However, the Bishop of Winchester as Legate of the Pope was really a more powerful man in the land than the primate, and being not a little vexed with his brother for having opposed his ambition, he determined now to take the opportunity which Stephen's violent conduct towards the bishops afforded him of humbling the king. The archbishop and almost all the bishops of England assembled at his summons, and the king himself was cited to give an account of his conduct. The legate declared the object for which the council was held. The Bishop of Salisbury had been made prisoner in the court itself, the Bishop of Lincoln had been captured in his lodging, and the Bishop of Ely had only saved himself by flight. "It was," he said, "an execrable crime that the king had thus been led away by evil advisers to allow violence to be offered to his liegemen, especially as they were bishops, who had come peaceably to attend his court. An injury had been done to heaven itself when, under pretence of the fault of the bishops, the churches had been robbed of their possessions. He felt deeply this transgression of the king against the law of God, and would rather suffer bodily loss and harm than that the episcopal dignity should thus be abased. The king had been admonished to make amends, and had

been cited to the council, nor had he refused to
come. Let, then, the archbishop and the bishops
consult together as to what was to be done, and as
for himself neither the friendship of the king who
was his brother, nor the danger of losing his possessions, not even the danger to life itself, should
prevent him from carrying it out." Stephen, on
receiving the summons, sent some of his barons to
the council to demand why he was summoned.
The Bishop of Winchester answered that as one
who was subject to Christ he was bound to give
account to the ministers of Christ for the crime
which he had committed, such as might be expected
of heathen rulers rather than Christian. If he would
appear at the council he might be sure of being
justly and leniently dealt with. Then Alberic de
Vere, a skilful orator, was sent from the king, who
laboured to make out as strong a case as possible
against the bishops,[1] while some of the barons who
accompanied him continually heaped abuse upon
the bishops. The Bishop of Salisbury was charged
with disaffection to Stephen, and of secret correspondence with the Empress. The Bishop of Lincoln
was said to have cherished an ancient grudge against
Count Alan, and his people were the beginners of
the fracas. Bishop Roger made a violent reply to
the charges made against him. Then arrived the
Archbishop of Rouen from the king, who declared
that it was against the canons for bishops to possess

---

[1] Bishop Alexander was not present.

castles, and that even if they were allowed to have them, as faithful subjects they were bound to hand over the keys of them to the king on his demanding them. Alberic de Vere added on the part of the king that he would appeal to Rome. The council, seeing Stephen show this bold front, was intimidated. The archbishop and the others besought him on their knees to have pity on the Church, and not to bring so great a mischief on the land as a quarrel between the secular and ecclesiastical authority. The king, misled by the advice of evil counsellers, did nothing to make amends for the outrage he had committed.[1] Soon after this Roger, Bishop of Salisbury, died, his end being hastened, as it was thought, by the harsh treatment he had received from the king. His immense wealth came to be applied, says the chronicler, "not to the honour of God, but to the use of King Stephen."[2] The Bishop of Ely made his escape beyond seas, and joined the party of the Empress, while Alexander, Bishop of Lincoln, avoiding all open partisanship, prudently waited to see what the events of the war now raging throughout the land between the partisans of Matilda

---

[1] *Willelm. Malmesb.*, 719-724 (E. H. S.) *Henric. Huntingdon, Histor.*, f. 223 (Ed. Savile). The author of *Gesta Regis Stephani* says the king did penance for his treatment of the bishops, but does not say that he made restitution.

[2] *Contin. Flor. Wigorn.*, p. 116 (E. H. S.) Roger was the most magnificent of bishops, "Ipse singulari gloriâ (quantum nostra ætas reminisci potest), in domibus ædificandis splendida per omnes posses- siones suas construxit habitacula, in quibus solum tuendis successorum ejus frustra laborabit opera."—*Willelm. Malmesb.*

and Stephen, would bring forth. In a council held shortly afterwards, it was ordered that bishops should not possess castles, but should devote themselves to the spiritual care of their flocks, lest the wolf should devour and destroy it.[1]

Before his seizure by Stephen, Bishop Alexander had, among his other works, carefully improved the fortifications of the strong castle of Lincoln,[2] but the strength of the place was speedily turned against the king, the Earls of Chester and Lincoln having surprised and captured it.[3] The citizens of Lincoln, wishing to curry favour with King Stephen, proposed to him at London that they should take advantage of the earls' security, carry the castle by surprise, and thus gain it for the king, as well as capture the two nobles. Stephen readily consented to this, but the castle was found too well guarded to be surprised. The Earl of Chester managed to escape through the besiegers, and at once took vigorous measures for the relief of the castle. About Christmas-tide (1140), Stephen arrived at Lincoln to assist in the siege of the castle. He continued to besiege it without success up to the Feast of the Purification (Feb. 2, 1141), when the Earls of Chester and Gloucester arrived to succour it, and a great battle was fought at Lincoln, which resulted in the complete defeat and capture of

---

[1] *Contin. Flor. Wigorn.*, p. 116 (E. H. S.)

[2] *Annal. Winton. Ann. Monast.*, ii. 51.

[3] Ralph, Earl of Chester, and William, Earl of Lincoln, were the sons of Lucia, Countess of Lincoln, by her two marriages.

Stephen. This defeat, as the chronicler tells us, was presaged by divers omens. The king on the morning of the Feast of the Purification had not, in spite of his numerous cares, neglected to hear mass. The cathedral had been turned into a fort, which was thought a great tempting of God's judgment, but it was still used for the purposes of a church. Bishop Alexander was the celebrant. When the king brought his waxen taper to offer on the altar, and reverently placed it in the hands of the bishop, it broke as he took it and fell to the ground. This was interpreted to imply the contrition in the heart of the king. But when the Sacred Pix, which held the consecrated wafer, and was suspended above the altar by a chain, suddenly fell upon the altar, the chain being mysteriously broken, this was thought to portend nothing less than utter ruin.[1] The king was defeated and captured, but ere long he was exchanged for the Earl of Gloucester, who had been captured by Stephen's partisans, and so, with varying success, war raged over unhappy England. All the chroniclers labour to depict the horrors of those days. The author of the *Gesta Regis Stephani* specially accuses the bishops of having done no little to aggravate the miseries of the land. The bishops were in an abject state of fear, like a reed shaken with the wind, and would

---

[1] *Henric. Huntingd., Histor.*, p. 224 (Ed. Savile). *Willelm. Malmesb., Gest. Reg. Angl.*, p. 740 (E. H. S.) *Roger de Wendover, Flor. Hist.*, ii. 228.

not give any protection.   They feared to strike with
the sword of the word of God these children of
Belial, but, in terror at these bold misdoers, they
either altogether submitted to them or only spoke
some mild and trifling sentence against them.
Some of them most unepiscopally occupied themselves in furnishing their castles with food and
armed retainers, and were more pitiless in plundering their neighbours than any of the barons' free-
booters.   Some of them, girt in armour and mounted
on their war steeds, joined in plundering expeditions,
and were ready to inflict prison and torture on their
captives to extort money, laying the blame of all,
not upon themselves, but upon their followers.   To
omit others (for all were not equally to blame), the
Bishops of Winchester, Lincoln, and Coventry, were
beyond all others publicly accused of these evil and
ungodly practices.[1]   This terrible accusation brought
against Bishop Alexander was no doubt exaggerated,
but yet had some elements of truth.   Henry of
Huntingdon, an archdeacon of his diocese, speaks of
him in terms which, to a certain extent, justify the
above description of his proceedings, but yet represent him as personally popular and acceptable
among his people.[2]   In the year 1145 Bishop

[1] *Gesta Regis Stephani*, p. 96 (E. H. S.)   See also *Willclm.
Malmesb., Hist. Nov.*, p. 731.

[2] It is perhaps important to observe that the panegyrical passages
respecting Alexander were written by Henry of Iluntingdon during the
bishop's lifetime, but the passage here referred to, in which censure is
mixed with praise, after his death.—*Henric. Hunt.*, f. 226 (Ed. Savile).

Alexander, glad, no doubt, to escape from the tur-
moils and miseries of England, went to Rome. He
was received there with the greatest respect. Such
visitors were ever welcome at the Papal Court. He
was a man of liberal and profuse expenditure, ready
with handsome presents and offerings to propitiate
the hungry crowd of officials who thronged around
the papal chair. On his former visit, some twenty
years before, the nephew of the great and wealthy
chancellor had so distinguished himself by his
liberality that he had gained from the Romans the
name of "The Magnificent." On the present visit
he kept up his character, and was received with the
greatest honour by Pope Eugenius. This was the
Pope who had been a pupil of St. Bernard, and to
whom that saint addressed his treatise *De Considera-
tione*, in which such terrible charges of venality,
corruption, and worldliness are brought against the
Papal Court. Alexander, whose experience of true
Church life was not great, would hardly be scandalised at these things. He spent his time at Rome,
and returned from there "in the highest favour with
the Pope and the whole court," and, according to
the chronicler, his return was heartily welcomed by
his people. "He was received with the greatest
reverence and joy." A great calamity had happened
during his absence. The fair church of Remigius,
which had escaped so wonderfully in the great fire
at Lincoln some years before, had been very

grievously injured by another fire,[1] and lay in a foul and disfigured state (deturpata). The spirit of the great builder was at once aroused. Alexander determined that he would restore his church, not to its pristine state, but to a much more splendid condition. The time at which his building began was the commencement of a change in the dominant style of architecture. The severity of the true Norman style, with its round-headed arches and stereotyped mouldings, was beginning to yield to new combinations. The round arches were made to intersect each other, and a richer style of adornment began. The builders, learning more of the mechanical art, aspired also now to carry their arches across wide spans, and causing them to meet at various angles, to produce that most beautiful feature of the vaulted stone roof. In these improved manners Alexander restored his cathedral. " He used upon it," says Henry of Huntingdon, " such subtle skill, that it seemed to be fairer than it was when it first came from the builders' hands, nor was it second to any building within the realm of England."[2] " He repaired it in a noble fashion," says Giraldus, " and was the first to use the firm and

---

[1] Henry of Huntingdon's account seems to imply that the fire had taken place during the bishop's absence abroad. Mr. Dimock (*Recorded History of Lincoln Cathedral*) points out from a Peterborough and Spalding chronicler, that there was a fire at Lincoln in 1141, but this may be two or three years too early a date.

[2] *Henric. Huntingd., Hist.*, p. 225. It will be observed that Henry of Huntingdon says nothing of the vaulted roof.

stable covering of stone vaulting."[1] The church of
Alexander remained the glory of the land until the
calamity of the great earthquake and the ruinous
condition into which the cathedral was thrown by it
brought out a still more famous builder in Hugh
of Burgundy. King Stephen had made various
attempts to capture the noble castle of Lincoln,
which had long been held by the Earl of Chester.
These attempts had been altogether unsuccessful.
The Earl of Chester was now nominally on the side
of the king, but still he held his strong castle of
Lincoln. By an act of treachery Stephen seized
him, and throwing him into prison, declared he
would keep him there until Lincoln Castle was
surrendered. The surrender was made. Then
Stephen, proud of his acquisition, came in the 12th
year of his reign[2] to Lincoln, and there was solemnly
crowned anew. It could not, indeed, have been the
case that the restoration of the cathedral was by
this time finished, yet Stephen may have received
his diadem there from the hand of the bishop.
Amidst the festivities and rejoicings men spoke
together of the boldness of the king. For it was
said that an ancient prophecy declared that no king

---

[1] *Giraldus Camb.*, vii. 33. This is adopted by John de Schalby
writing early in the century. In the western doorways which remain
" the foliage is more like some of the beautiful specimens in the Lom-
bardic Italian churches than the ordinary English Norman ; and when
we know that the bishop paid several visits to Rome, it is probable he
brought the designs from thence."—Sir C. J. Anderson's *Lincoln*,
p. 69.　　　　　　　　　　　　　　 [2] Christmas, 1146.

could enter the city of Lincoln without bringing
ruin on himself.[1]   The Christmastide of 1146 was
doubtless spent in festivities at Lincoln, and in the
month of August of the following summer Bishop
Alexander went to pay another visit to Pope
Eugenius, who, after having made a journey to Paris,
was sojourning at Auxerre.   The hot season, the
journey, perhaps the unhealthiness of the place,
brought on a low fever.   Alexander returned to
England still suffering from the disease, which
carried him off at the beginning of the next year
(1148).   In him the church of Lincoln lost a
magnificent prelate, a liberal benefactor to his
church, a fair specimen of the ecclesiastical baron of
his day, but scarcely to be regarded as approaching
to the highest type of bishop.   A letter of the great
St. Bernard, written to him on the occasion of one
of the Lincoln canons, named Philip, having entered
the Cistercian order at Clairvaux, manifestly points
at the too notorious worldliness of the bishop's
character: "We presume to exhort you in all
charity that you should not regard the glory of a
world which will quickly pass away, as though it
were stable and fixed, and thus lose the stable glory
of the real world; that you should not love your
possessions more than yourself, and thus lose both
yourself and your possessions; that no flattering

---

[1] *Henric. Huntingd., Histor.,* f. 225 (Ed Savile).   The same
appears to have been said both as regards Oxford and Leicester.   See
Chron. W. de Rishanger.

H

present prosperity should hide from you the adversity which will follow it ; that no temporal joy should be allowed to conceal the eternal grief which it begets, and thus beget that which it hides ; that you should not look upon death as distant, lest it should seize you unprepared, and life suddenly leave you whilst you are building upon its length."[1] We may trust that the bishop laid these wise and solemn words to heart before his summons came.

ROBERT DE CHESNEY (FOURTH BISHOP)—
1148-1167.

If not many episcopal acts can be found to be chronicled of Robert Bloet and Alexander, they were, at any rate, somewhat prominent figures in the history of their days, and their secular importance was considerable.   This cannot be said of Robert, the fourth Bishop of Lincoln.   In a secular point of view he occupies no conspicuous place, nor indeed is there much to be recorded of him for any great services done to the Church.[2]   Henry of Huntingdon, indeed, just at the close of his history, welcomes his advent

---

[1] *St. Bernardi, Ep.* lxiv.

[2] There is a *hiatus valde deflendus* in contemporary chronicles just at this point.   William of Malmesbury, Henry of Huntingdon, the continuator of Florence of Worcester, cease.   Roger de Hoveden does not become contemporary and valuable till towards the end of the century.   The valuable work of Benedictus does not begin till 1169. That of Ralph de Diceto, Dean of St. Paul's, does not begin to be original till 1159.

to the see with soft and laudatory words, which must,
however, be qualified by the fact that the archdeacon's
history was just about to appear under the very eye
of the new bishop. The name of the bishop is
written very variously in the chronicles. It is given
as Chennehai, Casnei, Cheynel, Cadney, Catineto,
Kaineto. But that the right form is Chesney is
evident from Henry of Huntingdon, who says, " His
surname is from the oak copse." His election would
appear to have been made by the dean and chapter
freely without the interference of the king.[1] Ralph
de Diceto says : " He was created Bishop of Lincoln
by the common consent of the whole Church of
Lincoln ;" and Henry of Huntingdon : " He was
elected Bishop of Lincoln."[2] Having filled the post
of Archdeacon of Leicester, he was well known to
his brethren, and being, from the character given of
him, probably of a quiet and unassuming nature, he
had made no enemies. " Every one," says Henry of
Huntingdon, " agreed that he was worthy of so great
an honour ; the king, the clergy, and the people, with

[1] A great variety of practice as to the appointment of bishops prevailed throughout all the period between the Conquest and Magna
Charta. Sometimes they were simply nominated by the king, as
Alexander appears to have been. According to Collier, the usual
practice was as follows :—" From the Conqueror's time to the reign of
King John it was the custom to choose bishops at a public meeting
of the bishops and barons, the king being present at the solemnity, and
that the election might pass through a regular form, a delegation of
monks or canons who represented the vacant sees, were sent up for that
purpose."—*Collier*, ii. 203.

[2] *Radulph de Diceto, Imag. Hist.*, 509 (Ed. Twysden). *Henric.
de Huntingdon*, f. 226 (Ed. Savile).

the greatest joy, welcomed his advancement, and, having received the benediction from the Archbishop of Canterbury, his coming to Lincoln was looked forward to with the greatest eagerness, and his reception, when he did come, both from clergy and people, exceeded all expectation."[1] Ralph de Diceto, Dean of St. Paul's, his contemporary, describes the new bishop as "a man of great simplicity and humility ;" and Gervase, the Canterbury Monk, also a contemporary, describes him as "a simple man, but not over wise."[2] Giraldus Cambrensis, whose testimony is perhaps not so much to be depended on, calls him "a generous man," but gives him a very bad character as a dilapidator of the property of the see. "He alienated estates from the Church by giving them to his nieces for marriage portions, thereby causing great scandal."[3] One recommendation, however, Robert de Chesney had which neither of his predecessors could boast. He was by birth an Englishman, though of Norman family.[4] We may therefore well believe Henry of Huntingdon when he tells us of the joy of the people at Robert de Chesney's appointment. It was not so common an occurrence even yet for an English-born man to rise to the highest rank in the Church. The new bishop also had another recommendation—he was young. Henry of Huntingdon

---

[1] *Henric. Hunting., Histor.,* f. 226 (Ed. Savile).

[2] *Radulph de Diceto,* p. 509. *Gervas. Dorobern.,* p. 1390 (Ed. Twysden).

[3] *Opera,* vii. 34. This is adopted in the notice of the Bishops of Lincoln, written by John de Schalby.   [4] *Giraldus, Op.* vii. 34.

calls him a youth, and expresses a devout hope that "God would cherish his youth with the dew of wisdom." Robert de Chesney was elected bishop not long before Christmas 1148,[1] and was consecrated by Theobald, Archbishop of Canterbury, some time in the following year.

It was the fate of Bishop Robert de Chesney, though by no means a prominent man in the history of his times, to be brought into the foremost place in a dispute which had the greatest possible influence in the future of the Church of England. The Norman Conquest allowed scope for the beginning of that series of encroachments by which Rome, in spite of the energetic resistance of some of the English kings, gradually enslaved the Church of this land, and brought it to that complete state of misrule, inefficiency, and debasement which at length led to the Reformation. The first step in this evil series was the admission of legates into England, having delegated to them the supreme and irresponsible authority claimed by the Roman Pontiff. A further advance in the same path was the conferring of a perpetual legatine authority upon the Archbishop of Canterbury, or, what was even worse, upon some other English bishop, so that the real ecclesiastical authority of the land was superseded, and the fountain of the controlling episcopal power was made to be at Rome. Then came the crusade against the married clergy, with the object of making them more

---

[1] Appropinquante natali.—*Hen. Hunt.*

completely the slaves of Rome, and the system of appeals to Rome from the decisions of English synods—a thing of which Henry of Huntingdon complains as utterly unheard of, and subversive of all discipline. But the most complete and entire overthrow of discipline, and utter paralysis of the power of bishops to correct abuses, was brought about by the rise of the system of monastic exemptions, granted arbitrarily by the Pope, which took its beginning from the dispute between Robert, Bishop of Lincoln, and the Abbot of St. Albans. It is true that the Cistercian order of white monks had been established in England since the year 1128, when its first monastery was built at Waverley, and the Cistercians were always specially and completely exempted from diocesan control. But the white monks were under a careful discipline and superintendence of their own arrangement. It was far worse when Benedictine monasteries or houses of canons strove by bribery or some undue influence to obtain from the Pope special exemptions for their own bodies, and thus to secure by the most shameless means a liberty of doing ill just as it pleased them. This rendered all discipline impossible, for the immunities of the monastery extended to all in any way connected with it ; and as each religious house eagerly and rapidly assimilated numerous parish churches, the tithes of which it held, while it became responsible for the duties of the Church, the bishops were everywhere thwarted and their power

scoffed at.   The annals of Evesham Abbey show
what excesses of wickedness were rendered possible
by this claim of exemption,[1] and the life of the great
reformer Grosseteste was one long-continued struggle
against this monster abuse.   The exemption of
Battle Abbey by the king from diocesan control, on
the ground of its being a royal chapel, seems to have
given the first hint to the abbots to make the
attempt at gaining for themselves independence ; and
about the same time (1152) we find disputes
beginning between the Archbishop of Canterbury
and the monks of St. Augustine ; between the monks
of Glastonbury and the Bishop of Bath and Wells ;
and between the Abbot of the famous Abbey of St.
Albans and Robert, Bishop of Lincoln.[2]   With this
last alone are we here concerned, and though every
student of history must feel the vast obligations he
is under to St. Albans for the numerous able
chroniclers which it produced, yet in its successful
struggle for exemption and independence, the abbey
inflicted a blow upon the English Church for which
not all the labours of its numerous literary monks
could compensate.   The ablest of the historical
writers of St. Albans (Matthew Paris) has left us a
minute account of the struggle between the Bishop
of Lincoln and his abbot,[3] which is beyond measure

---

[1] See *Annales de Evesham* (Ed. Macray).   Rolls Series.

[2] See Inett, *Ch. Hist.*, P. ii. ch. xi., where the whole subject is
very fully treated.

[3] In his *Life of the Abbot Robert*, from whence all the details which
follow was taken.   See also *Roger de Wendover, Flor. Hist.*, ii. 29.

interesting as a picture of the Church of that day. Robert, Abbot of St. Albans, was a man of great enterprise, spirit, and boldness. His opponent, on the other hand, Robert, Bishop of Lincoln, was evidently of a quiet and unambitious temper. The abbot saw clearly the immense value as regards power and dignity that the concession of independence would prove to be to him and his abbey; the bishop took, so far as we can perceive, no enlarged view of the matter. He was willing to do his best to retain a right which manifestly belonged to himself and his see; but he seems to have regarded it more as a piece of property than anything else; and in accepting the cession of a manor in lieu of his claim, he showed himself altogether below the situation. The attempt to obtain special privileges and exemption for his abbey seems to have been first suggested to the Abbot of St. Albans by the remarkable promotion to the chair of St. Peter of Nicholas Brakespere, the only Englishman who ever reached that dignity. This Nicholas was the son of one Robert de Camera, who had taken the cowl at St. Albans towards the close of his life, and was anxious that his son Nicholas, who had been bred to be a clerk, should be received into the society as a monk. The abbot was nothing loth, if Nicholas should be found competent. But the future pope, when submitted to the usual entrance examination, was found altogether deficient. "Go, my son," said the abbot, "and be diligent at your school, and perhaps hereafter you

may be found more fit." The young clerk departed
in confusion, and, taking the rebuff in good part,
went to Paris, where he studied diligently, and
gradually rising through one grade after another, at
length reached the throne of St. Peter by the title of
Adrian IV. He was known ever to have cherished
an affection for St. Albans in spite of its rejection of
him ; and when the Abbot Robert heard of his promotion to the highest dignity in the Church he was
glad and exultant, declaring to the brethren that now
should the ancient dignity of St. Albans be recovered,
and that they should soon see their abbey the first
in the land. The abbot straightway prepared for a
journey to Italy. Horses and money were got ready,
but especially that most important requisite, a store
of costly presents, and in particular three most beautiful caps and a pair of sandals embroidered with
exquisite skill by the hands of Christina, Prioress of
Margate. The abbot was fortunate in being entrusted
by the king with some matters to negotiate with the
Pope, and, in company with three bishops and their
retainers, he reached Italy in safety, and proceeding
southward found Pope Adrian at Beneventum. He
received the Abbot of St. Albans most graciously,
joked with him about his former rejection of him as
a monk, and accepting for himself the Prioress
Christina's caps and sandals, allowed the abbot to
distribute the rest of his presents among the
cardinals. In this happy conjunction of affairs for
St. Albans, it was clear that the rights of the Bishop

of Lincoln stood but a poor chance. The abbot
failed not to relate " with tears and sobs the various
oppressions, the plots, the violence, the imperious
demands, the ruinous rejections of suits, on the part
of the Bishop of Lincoln, and the intolerable pride
of the bishop's men, even mean persons." The pope
took pity on these manifold grievances, and
announced his intention of conferring upon his
beloved abbey " an extraordinary privilege." A bull
was issued which ran thus :—" We decree that all
who are dwellers in the said monastery, as well as
all those who are inhabitants of its dependent houses
(cells), or who are acting as guardians of its rights
in any vills (in custodiis villarum) shall be altogether free from all subjection to bishops, and shall
have no bishop whatever for the future, except the
Roman Pontiff." And in addition to this, says the
historian, " he gave us many other noble privileges,
so that no abbey in England was to be compared for
its privileges to St. Albans." It may be imagined
with what joy the Abbot Robert was received when
he returned to his monks, and, " entering the chapter-
house, told them the various adventures of his journey and its final success." Very soon the abbot was
to have a more public opportunity of displaying his
triumph. A synod was held at London in which the
archbishop and many bishops and abbots were present.
The Bishop of Lincoln was absent, fearing, it is said,
to hear what the abbot had brought from Rome, but
he was represented by some of his clerks. Then

Abbot Robert exhibited the Pope's letters, which first of all declared the Feast of St. Alban a day to be observed in all churches ; and after this, to which no opposition was raised, the abbot produced other letters which declared that the *Processions*[1] of the county of Hertford were to be made no longer to the cathedral at Lincoln but to the abbey of St. Albans.   At this the clerks of the bishop, aghast at the audacity of the claim, immediately lodged an appeal to Rome.   Both parties left the synod to prepare for the struggle, but Bishop Hugh of Durham, acting as peacemaker, procured a meeting between the bishop and the abbot at St. Neot's on the festival of St. Simon and St. Jude.   A composition, of which the historian does not give us the terms, was now made between the bishop and the abbot.   It was

---

[1] " This usage, known in our histories by the name of the Procession, was, if I am not mistaken, an honorary privilege granted to cathedral churches not long after the Norman Conquest, at least to those which had been built by the Normans : this was the case with that of Lincoln.   It was an acknowledgment made by the parishes of the diocese of their relation to and their dependence on the cathedral as the mother church of the whole diocese ; and being performed at Whitsun-tide, and by way of procession, came in due time to receive the name of the *Pentecostal* or the Procession.   And by an account yet remaining in the Registry of the Bishops of Lincoln, it appears that the ceremony was performed in this manner :—Each parish had a distinct sum charged on it, which at Whitsuntide was brought to the cathedral by some of the respective parishes, deputed by the whole, who came together headed by the respective archdeacons, in the way of a procession, and in the name of those whom they represented, offered at the altar of the cathedral church the sums charged upon their respective parishes."— *Inett.*   Russell, Bishop of Lincoln in 1491, caused the details of these processions to be entered in his Register.

probably somewhat unfavourable to the latter, as he quickly took occasion to send a handsome present of two magnificent gold and silver candlesticks to his friend the Pope. They were very gratefully received, and the Pope in return forwarded to the Abbot Robert the right of wearing "the episcopal ornaments," at the same time that he confirmed the privileges already granted. It thus became evident to the Bishop of Lincoln that so long as Pope Adrian lived he would have no chance whatever of success against the abbot, and he determined to bide his time. Soon afterwards the Pope died suddenly, it is said by poison. Then the Abbot of St. Albans, whose energy was equal to every emergency, sent a messenger in all haste to congratulate his successor, and to desire a continuance of the privileges granted by Adrian. This was readily acceded to by the new Pope Alexander. The Bishop of Lincoln betook himself to a less efficient ally—the king,—who was then in France, and having greatly prejudiced him against St. Albans (as Matthew Paris has it), and obtained his authority to act summarily returned, and with the advice of some of his brother bishops made a formal demand on St. Albans for the procession to Lincoln, and for the customary reception of himself and his train on their circuit through the diocese. The abbot stiffly refused both claims. Then the bishop appealed to the king's justiciary, Robert, Earl of Leicester, who summoned the litigants to appear before him at Northampton.

Robert, Bishop of Lincoln, came, accompanied by his kinsman, Gilbert, Bishop of Hereford, and a mighty crowd of his clerks. The Bishop of Hereford pleaded for his friend. The Abbots of St. Albans, he said, being within the diocese of Lincoln, have always been subject to the bishops of that see ; they have been blessed by them and made their professions of obedience there. Here is the profession of this very Abbot Robert. The Lord of Lincoln then can rightly claim the processions and the due refection at St. Albans, but the abbot flatly refuses to accord him this. Therefore let the justice of the king be done. The Abbot of St. Albans answered in a supercilious manner. It is probable there was some profession of obedience to the see of Lincoln, but there was always added at the end of it, a salvo of the dignities of St. Albans. The dignity and freedom of St. Albans existed of old, and were conferred upon it by King Offa, its founder. It soon became a mere squabble between the two parties as to the alleged ancient privileges of the abbey, and certain commissioners were appointed to investigate these. There now also was made public a letter from Pope Alexander to the abbot, in which, after reciting the favour he had shown him, he also states that not being able to deny the just claims put forward by the Bishop of Lincoln, he has appointed two judges, the Bishops of Chichester and Norwich, to hear the cause and take evidence, and transmit it to him for the final settlement.

This arrangement, however, came to nothing, as King Henry, hearing of it on his return from abroad, was very angry at the interference of the Pope, and cited all the parties to appear at the council which he was about to hold at Westminster in the middle of Lent, A.D. 1163. Long and bitter were the pleadings here on both sides. The abbot alleged ancient privileges and immunities of the abbey which, as he affirmed, had been at various times recognised and acknowledged by divers Bishops of Lincoln. He did not, however, plead the Pope's bulls of exemption, as the king was evidently in no mind to accept these. "You have no right," said Henry, "to make the church tributary to the Roman see. This cannot be done without my consent." The abbot declared that he had not done so. "Let us see then the copy of those privileges which are especially odious to the Lincoln people, and which they are wont to call 'horned' (cornuta)."[1] "Here they are," said the abbot, "but I solemnly declare they were not asked for by me nor at my instance. They were given freely by Pope Adrian to the church of St. Albans, in a village belonging to which he was born." This, if not actually a falsehood, was certainly a misrepresentation on the part of the abbot, who, by his sore complaints of the Lincoln oppressions, had induced the Pope to grant these privileges. When the Bishop of Lincoln's turn to plead came, he could

---

[1] They were called *cornuta* on account of the mitre with its two horns and the other pontifical ornaments with which they were adorned.

allege no written documents, but simply prescription and usage. The church of St. Albans had always been under the episcopal control of the Bishop of Lincoln; why should it be now exempted? "The abbot alleges," said the king, "that it was originally free, but that by the carelessness of his predecessors it became subject to your see; that now the Pope has restored it to its original state. Will you contend further about the matter, or will you agree to some compromise? Go, consult with your dean and canons." The bishop might easily perceive by this that his cause was lost, and after consultation with his clergy agreed to accept a composition. Then the king made the proposal for a compromise to the abbot. After some shuffling he agreed to give the manor of Tynghurst, of the value of ten pounds yearly, for the perpetual freedom of the abbey and its dependencies from the control of the Bishop of Lincoln, and for the right of procession from such parts of Hertfordshire as were within the see of Lincoln. This was duly confirmed by charters, the originals of which still remain at Lincoln. The king's charter declared that "Robert, Bishop of Lincoln, with the assent of his chapter, abandoned the controversy against Robert, Abbot of St. Albans, and the brethren, touching the privileges of the Abbey of St. Albans, and the 15 churches in its territory, and would never move it again, for the consideration of the vill called Tinghurst, with its church and pertinences to the value of land worth ten pounds yearly, to be held freely by the church of Lincoln for ever, the chapter of Lincoln consenting. And the bishop resigns all the right that he had in the said Abbey of St. Albans, and over the person of Robert, the abbot, and his successors, and over the 15 said churches, into the hands of me the king. Wherefore I will that henceforth it shall be free to the said abbey and churches to take the chrism, and the oil, and the benediction of the abbot, and all the other sacraments of the Church, without opposition from the Bishop of Lincoln, from whatever bishop they please, and the abbey shall remain free in my hands for ever, like the king's chapels. But the other churches belonging to the monastery in divers parts of the diocese of Lincoln shall pay due obedience to the bishop and his archdeacons, any privileges which the monks may claim as to these churches notwithstanding."[1]   Thus was this great controversy settled, and the evil principle of *imperium in imperio* formally sanctioned.   Henceforward bishops were baffled at every turn, and though the diocese of Lincoln was afterwards happy in being presided over by some of the most notable reformers of their day, yet, in spite of all their efforts, the evil system was too strong for them.   The Abbot of St. Albans was of course beyond measure triumphant.   He returned to his abbey amidst the acclamations of his monks, and at Easter following,[2] with the mitre

---

[1] *Dugdale, Monasticon*, vi. 1276.

[2] The controversy was settled March 3, 1163.

on his head, the gloves, the sandals—the distinguish-
ing mark of bishops—celebrated mass and went in
procession, and twice in the year convened the
synods of his new clergy, going at their head in the
episcopal ornaments.   Thus was St. Albans the
first in England of what are called the mitred abbeys,
the abbots of which obtained a dignity beyond their
fellows, and sat in the House of Peers as equals of
the bishops.[1]

The part which the Bishop of Lincoln bore in
this important dispute may have been an honest one,
but he does not seem to have fought the battle with
sufficient vigour and determination.   In acquiescing
in the cession of the rights of his see for a money
payment, he shows a want of appreciation for the
ecclesiastical bearings of the matter, and to a certain
extent justifies the reproach of Giraldus Cambrensis
against him, that he was an " enormous dilapidator."
Further than this, there is reason to believe that not
only in this case, where he was to a certain extent
driven to the concession, but also in other cases
where no such constraint existed, Bishop Robert de
Chesney sacrificed the property and privileges of the
see of Lincoln to feed and enrich monastic societies.
He must have sanctioned, if he did not actually
make, the grant of the procession and oblations
within the archdeaconry of Oxford to the Abbey of
Eynsham,[2] and he is distinctly accused by Giraldus

---

[1] Inett, *Ch. Hist.*, ii. 282.
[2] See Dr. Griffiths' note, Inett, *Ch. Hist.*, ii. 279.

I

of alienating from the see four churches and one prebend for the order of Sempringham.[1] This very curious monastic order, which had almost a local existence, not having extended much beyond Lincolnshire, grew up, as it were, under the patronage of the Bishops of Lincoln, both Alexander and Robert de Chesney having been benefactors to it. Its rule was founded on that of St. Benedict, but its special peculiarity was that it united in the same establishment houses of monks and houses of nuns. Every precaution was taken to secure an absolute separation between the two, but this did not prevent the order acquiring a very bad name, and, later on, Sempringham, the head house, had the reputation of being the most luxurious and disorderly house in England.[2] But had the order been most exemplary and promising, for a bishop to alienate churches from his cathedral and assign them to it, was a very questionable proceeding. The use which monastic houses made of parish churches was usually to rob them of their tithes and to starve them in spirituals. They also stood in the way of all episcopal discipline, and if they had obtained an exemption, absolutely

[1] *Giraldus*, vii. 34. Giraldus, however, also says that he gave to the church at Lincoln one prebend. He founded the religious house of St. Catherine's, near Lincoln, for the order of Sempringham. The churches which he alienated were Newark, Norton, Marton, and Newton. The prebend, Canwick.—(Mr. Dimock's note, *ad loc.*)

[2] Warton (*s. v.* Robert de Brune), quoting a MS. in Harleian Collection. We can forgive Sempringham a great deal for having been the home of Robert Mannyng of Brune or Bourn, the author of the *Handlyng Synne*, and *Piers Langtoft's Chronicle*.

defied it.   Hence the comment of Giraldus upon this alienation of churches to Sempringham is probably very well founded : " It did no small damage to the church of Lincoln and to his episcopal successors."   But Robert de Chesney must not be regarded altogether in this unfavourable light as an injurer or dilapidator of his see.   " He built," says Giraldus, who brings these heavy accusations against him, " the bishop's house at Lincoln at great cost, having obtained the lands whereon it had been situated."[1] Among the charters printed in Dugdale, is given the king's grant made to the bishop for the purposes of the building : " Henry, the king, to all his liegemen, etc., know ye that I have given and granted, and by these presents confirm, to the church of Lincoln, and to Robert, the Bishop of Lincoln, and his successors, for their buildings and their houses, all the land with the ditch of the wall of my bail in Lincoln on the east, through the cemetery of the church of St. Michael, as far as the cemetery of St. Andrew, and from the cemetery of St. Andrew as far as the wall of the town towards the east.   And this land

---

[1] *Girald.*, vii. 34. The expression *ubi sitæ fuerant* would imply that a bishop's house had stood on this site before. In the account of the fire in Lincoln, in 1122, in the *Margan Annals* it is said that the *Episcopium* escaped.   Probably, therefore, Robert de Chesney only rebuilt on a larger scale the former house of Remigius.   St. Hugh of Burgundy is also said to have built the Episcopal house (both by Giraldus and John de Schalby).   This may mean that he added to the buildings already existing, and especially, that he began the Great Hall, afterwards finished by Hugh de Welles.—(See John de Schalby, *Girald. Camb.*, vii. 200).

I have given to the church of Lincoln, and to the said Robert the bishop, and his successors, free and quit from all dues and all other things, and he is empowered freely to break through the wall of my bail for making his gate for entrance and exit towards his church, and so to build that his buildings may extend to either wall."[1] Thus Robert was not slow to imitate his predecessors in their love of building, and as Alexander had magnificently renovated the cathedral church and made it one of the most beautiful in England, so he, with similar zeal, determined to construct on a grand scale the palace of the bishop, who, even after the loss of Ely, ruled over a diocese far exceeding in extent any other in England. Nor did the bishop confine his building to Lincoln. He began, if he did not complete, the house of the Bishops of Lincoln at the Old Temple in London—the house afterwards made famous by the death of St. Hugh within it. We have the king's charter stating that he had "granted to the church of St. Mary in Lincoln, to Robert the bishop, and to his successors in the same church, the houses which belonged to the brethren of the Temple in London, in the parish of St. Andrew of Holborn, with the chapel and the gardens, and all their appurtenances, which the said Robert de Kaineto, Bishop of Lincoln, bought for a hundred merks of the brethren of the Temple, and for a' yearly payment to the same brethren of three gold crowns in

[1] *Dugdale, Monast.*, vi. 1275.

lieu of all service."[1] If to this we add the obtaining
for the see the concession of some "very useful
markets and fairs,"[2] it may be that as far as
temporal matters went, even according to the
account of Giraldus, the see of Lincoln was no great
loser by Robert de Chesney. These manifold works
would appear to have required means more than
even the rich revenues of the see could furnish ; or
possibly the bishop may not have thought it according to equity that works for the permanent improvement of the see should fall solely on one incumbent.
At any rate, Bishop Robert de Chesney contracted
a debt with Aaron, the Jew of Lincoln, for three
hundred pounds. This very considerable sum was
charged upon the see, the *ornamenta* of the church
being given by the bishop into the custody of the
Jew as security for it, from which unhallowed custody
it was one of the few useful acts of his unconsecrated
successor to redeem them.[3]

The latter part of the life of Bishop Robert de
Chesney was coincident with that most eventful
period in the history of our Church, when the ablest

---

[1] *Dugdale*, vi. 1275.

[2] "Sciatis me dedisse et concessisse pro Dei amore et petitione
Roberti Lincolniensis episcopi ecclesiæ S. Mariæ Lincolniensis in per-
petuum quod habeat mercatum suum in villâ suâ de Bannebiriâ in
unâquâque septimanâ in die Jovis, liberè, quietè et honorificè, ad tales
consuetudines quales habent alia mercata per Angliam."—*Carta Henrici
II.*, *Dugdale*, vi. 1276.

[3] *Girald., Op.* vii. 35.   Aaron, the Jew of Lincoln, was evidently a
person of great wealth.   Notices of his property occur in *Rotuli Lit.
Claus.*, pp. 187, 196, 479.

and most vigorous of our early kings was contending against the boldest and most unflinching of the champions of the Church in the person of Thomas of Canterbury. The papal intrusions which had already been sanctioned in England, and the vast power which the papacy had now reached in Europe, made this contest inevitable and its issue not doubtful. In vain did the king and the national party contend against the certain advance of the terrible power of the spiritual arm. The struggles of Henry II. only issued in the complete and degrading subjection of John. Throughout all the earlier part of this contest the king was well supported by the suffragan bishops of the province of Canterbury, and among the rest by the Bishop of Lincoln.[1] He was one of those who were present at Canterbury, when after a long and unseemly struggle as to who should take the leading part in the ceremony, Thomas was consecrated archbishop on the octave of Whitsunday 1162.[2] He was present, we know, at that council of Westminster (when the composition between him and the Abbot of St. Albans was made), at which the first strife broke out between the king and archbishop, on the point whether he and the bishops would promise to observe the ancient customs (*avitæ consuetudines*) of the realm without the addition of

---

[1] *Roger de Hoveden*, f. 282 (Ed. Savile). The Bishop of Lisieux had early given Henry the advice to gain over some of the suffragan bishops of Canterbury, and the Bishop of Lincoln was one of those who thus joined the king.—See *Roger de Wendover, Flor. Hist.*, ii. 316.   [2] *Gervas Dorobern.*, p. 1382 (Ed. Twysden).

salvo ordine meo.   He was probably one of those whose hearts failed them at the wrath of the king on that occasion.[1]   Again, at the council of Clarendon, when the stout heart of the archbishop himself yielded,[2] the Bishop of Lincoln would no doubt be of the number of those who were ready to welcome the "ancient customs," though he, as well as others, were very ignorant what those ancient customs were. Again, at the council at Northampton, when the king endeavoured to crush the archbishop by bringing charges of past illegal proceedings against him, Bishop Robert was one of the body of bishops who agreed that by a failure of justice in the matter of John, the Marshall, the archbishop had forfeited all his goods to the king.[3]   And when in the serious question as to the disposal of the revenues of the benefices which had been kept vacant during his chancellorship, the archbishop, in doubt as to his answer, consulted his suffragans, we have preserved to us in the pages of the chronicler Gervase, the answer which was made by the Bishop of Lincoln. After Gilbert Ffoliot, Bishop of London, had vehemently declared that Thomas ought to yield to the demands of the king, and Henry of Winchester had as vehemently declared for the liberty of the Church,

---

[1] "Conversi quidam ex episcopis minis et terroribus qui ab antiquo iram regis incurrerant."—*Gervas. Dorobern.*, p. 1382.

[2] The archbishop had sworn to obey the *avitæ consuetudines* previously to the Council of Clarendon, at Oxford or Woodstock, and the meeting at Clarendon was to declare the *consuetudines* and get them formally ratified.   [3] *Gervas. Dorobern.*, *Ib.*

Hilary of Chichester, much given to fine words,[1] somewhat enigmatically proposed a temporary submission. Then Robert, Bishop of Lincoln, spoke. "He," says the chronicler, "was a simple man, and not specially famous for his wisdom."[2] His words, however, are not devoid of plain good sense. "It is evident," said he, "that this man's (the archbishop's) life and blood is sought after. He will either have to give up the archbishopric or his life. And, for my part, I don't see what good his archbishopric will do him if it is to cost him his life."[3] We may easily infer from the spirit of this utterance that the bishop did not sympathise with the bold struggle which Becket was making against the secular power, and that he inclined to support the cause of the king. But Robert de Chesney was no Gilbert Ffoliot to take a prominent and decided line. He earnestly besought Becket to yield to the king. He is said even to have been moved to tears in the violence of his entreaties.[4] When all proved ineffectual, and Becket in a foreign land fought with all the ardour of his fiery soul against the king and the national party, he would have no support from the mild temper of the Bishop of Lincoln. But the bishop did not live to see the bitterest part of the struggle, nor its tragical termination by the murder

---

[1] "Gloriosus in verbis." He afterwards grievously broke down in his Latin when speaking at Rome, and his *oportuebat* made all the curia laugh.   [2] "Simplex homo et minus discretus."

[3] *Gervas. Dorobern.*, p. 1382.

[4] *Milman*, iii. 474, quoting De Bosham.

of Becket. He died on the 27th December 1166,[1] and left his see exposed and undefended to the attacks of the spoiler. Henry was not unwilling to solace himself for the trouble which he was suffering from the violent archbishop by deliberately robbing the see of Lincoln for many years.

VACANCY OF THE SEE. GEOFFREY PLANTAGENET, TITULAR BISHOP—1167-1183.

According to William of Malmesbury, it was during the evil reign of William Rufus, and under the advice of Ralph Flambard, the notorious spoiler and pillager of the Church, that the custom first began of the king keeping bishoprics and abbeys vacant, and seizing upon their revenues for himself. He thus writes :—" It was under his (Ralph's) advice that when the death of a bishop or abbot was heard of, straightway a clerk of the king's was despatched, who took an inventory of all that he found, and brought all the revenues which afterwards accrued into the royal treasury." " This seemed the harder, as in the time of William I. all the rents were carefully kept to be given up to the new incumbent when appointed."[2] In the reign of Henry I., who was anxious to conciliate the people on account of his

---

[1] The date is variously given. I follow Mr. Dimock's opinion. See his note, *Giraldus Camb.*, vii. 36.

[2] *Willelm. Malmesb.*, *De Gestis Regum*, iv. 314.

defective title, this custom was deliberately and formally abandoned. In the Charter of Liberties, issued by him at his coronation, it is said: "Inasmuch as the kingdom was oppressed with unjust exactions, I, having regard to God, and for the love which I bear towards you, in the first place make the holy Church of God free, so that I will neither sell it nor put it to farm, nor at the death of an archbishop, a bishop, or an abbot will receive anything out of the lordship of the Church, or from its men, until the successor enters upon it."[1]   In the second charter of Stephen this is even more particularly confirmed. "When the sees shall have become vacant of their proper pastors, I will commit them and the whole of their possessions to the hand and custody of clerks, or of honest men of the same church, until a pastor be canonically appointed in succession."[2]   How then came it to pass that in the inquiry made for the *avitæ consuetudines* of the realm at the council of Clarendon, the following was reported by the barons and bishops to be one of them :—"When an archbishopric or a bishopric shall have become vacant, or an abbey or a priory in the lordship of the king, it ought to be in his hands ; and he shall receive from it all the rents and outcomings as though they were of his lordship."[3]   The explanation, probably, is that the practice of the earlier kings having been in con-

---

[1] Stubbs, *Select Charters*, p. 97. This charter was afterwards made the foundation of the Magna Charta.

[2] Stubbs, *Select Charters*, 115.   [3] Stubbs, *Ib.* p. 133.

tradiction to their charters (as we know that it was), the *consuetudo* is taken from this, and not from the formal and legal document.   If so, it cannot but be held that Becket was fully justified in objecting to put his seal to the constitutions of Clarendon.   But inasmuch as all the bishops of England, with the exception of Becket, did fully agree to them, they would seem to have cut away the ground from under their feet for objecting to the enforced vacancies of sees, and to the absorption of their revenues by the king ; and Henry had a legal or technical justification for keeping the see of Lincoln vacant for so many years. The moral question is altogether different.   The iniquity of keeping such a diocese as Lincoln for so long without a chief pastor could hardly be surpassed. Indeed, had there not been anything to interfere with Henry's grasping inclinations and disregard of the obligations of religion, it is probable that Lincoln would not have been allowed the semblance of an election of a bishop even so soon as it actually came about.   But after the murder of Archbishop Becket the Church gained enormously in power, and the king, with enemies on every side of him, found himself in no condition to make that imperious stand against it in which he had begun the dispute with Becket.   At Avranches, in 1172, he practically abjured and abandoned the constitutions of Clarendon,[1] and having sworn to " renounce all customs and usages prejudicial to the Church," he was urged by

---

[1] *Collier, Ch. Hist.,* ii. 319.

the Pope's legates to prove the sincerity of his oath by
filling up the numerous vacant sees in his dominions,
whose revenues he was receiving.   The necessity for
this became absolutely pressing in the next year.
His eldest son, who had been crowned king by the
mistaken policy of his father, united his fortunes to
those of the King of France, and openly declared war
against his father.   His mother and brothers seconded
him, and a large number of the nobles espoused his
cause.   But the Church supported the old king.
Almost all the bishops were with him,[1] and hence
it became necessary that Henry, if he would preserve these valuable allies, should allow elections
to be made to the vacant sees.   According to Roger
de Hoveden, the king himself nominated to the
Archbishopric of Canterbury, the bishoprics of Bath,
Winchester, Hereford, Ely, and Chichester ;[2] other
authorities say that the elections were free.[3]   But
whether, indeed, this were so in the cases mentioned,
in the case of Lincoln, which was also filled at the
same time, it could hardly have been that the election
was in reality a free one.   For there the person
elected was the natural son of the king, a young man
under twenty-one years of age,[4] only in deacon's
orders, who held the post indeed of Archdeacon of
Lincoln, but who did not affect to be anything but

---

[1] *Benedictus, s. a.* 1173.   [2] *Hoveden,* f. 307 (Ed. Savile).
[3] *Matt. Paris, Hist. Maj.,* p. 127 (Ed. Watts).
[4] If he was born in 1159, as some authorities say, he was only
fourteen.

the courtier and the soldier.[1]   It is needless to cast so
great a slur upon the Chapter of Lincoln at that period
as to suppose that Geoffrey Plantagenet could have
been their *bonâ fide* choice for the bishopric.   They
might, indeed, have preferred to have any head, however unsuitable, rather than suffer the simple spoliation to which they had been exposed now for seven
years.   Nor was Geoffrey Plantagenet without his
good qualities.   Still it is more reasonable to adopt
the view of Giraldus in another place, that "after the
revenues of the bishopric had for many years been
most scandalously carried into the treasury, Geoffrey
succeeded, the son of King Henry, being promoted to
the highest chair from the archdeaconry of Lincoln
by his father's management *(patre procurante)*."[2]
But though the election of Geoffrey had been thus
skilfully brought about, there needed his acceptance
and confirmation by the Pope, in the then state of
Church affairs, before he could be consecrated.   And
here great difficulties presented themselves.   Henry

---

[1] Giraldus Cambrensis, who was a great admirer of Geoffrey's, and
who wrote his life, gives him a very good character.   "He had been
used to letters and study from his youth, and being designed for the
religious profession, he went through the lower orders and was made
one of the clergy with very great fitness.   Among other honours which
he reached when a youth he was made Archdeacon of Lincoln, and,
as royal blood may be assumed to be precocious in virtue, when the
see became vacant, he was elected Bishop of Lincoln by the unanimous
consent of his brethren and his father's permission."—*Anglia Sacra*,
ii. 378.   The assertion sometimes made that Geoffrey was the son of
fair Rosamond will not agree with the chronology.   Walter Mapes
gives his mother's name as Ykenai.   See Raine's *Fasti Eboracenses*,
i. 252.   [2] *Opera* vii. 36.

the son, in conjunction with the King of France, was at this moment more powerful at Rome than Henry the father. The elect of Lincoln was a firm sup-porter of his father,[1] and hence his confirmation would be most strongly opposed at Rome. A protest had been made by the younger Henry, and an appeal lodged when the appointments to the sees were made,[2] and when the new bishops repaired to the Papal Court they found great difficulties in their way. "The new King of England," says the Abbot Benedictus, "wishing, if possible, to hinder their elections, sent his messengers with the messengers of the King of France, to Alexander, the chief Pontiff, charging him, and begging him not to confirm those elections, because they had been made against his will and consent."[3] The Pope, however, who dreaded both parties, took a middle course. He accepted Richard, Archbishop of Canterbury, con-secrated him, and gave him the pall ; but the other elects he would not confirm, declaring he would do nothing in the matter until the king and his son were at one again.[4] When this news was brought back to England, Geoffrey Plantagenet was excited to great wrath thereby. He immediately started for Rome

[1] Immediately on his election he raised a large subsidy in his diocese, which he afterwards restored. Then, with levies raised in Lincolnshire, he took an energetic part against the king's enemies, taking the castles of Roger de Mowbray in the Isle of Axholme and Yorkshire, and check-ing the advance of the King of Scotland, who had invaded Yorkshire. —*Giraldus, Vita Galfridi, Anglia Sacra*, ii. 376.

[2] *Roger de Hoveden,* f. 307 (Ed. Savile).   [3] *Benedictus, u. s.*

[4] *Epist. Reginaldi Bathon. electi in Benedictus.*

himself, determining either to make a personal appeal to the Pope, or to authorise some influential friend to represent his cause.[1]   Peace was soon made between Henry and his sons, and the Pope's confirmation of the new bishops-elect, with the exception of Geoffrey, being no longer delayed, Richard, Archbishop of Canterbury, consecrated them at Canterbury (1174). But no confirmation of the election of Geoffrey Plantagenet had yet been granted by Alexander, and his election being thus incomplete, the power in temporal matters connected with the see, which he might exercise previous to his consecration, would be invalidated.   As it is evident that this was that to which both he and his father looked, and that there was no real intention on the part of either that he should be consecrated, doubtless every effort would be made to procure this confirmation from the Pope. At length, in the summer of 1175, when the king was holding a council at Woodstock, the confirmation of Geoffrey's election to the see of Lincoln arrived. Then the king, his father, suddenly discovered that he was too young to be consecrated. " He had not reached the years of the fitting age, and he knew not how much was necessary to the right administration of the episcopal office when conferred upon any."[2]   It might perhaps have been desirable to have entertained these considerations before, and

---

[1] *Matt. Paris, Hist. Maj.*, p. 131 (Ed. Watts).

[2] *Benedictus, s. a.* 1175.   Geoffrey was born in 1152, and therefore was at this time twenty-three years of age.

to have reflected that if Geoffrey were too young for consecration he was also too young for election. But the king, having now put him in possession of the revenues of the see, was suddenly afflicted with qualms of conscience, which were highly convenient to the elect, with his martial and unecclesiastical tastes.[1]   It was necessary, however, to keep up appearances, otherwise the Pope might withdraw his confirmation, or the bishops in England who were necessary to the king, might murmur too loudly. The elect, who was as yet unfit for consecration, should do all he could to qualify himself. He was to go to Tours, and there diligently to exercise himself in the schools, and improve his mind "until he should be made worthy of the dignity of so great an honour."[2]   The young bishop-elect thus sent to school would probably assume the liberty of making his studies as light as he felt inclined. His time was no doubt principally occupied in the military pursuits for which he showed such great aptness, and in attending on his father, to whom he was ever faithful and affectionate. Nor did he altogether neglect his church of Lincoln. He paid off the sum of £300 due to Aaron, the Jew, which had been borrowed by Bishop Robert de Chesney, and he expended large sums in increasing

---

[1] William of Newberry says of him that he was "amplissimis contentus reditibus, ut liberius vacaret deliciis, canonicæ consecrationis tempus protraberet, ovesque dominicas nesciens pascere et doctus tondere, multo tempore Lincolniensi ecclesiæ sub electi momine incubaret."—ii. 22.   [2] *Benedictus, u. s.*

the adornments of his church.   Among other gifts
he bestowed upon it two magnificent bells, and was
zealous to bring distinguished persons to become
members of the chapter.   He also recovered some
estates which had been alienated from the church.[1]
But from consecration to the episcopal office, in
spite of his studies at Tours, he altogether shrank,
and when at length Pope Alexander, who seems to
have kept a watchful eye upon England, would
endure this no longer, he preferred to resign his
claim to the see rather than seek the higher orders
of the Church.   Giraldus says that he did this freely
and without any compulsion,[2] in order that he might
the better attend upon his father, but we have the
more reliable authority of Benedictus to the contrary.
"The Pope," says the Abbot of Peterborough,
"wrote (1181) severely to Richard, Archbishop of
Canterbury, that, without any delay or excuse, he
should compel, by ecclesiastical censures, Geoffrey,
the elect of Lincoln, son of the King of England, to
resign his rights as elected to the see, or without
further delay to receive the order of priest and the
dignity of the episcopal office.   Geoffrey, therefore,
being put in a difficulty, and feeling himself unfit,
consulted his father.   He knew that he was not
competent for so great a charge, and so would
rather hold back from being a bishop than impose

---

[1] *Girald. Camb., Op.* vii. 39.

[2] *Anglia Sacra*, ii. 380.   So also *Hoveden*, and *Roger de Wendover, Flor. Hist.*, ii. 409.

K

upon himself an intolerable burden. Therefore he wrote to Richard, Archbishop of Canterbury, as follows :—" It has pleased his apostolical majesty to enjoin your holiness that you should call upon me at a fixed time, to undertake the order of the priesthood and the dignity of a bishop. I, however, considering that many bishops, of maturer years and greater wisdom than I can boast, are scarce equal to the charge of such an office, and cannot perform the duties of it without peril of souls, fear to impose on my youth this burden, too heavy even for those much older ; and this I do, not from any levity of mind, but out of reverence to the sacrament of orders. Having, therefore, consulted with my father, my brothers, and several bishops, I have otherwise disposed of my life and condition, wishing to serve in war for a time under the command of my father, and to abstain from episcopal matters. I therefore resign all my right of election and the bishopric of Lincoln, spontaneously, freely, and entirely into your hands, holy father, craving of you absolution, both from my election and my claim to the see, as my metropolitan, and the special delegate of the apostolical see in this matter." A similar letter he also wrote to the Chapter of Lincoln.[1] It may truly be said of Geoffrey that nothing in his connection with

---

[1] *Benedictus, s. a.* 1181. William of Newberry says : " Rex peni-tentiâ ductus quod delicatum juvenem, et tanti honoris apici minus congruentem carnali affectu ita promovere voluisset, eo tandem ad refu-tandum jus et nomen electi prudenter inducto, Episcopatum rursus in Fiscum reduxit."—ii. 22.

the see "became him like the leaving of it." He had, it is true, absorbed the revenues of the bishopric for some seven years, but far better that he should at length leave his anomalous position, than make his power over the see perpetual by an unworthy consecration, which no doubt he might have easily procured. The tender and faithful care which he afterwards bestowed upon his father (who had made him his chancellor and heaped benefices upon him), and the conspicuous and not over creditable part which he played in the troubled affairs of England when advanced to the high dignity of Archbishop of York, are told at length by Giraldus in his interesting life.[1]   The church of Lincoln, long despoiled and oppressed, might now heave a sigh of relief, and look forward to the appointment of one who should be, not only in name, but in reality, a bishop and pastor of the long neglected flock.

WALTER OF COUTANCES, FIFTH BISHOP—
1183-1184.

The resignation of his claim to the see by Geoffrey Plantagenet took place in 1182 (January 6), and yet again there was a vacancy in the office of chief pastor of the church of Lincoln. The king,

---

[1] A full account of Geoffrey Plantagenet will be found among Mr. Raine's valuable *Lives of the Archbishops of York.—Fasti Ebora-censes*, i. 251, *seq.*

engrossed in his wars, and eager to obtain subsidies
from every possible quarter, once more laid his hands
upon the tempting spoil, and forgot his solemn obligations towards the Church of God. No wonder
that the hearts of religious men in the diocese were
utterly in despair, no wonder that prophecies were
uttered, and obtained general belief, that never again
should a bishop of Lincoln offer the holy sacrifice in
the cathedral church of Lincoln.[1] At length, however, after a delay of nearly a year and a half, the
king vouchsafed to allow another election to be made
to Lincoln, and sent from Normandy his mandate to
the Chapter, that they should proceed to choose a
bishop. It is probable that at the time of sending
he did not designate any person for the office, but
allowed the Chapter to choose, reserving to himself
the right of approval. The Chapter at once met and
unanimously, as it seems, chose for their bishop
Walter de Coutances, Archdeacon of Oxford, "a
clerk, and of the household of the lord king."[2]
Henry, on hearing of the election, was very angry.
He would not allow the election, he said ; it was
against his will and consent. Walter should never
be consecrated, and he appealed to the Pope.[3] What
was the cause of this outbreak of ill-temper ? Doubt-

---

[1] A lay brother of the monastery of Thame (built by Bishop Alexander) is said, by Giraldus, to have made this prophecy. Benedictus
speaks as though there were many prophecies to this effect.

[2] *Benedictus, s. a.* 1183.

[3] *Benedictus, u. s.* Giraldus is in flat opposition to this, saying
that it was by the king's procuring that Walter was elected.

less the Chapter of Lincoln thought that they had chosen the man of all others most pleasing to the king.   They intended, no doubt, to pay him a compliment by their choice, and by fixing on one whom they knew to be a favoured servant of his to obviate all difficulties which might arise.   Walter de Coutances was the king's vice-chancellor.   He had been constantly employed on his affairs.   In 1177 he formed one of the embassy which went to the King of France about the marriage portion which he had promised to give to his daughter, who had married the son of King Henry.[1]   There could have been no personal objection to Walter, as his immediate promotion to a higher place proves, but the objection probably was simply a selfish one.   Henry did not want to lose a useful and trusted servant, so he sullenly refused his consent.   But the unexpected death of his son, while in arms against him, which threw him into transports of grief, seems to have altered his mind.   There was no longer any opposition to the choice of the Lincoln Chapter.   Walter was ordained priest by John, Bishop of Evreux (June 11), who had formerly been a clerk in his office in the king's service, and after a few weeks (July 5) was consecrated Bishop of Lincoln at Angers, by Richard, Archbishop of Canterbury, in the Church of St. Laudus.[2]   There does not seem to

---

[1] *Benedictus, s. a.* 1177.

[2] *Benedictus, s. a.* 1183. *Matt. Paris, Hist. Maj.* p. 140 (Ed. Watts.) *Ann. de Theokesberiâ, Ann. Monast.* i. 53.

have been any confirmation by the pope asked or waited for. Not long after the consecration, the king made up his mind to part with his old servant and friend. Leave was given to Bishop Walter, some time towards the approach of winter, to go and take possession of his see. He made his solemn entry into Lincoln on the 10th December (1183), and was enthroned the following day. The chronicler tells us that he was received in the most enthusiastic manner. " Both clergy and people exulted and sang hymns and canticles."[1] It was within three weeks of seventeen years since the last Bishop of Lincoln had expired. For seventeen years in that vast province of England, no episcopal acts had been done. No consecrations, confirmations, or orders had been ministered. No effectual supervision of the clergy had existed. What wonder if, when we have to pass in review the clerical state of the period, we shall find many terrible scandals existing. The new bishop, conducted in solemn procession to his cathedral church, was enthroned by Herbert, Archdeacon of Canterbury, whose peculiar office this work was ; and on the same day, anxious to impress men's minds that a better state of things had indeed begun, and that those melancholy prophecies as to no Bishop of Lincoln ever again saying mass in the cathedral were mere idle dreams, Bishop Walter, " fortifying himself with the sign of the cross and armed with the Catholic faith,"

---

[1] *Benedictus, u. s.*

approached the high altar, and with great pomp celebrated the highest rite of the Christian religion, Baldwin, Bishop of Worcester,[1] who had accompanied him, acting as his assistant. "Thus was the mind of the false prophets confounded, and the Catholic faith strengthened."[2] All could now rejoice and congratulate themselves that after the long interregnum there was once again a bishop in the see of Remigius, and that the full ecclesiastical establishment was once more to be seen in the cathedral. What qualities Walter of Coutances would have displayed as Bishop of Lincoln, we have but little means of judging. His occupancy of the see was so short that he had scarcely the opportunity of showing how he would have applied himself to the vast task which had been entrusted to him. Giraldus, who knew Lincoln soon after the time of Bishop Walter, speaks of him as "a man affable and liberal, who was excellently well learned in letters, and in secular things and the affairs of the curia skilled beyond measure," but he notes to his disadvantage one matter, in which he says "he injured his church greatly and offended not slightly his Chapter." This was his confirming and sealing the grants of the churches which his predecessor, Robert de Chesney, had made to the Order of Sempringham.[3] About six months after his con-

---

[1] Promoted to be Archbishop of Canterbury the year following.

[2] *Benedictus, s. a.* 1183. *Guil. Neubridg.,* iii. 8.

[3] *Anglia Sacra,* ii. 418. Giraldus and John de Schalby say that though called Walter of Coutances, he was in reality of Cornwall, and

secration to Lincoln, Walter was translated to the
archiepiscopal see of Rouen, which he occupied till
the year 1206.   William of Newberry, censuring
the bishops of this period, instances the case of
Walter of Coutances as that of one who was guided
only by ambition and the love of dignity and pre-
eminence.   For this reason, he says, he chose the
Archbishopric of Rouen before the bishopric of
Lincoln, although the revenues of Lincoln were far
greater.[2]   Would it not, however, have been equally
reprehensible had the love of the greater revenue
been the motive for keeping him at Lincoln?

We now approach a new era in the history of
the see of Lincoln.   After a succession of bishops
who were for the most part courtiers or states-
men, and none of whom made any mark on the
ecclesiastical history of their day, we come to one
alike distinguished by his sanctity and the independent and manly tone which he adopted
towards the kings, who were wont to oppress and
intimidate churches and Churchmen at their will;
who excelled his predecessors in his munificent
adornment of his see, but excelled them still more
in his exalted life and noble aims.   But before we
proceed to the welcome task of narrating the life
of Saint Hugh, it will be well to consider somewhat
the characters of the kings with whom he had to
deal, and of the clergy whom he sought to elevate.

of the ancient British blood.   Mr. Dimock is of opinion that this merely
implies that he was of a Norman family settled in Cornwall.

   [1] *Guil. Neubridg.*, l. iii. c. 8.

CHAPTER II.

THE KINGS AND CLERGY WITH WHOM ST. HUGH HAD TO DO.

As regards the first of these kings, Henry II., those singular inconsistencies which abounded in this prince are scarce capable of explanation, without some solutions such as those furnished by this narrative. The one great purpose, indeed, of the reign and policy of Henry II. is sufficiently clear. It was to consolidate the kingly power in his own hands. But it would be altogether wrong to regard Henry simply as a far-seeing statesman, or to attempt to account for all his actions on pure principles of policy. He was a violent, selfish, headstrong man, much swayed by his passions, but withal, clever and sagacious enough to see clearly in what way his selfish aspirations after power would best be gratified. At the same time, he was so resolutely bent to obtain his ends, that the lower motives of his nature were often forced to yield to the higher and more subtle springs of action. "His moral character, his self-will and self-indulgence, his licentious habits, his paroxysms of rage, his covetousness, faithlessness, and cruelty, did not come into any violent collision with his political schemes, or if they threatened to do so, were kept in abeyance until the threatened necessity of policy was satisfied. That they were so restrained, proves that this leading purpose is not to be regarded as imaginary. That they did sway him on almost every recorded occasion of his life in which they did not clash with this purpose, is so certain as to prevent our listening for a moment to any who represent him as a beneficent, unselfish ruler. His ambition may not have been the one which his moral character and circumstances lead us to expect; but to say this is merely to repeat that that character was rather a compound of inconsistent qualities than a balance of opposing forces."[1] This inconsistency and these bizarre contradictions of Henry's character are best illustrated by his relations to the Church and to Churchmen, whose power and influence were, in his age, growing at so wonderfully rapid a rate. The lives of St. Thomas Becket and of St. Hugh represent him under aspects which appear at first sight entirely irreconcilable, but which, on a closer study, may be made mutually illustrative. Henry lived in the century between Hildebrand and Innocent III., the period of the most portentous up-growth of ecclesiastical power. Unconscious himself of this growth, believing that he could control ecclesiastical opposition as successfully as he had done the opposition of

---

[1] Stubbs' *Preface to Benedictus*, where a most masterly dissection of the character and era of Henry II. is to be found.

the great feudal chiefs, Henry came into collision with
a force he had not rightly gauged and estimated, and
was vanquished, or at least checked and hampered
by it.   In such a character, so violent and undisciplined, so eagerly set upon compassing its ends, so
keenly alive to the value of failure and success, we
might naturally expect that a humiliation inflicted
through, and on account of Churchmen, would exasperate him bitterly against all Churchmen and matters
ecclesiastical.   But he whose passions had been
excited to fury by Becket's opposition, who had been
made to feel and to bend before the potent arm of
the Church, yet, nevertheless, does not turn angrily
from all Churchmen after having been (as he held),
so grievously deceived and betrayed by them, but
even cherishes and treats as his intimate friend a
thorough and earnest Churchman.   Painfully convinced of the power of the Church, and taught that
the attempt " to apply the principles of law and order
to the clergy, in a way that was not sanctioned by
the public opinion of his day," [1] was impracticable, and
that he must needs yield before this powerful antago-
nist, he yet, though raging against the Church, did
not altogether revolt from it (as William Rufus
had done, and as his son John afterwards did), but
even to a certain extent cherished and endowed it.
Yet his support was still fitful and niggardly ; his
deference to Churchmen partial and occasional ; the
influence of religion on his life scarcely appreciable.

[1] *Stubbs, u. s.*

"He had little regard," says Professor Stubbs, "for more than the merest forms of religion ; like Napoleon Bonaparte, he heard mass daily, but without paying decent attention to the ceremony.   During the most solemn part of the service, he was whispering to his courtiers, or scribbling, or looking at pictures. His vows to God, he seems to have thought, might be evaded as easily as his covenants with men ; his undertaking to go on a crusade was commuted for money payments, and his promised religious founda- tions were carried out at the expense of others.[1]   His regard to personal morality was of much the same value and extent.   He was at no period of his life a faithful husband, and when he had finally quarrelled with Eleanor, he sank into sad depths of licentious- ness."   How could a man who was thus, on grounds of policy, embittered against the Church, and who was personally disinclined to the restraints of religion and morality, be yet a friend to the devout and

---

[1] Ralph Niger's account of this is very characteristic.—"Juratus se tria monasteria constructurum duos ordines transvertit, personas de loco ad locum transferens, meretrices alias aliis, Cenomannicas Anglicis substituens."   This refers to the Amesbury transaction.   The Waltham one was much of the same kind.   Giraldus also is severe on this shabby business, and is unable to say what the third monastery was, by the construction of which his vow was fulfilled, unless it were the charter- house at Witham.—(*Giraldus de Inst. Pr.* ii. 7).   *Stubbs*, note. *Ralph Niger*, a chronicler of this era, was born at Bury, in Suffolk, and wrote several historical pieces.   His *Chronicle* contains very little connected with English affairs, and that little is taken from Geoffrey of Monmouth, William of Malmesbury, and Henry of Huntingdon.   He was exiled with his friend and patron Archbishop Becket, and in his indignation wrote a bitter invective against Henry II."—*Hardy, s. v.*

ascetic Saint Hugh, delight in his conversation, and
affect his company?   One explanation of this may
doubtless be found in considerations of policy.
Henry II. might not be fully enlightened as to the
power which the Church had in his time acquired
of resisting even his own imperious will, but he, like
the Conqueror, was fully aware of the strength
which was derived by the central authority in its
contests with the barons, from the support and
good-will of the Church.   The Church represented
the people.   It was through the Church that the
voice of the people was heard ; it was by the Church
that the power of the people was felt.   Now, when
the king was occupied in putting down the power
of the barons, he was acting for the people, and
therefore in alliance with the Church.   He naturally
turned to the Church for support, nor would he
turn in vain.   The life of St. Hugh remarkably illustrates the position which the great Church
dignitaries held of protecting the people from
their feudal oppressors.   Henry, whose great object
was to abate baronial independence, was neces-
sarily driven into alliance with those who could
help him so effectually in this respect.[1]   This will
account for a certain amount of favour and respect

---

[1] Stubbs' *Introductory Sketch to Select Charters*, p. 31.   " The clergy
may be roughly divided into three schools—the secular or statesman
school, the ecclesiastical or professional, and the devotional or spiritual.
Throughout the whole period, the first of these schools was consistently
on the side of the king, the last as consistently on the side of the nation.
No division of the clergy ever sympathised with the feudal party."

shown to Churchmen, while the deep-seated desire
which possessed the king of making Church, as well
as barons, dependent on him, explains those outbursts
of fury and menace against ecclesiastics which seem
inconsistent with it. But the life of St. Hugh
throws also other light on the character and conduct
of Henry II. There is no reason to suppose that
Henry was a disbeliever in Christianity, like his son
John, and yet he utterly refused to restrain and
govern his life by the laws of the gospel. This
inconsistency, however, sat lightly upon him, for it
would seem that he had adopted the theory that
his religion and salvation could be done vicariously.
His friendship with St. Hugh, and the interest
which he had secured in his prayers and merits were
to be the deliverers of his soul. This is remarkably
illustrated by that strange passage in the life of St.
Hugh, which tells us how Henry in danger of shipwreck put up his prayers to heaven, pleading the
merits and virtues of St. Hugh, and was instantly
delivered. The theory of a good many kings of
that era was, that a certain amount of hard fighting
against the Saracens would secure them salvation in
spite of their murders and rapines. Henry's theory
would seem to have been a still more convenient
one. He would appear to have held that it was
not needful to distract his kingdom and endanger
his power by a rash military expedition to a distant
land. It was sufficient for him to be on friendly
terms with a saint at home, and all would be well.

Thus the friendship of Hugh was valuable to him, both for the requirements of present policy, and for a provision for the future. And this would seem to account for the fact of the popularity of Churchmen with men of the world in those days being in proportion to the asceticism of the lives of the Churchmen. There was no other notion of religion then save asceticism, and the more extreme and bizarre the asceticism, the greater the reputation for religion. Men hoped to get a share in their intercessions, or the transfer of a portion of their merits, and hence they encouraged, applauded, and revered the self-immolation of the Carthusian and the anchorite. St. Hugh was more venerated for his Carthusian austerities and his ministrations to lepers, than as a wise and holy bishop, or the enlightened patron of ecclesiastical art. In yet another point does the life of St. Hugh illustrate the character of Henry II. With all his ambitious schemes and his constant turmoil of business, Henry was extremely fond of a joke, and enjoyed a touch of humour beyond measure. Hugh of Avalon, Carthusian though he was, was full of humorous sallies, and of a keen and biting wit. On this ground his companionship was highly appreciated by the king. Many anecdotes of Hugh's "good things" will be found in his life. Walter Mapes has preserved one which may illustrate the style of his wit. On one occasion Hugh was going to see the king, when he found a number of men in high wrath, and giving vent to all sorts of

uncourteous expressions as to his Majesty.   Struck
with astonishment, the bishop demanded, " Who are
ye that venture to talk thus ? "   They answered, " We
are foresters, and the king .won't admit us into his
chamber."   " If you are foresters," said Hugh, who
hated all that appertained to the cruel game-laws
of that period, " clearly your business lies out of
doors, not within."[1]   Henry, hearing the joke, burst
into a loud laugh, and came out to greet the bishop,
on which Hugh, wishing to blend a word of warning with his humour, said to him, " Mark this
parable.   The poor whom these men torment shall
go into the palace of delights, while you and your
keepers shall be kept outside."   At this the king
laughed louder than ever, being anxious, perhaps,
to see nothing but the joke.[2]   Nor does the life of
St. Hugh fail to illustrate the characters both of
Richard and of John, as well as that of their father.
The popularity which has always more or less
attached itself to Richard from his exploits in the
·Holy Land and his name of Cœur de Lion, was
very little deserved by his conduct as a king.[3]   His
unscrupulous grasping and exactions for his wars,
his neglect and contempt for England, his brusque

---

[1] *Forestarii foris stent.*   It is not easy to give the equivalent of the
joke in English.

[2] *Mapes de Nugis Curialium*, p. 7 (Ed. Camden Soc.)

[3] " Richard's absence from England, his imprisonment, still more
the vileness of his successors, have invested him with a halo not justified
by a single act of his as a prince or a king.   Of such stuff are heroes
manufactured."—*Brewer*, note to *Preface to Giraldus Cambrensis.*

and violent way with his clergy all come out in this
narrative ; as does also his appreciation of a straightforward and honest reproof, such as none but St.
Hugh could administer, and the better side of his
character which this frank dealing brings to light.
The miserable character of John is not relieved from
any of its baseness by that which is recorded of him
here. His incurable levity and utter absence of
reverence are remarkably illustrated. He, too, is
seen sharing with his father and brother a readiness
to allow a retort from an inferior without taking
offence. He could even " relish a sharp reply,
though he himself was the subject of it,"[1] and St.
Hugh was not the man to disguise his opinion of
his ill-deeds. So much for the kings with whom
this history is concerned. We turn next to the
clergy, and inquire what information we can gain
from it as to the seculars and the regulars in the
English Church of that day. What was the state
of the clergy at the period comprised within the
life of St. Hugh ? It so happens, that we are in
possession of a somewhat full and elaborate sketch
of the clergy in England and Wales, in the latter
part of the twelfth century. Giraldus di Barry, the
contemporary, friend, and biographer of St. Hugh,
has given us, in his *Gemma Ecclesiastica*, a lively and
telling picture of clerical life. This treatise was

---

[1] *Brewer, Preface to Giraldus Cambrensis.* Mr. Brewer well points
out Shakspeare's appreciation of this characteristic of John as exempli-
fied in the first act of his play of King John.

intended as a sort of archdeacon's charge to the
clergy of St. David's ; but as the experience of the
writer was very varied, and had extended to the
whole of England, as well as France and Italy, and
in particular as he had resided several years at
Lincoln, we may fairly take his words as applying
generally to the ecclesiastical practices of his day.
Giraldus commences, as indeed we should expect
from the general tone of all writers of the period,
by treating the ministerial work of the priest in the
Holy Eucharist as the most important part of his
office, and a great portion of his treatise is occupied
with the many revolting details which spring naturally from the material view of the Holy Sacrament.
He discusses what is to be done when mice eat the
host, or spiders fall into the cup ; how the holy
elements are to be considered as performing the
functions of ordinary food ; what steps are to be
taken when any of the sacred liquid is accidentally
spilled, etc.   Amidst numberless trivial stories as to
the elements, indicating their conversion into human
flesh and blood in various ways, we have it incidentally noted that the churches in that day were sometimes suffered to fall into very grievous disrepair,
and even to be without roofs, and that it was held
to be the duty of the parish priest to keep them in
repair.   A custom is also mentioned of claiming
the books used in the church as the property of the
priest, so that at his death they were divided
between his children or nephews.   Giraldus contends

that at least two or three pairs of the better sort
ought to be kept in the churches, while the others
might be given away by the will of the priest.[1]
This implies the very considerable value of missals,
antiphonals, and lectionaries in that day. So completely material is the view taken of the Eucharist,
that it is held that certain material conditions, even
under circumstances of the greatest necessity, are
required for a valid sacrifice, as for instance a fitting
table.[2] On the other hand, the writer does not hold
that the officiating priest must of necessity be
fasting, inasmuch as the holy rite was at first instituted after supper, and was commonly celebrated
late in the primitive Church. This opinion will be
found to be illustrated by the practice of St. Hugh,
as recorded in his life. The power lodged in the
priest's hands as being the sole dispenser of the
sacrament of life, was, as we find from this treatise,
frequently abused for the purposes of gain. The
miserable pittance on which the parish priest of the
Middle Ages was compelled to live, while the
wealthy monks absorbed his lawful inheritance by
the practice of procuring for the monasteries the
advowsons of churches, which were then served for
them by some poor priest at a very low payment,
may go far to excuse some of the practices which
are stigmatised under the name of simony. But
that this abuse prevailed to a fearful extent, and

[1] *Gemma Ecclesiastica*, chap. x.
[2] *Ibid.*, chap. vii.

that all sacred things were bought and sold in the twelfth century, there can be no doubt. The poems of Walter Mapes, the testimony of St. Bernard, agree strictly with the complaints of Giraldus. One method by which the priest was wont to augment the offerings of the faithful, was by using several gospels at a mass, and in particular, selecting such gospels as he thought most likely to please those for whom the mass was being celebrated, as it was the custom to make an offering at the gospel. In France, says Giraldus, these various gospels were wont to be said before the mass, and such masses are called in derision *conflatæ*; but in England they were said after the mass, "because lay people and soldiers are wont to make an offering at those gospels which they particularly desire and venerate." Another plan was to begin a mass and say it down to the offertory, then to begin another and bring it to the same point, and then another, as long as the congregation could be got to offer. Such tricks played about the holiest things give us a very low idea of the reverence and devotion of the time. There is a story told by Giraldus of St. Hugh in connection with these practices. St. Hugh, he says, once went into a parish church to hear mass, when, after the consecration, the priest began to read a number of gospels one after another. The bishop listened for some time, and at length exclaimed, with a touch of his habitual humour, "What will this good fellow have for to-morrow, if he expends all he knows to-day?"[1]   One almost shrinks from setting down the various stories told of the manipulation of the holy mysteries for the purposes of gain. Priests were wont to say masses, not once only, but many times in the day ; thus, as Giraldus points out, showing great irreverence.   And the object for which this was done makes the matter much worse. In some places; he tells us, the first offertory was due to the monks, the second to the priest.   A lady coming to return thanks after childbirth, was requested by the priest not to make any offering at the first offertory, as a monk was in the church ready to pounce upon it, but to reserve her offering for the second mass, when it would belong to him. Another practice was to add to the mass of the day some other of which the people present were fond, as, if soldiers were present, they would tack on the mass of the Epiphany, which, it seems, was a special favourite with them on account of the Gospel of the Three Kings.   When any had lost a friend, the priest in the confessional would make a Tricenary or series of masses for thirty days obligatory on them, and thus it would frequently happen, that in addition to the other daily masses, the Missa Fidelium had to be said.   And this Missa Fidelium was made the source of great profit.   For, by undertaking for each one who desired it, to say a Tricenary, and then making one Missa Fidelium do for all, the priest was able to get his fees many times multiplied,

---

[1] *Gemma Ecclesiastica*, chap. viii.

whereas, instead of promising a separate Tricenary to each, he ought merely to have undertaken to commemorate the names of their friends in the Missa. But we have not yet exhausted the sacerdotal tricks in this matter. In order to get more offertories, the mass belonging to a season was added to the mass of a special festival, whereas the special festival ought to have displaced it altogether. Persons yet alive were encouraged to institute *anniversaries* for themselves, and to have the Missa Fidelium celebrated. But, worst of all, the Holy Sacrament was used for the purposes of magic, and masses were celebrated over waxen images, with imprecations, devoting the person whom the image represented to death within a certain time. This last horrible abuse, we may trust, was not generally prevalent, but peculiar to the fierce and relentless character of the Celt. These abuses of the Holy Sacrament for the sake of gain, Giraldus says, were more common among the rural parish priests than among others. They were worse than Judas, he says, for he, believing Jesus to be merely a man, sold him for thirty pieces of silver, they, believing him to be both God and man, sell him for a penny. Christ was offered once for the sins of all, but they will offer him as often in a day as they can get any one to pay them for it. They are like the hired mourners among the Lombards, who will lament any one whose friends and relatives choose to pay them. They are, in fact, nothing but idolaters, "inasmuch as they adore money rather than God, and will not be moved to offer services by their duty to God, but by their devotion to gain."[1] One great cause of this greediness of gain among the priests was, according to Giraldus, their practice of having wives or concubines, who demanded fine clothes to go to the markets in, riding upon palfreys, and sometimes attended by the priest on foot as a lacquey, while the children were to be smartly decked, and the house handsomely furnished. From the general tone of his remarks on this matter, we should gather that the *focaria* was an almost universal inmate of the priest's house. This, indeed, we know to have been the case throughout the Middle Ages, and probably about as much at one period as another. The attempt to refashion human nature, made by Hildebrand for the purposes of his own ambitious policy, has never had even the semblance of success.[2] Giraldus, indeed, has the good sense to see that the forbidding of lawful matrimony to priests was the greatest triumph which the devil had ever achieved,[3] but, inasmuch as the indulgence was forbidden, he felt it his duty as a church official to preach against it. There is reason to believe that St. Hugh took a

---

[1] Dist. II., chap. xxv.

[2] "In vain legate, archbishop, and bishops put forth their decrees. The old custom of England was too strong for them, and the king no longer gave his countenance to the innovation. By his leave, when the bishops were gone home, the priests kept their wives as they did aforetime."—Freeman, *Norman Conquest*, v. 236.

[3] Dist. II., chap. vi.

very common sense view of this matter, and did not attempt any wild crusade against the *uxorati sacerdotes*. Another phase of the clerical life of the twelfth century which is largely illustrated by Giraldus, is the grotesque ignorance which prevailed among the clergy. He gives some curious instances:—A certain priest preaching about Barnabas said " he was a good and holy man, but he was a robber," confounding Barnabas with Barabbas. Another described the Canaanitish woman as partly a dog, partly a woman, thinking her name to be derived from *canis*. At the festival of SS. Simon and Jude a clerical orator declared that one of the two was a good man, the other a traitor, nevertheless he was to be honoured on account of his fellow, being innocent of the fact that there was more than one Judas. The Latin equivalent for a " broiled fish and a piece of honeycomb" was transformed by another into an " ass-fish and beans covered with honey." Being asked what an " ass-fish" was, he replied that if there were a dogfish there must, of course, be an " ass-fish," though it was not found in these parts. The word in the Vulgate for a " fire of coals" (*pruna*) another explained as meaning " plums." The two debtors who were forgiven, one 500 pence and the other 50, were commented on as having both been forgiven 50. One of the congregation was bold enough to suggest that in that case they were both forgiven the same amount. " No," said the priest, " the one were Angevin pennies, the other English." The congregation of another priest were much astonished to hear on St. John's Day that St. John had first introduced the Latin tongue into England. This, it seems, the priest had deduced from the name of the festival, " S. Johannes ante portam Latinam," translating *ante portam* as " first brought." Explaining the gospel, " Say ye, The Lord hath need of them" (*his opus habet*), a priest said that it meant the Lord hath hyssop (*hisopus*). Another, confused in the same way by the words running together, asked what was meant by *busillis*. The learned man to whom he applied was fairly puzzled until the priest showed, at the bottom of his missal page, *in die*, and at the beginning of the next, *bus illis*. A somewhat more serious fault was his who argued from the words " Fornicators and adulterers God will judge," that no other evil-doers were to be judged. A very large number of instances are brought together by Giraldus to illustrate the ignorance of Latin which prevailed even among the higher clergy—bishops and abbots —but these are not easily producible in an English dress. According to him, a great part of the prevailing ignorance of theology arose from the new-fashioned importance given to the studies of law and logic. This is a complaint often echoed by writers of the day. A similar one is sure to be heard upon every change of studies in the centres of learning. But there were, perhaps, worse evils prevalent among the parochial clergy of that day than ignorance or even simony. William of Newbury tells us of more than a hundred homicides committed by clergy, and he freely lays the fault of all this disorder on the bishops. "How many clerks," says he, "have been deprived of their office in England? The bishops will defend the liberties of the clergy, and contend for the dignity of their order, while they are not careful to correct and repress their vices. They think that they are performing well their duty to God and the Church if they defend against all public censure those criminous clerks upon whom they themselves either refuse or neglect to inflict canonical censures, as their office ought to make them ready to do. From which cause the clergy, called to the Lord's inheritance, and as stars placed in the firmament of heaven, who ought to shine above the earth both in life and in word, having impunity to do whatever they please, are led into license and liberty, and throw off all reverence for God, whose judgment seems to tarry, and for rulers, inasmuch as the bishops care not to check them, and the prerogative of their sacred order exempts them from secular jurisdiction."[1] The bishops, according to the same authority, were occupied about other matters. "They care nothing for the pastoral office, but are occupied in obstinate and empty disputes about precedency, and getting

---

[1] *Guil. Neubridg.*, Lib. ii. c. 15. "The authority of William of Newbury," says Sir T. Hardy, "as a contemporary writer is especially valuable, for he has preserved many anecdotes of distinguished persons. His work, too, bears internal evidence of having been written whilst the occurrences which are therein recorded were in actual progress."— *Catalogue of British Hist.*, ii. 515.

the first place in honour and dignity."[1]   In some prelates, who loved money well, this fondness for precedence was even stronger than that other strong passion.   Such (says William of Newbury) was the case with Walter de Coutances, St. Hugh's predecessor in the see of Lincoln.   He succeeded to the see after it had been vacant for some seventeen years, but almost immediately left it for the see of Rouen. The chronicler observes :—" It is well known that as much as the church of Rouen excels that of Lincoln in dignity, so much does it fall short of it in temporal advantages.   Yet the man who, on account of its most ample goods, had much courted the bishopric of Lincoln, preferred to leave it that he might ascend higher, though to less wealth, rather than to retain it and sit in a lower place, though with greater riches.   And, indeed, he is said to have long hesitated whether he should choose eminence or wealth, and to have carefully deliberated with himself, but at length eagerness for the higher place overcame the love of ample goods."[2]

From another writer of the twelfth century we gain no higher notion of the state of the clergy of that period than from Giraldus, Walter Mapes, and

[1] *Guil. Neubridg.*, Lib. iii. c. 1. This is said on occasion of the famous quarrel for first place between the two archbishops in the Council of London, 1175. York, coming early, had seized the place of dignity, but after a violent and unseemly quarrel of words he was expelled bodily by the suffragans of Canterbury, and preserved his torn cope to show the violence to which he had been subjected.

[2] *Guil. Neubridg.*, Lib. iii. c. 8.

William of Newbury. " Nigel Wireker, a monk of
Canterbury, has left us a book, *De Abusu Ecclesiastico*,
and in it has sketched a picture of the state of the
Church as drawn by a sincere and by no means
prejudiced monk. The following of secular pursuits
by the superior clergy had the double effect of laying
open the spiritual offices to unworthy persons, and of
perverting religious endowments to mere secular uses.[1]
Immorality and simony were crying sins in the portion of the clergy that was supposed to be devoted
to spiritual duties, and these were rather encouraged
than restrained by their poverty. The superior clergy
were generally free from these stains, but ignorance,
meanness, avarice, and servility were common amongst
them. There was a paralysis of discipline in the
Church. The hands of the bishops were tied by the
sufferance of appeals to Rome, contrary to the ancient
custom of the realm ;—the evil which had called for
the constitutions of Clarendon, the old evil, foreign
to the English Church, which had been gradually
creeping in since the Conquest. It was practically
in the power of any contumacious priest to lodge an
appeal to Rome, which at once removed him from
the authority of his diocesan, and placed him, whatever his merits might be, under the protection of the
holy see. Neither the spiritual nor the law courts
could try him ; no bishop would subject himself to

---

[1] This account of the strictures in Wireker's book, which only exists
in a rare MS., is taken from Professor Stubbs' *Introduction to Epist.
Cantuarien.*, p. cxvii.

the annoyance and expense of a suit which would almost for a certainty be decided against him. All-powerful money could purchase, or wearisome pertinacity extort, a mandate ; pains and penalties would follow the refusal of a bishop to obey ; from that moment he ceased to be a judge, and became a defendant, and that under a charge on which the Italian lawyers never acquitted a bishop. The great proportion of English cases which are found in the Decretals of Gregory IX., and the space that English letters occupy in the letters of Alexander III. and his successors, which are, of course, only picked cases and letters of supposed importance, speak more completely than any complaints of the historians, of the paralysis of judicial power in the English Church. Although Hubert of Canterbury was neither a learned man nor a great theologian, he did his best by the means of councils and legatine visitations to remedy the evils that he saw existing. He failed under circumstances in which St. Hugh of Lincoln and Baldwin of Canterbury failed too." And the monstrous evil of looking to Rome not only had this bad effect of the paralysis of discipline both among the secular and regular clergy. It had also a distinctly bad effect on the character of the bishops, making them mean and time-serving schemers as regards the pope, and false towards the king ; yielding only under the influence of fear, and with an ulterior design of protecting themselves from the consequences of any promise which they had made by the secret thought of that dispensing power of the pope which they could invoke in any difficulty, if not against ecclesiastics, yet certainly against the lay and secular authority. How different from this was the bold-spirited and sincere dealing of St. Hugh with the three monarchs with whom he was specially brought into contact. It is but fair to take into consideration the character of the prelates of that day, that we may estimate rightly the value of such an example.

Hugh was completely above worldly motives, and earnestly set to perform his office aright, though, no doubt, there were many hindrances in his special circumstances to his efficient performance of it. As far as personal character went, there could not have been a greater boon to the Church than the example of the simple, sincere, and upright Burgundian monk, but when we estimate his probable influence on the unlettered and undisciplined clergy described by Giraldus and others, we are doubtful as to its extent in the way of discipline and correction of morals. There was first of all the one great and all-important drawback of Hugh's foreign birth and education, and his ignorance of the language and manners of the race over whom he was called to preside in spiritual matters. Mr. Freeman, in his admirable and exhaustive history of the Conquest, has well shown both the policy adopted by William and followed up by his successors of putting foreigners into all the higher places of the Church, and also the effects of that

policy on the well-being of the national Church.   In
some respects these men, no doubt, did much to raise
the Church, but in their immediate teaching power
they were greatly hampered by their foreign origin.
" While William was asserting the rights of the
English Crown he was using its powers to fill all
offices of trust, temporal and spiritual, with men of
other lands and other tongues.   From his own point
of view most of the appointments were wisely and
conscientiously made, but every Norman bishop or
abbot was none the less a badge to show that England was a conquered land.   Lanfranc never became
a naturalised Englishman.   His destiny made him
first Norman and then English, but we may suspect
that he never heartily assumed either character.   In
his eyes Normans and English alike were simply
instruments for carrying out designs in which Normandy and England seemed but as small specks on
the globe."[1]   Lanfranc had himself pleaded this
objection to his appointment when he went through
the accustomed *Nolo episcopari.*   He writes : " Ad-
versus hoc imbecillitas mearum virium morumque
indignitas prolata in medium nihil profuit : excusatio
incognitæ linguæ gentiumque barbararum nullum
apud eos locum invenire prævaluit."[2]

We shall find St. Hugh, perhaps, with greater
sincerity, making the same complaint immediately on
his consecration.   And in addition to his ignorance

[1] Freeman's *Norman Conquest,* iv. 440.
[2] *Ep. Lanfr.* (Ed. Giles), i. 19.

of the English language and customs, St. Hugh had
to contend in the administration of his episcopal
office with the ascetic tastes and love of cloistered
seclusion which his early life had engendered. The
long and frequent retreats which he made from his
public work were perhaps absolutely necessary for
himself, but they were singularly inopportune and
unfortunate for his diocese. In his time, indeed,
the monastic system was everywhere falling into
disrepute, and though the order to which he belonged,
the Carthusian, maintained an exceptional popularity
and regard, from its consistent asceticism,[1] yet men
could not have been pleased or edified at seeing the
great prelate, whose influence was so valuable, constantly and determinedly lapsing into the monk.[2]
Two of St. Hugh's immediate successors, Hugh de
Welles and Robert Grosseteste, were both noted for

---

[1] Walter Mapes, the bitter foe of the Cistercians and of monks generally, has nothing but praise for the Carthusians.

[2] "From the end of the twelfth century until the Reformation, from
the days of Hubert Walter to those of Wolsey, the monasteries remained
magnificent hostelries ; their churches were splendid chapels for noble
patrons ; their inhabitants were bachelor country gentlemen, more
polished and charitable, but little more learned or more pure in life,
than their lay neighbours ; their estates were well managed and enjoyed
great advantages and exemptions ; they were, in fact, an element of peace
in a nation that delighted in war. But, with a few noble exceptions,
there was nothing in the system which did spiritual service : books
were multiplied but learning declined ; prayers were offered unceasingly,
but the efficacious energy of real devotion was not found in the houses
that it had reared. The monastic body had sacrificed the opportunity
of doing good work for the triumph of a moment. The great prize of
their ambition, the government of the Church, fell from their hands."—
Stubbs' *Introd. to Epist. Cantuariens.*

their special antipathy towards monks, and their severe treatment of the monasteries. The abuses of the system, coupled with the constant claim for exemption from the jurisdiction of the bishop, had, in fact, become intolerable. They both attempted to bring about a restitution of the tithes, of which the monks had systematically robbed the parish churches, and the enforcement of spiritual duties upon these inactive and selfish communities. In doing this, though they incurred the odium of the regulars, they had the hearty sympathy both of the secular clergy and of the laity. But Hugh was ever regarded as a genuine monk, and to him, as having the interests of monasticism thoroughly at heart, we find the great monasteries in their contests with their bishops appealing. This was the case in the great Canterbury dispute, which dragged its weary length along under Archbishops Baldwin and Hubert. The monks of Christchurch write to Hugh, as one certain to be on their side, as against the archbishop. He is the patron of whom, though others fail them, they can be sure. The character which thus attached to Hugh can hardly have been useful to him in working his diocese. Under considerable disadvantages and drawbacks, then, his work had to be done, and yet with all this he contrived to do it so well, that in the estimation of all he held the place of the foremost bishop of England. The great secret was the thoroughly genuine, simple, straightforward, and courageous character of the man, without fear

M

or favour, which triumphed over every difficulty, and shone under every disadvantage. And if it were indeed the case, that the prelates of his day were distinguished by their excessive greediness for money, as Walter Mapes and the other satirical writers of the time assert,[1] then the utter contempt for money which St. Hugh displayed, and the profuse liberality which distinguished him, must have been an enormous help to him in raising him in the estimation of his fellows. He stood out, indeed, in his generation, as so far exalted above everything petty, small, and mean, that he could not fail to attract the eyes of all upon him. Many of the bishops, his contemporaries, were certainly the servile flatterers of royalty. Hugh, so far from being a flatterer of the king, treated one king after another in so straightforward and unceremonious a fashion, scrupled so little to oppose their claims and to denounce their proceedings, that he must have been the very wonder of his age for moral courage.

---

[1] The Metrical Life of St. Hugh, after giving some anecdotes of the bishop's generosity, thus reflects upon the prelates of his day :—

> " O pietatis opus ! Quam rara potentibus ista
> Gratia ! quam longè dominis aliena modernis.
> Si bos debetur de jure, duo rapiuntur
> De facto. Jus est quicquid dominatio jussit :
> Non est jus aliud quod curet Curia. Nullus
> Villicus esse potest potior, quam qui nequit esse
> Nequior. Et frustra miseros condemnat agrestes ?
> At dominus fovet ejus opus ; servoque petente
> Quæ sua sunt atrox et inexorabilis aurem
> Obstruit, et viduæ lacrimas irridet inanes."—L. 823-833.

Possibly, it may be thought, that in the brusque opposition which Hugh offered in the matter of supplies in the time of Richard, and in the contemptuous and repellent fashion of his demeanour towards Archbishop Hubert, he somewhat forgot the humble and patient character of the saintly Churchman. But a little attention to the state of the period, as sketched for us by good authorities, will serve to alter these views. Matthew Paris tells us that by the raising of money, first of all for the Crusade, then for Richard's ransom, and afterwards for his long protracted war with the King of France, England had been so spoiled, that " no man had left to him so much as a belt bound with silver, no woman had a necklace, no nobleman a ring, nor had the Jews even any treasure remaining. In the king's treasury there were nothing but keys and empty vessels." Hugh was therefore altogether justified in refusing to lend himself in any way to these ruinous extortions. Nor was it unnatural that he should bitterly resent the part which Archbishop Hubert took in helping to fasten these burdens upon the Church, and in conducting the secular taxing, as the king's representative and justiciary. For Hugh held as a matter of principle, that secular work was altogether unbecoming an ecclesiastic, and though he appears to have, at least, tolerated this in the case of William Longchamp, the Bishop of Ely, the king's chancellor at the beginning of his absence, yet he never could have approved of it. Nevertheless Hugh's bitterness against Archbishop Hubert, and especially his refusal to be reconciled to him on his death-bed, is certainly one of the weak points of his character.   Professor Stubbs says of Hubert, " He was not perhaps the best conceivable minister for Richard, but he was probably the best, if not the only one, possible.   He was a true patriot, a man of honest purposes, and of pure life."[1]

Giraldus Cambrensis has left us a lively sketch of six prelates of his era, whom he selected as specially representative men.   Of these the first mentioned, Henry, Bishop of Winchester, and brother of King Stephen, somewhat resembled William Longchamp in the temporal state and magnificence with which he was surrounded.   Every marvel of nature and art was around him, but yet, says Giraldus, " although surrounded and mixed up with worldly pomp and vanity, yet in his mind there was nothing of pride, in his look nothing of haughtiness, nothing in his demeanour or dress, which did not agree with the religious profession."   The next of Giraldus' six bishops is Archbishop Thomas Becket, whose extreme claims for the pre-eminence and independence of the spiritual power, Hugh accepted to their utmost extent, and even perhaps carried further than Becket himself.   Bartholomew of Exeter and Roger of Worcester are two more of the selected band of prelates.   The former of these was famous for his learning and legal lore, the other both for his

---

[1] *Introd. to Epist. Cantuar.*, p. cxvi.

high birth and dignity of character, which gave him
great weight with all the first men of the land.
There was a certain resemblance between Bishop
Roger and Bishop Hugh, both being very ready
with witty sayings, a quality which the Plantagenet
kings, who were of a free and genial disposition,
greatly relished.   When the dispute arose between
the Archbishops of Canterbury and York, which
ended in a regular fight, the Archbishop of York
made his complaint to the king, exhibiting at the
same time his torn cope, to testify to the violence
which had been used towards him.   The Bishop of
Worcester suggested that the cope was of considerable antiquity, and that not much violence was
required to tear it, inasmuch as it could scarcely
hold together of itself.   As the Archbishop of York
was rather remarkable for his meanness, this sally
caused much mirth to the king and courtiers.   On
another occasion, some were accused before the king
for having spoken unfitting words of him, and dis-
respectful to his Majesty.   The bishop, who knew
the royal temper, suggested to one of the accused
his line of defence.   Taking the bishop's hint, he
answered,   "It is very probable that we did say
them, and if the wine had held out we should no
doubt have said many more."   This, which fell in
with the royal humour, caused a laugh, and the
culprits escaped.   But the bishop who is selected by
Giraldus, specially to be classed and compared with
Hugh of Lincoln, is Baldwin, Bishop of Worcester,

and afterwards Archbishop of Canterbury. "These two were both monks," says Giraldus, "one of the Cistercian, the other of the Carthusian, order. Their goodness and religious temper were alike ; they were both well learned. But their characters were very different. Baldwin was slow and sparing in speech, Hugh's words were full of sprightliness and wit. The former was melancholy and timid, the latter full of hilarity, confident, and facetious. One was Diogenes, the other Democritus. One could scarcely be moved to anger, the other excited by very little. The one gentle, the other rough. The one luke-warm, the other hot. The one lax, the other strict." This character of Hugh by a clever, though eccentric contemporary writer, and one who loved the bishop well, is worthy of notice. Giraldus, however, was a man not easily satisfied ; very few whom he has touched escape altogether free from censure. Even Hugh, who is represented by him as so saintly and upright, has to suffer some abatement. "The Bishop of Lincoln," he says, " whom we have spoken of as warm and strict on his first commencing his episcopate, considering with himself that the head of the Church upon earth was but feeble, and that he had in this country no superior to support him with his authority, nor any equal to join with him or give him strength ; holding that every part ought to agree with the whole, thought it better and safer to conform to the patience and modesty of his fellow bishops. Hence in many things he purposely chose

to yield to overbearing power, rather than by standing alone against it, to put himself and his friends,
whom he had settled well in the land, in danger by
more wholesome plans." Thus he will not allow
Hugh in the world to come "the bright and rosy
crown," but merely, "the white crown of the hue of
the lily," because he would not, like St. Thomas,
contend to the death for the right.[1] It will probably
appear to the readers of the following life that these
strictures are eminently unjust ; that if the writer of
the *Magna Vita* is to be trusted, Hugh was not in any
way guilty of unworthy compliances,[2] but rather erred,
if at all, on the other side. At this point, therefore,
arises the question, How far is the writer of the *Magna
Vita* of St. Hugh to be trusted, and to what degree
is the very remarkable narrative put forth by him
to be literally taken ? Mr. Dimock, the editor of
this and of other lives of St. Hugh, and to whose
learned labours, indeed, we may be said altogether
to owe our knowledge of St. Hugh, considers the
writer of the *Magna Vita* a most trustworthy nar-

---

[1] *Giraldus, Vita Remigii. Opera*, vol. vii. p. 43 *seq.*

[2] Both Mr. Dimock and Mr. Freeman observe and comment upon
the inadequate and grudging character of the commendations given to
St. Hugh by Giraldus (Preface to vol. vii.) The former suggests in
his *Preface to the Magna Vita* a special reason for this. "It is very
probable that the cause of these disparaging remarks of Giraldus was
the fact that Hugh for some reason or other had thrown obstacles in
the way of Giraldus' institution to the church at Chesterton, to which
he had been presented. In a letter preserved he expostulates strongly
with the bishop for keeping him out of his preferment, and says that
he is truckling to the Court," etc.—Mr. Dimock's note to *Preface to
Magna Vita.*

rator.   He was no doubt a member of Hugh's
household during the latter part of his life, and eye-
witness of many of the things of which he wrote.
After his patron's death, in the year 1213, he
became Abbot of Eynsham, which was in the
patronage of the Bishops of Lincoln.   In the *Dunstable Annals* he is said to have ·been deposed by
Hugh de Welles, Bishop of Lincoln, in 1228, for
perjury, and manifest dilapidations of the property
of the abbey.   Mr. Dimock thinks, however, that
he is " able to produce very conclusive evidence of
his strictest truth and honesty as Hugh's biographer."
It is on the question of the alleged miracles wrought
by Hugh, that the greatest doubt will be felt as to
the truthfulness of the narrator ; but as it is not
proposed to relate these miracles in the following
life, we need not stop to discuss the value of his
testimony in such a matter.   He has certainly preserved us the bishop's own very disparaging view of
miracles, which is a great proof of his candour.
But that he was no enthusiastic upholder of the
truth, may be inferred from the excuses, and even
commendation, which he records for Hugh's manifest
breaking of an oath in his younger days, when he
entered the Grande Chartreuse, after having taken
a pledge to the Prior of Villarbenoit, that he would
not do so.   We should hardly be inclined to accept
the account of a miracle as a matter of fact, on such
testimony as this.   But for all the ordinary events
of Hugh's life, and especially for those of his latter

years, this writer may probably be trusted. He has no doubt drawn his hero as somewhat too perfect, but this we may readily excuse. Contrasted with most other writers of the Lives of Saints he stands well. He exhibits far more traces of humanity than are to be found in most of them. And we cannot but be profoundly grateful to him for having left us the lineaments of such a character as St. Hugh, and for having preserved those graphic historical episodes which are to be found in no other writer.

It can, however, hardly be said that the writer of the *Magna Vita* has left us, in the strict sense, a life of St. Hugh. The outlines of his earlier life are preserved, and the events of the few last years are pretty fully given, but for the ten or twelve years which followed after his elevation to the episcopate very little is supplied. This is the more to be regretted, as the earlier years of the reign of Richard, and the intrigues, struggles, and divisions, prevailing in England at that time are but very imperfectly understood by historians.

It is not, indeed, easy to ascertain from the historians of the period to which of the two great factions of that day, that of William Longchamp or that of Prince John, the Bishop of Lincoln inclined.

We find William Longchamp, after his banishment, sending the Papal bull, which was launched against his enemies, to Bishop Hugh to execute. This would seem to mark him out as his friend.

But, at the same time, we are told that Hugh refused
to execute it. He joined, however, afterwards with
the other bishops in excommunicating John. Some
of William Longchamp's most violent proceedings
were in the diocese of Lincoln. He besieged with
an armed force the Castle of Lincoln.[1] What part
did the bishop, who was not one to remain quiet or
to shrink timidly from taking a side, play in these
matters? We should have been glad to know; but
the writer of the *Magna Vita*, and those who compiled from him, evidently think the getting possession of the tooth of a saint of far more importance
than these political events. The Life of St. Hugh
by Giraldus, exhibits the bishop still more markedly
from the point of view of the saint, rather than the
human being, and so is not specially valuable to one
endeavouring to construct an historical life of him.
This, also, is the case with the report of the Papal
commissioners, who recommended Hugh's canonisation, preserved among the *Harleian MSS.*, and in the
Legenda drawn up from this, to be read in Lincoln
Cathedral on St. Hugh's Day.[2] It is, indeed, most
difficult to know how to treat these solemnly attested
records of miracles. It is impossible to credit them
upon the testimony of men who were interested in
establishing them, who were *à priori* disposed to
expect a miracle, and who would have thought it
impious to exercise the critical faculty in the mat-

[1] *Roger de Hoveden* (Ed. Saville), pp. 399, 402.
[2] Printed in vol. vii. of the Works of Giraldus, Appendix D.

ter.[1] Testimony of this class, however respectable, and however multiplied, is not sufficient by the very nature of the case, to overcome the *à priori* improbability attaching to a miracle. But it is invidious and irksome to be ever accusing men, probably sincere, of fiction and deceit, and it seems almost hopeless to attempt to sever the true from the doubtful in the case of an alleged miraculous occurrence. Such alleged facts are therefore, it seems, best omitted altogether from what aspires to be a veracious history, and neither harshly condemned nor critically examined. Happily in the case of St. Hugh, there are quite sufficient facts recorded of him into which the miraculous element does not at all enter, to enable us to give a full delineation of his character, and to represent him as a real man, moving and acting among real men. There are a great number of saints of whom this would be simply impossible, but this man was too genuine, too true and simple-hearted, too great and marked a character, to be altogether obscured, even by the most devoted labours of the hagiologists. The "one touch of nature" will come out in spite of all. We have before us the man, ardent, impetuous, fiery, scornful, jocular, tender, loving, devoted ; with his whole soul given to God ; the champion ready

---

[1] Mr. Freeman says : "In an age where a certain phenomenon is looked for, that phenomenon is sure to be found. An age which expects miracles is sure to find miracles, as an age which believes in witches is sure to find witches."—*Preface to Giraldus*, vol. vii. p. 67.

to do battle with kings and nobles, and judges and officers ; but unable to resist the appeal of the poor ; the despiser of ease and wealth, the servant of the leper and the beggar ; the man who truly lived the life of Christ upon earth, and illustrated and adorned the religion which he professed.

CHAPTER III.

HUGH'S LIFE UP TO THE PERIOD OF HIS CONSECRATION.

HUGH, afterwards so famous for his saintly virtues and his architectural taste, was born at Avalon, near Pontcharra, in Burgundy, close to the Savoy frontier, probably in the year 1135. He came of a noble family. His father was Lord of Avalon, and boasted a long line of ancestors renowned for religious devotion no less than for gentle blood. The name of his father was William, which was also the name of his eldest brother, who succeeded to the lordship. His mother, who died when Hugh was quite young, was called Anna. Moved either by grief for the loss of his wife, or by higher motives, Hugh's father, the Lord William, determined to quit the world, and devote himself to a " religious" life. But, unwilling to leave his child of tender age uncared for, he resolved to take him with him to the cloister which he had selected for himself. " He would have him taught to carry on warfare for God before he learned to live for the world,"[1] says his biographer. At the

---

[1] *Magna Vita*, p. 8.

age of eight years,[1] therefore, Hugh entered with his father a Priory of Regular Canons at Villarbenoit. As the place was close to Avalon, it may very probably have been the case that the religious house had been founded by one of the ancestors of the Lord William, as we are informed it had been enriched by himself. It was in immediate connection with the church at Grenoble, and consisted of six or seven canons. The young noble thus early cloistered was not, however, treated as the spoiled child of the monastery. His biographer, indeed, gravely tells us : " His infant body was made familiar with the scourge of the pedagogue, the fetters of discipline restrained all boyish emotions in him, so that he was made to excel in virtue ; and the whole of his life, from his birth to his death, was one entire martyrdom."[2] Possibly, indeed, the school may have been somewhat strict, but that the above is not a fair account of it is clearly shown by the bishop's own reminiscences of his young days quoted immediately afterwards by the same writer. There were many children of nobles there, he says, under the care of one of the canons, famous for his learning and devotion. They were instructed both in secular and in ecclesiastical lore, and Hugh was specially an object of attention to his master, who strove, both by coaxing and good advice, to incline him to an ecclesiastical life. He was ever endeavouring to keep him, by "various arts," from the games and tricks which delighted his

---

[1] Giraldus says ten, vol. vii. p. 89.   [2] *Magna Vita*, p. 8.

companions, and would interrupt him in the midst of
his sports by telling him that such things were not
for him. They might be well enough for others, but
they were beneath his dignity. "Hughy,[1] Hughy,"
he would say, "I am bringing you up for Christ.
Sports are not your business."[2] A skilful appeal to
pride would doubtless do more in influencing a
gallant young nature than the fear of the scourge.
Judging from Hugh's adult character, it can hardly
be doubted that one who showed so much vigour,
and such a keen sense of humour in after life,
must have been a lively and playful boy. But his
father's precepts and example, the skilful handling of
the canons, combined with his own pure and good
disposition, to make serious impressions take firm
hold of him, and Hugh soon determined to forego
all that the world had to offer for the sake of making
a "profession" of the regular religious life. His
devotion to his studies, his pure and faultless morals,
were remarkable, and he was no less distinguished
for an extreme sharpness of wit, which enabled him
to master readily everything which he attempted.
His memory was powerful and unfailing, which aided
him to take part in the numerous services of the
monastery without ever making a mistake or pause.
This, in after life, when a bishop, he was fond of
recalling with pride. He was often condemned to
listen to blunders made by the officiating priests, and
he would always rebuke them for this afterwards by

[1] Hugonete.   [2] *Magna Vita*, p. 10.

telling them that in his youth he never made a hitch (*morantia*) in the service.[1] No disturbance or confusion could ever put him out, or make him lose the clear grasp which he held of the matter in hand. Another most amiable trait is recorded of Hugh's boyhood. His father had become very infirm, and needed much care and devotion. Hugh supplied this with unremitting solicitude till his death. At the age of nineteen he was ordained deacon by the Bishop of Grenoble, and gave himself with great earnestness to the duties of his office. He preached zealously to the people, and made a deep impression on many. The prior of the canons, who discerned Hugh's great power and personal influence, wished to make use of it by stationing him in a *cell* or separate station, where he might minister to the people around. There was considerable danger in this for one so young, and Hugh, with great prudence, prevailed on a priest of more advanced years to be his companion in the cell of St. Maximin, of which he was styled the prior.[2] In the administration of his parish he has himself recorded how he dealt with a stubborn and notorious offender. By showing that firmness and decision which remarkably distinguished him in after life, he succeeded in bringing him to repentance. But the useful occupations in which Hugh was now engaged did not satisfy his mind. He craved for something higher, more romantic, more difficult, in the way of religious life. While all

[1] *Magna Vita*, p. 13.   [2] *Giraldus*, vol. vii. p. 91.

men's tongues were declaring his praise, he himself did not consider that he had even made a beginning in true devotion. For Hugh had completely imbibed the prevalent opinion of his age, that there was no true religion without complete self-immolation ; that the body must be reduced to the state of the greatest misery compatible with existence before the soul could reach the true heights of perfection.[1] Now, in the neighbourhood of the religious house in which Hugh was professed were the head-quarters of the most ascetic order of monks that the Church has ever seen, and towards these, as heroes of the faith, Hugh's heart continually yearned with ardent desire and longing. He prevailed upon the prior of his convent to accompany him on a visit to the convent of the Great Chartreuse,[2] carefully concealing from him, meanwhile, his wish to become an inmate of that famous abode of ascetic religion. Arrived there, everything impressed him with the profoundest ad-

---

[1] The writer of the *Magna Vita* says nothing of the dangers and scandals to which Hugh was exposed in the cell of St. Maximin ; but in the poetical Life of St. Hugh these are dwelt upon at much length. We are compelled to gather from the account that the state of morals of the canons and canonesses was so bad that Hugh could not live among them with safety to his soul.

    " Sic Hugo, contemplans cœlestia,, dum mulierum
      Vipereo nexu fratres videt illaqueari,   '
      Quos salvare nequit pereuntes deserit : unus
      Mavult salvari quam cum plerisque perire."
Metrical Life (Ed. Dimock), 273-7. The Life by Giraldus also speaks of the danger from female snares, vii. 91.

    [2] The order of Carthusians, so called from their first famous monastery on the mountain of the Grande Chartreuse, near Grenoble.

miration. The situation of the place, aloft in the
clouds, far above earth and near to heaven, touched
him with awe.   In that deep and unbroken solitude
what glorious opportunities were there for communing
with God!   Then there was the rich library, affording
abundant materials for sacred study and meditation;[1]
and the inhabitants of the place, bearing visible
tokens, in their appearance and manners, of mortifi-
cation of the flesh, serenity of mind, and purity of
spirit.   There was the happy union of the separate
and the common life—each monk remaining in his
separate cell, while all belonged in common to the
one monastery.   Here there could be no such dangers as those to which Hugh had been exposed in
the cell of St. Maximin.   Here all the way was
made plain for the servant of God.   He was soon,
however, to discover that all these advantages did
not avail to keep out spiritual pride.   One of the
Carthusian monks, to whom he ventured to hint his
desire to cast in his lot with them, sternly reproved
his presumption, and contemptuously told him that
the life was too high, the struggle too severe, for
such as he was.   Others, however, of the brethren

---

[1] It would seem from this that the Carthusians encouraged study
and provided books for the monks. Some of the religious orders did
not tolerate this. The Cistercians obliged the monks to spend all the time
to be spared from devotion in manual labour. The Franciscan friars
were not allowed to possess a book. It is singular that this last order
produced more learned men than any other, whereas the Cistercians, to
whom it soon became apparent that hard manual work and poor fare
were incompatible, rapidly became the most luxurious of the monastic
orders.

encouraged Hugh in his aspirations. The great difficulty he foresaw would come from his prior, who was by no means likely to sanction the departure of so promising a son. Accordingly, Hugh concealed his desire from him as long as possible, and, when it was discovered, had to hear, as he had expected, most moving appeals and entreaties to him to forego his purpose. The prior pressed it upon Hugh, on the ground of his obedience, that he should take a solemn oath not to enter the Carthusian Society, and in an unhappy moment Hugh consented to do this. Possibly, he may have taken the oath in good faith, but if so, he very quickly broke it, and escaped like a criminal to the Chartreuse, where he was received with ready welcome. No plain person would hesitate to pronounce this a sinful action, yet the biographer of Hugh, in his too eager desire to make everything redound to his honour, pretends that he acted by an inspiration from on high.[1] What is more remarkable is that the saint himself, when appealed to in after life as to whether he had ever felt any scruple as to thus breaking his oath, declared that it had never caused him any regret but only joy. No doubt there is something to be alleged in excuse for Hugh as to this transaction. In the notions of those days plain morality held but a very low place as compared with the glories of the " spiritual life,"

---

[1] It is somewhat remarkable that this Abbot Adam who wrote the *Magna Vita* of St. Hugh was himself afterwards convicted and deposed for perjury.

and Hugh may have been utterly unable to see how any irregularity which led directly to great spiritual triumphs was to be condemned. Having thus become a member of this ascetic order, Hugh applied himself with fervour to the performance of the discipline enjoined by its rule. He especially gave himself to advancement in sacred study, and to acquiring an intimate knowledge of the Holy Scriptures, in which the monks of this order were reputed to excel.[1] His charitable disposition was also exercised in the care of an aged monk, who was unable to leave his cell, and who was tended by him with the utmost solicitude. This old man prophesied that one day Hugh would be raised to the dignity of bishop. Being admitted after a time to the office of the priesthood, Hugh increased his fasting and discipline to such an extent that he permanently injured his health by it. The doctors used to ascribe the corpulence which affected him in after life to these early severities. There is no doubt that Hugh soon became one of the most distinguished and eminent among the monks of the Great Chartreuse. When the Archbishop of Tarentaise came to take up his abode at the convent, it was Hugh who was specially appointed to attend

---

[1] In the midst of his austerities, however, Hugh had his little amusements. In the Life by Giraldus we are told that at the Chartreuse "the little birds and the mice of the woods, which are commonly called squirrels, were domesticated and tamed by him to such an extent, that they would leave their woods, and regularly at the hour of supper would come to share his meal with him, not only getting on his table, but eating out of his hand and his plate, and making themselves completely his companions."—vii. 91.

upon him. His clever and shrewd character was recognised in the appointment which he received from the prior of bursar to the monastery. This office, which involved the providing of all things needed by the establishment for their diet, their services, and their library, obliged Hugh to be in constant communication with the outer world ; and his reputation grew among all men, not only for his spiritual-mindedness and his learning, but for that tact and ready wit which especially distinguished him afterwards in his episcopal life.

But a great change was now to take place in the life of Hugh. He was to be brought out of the position of comparative obscurity in which he was, to be himself the head of a religious house, the favourite of the most powerful monarch of the day, and on the road to the highest preferment. Of the character of Henry II. enough has been said in the preceding chapter. His occasional pious professions and movements contrasted but strangely with an ill-regulated and wilful life, and these same pious movements were but of rare occurrence, and of very limited and paltry extent. He had made a vow, it seems, to found three abbeys, and then, after having made the vow, he sought how to carry it out at the least expense possible. At Amesbury and Waltham he had simply reconstituted the religious foundations by turning out the old inhabitants and introducing religious of a different order, and his third monastery he now attempted to found in a wild spot at Witham,

in Somersetshire, by merely making a grant of the
place to a few Carthusian monks, and sending them
there to establish their monastery as best they could,
without any effective help from himself. The consequence was such as might be expected. They
miserably failed to form a religious house. The first
prior, scared by the threatening aspect of the country
people, who looked upon the monks as so many
robbers come to spoil them of their goods, fled away
in terror. The second, overwhelmed by his difficulties, died at his post, and Henry's grand foundation
of Witham was on the point of collapsing, when a
certain nobleman of Maurienne bethought him of
telling the king of a method by which he was confident that he could turn the threatened failure into a
brilliant success. " There is," said he, " in the house
of the Great Chartreuse, a certain monk illustrious
for his noble birth, but still more distinguished by
his character, by name Hugh of Avalon. Furnished
with every sort of virtue, this man is beloved by all
who know him, and his very look is enough to turn
all men's affections towards him. His words, when
he speaks, are like those of an angel. This is the
man whom you should seek to obtain as the founder
of your abbey. The whole Church of England would
be a gainer if he could be induced to come. But you
must expect to find this no easy thing. The brethren
of his house will neither be willing to part with him,
nor he to leave them. You must send an influential
embassy for him, and use all your power to get him.

If you succeed, the beauties of his character and temper will be found to conciliate and attract all, for he
looks upon all mankind as his own bowels, and cherishes all with the love of a universal charity."[1] Acting
upon the advice thus given, Henry II. despatched
Reginald, Bishop of Bath, with a number of influential
companions, to solicit Hugh to leave the Chartreuse,
and come to take upon him the government of the
struggling foundation of Witham. Anticipating a
good deal of difficulty, the envoys persuaded the Archbishop of Grenoble to go with them and take part in the
negotiation. When the proposal was made, the prior
of the Chartreuse absolutely refused ; Hugh was also
unwilling to go, but left it to the prior. The latter
was at length persuaded to leave it to the Archbishop
of Grenoble, his diocesan. The bishop, who was
already gained to the king's side, decided that Hugh
was to go. And so this important matter, which
the writer of Hugh's life evidently thinks equal to
the negotiation for the fate of a nation, was settled.
Arrived at Witham, Hugh found everything in a
wretched state. The monks were dwelling in poor
huts made of twigs,[2] while the inhabitants of the

---

[1] *Magna Vita*, p. 54.

[2] It might seem at first sight that the Carthusians who affected the
extremest asceticism need not have been dissatisfied with the very
meanest dwellings. The poetical Life of Hugh gives another view of
the matter which is worth quoting :—

   " Parvula tecta videt, contristaturque videndo :
     Non quia divitiis velit uti, sed quia posse
     Vult uti. Nec enim regnum cœleste mereri
     Mens hominis compulsa potest ; mentisque coronat

place still held the houses and lands which had been
granted for the monastery, no provision having been
made for them elsewhere.   It was Hugh's first care
to procure their removal, with full compensation for
that which they were obliged to give up.   The king
made considerable difficulty about this, but yielded
at length to Hugh's firmness and persistency, and
when the buildings had thus been acquired by him,
he still hung back from allowing the monks to treat
them as their own, until Hugh insisted that without
this nothing could be done.   The niggardly spirit in
which Henry was bent upon dealing with this
foundation of his own creating, was still further
apparent, when Hugh attempted to erect buildings
suitable for the monastery.   The building soon came
to a standstill for want of funds, and twice were
some of the brethren sent to the king to ask the
necessary help, and twice did they return with
nothing but fair words and promises.   The work-
men were mutinous and found fault with the prior,
and some of the monks also were indignant with
him for not having himself gone to the king and constrained him to furnish the required supplies.   One of
the monks, named Gerard, boldly reproached him with
this neglect, and said, that if he was too timid himself
to say what was fitting to the king, he would go with

Paupertas, non materiæ defectus, egenos ;
Libertas perit arbitrii, cum nulla facultas
Suppetit utendi ; nec habent jejunia laudem,
Passio non confert meritum, nisi sponte feratur ;
Nulla necessariis debetur gratia rebus."—436-444.

him, and boldly declare the real state of the case. To this Hugh agreed, and taking with them another of the most distinguished of the monks, they repaired to Henry. ·After explaining to him the state of the case, the king as before made fair promises but gave nothing. Then the honest old monk Gerard could no longer contain himself. He denounced Henry as heartless and penurious, and declared that for himself, he would sooner go back to starve among the rocks of the Chartreuse, than live in the kingdom of so mean and dishonourable a prince. Henry, who knew well that he had deserved all this, and who was by no means easily offended at plain language, merely turned to Hugh and asked him if he was of the same mind. "No," said Hugh, "I believe better things of you, and am confident that you will carry out the salutary purpose which you have entertained." At this the king was greatly delighted, and declared that Hugh was the man after his own heart, and the necessary supplies were at once forthcoming. The credit of obtaining them, however, seems rather to rest with the honest old monk who had spoken so plainly, than with Hugh who had thus skilfully played the courtier's part. By his address on this occasion, Hugh laid the foundation of that friendship with Henry which continued unbroken until that monarch's death. There was no one, says Hugh's biographer, whom he more delighted to consult, no one to whose counsel he more readily listened. So great was the

intimacy which sprang up between them, that Hugh
was thought by many to be a natural son of Henry's,
a fancy which was supported by the great likeness
of feature which there was between them. The
intimacy, however, may be very easily explained,
without having recourse to this supposition. Henry
II., whatever were the irregularities of his life and
the defects of his moral character, was a prince of
the greatest talent and acuteness. He easily perceived that in Hugh he had found a counseller, who
was not only pure and disinterested, but of extreme
shrewdness and insight, and he had the sense to
make full use of so valuable a helper.[1] Nor did
Hugh fail to use the influence which he had obtained
over the king to good and salutary ends. Often did
he mitigate his sternness and obtain pardon for
offenders ; often did he induce him to give benefac-
tions to churches and religious houses ; and most
earnestly did he protest against that evil practice,
of which Henry was conspicuously guilty, of keeping
bishops' sees and rich abbeys a long time vacant,
that he might appropriate the revenues for himself
and his courtiers. A circumstance which occurred
about this time contributed towards fixing and confirming Hugh's influence over this wayward prince.
Henry, in one of his frequent passages between
England and Normandy, was in imminent peril of

[1] Henry was in the habit of hunting frequently in the forest where
Witham was situated, on all which occasions he was wont to be the
guest of the Prior of Witham and to hold much converse with him.
—*Giraldus* in *Anglia Sacra,* ii. 419.

shipwreck. At the moment of extreme danger he bethought him of Hugh, and prayed that for his sake and for his merits he might be spared. The tempest abated, and the grateful king attributing this to the merits of the saint, held him in still higher honour than before. Meantime the buildings at Witham advanced apace. Two houses were soon completed, one for monks, the other for lay brethren. The prior was the admiration of all for his great devotion, and it was thought that he prayed even in his sleep, as he was often heard to mutter "Amen." He provided suitable religious readings for the monks at meals, and in his own diet he showed the greatest abstinence, being usually content with water as his only drink.[1] Under his earnest and enlightened rule, Witham soon attained to the highest reputation for religious discipline, and eminent men began to resort thither for the advantage of living under the direction of one who was at once so learned, so wise, and so good. Hugh was not over forward to admit every applicant to the order. He was determined that the strict discipline of the Carthusians should be fully preserved, but even with all his caution, some were admitted who after-

---

[1] At Witham, as well as at the Great Chartreuse, and afterwards at Stow, Hugh showed a singular power of attracting the affection of birds. This is ascribed by Giraldus to his especial sanctity. "A certain little bird," he writes, "which is called *Burneta*, was so tamed and domesticated in his cell that every day it came to his table, as though it had discovered the innate kindness of the man, and took its food from his hand and his plate."—*Giraldus, Op.*, vii. 93.

wards deserted him and brought some scandal upon
the order.   Those who had once deserted the house,
where they had been voluntarily received, Hugh was
inflexible in refusing to re-admit, though they sometimes sought for this.   Having now finished the
building of the monastery, and filled it with obedient
and observant monks, Hugh applied himself to
obtaining all that was needed for the edification and
well-being of the establishment.   He sought eagerly
for manuscripts of good books, and above all he was
desirous of obtaining a copy of the Scriptures entire,
which he regarded, says his biographer, as "the best
comfort and recreation in peace, the best weapon
and armour in war, as nourishment in time of famine,
medicine in time of sickness."[1]   In one of his friendly
interviews with the king Hugh mentioned the dearth
of books as a great trouble to him.   "Why not set
your brethren to copy some?" said the king.   "We
have no parchment," replied the prior.   "How
much money would supply that want?" said his
Majesty.   "One silver mark would last us for a
long time."   "Oh!" said the king, "your demands are
immoderate indeed."   Whereupon he ordered ten
marks to be given to Hugh for the purchase of

[1] In connection with the love of the Scriptures here attributed to
Hugh, it is interesting to observe that there are now in the library of
Lincoln Cathedral some splendid MS. volumes, said, in a contem-
poraneous catalogue, to have been given by him to the Church; among
which are "two great volumes" of sermons extracted from the Latin
Fathers, and a splendidly illuminated Psalter, with a very large and
full comment on the Psalms.

parchment.[1]   This, indeed, was not the whole extent of the literary help which Henry designed to
give to his new foundation at Witham.   But having
been at the expense of the munificent donation of
ten marks, he sought to make his next present
somewhat less costly to himself.   Accordingly he
inquired carefully where a good copy of the whole
Bible (*bibliotheca*) could be found, and having heard
that at the monastery of St. Swithun's at Winchester
there was a very fine copy, he sent for the prior of
that house, and blandly told him that he should be
very much obliged to him if he would give him the
book.   The prior, hoping no doubt to experience
some substantial benefit from the king's promises,
readily gave him the volume, and Henry at once
despatched it to the favoured house of Witham.
Great was the joy of Hugh and the brethren.   They
examined the splendid manuscript with admiration,
and they liked it all the better because there was
room for some of their own work to be added to it
in illuminations and ornament.   The satisfaction,
however, which they derived from the present was
destined to be short-lived.   It chanced that one of
the monks of Winchester paid a visit to Witham,
and he at once told the whole story how the king
had begged the book from their prior.   He very
politely added that he was glad that so good a use
had been made of their much-loved manuscript ; but
he also said, if you would desire it in any way dif-

[1] *Magna Vita*, p. 92.

ferently copied, we shall be only too glad to make
you another copy and thus get back this, upon
which we have spent immense pains to fit it exactly
for our own use.   At this speech, Hugh, who was
quite ignorant how the book had been obtained,
was struck with amazement, not unmixed with
vexation and annoyance.   "Is it indeed the case,"
he said, "that the king has thus robbed your church
of so important and necessary a treasure?   You
shall have your Bible back without a moment's
delay, and I entreat you to make the most ample
apologies to your society, and to assure them that
we were utterly ignorant of the way in which the
book was obtained."   Upon this the Winchester
monk was seized with terror.   He pictured to
himself the wrath of the king if his false liberality
should be detected, and the reproaches of his brother
monks, if he should bring this danger upon them.
But Hugh was not to be turned from his purpose.
"Is it indeed the case," he said, "that you hope for
any substantial favour from the king for having
made him this present, and if so, do you not think
it was somewhat of an unseemly way of obtaining
it?"   The monk assured him that greatly as they
loved the book, all the monks had gladly joined in
giving it up to please the king.   "Then," said
Hugh, "we must preserve their satisfaction as well
as we may.   The king need know nothing about it
if you take it back secretly, but if you decline to do
this, I tell you plainly that I shall restore it to him

who gave it to me." Upon this, the monk took
possession of the volume and carried it back again
to Winchester, that society being even more pleased
with the kindness of Hugh in sending it back, than
in the return of their sacred treasure.[1] Certainly
the story is much to Hugh's credit, but perhaps it
would have been even more so had the gift been
returned to the king direct, could this have been
done so as to save harmless the Winchester monks.
From the kindly interchange of civilities which thus
took place between the monasteries of Witham and
St. Swithun's, at Winchester, a great friendship grew
up between the two societies. Several of the Winchester monks appear to have resorted to Witham as
a *retreat*, for the benefit of the stricter discipline
exercised there, and the author of Hugh's life specially mentions that it was at the request of two of
these that he undertook the task of compiling a
history of the saintly bishop.

[1] This magnificent MS., with its splendid illustrations, is still in the
library of the cathedral church at Winchester.

CHAPTER IV.

HUGH'S ELECTION AND CONSECRATION TO THE SEE OF LINCOLN.

AFTER the translation of Walter de Coutances in 1184, there was yet another vacancy of nearly two years in the chief pastorship of the persecuted church of Lincoln.   It seemed as though Henry could not bring himself to allow the vacancy to be filled without at any rate securing some profit to himself from its occurrence.   And yet at this time there were around Henry some better influences than those among which he had passed the greater part of his life.

Reginald, Bishop of Bath, is specially mentioned by the writer of St. Hugh's life, but it is by no means improbable that Hugh himself was the influential adviser who determined the king to fill up the vacancy, and that the very circumstance of his having pressed this upon the king may have suggested himself as the most fitting person for the important post.   In May 1186 the king was holding a council at Eynsham, near Oxford, with his bishops and barons, on various important matters of state.   He repaired each day to the Abbey of Eynsham to meet his councillors, returning in the evening to the palace of his manor of Woodstock, only a few miles distant. Having determined to fill up the vacancy at Lincoln, he ordered the canons of Lincoln to repair to him at Eynsham, and to make their election. These important personages obeyed the royal mandate. " There were in that church," says the author of the *Magna Vita*, " many personages of prominent importance, who were accustomed also to frequent the palace and the court. They were men of great renown in secular things, of high acquirements in literature, and abundantly furnished with worldly riches. Many of them, indeed, considered no bishopric, however large, greater than their own greatness, and indeed they were heaped up with revenues more ample than those of large sees. Nevertheless, there were some among them, who, either out of regard to the apostle's words as to the office of a bishop being a good work, or it may be from secular ambition and regard to the honour and power which they might gain, would not have refused to be made bishops if they had been very hardly pressed."[1] The irony of this description of the Lincoln canons should be qualified by the remembrance that a regular is here writing of seculars ; and that secular canons, even more than the secular

---

[1] *Magna Vita*, p. 102. Godfrey de Luci, one of these canons, shortly afterwards refused the bishopric of Exeter " quia non videbatur sufficere ei ad impensas suas."—*Benedictus.*

parochial clergy, were an object of contempt and dislike to the true monk. This body, then, of rich and magnificent Churchmen, was now called upon at Eynsham to choose a bishop to preside over their diocese. They had no doubt had many discussions and not a few intrigues and schemes on the important subject. A small body of Churchmen charged to execute a trust, and bent in doing this so to act that each may serve some fancy or interest of his own, without too openly offending against public opinion, is perhaps of all bodies the one least qualified to make a good selection. In one point the Lincoln canons seemed to be tolerably unanimous. They desired to have one of their own body to preside over them. They hoped that they might find among themselves one not distasteful to the king. They first presented Richard their dean, the king's treasurer, then, when he was declined, Godfrey de Luci, one of the canons, and of the king's household. He also was refused. They then tried the Archdeacon of Canterbury, who was also a canon of Lincoln. But this dignitary was not more acceptable than the others.[1] Henry had, in fact, long before made up his mind as to the man he would have as bishop, and this allowing the

---

[1] "Henry," says Professor Stubbs, "recollecting his sad experience with St. Thomas, refused to reward with the episcopal dignity those who as lawyers and ministers had been his faithful servants."—*Preface to Epist. Cantuar.*, p. lxxx. Herbert, Archdeacon of Canterbury, was shortly afterwards elected Bishop of Salisbury and approved of by the king, but an appeal was lodged against his election by some of the clergy on the ground of his being the son of a concubine, and he was not consecrated.—*Benedictus, s. a.* 1186.

canons to occupy themselves in elections was but a mere decent preliminary to the appointment of the clerk long ago selected.   It is probable that the king's conscience was uneasy as to the ills that he had inflicted upon the diocese of Lincoln by the enforced vacancy of the see, and now he thought by procuring it an exceptionally good bishop he would do something to compensate for his spoliations.[1]   He was desirous, however, that the man whom he had designed for the post should approach it by a canonical election, and not by the mere exercise of his will.   Accordingly he directed some to go to the canons as friendly advisers, and to say to them that it would be far the best course if they would at once choose a clerk who was conspicuous above all by his learning, piety, and zeal, namely, the prior of Witham.   The canons received this advice with a scornful smile (*derisionis cachinno*). Who was the prior of Witham that they should think of. him?   An obscure foreign monk whose

---

[1] Thus *Roger de Wendover* and *Matthew Paris*.   Tenuerat rex ecclesiam Lincoln in manu per multos annos pastoris solatio viduatam, quem *volens excessum redimere* honestè procuravit ut per electionem vir prædictus ad illius ecclesiæ regimen vocaretur.   *Wendover, Flor. Hist.*, iii. 176.   *Matt. Paris, Hist. Maj.*, p. 203 (Ed. Watts).   Giraldus Cambrensis says that he made Hugh bishop Ad redimendum sic famam suam, quia multos ante indignos episcopaverat.—*Anglia Sacra*, ii. 429. Benedictus says that the canons presented the three clerks mentioned to the king as men of approved life and honest conversation, that the king might select one of them, but that Henry answered, Illos satis divites esse, et se de cœtero nunquam daturum episcopatum alicui pro amore vel consanguinitate vel consilio, vel prece, vel pretio, sed illis quos elegerit sibi Dominus.—*Benedictus, s. a.* 1186.

manners and language were absolutely strange to
them! That such an one should be selected to
govern the most important diocese in England! to
preside over a people of whose habits and whose
tongue he was absolutely and entirely ignorant!
They were, says Hugh's biographer, "struck with
horror" at the notion. And no wonder. For, as
far as the canons knew anything of the matter, it
might well seem about the worst appointment that
could possibly be made. The king, a man of keen
discrimination, had penetrated the secret of the
powerful cast of Hugh's character, and the high
order of his abilities, but the world in general knew
nothing of it. How should it? Probably Hugh's
name even was unknown to many of the Lincoln
canons, and though his biographer talks wildly about
their being swayed by carnal judgment, and so on,
yet it seems clear that no canon of ordinary prudence and sense of responsibility, could, voluntarily,
and without further information, have voted for
Hugh. They soon found, however, to their dismay,
that the advice which had been given thus, and at
which they had scoffed, meant somewhat more than
they were at first inclined to attribute to it. They
discovered that the king was resolutely bent to have
Hugh as bishop. This changed their views very
speedily. There was really no means of resisting the
will of a prince like Henry II. in such a matter.
Elections of bishops were nominally and formally
free ; in reality the bishops were appointed by the

Crown, just as in modern days by the Prime Minister. Accordingly, the canons of Lincoln very speedily elected Hugh of Avalon, prior of Witham, to be bishop of Lincoln (May 1186). They chose to the supervision of that great see—containing eight arch-deaconries and nine counties—a foreign ascetic, now upwards of fifty years of age, without any experience of parochial life, without any knowledge of England, simply because the king, pleased with his ready wit, and believing in his great ability, willed to have it so. It was a perilous risk, and might have involved the electors, constrained though they were, in a terrible responsibility. The excellence of Hugh's after life and work as a bishop well excused both the canons and the king. As a noble, straightforward, dauntless, and holy man, giving in his high post a bright example, and exercising a salutary influence over all around him, it was a happy day for the Church when he was appointed to a position of dignity and power.

The choice of the canons was approved by the king, and confirmed by the metropolitan Archbishop Baldwin, while the person principally interested was quietly abiding in his monastery, in complete ignorance of what was going on. It had probably been assumed by the king and bishops that all that was necessary for procuring his accession to the see of Lincoln was done when his election had been procured. But, if so, they quite misunderstood the man. Hugh had no intention of giving utterance to a childish and

unmeaning *nolo episcopari*, and then meekly submit-
ting to that which in word he disclaimed.   He did
not shrink from the labour and responsibility of the
episcopate, but his pride and sense of dignity revolted
from being chosen by an election which was in any
manner constrained.   When, therefore, the messengers who brought him the news of what had been
done at Eynsham, requested Hugh at once to present
himself to the king and archbishop, the prior of
Witham calmly refused.   He did not wonder, he
said, at the king desiring his promotion.   He had
brought him from abroad, and naturally took an
interest in his advancement.   Nor was he surprised
at the archbishop wishing the same, for Archbishop
Baldwin, almost alone of the bishops of England,
valued the regular discipline, and would thus naturally wish his suffragans to be chosen from among the
regular clergy ; but he would have the canons of
Lincoln clearly to understand that no such election
as that which they had just made could have any
weight with him.   The election of a bishop was a
solemn thing, to be done in chapter of the clergy
after the invocation of the Holy Spirit, and not
amidst the intrigues of the court, or the distraction
of a large meeting of the magnates of the land.   Let
the canons treat, as he did, the proceedings at Eynsham as utterly null and void.   Let them assemble
in their Cathedral Church, and in due and canonical
fashion make a solemn election, uninfluenced in any
way by the wiles or wishes of others, and unfettered

by any previous acts. He would return no other answer but "God be with them." The messengers quickly perceived that these words were the sincere and genuine resolves of the prior, and returned to the canons to tell them of the bold and undaunted bearing, and the high sense of ecclesiastical dignity exhibited by Hugh. The report was received with the greatest satisfaction. Doubtless some thought that here they had found a second Thomas Becket, and that the king was again forcing into a high ecclesiastical position one who would boldly contend against him with the power of the Church. Those who had before made the election grudgingly and unwillingly, thinking that they were choosing to so high a dignity some mean and pliant foreigner who would be a mere tool in the hands of the king, now entirely changed their view. Here was a man who showed himself altogether without fear of angering the king, who would enforce the usages of holy Church, and the free and unbiassed election-rights of the clergy, in the face of all authority. Such an one would they have to rule over them. Accordingly they at once unanimously re-elected Hugh in their chapter, and despatched a more dignified embassy than the former to acquaint him with the fact. Every one supposed that all was now happily accomplished. But another impediment arose. The dignity of the Carthusian was not yet satisfied. The election might be regular enough, he said. The king and the archbishop were doubtless the heads of State

and Church in the kingdom, and their wishes ought
to be respected. But there was one who was to him
a greater man than either of them, and he certainly
could not accept this dignity until the head of his
order, the prior of the Great Chartreuse, had been
consulted and had given his sanction. And so the
King of England, the Archbishop of Canterbury, and
the electing chapter, had to despatch a humble
embassy to the Alpine monastery, to solicit the favour
of the prior's permission for one of his children to
accept one of the highest dignities in the English
Church. We need not wonder at Hugh's being a
popular saint in his own order, but it is a question
whether this proud humility altogether became him.
It was well to assert his dignity, and to refuse to recognise a constrained and prejudiced election. It was
scarcely as well, when he had been canonically elected,
and had made up his own mind as to accepting the
office, to insist upon this solemn offering at the shrine
of the Carthusians. Of course the monastery of the
Chartreuse gladly gave the required permission, and
Hugh prepared himself for his consecration. His
preparation was a devout and spiritual one. He
looked upon the dignity that was coming to him (as
his biographer tells us) as the sailor looks upon the
black clouds gathered together for the storm. But
he did not shrink back on account of the danger, but
bravely prepared himself for it. It had been early
predicted to him that he should be a bishop, and he
had always believed it. The thought was therefore

not a new one. He had probably considered the special difficulties to the right performance of the episcopal office in England. No man knew better the character of the king. Of the rough licentiousness of the nobles, the corruption of the clergy, the ignorance of the common people, he had, doubtless heard, though his experience of all these was as yet but small. These things did not frighten him. He had a religious distrust of himself, but he had no fear of man before his eyes. Three months elapsed between his election and consecration. At the end of that time he left his Somersetshire home—the monastery which he had made, and where his days had passed in religious peace and quiet,—and proceeded towards London to receive consecration from the archbishop. But the elect of Lincoln still preserved in his journey the ascetic habits of the Carthusian. His clerks attended him decked in rich attire, and with gilded trappings to their horses, while Hugh, in monk's garb, bestrode his mule, and carried, strapped behind him, in a huge bundle, his baggage and bedding. Great was the confusion and vexation of the courtly clerks at this, in their eyes, unseemly exhibition. In vain, however, either by serious remonstrance or jocular remark, did they try to induce the ascetic to allow his bundle to be removed and placed among their baggage. Hugh had as great a pride in exhibiting his contempt for show, as the others had in exhibiting their magnificence. Thus the clerks had to endure this practical comment

upon their luxurious habits as they journeyed along
the southern roads.   To enter, however, in this guise
the town of Marlborough, where the king with his
prelates and barons was then holding a great council,[1]
was more than the equanimity of the clerks could
endure.   So a dexterous member of the party contrived, in the twilight, to cut the fastenings of the
hated bundle without Hugh's perceiving it, and
secretly to abstract it.   From Marlborough, after
taking part in the council held there, the bishop-
elect, with his attendants, proceeded to London,
whither, after the council was finished, Archbishop
Baldwin also proceeded.   Here, on St. Matthew's
Day (September 21, 1186), the primate consecrated
Hugh to the see of Lincoln, and William to that of
Worcester, in the Chapel of the Invalids at Westminster.[2]   The king testified his satisfaction at the
man of his choice having reached this high dignity by
making munificent offerings, and by bearing the whole
expense of the ceremonial.   No time was lost between the consecration of Hugh and his enthronisa-
tion in his Cathedral Church.   He must have left
Westminster almost immediately, as at least five days
would be required for the journey, and on Michaelmas
Day, September 29, he reached Lincoln, accompanied

---

[1] *Benedictus, s. a.* 1186.

[2] *Benedictus, s. a.* 1186.   *Capellâ infirmorum*, are the words used.
St. Matthew's Day fell on a Sunday in the year 1186, which proves
among other things that the date of 1185 implied in the *Magna Vita*
is incorrect, bishops being invariably consecrated on a Sunday.   See
Mr. Dimock's *Introd. to Magna Vita*, p. xxv.

by Gilbert, Bishop of Rochester, and Herbert, Archdeacon of Canterbury, one of the canons of his
church, and received by the clergy and people with
solemn ·procession.   On the same day he was enthroned by the Archdeacon of Canterbury.   The
usual fee for the ceremonial, which consisted of the
horse used by the bishop in riding to his cathedral [1]
and the cope used in celebrating, was demanded by
the archdeacon, but Hugh, who seems to have considered it a matter of principle to oppose all usages
which had any smack in them of worldly profit or
show, indignantly refused the demand.   "As much
as I gave for the mitre, so much, and no more, will I
give for the chair," said he ; and the archdeacon had
to be content with performing his work gratuitously.
But that this refusal proceeded from no niggard spirit
was quickly proved by the new bishop.   His steward
suggested that for the feast of installation some of
the deer in his park at Stow should be killed, and
asked how many it would please him should be taken.
Hugh replied, let them take 300, and if more be
required they can take those also.   The astonishment of the steward at this wholesale massacre must
have been considerable.   The king and courtiers
heard of it, and were hugely amused at the simplicity
of the man.   But Hugh meant that all the poor of
his cathedral city should feast with him, and no more

---

[1] Mr. Dimock observes in a note to the *Magna Vita* that no horse
was used at Lincoln. From an old MS. in the Registry it appears
that Hugh slept the night before his installation at St. Catherine's
Priory, and thence in the morning walked barefoot to the cathedral.

fitting or more politic way of recommending himself
to his people could have been devised. The preservation of game, with all the terrible forest laws
of the Norman kings, was the crying grievance
of the day. The great Churchmen shared in the
odium which belonged to these tyrannical oppressions.
But in Hugh's first act the people might recognise
a man of another sort—one who valued not the
baronial privileges or the worldly possessions of the
see, but who came among them to work for God, and
to win souls. And so the good folk of Lincoln ate
contentedly of the fat venison, and praised God for
the pastor He had sent them.

Nor were they long left without more certain
proof of the temper of the man who had come among
them as their chief pastor. One of Hugh's first acts
was to publish certain *decreta*, in which he at once
addresses himself to the correction of some of the
abuses which were most rampant among his clergy.
"Bishop Hugh," says the Abbot Benedictus, "remaining in his diocese, laboured to edify the people
committed to him by his conversation and the word
of paternal exhortation, and in his synods enjoined,
in virtue of their obedience, both his clergy and
people to keep without fail the following decrees :—

"1. That nothing should be given or received for
administering or for hastening the administration of
justice.

"2. That nothing should be given or exacted of
the priests-vicars for their office.

" 3. That the archdeacons and their officials should not presume without regular trial to fine any church, or clerk, or any one else.

" 4. That no layman or other person, not a priest, should have the celebration of masses inflicted on him as a penance.

" 5. That no annuals, or tricennials, or any other fixed masses,[1] should be celebrated for temporal gain.

" 6. That no one be admitted to the performance of the priestly office unless it shall have been proved that he was ordained canonically by the Archbishop of Canterbury, or by one of his suffragans.

" 7. That all who hold benefices should have the tonsure.

" 8. That no clerk should sue another clerk in a secular court for matters ecclesiastical."[2]

John de Schalby also informs us that the bishop published letters to his archdeacons, and to the Dean and Chapter, ordering the first to enforce the attendance of all the clergy at the Mother Church of Lincoln, with due and fitting offerings, at the Feast of Pentecost yearly ; and charging the latter, if not resident, to appoint and provide for vicars to fill their places.[3]

Such were the first utterances of the new bishop, and men might perhaps not inaptly judge from these of what nature his administration of the diocese

---

[1] *Missæ ex conventione.* The reader will not fail to observe how directly these and the other decreta meet the abuses mentioned by Giraldus.   [2] *Benedictus, s. a.* 1186.   [3] *Giraldus, Op.,* vii. 200.

would probably be.   They soon learned to reverence
him for his straightforwardness, honesty, and upright-
ness, although it was a time when all moral qualities
were in very low repute, and nothing was very highly
esteemed save a senseless and excessive asceticism.
Hugh, indeed, was an ascetic as rigid as any, but he
was something also far beyond this.   He was a man
who took a wise, politic, and shrewd part in the
affairs of the world, with a view of furthering the
interests of the Church and of religion, and as to the
miracles of which so much was thought and said by
the men of his day, he neither desired them to be
imputed to himself, nor did he value them when
asserted of others.   In a remarkable passage of the
Magna Vita the writer tells us, " he had learned
from the founders of the Carthusian order to cherish
with all his soul gravity and humility.   So that he
was as far as possible from admiring or emulating
prodigies of miracles, though he paid a proper respect
to them when related of holy men.   For he was
wont to refer these things to the desire felt by the
narrators of commending the person to whom they
were attributed, and to the profit likely to arise to
those who admired such things ; but for himself, the
holiness of the saints was a sufficient miracle for him,
and a sufficient example.   The one universal miracle
which was ever present to his mind was the remembrance of his Creator, and the thought of the stupen-
dous multitude and inexplicable greatness of His

mighty works."[1]   This indicates a mind greatly in
advance of his age, and which had true conceptions
of the grand and spiritual nature of religion.   It
would, indeed, have been a real misfortune for the
Church had such a man been allowed to consume
his days in the solitude of an obscure monastery,
and if all the good work which he had in him to do
had been confined to a few recluses.

[1] *Magna Vita*, p. 97.   This passage seems abundantly to justify
the omission of the alleged miracles from a life of the bishop ; one is
forcibly reminded of the letter of Gregory the Great to Augustine,
reproving him for boasting of miracles.

CHAPTER V.

HUGH AS BISHOP—ILLUSTRATIONS OF HIS PERSONAL CHARACTER.

THE residence of the newly consecrated Bishop of Lincoln was at his manor of Stow, near Lincoln, which Robert Bloet, one of his predecessors, had made meet for an episcopal abode by the transfer of the monks of St. Mary's to Eynsham, and the appropriation of their domain. It was here that, immediately after his arrival, Hugh became acquainted with his famous swan, which occupies so prominent a place in all histories and representations of him. As the account of this strange creature is given to us by two credible eye-witnesses, we are bound to reproduce it, and we prefer to do this in the very words of the original narrators, as the giving a modern form to the story, or attempting to explain it,[1] would, as it seems, be altogether out of place. " It was," says Giraldus Cambrensis, " on the very day that Hugh was enthroned at Lincoln that at his manor

---

[1] Nevertheless, somewhat of explanation is certainly supplied by the facts recited above of Hugh's having great skill in taming birds, both at the Great Chartreuse and at Witham.

of Stow, where woods and lakes are agreeably blended, there was noted the appearance of a swan never seen there before. Within a few days after its coming, the new bird had killed all the other swans in the waters there, being much bigger and stronger than any of them, sparing only one of the female sex, which he took to be his companion. Its size and strength were as much greater than those of an ordinary swan as the swan excels a goose. In all other points, however, it resembled a swan, as regards look and the pure white of its feathers, save that on its beak it had not the swelling and the black mark of other swans, but its beak was straight, and of a beautiful yellow, as were also its head and the upper part of its neck. This royal bird, remarkable both for its beauty and its size, coming to that place just at the same time that the bishop came, at once showed itself disposed to be tamed, and was brought to him in his chamber to be admired. Immediately it took bread from his hand and ate it, and seemed to cling to him as a friend, putting off its wild nature, and being quite unmoved by being touched, and not frightened by the noise of the crowds that pressed around to gaze at it. It was wont sometimes, when fed by the bishop, to thrust its head and long neck into his wide sleeve and right up to his bosom, and here it would seem to mutter as though holding a friendly conversation with its master. The servants and keepers asserted that when the bishop was about to return home after a long absence, for

P

three or four days the bird would seem to be
possessed with special activity, flying about on the
water, beating it with its wings, and crying with a
loud voice. Sometimes it would leave the lake and
go to the palace or the gate, striding along with
great steps, as though going to meet its master. It
is indeed easy to understand that the preparations
and the going and coming of servants might indicate to it the bishop's near arrival, especially as these
birds are of a subtle nature, and omens have often
been drawn from their doings. The strange thing is
that it would not make friends or show itself tame
to any one except the bishop, but was wont, as I
have often seen with wonder, to stand near its
master, and to keep all from approaching him by
threatening with its wings and beak, and crying out
its tones with a most high-sounding voice. It
seemed clearly to show that it belonged to him alone,
and was manifestly sent to him for a sign." Thus
far Giraldus, but the author of the *Magna Vita* adds
other particulars of this strange bird. He, as one of
the bishop's household, as well as others in the house,
were not a little annoyed by the excessive and dog-
like care with which the swan guarded its master.
" For when the bishop was asleep, and it was necessary for us for any matter to pass his bed, none
could evade the creature's vigilance ; it would spring
up and pugnaciously oppose any one who wished to
slip by. If threatened with any violence, it straightway gave utterance to a most furious clamour, so

that, from fear of disturbing the bishop's rest, things of importance were omitted if they would take us past his couch. No coaxing or blandishments had any effect upon the creature ; it seemed out of devotion to the bishop to be at enmity with every one else. When he was absent, indeed, it would condescend to come to the bank of the lake and receive its food from the bailiff in a tame and friendly manner, but immediately after being fed it would retreat. A most strange thing was it that the very person whom for a year or more it had approached familiarly to get its food, it would, when its lord came, drive away from approaching it just as much as the other servants whom it had never seen before. The bishop would sometimes be absent from Stow for two years together, but at the end of this period it would meet him, not as one who had forgotten him from his long absence, but rather as one tired out with longing for him, as it would show by the welcome which it gave him, by its strange gestures and sonorous voice. The keepers and the neighbours used to say that even if no one in those parts had any suspicion that the bishop was likely to come, they were able to divine his approach by the beating of the swan's wings, and by other of its strange ways. No sooner did his luggage carts and the servants who preceded him make their appearance, than the creature would leave its lake and straightway quickly penetrate to the interior of the palace. Surrounded on its entry by crowds of spectators, it would, as soon as it heard

the voice of its patron entering, give clamorous vent
to its shrillest tones, then running to him, and as it
were saluting him, it would follow him into the
upper story to his inner chamber, going through the
intervening cloister, and up the stairs, clapping its
wings the while, and modulating the tones of its
voice in token of the joy which possessed it.   When
it got to the bishop's room, it could not be made to
leave except by violence.   It used to be fed from
his hand with plenty of bread cut in pieces about
the size of one's finger.   These were its constant
habits for nearly thirteen years.   But when about
the time of Easter, before his death, the bishop paid
his last visit to Stow, the swan did not go to meet
him as it was wont, nor fawn upon him, nor could it
be got out of its pond where it was swimming.   It
remained on the water, looking sad and sick, without
any of its usual activity.   When all wondered at
this, the bishop ordered that it should be brought
in, even against its will ; and for three days it was
pursued in vain.   At length it was taken in a retired
bed of reeds, where it had concealed itself.   Being
brought to the bishop, it hung its head and had all
the ways of a sick creature, so that every one was
greatly amazed.   The bishop soon left that place,
and in six months after died, and was never again
seen by his favourite bird, so that it was easy to
understand from the event what these mournful gestures of the swan portended.   They were his sorrow-
ful farewell to his master.   After the bishop's death

it remained a long time at the same place."[1] Such was the famous swan of St. Hugh, one of those weird creatures which meet us strangely in history, and of which, at so long an interval, it is perhaps impossible to give a rational account.[2]

The bishop had the gift of keen perception, and what we call common sense, in a remarkable degree, and this, united with a deep sense of his holy office, and a spirit of profound devotion, led him, immediately after his consecration, to seek the most fitting help which he could procure for the administration of his diocese. None could be more conscious than Hugh himself how little he was fitted, by his birth and early training, for the government of a huge diocese like that of Lincoln. Ignorant of the language and habits of the people,[3] ignorant of· the laws and customs of the land, he had to contend against many most serious deficiencies. But he had, after all, the most necessary qualities for the episcopal office. He

[1] *Magna Vita*, p. 118.

[2] Sir C. J. Anderson thus attempts to explain this strange story :— "From the minute description of its bill, the bird appears to have been one of the wild species, or hooper. Such predilections in birds and animals are not unexampled. We have known a gander which attached itself to a farmer in this county, which used to accompany him daily for a mile and a half, when he went to look after his cattle in the meadows, waddling after him with the greatest diligence and satisfaction, and whenever he stopped fondling his legs with his neck and bill."—*Lincoln*, p. 76.

[3] Two instances are mentioned in the *Magna Vita*, one of a man of Kent, the other of a Huntingdonshire woman, in which Hugh was obliged to have recourse to an interpreter. But, no doubt, this must ordinarily have been the case.

had a zeal for holiness, a keen sense of justice, a
shrewd and discerning mind, and an utterly fearless
spirit. These would assuredly lead him to supply
what was lacking of the more accidental qualifications.
His first step was a very wise one. It was to apply
to the Archbishop of Canterbury to recommend to
him some learned and discreet clerks to assist him in
his work. "I thank God," he said, "that to will is
present with me, but how to perform that which I will,
I find not. Not only in myself am I unable, but I
know not where to look for help. I am a foreigner,
without knowledge of the natives of this land, ignorant in what they excel, and what are their favourite
pursuits and studies. You, on the contrary, are well
experienced in all this, as one born among them and
. for many years in office over them.[1] I appeal to you,
not only for myself, but also as a matter personal to

[1] "Archbishop Baldwin," says Professor Stubbs, "was a man of
singular sanctity, courage, and honesty. He was one of the most distinguished scholars of his time, and has left behind him works which
attest his proficiency in the studies of the day. According to Giraldus
Cambrensis, who knew him well, though it is not easy to decide how
far he speaks the truth, he was an austere melancholy man, slow to
anger and temperate in the show of it, wanting in severity and firmness.
He was, in fact, a Cistercian of the best sort, a man who lived but
little for the world and that little to make it better. As archbishop,
instead of playing into the hands of the monastic party, a course which
would have ensured for him a much more quiet life, he tried to do his
duty. The errors of temper, harshness, arbitrary severity, and want of
tact, of which he cannot be acquitted, are not perhaps really inconsistent
with the character drawn of him by Giraldus. They seem to be exactly
the faults into which an unworldly man would be hurried by the influence of unscrupulous and interested advisers."—*Introd. to Epist.
Cantuar.*, p. xxxiv.

you, inasmuch as you are responsible for putting me into this office, to give me as assistants some men whom you yourself have well proved, and who have had you for their example, to share with me the labours and cares of the pastoral office." To this request Archbishop Baldwin lent a ready ear, and from the body of clerks who were in his service, transferred to the Bishop of Lincoln Robert of Bedford and Roger de Roldeston, who are both described as men of high character,. and very useful to the bishop. Roger became Dean of Lincoln in 1195, and remained in that office till 1223, so that with him the bishop must have been in the closest and most constant communication in his great work of the renovation of the cathedral. Other men of mark and high qualities Hugh attracted to his church, but the reputation which he himself speedily acquired was so brilliant, and men's mouths were soon so full of the Bishop of Lincoln, that the minor luminaries of his church were forgotten.

One of his very earliest acts was to take a firm and decided stand against that great and crying abuse which more than any other pressed upon England at that time—the iniquitous forest laws. Well does the writer of the *Magna Vita* exclaim, that of all the pests of the land, there was none comparable to the tyranny of the foresters, to whom "violence was instead of law, rapine a matter of praise, equity a thing to be hated, and innocence the greatest guilt."[1] This

---

[1] *Magna Vita*, p. 125.

pest, he says, was depopulating the land, and, indeed, when one comes to examine the nature of these vile laws and customs, one is lost in amazement that any nation could have submitted to them so long. It would seem that the Anglo-Saxon kings had assumed that the king had sole right over all wild and unenclosed woodlands, and after the Conquest the Norman princes took advantage of this, not only to claim the right but to enforce it by a code of laws of a most savage character. In the time of Henry I. an extension of the king's claim was made to *all* forests, whether enclosed or not. The king was held to be the sole hunter-in-chief throughout the land, and none had a right of hunting save by concession from him. We have the forest-assize or code of laws passed by Henry II. at Woodstock still remaining, and nothing can be more flagrantly unjust than its provisions. None are to have bows and arrows or hunting dogs in their own forests without the king's warrant. None are to allow their coverts to be injured or destroyed, though they may not themselves hunt in them, but they may take a certain amount of firewood from them. They are to keep foresters at their own expense to look after the king's rights; and if any covert is destroyed, the destroyer is liable to be put to death, but if he can't be discovered, then the forester shall suffer. The king's woods are to be *agisted* or stocked with cattle before any other woods are allowed to be, and each county is to be at the expense of protecting them and gathering the payments for the king. If clerks are found in pursuit of game, or *trespassing in the forests*, they are to be seized by the foresters and imprisoned ; for the third instance of trespass capital punishment is to be inflicted. Dogs are to have their claws cut off; no tanner or felt-monger is to be allowed within the precincts of the forest ; and all males of twelve years of age are to take an oath to observe the king's laws. But not only were these statutes enforced by oath ; there were regular forest judges who went their circuits at the same time that the other judges visited the counties, and all arch-bishops, bishops, earls, barons, and esquires were bound to attend on them and plead in their courts.[1] Henry II. was an ardent and devoted hunter, and we constantly find him performing important acts of government and policy at some one or other of his hunting lodges, as Clarendon, Woodstock, and Marl-borough. When, therefore, the newly made Bishop of Lincoln ventured to thwart the king's foresters, whom the law invested with so great a power, and whom custom and terror and the king's support made still more formidable, he gave a signal proof of courage, and of that love of the right and just which nothing could daunt. Hugh's biographer does not supply us with the exact circumstances of the case, but describes the act of the forester as an infringe-ment upon the liberties of the bishop's men and the

[1] See Stubbs' *Select Charters*, p. 149 *seq.*, where the Woodstock assize is printed from *Benedictus*.

privileges of the Church, for which the bishop's punishment was the sentence of excommunication. On hearing of this the king was inflamed with furious anger. But the dauntless spirit of Hugh did not quail. On the contrary, he immediately added another proof that he was not to be swayed from the right course by the fear of man. One of the prebends of his church just then fell vacant, and this, according to the evil custom of those days, might easily have been held by a layman, who would only be charged with a small payment to a clerk-vicar to perform his duties in the cathedral. The courtiers applied to the king for a letter directing the bishop to grant it to one of them. At the same time they pretended that by doing this they were doing the bishop himself good service, inasmuch as they were affording him an opportunity of making his peace with the king by a kindly and gracious act. Henry himself was also anxious to give the bishop this opportunity of atoning for his presumption in the matter of the forester. But they little knew the man with whom they had to deal. Hugh would not swerve either to the right hand or to the left for fear or favour. Henry gave the letter asked for. He was at this time at Woodstock ; the bishop was at Dorchester, only distant some thirteen miles. The reply which Hugh unhesitatingly gave was : "Ecclesiastical benefices are not for courtiers, but for ecclesiastics. Those who hold them must serve, not the palace or the treasury, but the altar. The king has wherewithal to compensate those who work for him and fight his battles. Let him allow those who serve the King of kings to enjoy their fitting remuneration, and not to be deprived of it."[1] With these words he sent the king's messengers back to their master. Of course Hugh's enemies at court took advantage of this refusal to urge on the king the audacious ingratitude of the man whom he had recently promoted. Henry sent to summon the bishop to his presence. In the meantime he prepared a little scene to try whether Hugh's boldness were really as great as his words seemed to indicate. He mounted his horse, with his courtiers, and they proceeded in a body to a pleasant glade in the Woodstock manor, where the king bade them dismount and recline on the grass in a circle round him. The bishop on his arrival was brought to the group. The king had given directions that none should notice him on his coming, nor offer him any salutation. The strange silence and inattention served to amaze Hugh, but not for a moment to daunt him. Placing his hand on the shoulders of a magnate who was sitting next to the king, he gently moved him aside to make a place for himself by Henry's side. Still the rigid immobility of king and courtiers continued. Presently Henry asked for a needle and thread, and began to stitch vigorously at a bandage which covered one of the fingers of his left hand. Still not a word. The bishop looked on for a

[1] *Magna Vita*, p. 126.

moment, and then, with his quick sagacity, interpreted the whole affair. He instantly decided how to treat it. Looking at the king, he quietly said, " How like you are now to your kinsfolk of Falaise." Henry stopped his stitching, clasped his hands, endeavouring to repress a laugh, but the joke was too good for him ; he bent his head to the ground, and broke forth into a loud peal of laughter. The courtiers, struck with amazement at the bishop's audacity, were fairly perplexed, but some, led on by the merriment of the king, began to laugh in concert. The king, as soon as he could speak from laughing, seeing the puzzled look of the faces round him, vouchsafed to explain, with infinite relish, the saucy speech which had been directed against himself. " Know you," says he, " what sort of an insult this strange fellow has offered to us ? I will explain it to you. Our great ancestor, Duke William, the Conqueror of this land, was born of a mother of no very high extraction, who belonged to a town in Normandy somewhat notorious, namely Falaise. This town was very celebrated for its skill in leather-stitching. When, then, this scoffer saw me stitching my finger, straightway he declared me to be like the Falesians, and a kinsman of theirs."[1] Having thus explained the bishop's joke, Henry, not the least offended by it, proceeded calmly to remonstrate with him for having excommunicated his chief forester, and for having treated his request with so little

[1] *Magna Vita*, p. 129.

ceremony as to refuse it without any qualifying
expressions. The bishop answered : " I know well,
sire, that you took great pains to get me made a
bishop. I would, then, in return free your soul from
the danger which would threaten it if I were careless
in executing the trust committed to me. It was
needful for the good of the Church to censure that
oppressor of the Church, and to refuse the prebend to
one who sought it unjustifiably. Truly I held it not
necessary to communicate with you on these matters
personally, inasmuch as I felt confident that as they
were right you would at once approve them."[1] This
skilful and delicate flattery availed completely to
soothe the king. He approved all that the bishop
had done, only he desired that his forester might
obtain absolution. This, however, the bishop did
not grant him until he had received severe discipline
in the shape of a good flogging, a discipline which,
as Hugh's biographer tells us, resulted in making
him the bishop's firm friend for the rest of his life.
The courtiers, also, were no less happily impressed
by the bishop's boldness and vigour. No more
petitions for prebends assailed him henceforward.
On a similar ground to that on which he refused to
allow courtiers a share in the emoluments of his
cathedral church, Hugh also declined to make
these appointments complementary additions to the
salaries of any clerks, however eminent, who could
not perform the fitting residence, and execute the

[1] *Magna Vita*, p. 130.

duties of the office. On one occasion a famous
doctor of Paris having paid the bishop a very fine
compliment on the number of distinguished clerks
whom he had succeeded in getting together, added
modestly that he should esteem it an honour to be
one of them, even in a very humble capacity. "We
should be most happy to have you," said the
bishop, "if you would come and reside among
us, and if also you would not neglect morals for
the sake of learning."[1]   This was a home-thrust,
as the doctor was more celebrated for his learning than his discipline, and is said to have produced a wholesome effect.   Indeed the bishop was
not likely to be tempted by the mere reputation
of learning.   He loved far before learned men
those of a pure and peaceable spirit.   He held
nothing so detestable as turbulence, nothing so
desirable as gentleness and love.   Had Hugh's
judgment and advice been followed, the long
quarrel which vexed and troubled the English
Church in his day might have been altogether
avoided.

A merely general account of this dispute must
here suffice.[2]   It arose from the attempt made first
by Archbishop Baldwin, and then by Hubert Walter,
to found a house of secular canons which should

---

[1] *Magna Vita*, p. 132.

[2] Those who desire to see the details minutely and clearly traced
out may consult Professor Stubbs' *Introduction to Epistolæ Cantuari-
enses*, a bulky volume, which is entirely occupied with the numerous
letters which survive on the subject of the quarrel.

gradually supersede the monastery of Christ Church, Canterbury, in the position of metropolitan chapter, and being more under the control of the Archbishop and less fortified with privileges and immunities, be easier to manage and control. The monastery, seeing in the contemplated foundation a most dangerous rival of its power and importance, fought with the utmost vigour and perseverance against the threatened institution. Kings Henry and Richard supported the Archbishop, and so it came about that the quarrel assumed the character of a great duel between the secular clergy, supported by the king and the law, and the regular clergy, supported by the pope. Which of these was henceforth to govern and control the English Church? The quarrel was not one merely of recent date. Ever since the days of Dunstan monachism had been aggressive and self-asserting, claiming to control the whole Church. At the Norman Conquest the monasteries were at first upholders of the national spirit and feeling, but this soon ceased. " So long as the pope and king were on the same side, the monks and the nation were opposed to both alike; when the pope and the king quarrelled, the nation sided with the king, the monks with the pope; hence the monasteries became more papal as the State became more national, and the same series of events made them less English without becoming more Norman, and more papal without becoming more loyal."[1] The

[1] Stubbs' *Introd. to Epist. Cantuar.*, p. xxi.

monastic cathedral is said to have been an institution
peculiar to England.   Hugh, in his own cathedral,
had knowledge of one which was not, like that of
Canterbury, connected with a monastery, but had a
body of secular canons.   But Hugh was a monk of
the strictest order and the greatest devotion, and the
monks might consequently expect to find in him a
zealous patron and friend.   He was one of those
named earliest by the pope as a commissioner to
arbitrate in the dispute between Baldwin and the
Canterbury monks, and there are several letters in
the collection remaining addressed by the monks to
him, calling upon him, as their friend and supporter,
to uphold their cause.   The bishop, however, was not
led away to become a partisan of either side.   He
saw that the archbishop's design was impolitic and
perhaps unjust, inasmuch as for his new foundation
he proposed to alienate violently some of the property of Christ Church.   He saw also that the monks
were not to be justified in the violent opposition with
which they continued to contend against their ordinary, even after all the concessions which justice
required had been made by him.   Thus he warned
the archbishop before the commencement of the work
that much mischief would be sure to follow from it,
that he would experience the injustice and arbitrary
interference of the pope as well as the bitter ill-will
of his chapter ; and in the course of the dispute he
spoke his mind plainly to the monks, telling them
that they did wrong by their quarrelsome conten-

tiousness, and that they ought to submit to the archbishop.[1]

Hugh not only saw the importance of the existence of unanimity between the bishop and his chapter, but he took care that this should be realised in his own case.   With his own canons he never quarrelled, believing that while the house was thus at peace within itself no external authority either secular or spiritual need be dreaded.   That the concord which reigned in the church at Lincoln was due principally to the tact and straightforward dealing of its head can hardly be doubted if we remember the sketch of the character of the Lincoln canons which has already been given.   But the good bishop did not claim any merit for it himself, but rather put it down to their credit.   " His masters," as he used to call his canons, did not, he said, live with him in peace because they thought him gentle and mild.   " For indeed I am rougher and sharper than pepper, and often when presiding over their chapter a very little thing will make me furiously angry.   But as they have got me, they know they must put up with me, and they make a virtue of necessity.   Indeed, I have much to thank them for. They have never opposed me in anything since the time I first came to reside amongst them.   When we leave the chapter there is not one of them, I

---

[1] Thus one of them writes : " Perrexi ad episcopum Lincolniensem qui multa aspera mihi dixit, et ultimo in fide laudavit ut prosternerem me ad pedes archiepiscopi."—*Epist. Cantuar.*, p. 283.

believe, who is in doubt as to my affection for him,
nor have I any reason to think that I am not loved
by each one of them."[1]   The admirable temper
which the bishop thus displayed in the more formal
and important part of his intercourse with his canons
and clergy was altogether of a piece with. his kind
and genial manners at times of relaxation.   The
strict asceticism in which his life had been passed,
and which he ever regarded as the highest and most
happy state, did not prevent him from taking a part
at fitting seasons in festivities, and encouraging
hilarity and gaiety.[2]   His biographer tells us that
from early habit he never ate meat, but that he was
fond of fish,[3] and that he took wine habitually as a
necessary support for his weak frame.   At table he
was full of fun and very fond of a joke, but if it happened that any professional buffoons, players, or
minstrels were present he was more than usually
grave, in order to keep the merriment within due
bounds.[4]   The rigours of his early life had very much

[1] *Magna Vita*, p. 136. No doubt the bishop was very careful in
the selection of his canons. Roger de Wendover says : "In ecclesiâ
Dei cathedrali electos collocando personas vivis ex lapidibus habita-
culum Deo construxit."—*Flor. Hist.*, iii. 157.

[2] We are specially told by Giraldus, who had plenty of opportunity
for observing, that the bishop's retainers were grandly clothed, and that
his housekeeping was on the most liberal scale.—*Girald. Camb., Op.*,
vii. 107.

[3] King Richard was probably aware of this when he sent the bishop,
on the occasion of his visit to Roche d'Andelè, a grand pike.—*Gir.
Camb.*, vii. 105.

[4] It would seem that the *histriones* and *musici* were sometimes
admitted by the bishop to his own table, as well as met with by him at

impaired the bishop's constitution, and had involved him in maladies which he did his best to remedy afterwards by the use of a more generous diet, but in spite of these weaknesses he was so strong, and gifted with so much endurance, that in long Church ceremonials he invariably tired out all his assistants and was usually obliged to have relays of priests to relieve one another, while he himself remained fresh and vigorous. He would sometimes sit from early morning until late into the darkness of night without breaking his fast, intent upon his labour. But though he was thus careless of himself, he had thought for others, and during the hot weather would oblige the priests who said mass at great Church ceremonials to take some food before the celebration, though this was utterly shocking to the prejudices of his day. Rising in this, as in most other matters, superior to his time, Hugh would reprove the scruples of those who regarded such a direction with horror. " They had " he told them, " but a weak faith, and a poor amount of discretion, inasmuch as they could neither obey without hesitation when they were commanded, nor could perceive the reasonableness of a wise and prudent command."[1]

That the allowance to break the customary fast in the celebration of the Eucharist was not

the tables of great men where he was being entertained. "Sive ad propriam sive ad mensam resideret alienam. Tunc maximè gravitati studebat."   [1] *Magna Vita*, p. 140.

due to any irreverence or carelessness in the matter
of the sacraments, Hugh proved by his practice as regards confirmation.   In those days there
was no systematic arrangement for confirmation,
but children were brought to the bishop to be
blessed, on any of his progresses, wherever he could
be met with.   Many bishops were in the habit of
performing the rite very perfunctorily and even
without descending from horseback,[1] but no fatigue,
or hurry, or bad weather could prevent the Bishop of
Lincoln stopping his journey when appealed to for
the performance of this function, and, descending
from his horse, carefully going through it with all
the solemnity of which the circumstances admitted.
On one occasion he had been occupied the whole
day in the consecration of churches and confirming,
when just as it was growing dark at night and his
tired attendants were hoping for a little refreshment,
a fresh band of children was descried trooping in for
the blessing.   The bishop, fasting though he was, at
once addressed himself to this new labour, and continued unceasingly till midnight, occupied in it.

---

[1] Hugh's biographer fortifies this somewhat startling assertion with
the narration of an instance which he had himself seen.   "It was not
without shame and pain that I once saw a bishop, young in age,
vigorous in strength, when there were no difficulties of place nor stress
of weather, and no occasion for haste, sitting on his horse sprinkling
children with the consecrated chrism.   The children were screaming
and terrified among the prancing horses, while those who were in charge
of them were buffeted by the bishop's retinue for not preserving better
order, the bishop meanwhile being utterly unconcerned about the whole
matter."—*Magna Vita*, p. 140.

Another story is told of an old man who, coming too late for the confirmation in his own church, was bid by the bishop to follow him to another neighbouring church, where he was about to repeat the ceremony. The old rustic, indignant at this extra labour, sat down and refused to stir, at the same time praying aloud that the bishop might be held responsible for his loss of the means of grace which he thus suffered. Hugh, although already starting for his next appointment, could not endure to leave one in this evil frame of mind ; he returned to him, remonstrated with him for his frowardness, and ended by confirming him. On which his biographer very naturally observes that the convenience and profit of many were allowed to be interfered with by the laziness and evil temper of one.[1] The bishop was probably of this mind himself, for it is recorded in his Life by Giraldus Cambrensis that after confirming this contumacious peasant, he administered to him a severe slap in the face, telling him that this was an appropriate punishment for having so long delayed to seek the holy rite.[2]

So careful, indeed, was the bishop that the children who were brought to him should be properly attended to that he would not only "terribly chide" his attendants for any lack of duty in this respect, but even with his own hands would give them sound blows if they were not careful. Hugh indeed, like all men of a pure and genial spirit, was intensely

[1] *Metrical Life*, lines 735-765.   [2] *Girald. Camb.*, vii. 95.

fond of children, and this love evoking, as it always does, in the children themselves a corresponding affection, often seemed to the bystanders, little versed in childlike ways, to have miraculous powers ; so eagerly did the babies who were noticed by him smile upon him and stretch out their hands towards him. Nor was the bishop's care of children confined to mere affectionate notice of them. In many instances he cared diligently for the education and training of those who had been brought into connection with him, and two are specially mentioned by his biographer, Benedict of Caen, and Robert of Noyon, for whom he was the most affectionate of patrons. A happy manner of attracting and influencing the young was ever conspicuous in him. A youthful acolyte of his, vain of his good looks and becoming curls, could not be induced to submit to the accustomed tonsure. Hugh settled the matter for him by himself taking his curls in hand and snipping them off with a scissors. The kind act, instead of the severe discipline which he expected, touched the heart of the youth. He forswore vanity, became a monk, and was afterwards ordained deacon by the bishop. The overflowing love and charity which was in Hugh must needs find a vent by every possible channel. Of these none was more remarkable than his tender care and love for the most afflicted of their kind, the poor suffering lepers. The fearful scourge of leprosy which for many centuries was the plague of Eastern England, and of the prevalence of which at Lincoln in particular traces still remain,[1] had the effect of making those afflicted with it not only personally loathsome, but also the objects of general proscription and avoidance, as those suffering under a divine judgment. Hugh earnestly addressed himself to meet and remove, as far as his influence could, both these evils of it. He zealously gave personal service and care to the lepers ; with his own hands he would wash their feet ; he would kiss them ;[2] he would take up his abode in the hospitals appropriated for them and console their miseries with the tenderest words, eating out of the same dish with them, while those who accompanied him were often overcome with horror at the bare sight of their loathsome sores ; and in order to remove the prejudice which regarded such persons as the special objects of divine vengeance Hugh used to preach that those who were called to bear such sufferings were especially blessed, and the recipients of the highest gifts. " The blessed Saviour of mankind," he would say, " had represented Lazarus

---

[1] *e.g.*, The site of the Malindery or Lepers' House is still known and marked by its name, and in the neighbouring church of Bracebridge may be seen a leproscope, or hole cut in the wall to enable the leper standing outside to see the service of the altar.

[2] On one occasion of his kissing a leper at Newark, William de Monte, chancellor of the cathedral, who was with him, wishing probably to suggest that such an extreme proceeding was not defensible unless some good came of it, said, "When Saint Martin kissed the leper he healed him." The bishop replied at once, " Martin by his kiss brought bodily health to the leper, but the leper by his kiss brings to me the health of the soul."—*Girald. Camb.*, vii. 107.

as received into Abraham's bosom, and His delight while on earth was to tend and minister to every form of human woe. What greater privilege could there be than thus to follow Him, and how could those be looked upon as unfit for our regard to whom He would have readily ministered?"[1]   And as there was this readiness in the bishop to give his personal service to the afflicted, so, as might be expected, in the matter of almsgiving for the needy he was most profuse and generous. For besides, says his biographer, all extraordinary calls, which he never refused, he regularly set apart a third of his whole income to be expended in works of mercy. The man full of love and tender care for the suffering is often found to be endued with the greatest courage and boldness in danger. So it was with St. Hugh. On several occasions, when violent tumults arose, and he was threatened by angry men with weapons in their hands, he showed so unmoved a constancy that by its power he quelled the tumults and reduced the turbulent to submission. We are without the details of these riots, but one is said to have taken place within the cathedral at Lincoln, in which both clergy and laity took part; another, in the district of Holland in Lincolnshire, was a tumult of soldiers and armed retainers; while the third, in the town of Northampton, was due to the fury of the angry burgesses. It is not improbable that some exercise of the bishop's discipline, which, as will be

[1] *Magna Vita*, p. 164.

seen, he applied with no sparing hand, and with no
regard to persons, may have produced these out-
breaks.   But, whatever their origin, they only served
to prove that the bishop was utterly inaccessible on
the side of fear, and that open resistance would only
serve to make him more firmly set to carry his point.
It was alike to him whether an armed mob assailed
him or royal displeasure threatened him.   He had
his own views as to what was right and seemly, and
no earthly considerations could make him shrink
from them.   This was specially evidenced in a
matter to which Hugh attached the utmost importance, viz. the decent and devout performance
of the funeral rites.   Just in the same spirit that
he protested against the neglect of the suffering
living body by his care for lepers, so did the bishop
emphatically rebuke the careless treatment of the
dead, which was too prevalent in that age.[1]   " How
different," he would say, " is the regard in which God
holds the dead from that with which man treats
him !   No sooner has death taken place than those
who are nearest to the dead are anxious to get rid
of him and put him from them, while God employs
the heavenly angels to guard the spirit which has
gone forth, and commissions His chief ministers on
earth, His priests, to take charge of and do honour
to the body.   He bids them carry to him the image
of His crucified Son, the incense and the taper, to

---

[1] We frequently hear of dead bodies lying neglected in the streets,
with no one to bestow any care on them.

sound the solemn voices of the Church, to raise the chant and the hymn, to open the doors of the church, and deposit the corpse near the altar, to cover the bier with costly vestments, to surround it with candles and acolytes, and having made a solemn memorial of the all-prevailing sacrifice, to deposit the body in its tomb prepared for its re-occupation hereafter by the spirit."[1] So great did he esteem the privilege of officiating at funerals, that he used to claim it for himself as a special honour, and distinctly inhibited all parish priests from performing the funeral service without him when he was near at hand. For the performance of this office he would stop on a journey, and joining himself to the officiating priest would take a part in the ceremonial, and when he chanced to be in a large town and there were many corpses to be buried, he would perform the rites for one after another without cessation, however many there might be.[2] The great men who expected the bishop at the banquet would murmur in vain at being kept waiting. Nothing could induce him to omit or hurry over the solemn task which he

---

[1] *Magna Vita*, p. 226.

[2] In connection with Hugh's zeal for burying the dead may be mentioned his manner of consoling the living for the loss of friends. "What is it that you are doing?" he would say to the mourners. "By the holy nut" (his usual form of adjuration)—"By the holy nut, our lot would indeed be too miserable if it were not allowed to us to die." —*Magna Vita*, p. 368. Hugh used to punish severely the clerks about him if they neglected to inform him of any needing burial. Various anecdotes are recorded on this subject in the Life by Giraldus.—*Op.* v. vii. pp. 98-102.

had imposed on himself. On two occasions, at Rouen, he had the boldness to keep kings waiting while he was occupied in this work, first Henry II. and afterwards Richard. In vain anxious messengers were despatched to the bishop, bidding him hurry, for the king was impatiently waiting for his dinner. "I am occupied," he said, "in the service of the King of heaven, and I cannot neglect it for that of an earthly monarch."

A still greater proof of true courage, because it shows a moral courage very rare in the men of his generation, was the way in which Hugh behaved when invited to inspect an alleged miracle. A priest once called upon him to inspect a miraculous appearance in the chalice, where it was said that the actual conversion into flesh and blood of part of the host could be seen with the bodily eyes. Hugh indignantly refused to look at it. "In the name of God," he said, "let them keep to themselves the signs of their want of faith." He wanted no material proof of the virtue of the blessed sacrament; neither would he suffer his attendants, who were eagerly curious to examine the prodigy, to inspect the chalice.[1] To a man so far raised above the common level, the ignorance and materialism of the priests with whom he had to do must have been a constant source of annoyance. The bishop, of course, could only work with such instruments as he could find, but in order to do the best possible with them he was ever

---

[1] *Magna Vita*, p. 245.

very careful and scrupulous as to the admission to benefices, and for the promotion of discipline. "Omitting," says his biographer, "no part of fatherly care, he ever strove to pour oil and wine into the weak characters of those committed to his trust, restraining by severity those whom he could not heal by gentleness. The churches of his diocese he laboured with all his might to raise to their due state. He took great pains to admit to their government men who were commendable for knowledge and good living, and those who were lacking in these qualities with all his energy he repelled from entering them. 'I wonder,' he used to say, 'at those who speak of it as a matter for rejoicing when prebends or churches in their gift become vacant. For myself, I say truly nothing in my life afflicts me with such anxiety as choosing fit persons for such offices. Nor have I ever been so grieved as when, on the advice of others, I have conferred ecclesiastical benefices on those who, after they have received the good things of the Church, have shown themselves but drones.'"[1] The bishop had been very grossly deceived in recommendations and testimonials by some in whom he thought he could place confidence, and after that had acted more from his own judgment and opinion alone. It certainly was not from any want of natural acuteness, or of skill and knowledge

---

[1] *Magna Vita*, p. 246. The same overpowering sense of the responsibilities of patronage was frequently expressed by Hugh's great successor, Grosseteste, though in almost every other respect these two great bishops are a contrast one to the other.

of ecclesiastical laws, that Hugh was thus often deceived. No one, it was said, held more tenaciously to truth and right, but no one was more keenly awake to all the ramifications and subterfuges of tricks and fraud. The lawyers used to ascribe it to miraculous powers that without any previous training or experience he could at once master the intricacies of a complicated case, and show himself more acute therein than the subtlest advocate. Hence everybody wished to have their causes tried before the Bishop of Lincoln, and hence also the pope, who was ever conducting by his delegates an immense mass of litigation, constantly appointed Hugh as a commissioner to investigate, report, or decide on contested matters. Hugh disliked all such employments beyond measure. He chafed under the amount of forensic work imposed upon bishops, which took up nearly all their time. He groaned under this, which the lordly prelates of his day loved, as an intolerable cross. For him state and pomp and power had no charms, and the real solace and happiness of his life were those times when he could cast away all the trappings of state and all the insignia of his high office, and become once again the poor Carthusian monk in his cell at Witham.

CHAPTER VI.

HUGH AS BISHOP—ILLUSTRATIONS OF HIS DISCIP-
LINE—HIS RETREATS AT WITHAM.

THOUGH ever earnestly longing for quiet and heavenly contemplation, Hugh was not the man to shrink from the responsibilities of his high office and from the exercise of discipline. Rather, it may be, that the impetuous and decisive nature of his character inclined him to give to his disciplinary acts somewhat of a violent and excessive strictness, which gained strength from the notion that grew up and was extensively held that the Bishop of Lincoln's words never fell to the ground, and that the object of his anathema was certain to incur irremediable destruction. The writer of his Life has given us several instances of this, but, writing as he did, with the avowed belief in the bishop's inevitable stroke, it may be that he has omitted other instances which told the other way; for however highly we may rate the bishop, we are not prepared to ascribe to him the attributes of infallibility or omnipotence. Some of these instances which illustrate the manners of the time shall now be detailed, though with no approval of the spirit in which they are related, nor, indeed, with complete belief in the accuracy of the narration.

The subject of the bishop's discipline is thus introduced :—" So ready was he, according to the apostolic pattern, to take vengeance on all disobedience, and so quickly did punishment from on high follow upon his vengeance, that, as he would never spare those who contumaciously offended against God, so, whosoever was smitten by him with the spiritual sword, quickly, if he did not repent, would perish by the destruction of the body. Those who were rebellious, and the violators of ecclesiastical law, who insolently presumed on their power, and sometimes audaciously threatened him, he would upbraid with a terrible voice—' How dare ye presume on your strength and your arms against the hand of the Omnipotent, which has given to us, though unworthy and weak, weapons of such great power that no human armour can equal them. Your darts cannot penetrate our breastplates, our helmets fear not your swords ; but our swords can pierce through all your defences. You may wound the flesh, but you cannot touch the soul ; our sword both destroys the body and devotes the souls of those whom it strikes to a death which is not transitory but eternal.' But now if I should endeavour to set forth severally how many he handed over to a reprobate death by his anathema alone, by what a terrible end the greater part of the despisers of the divine

law perished, who, according to their hard and
impenitent heart, heaped up unto themselves wrath,
and, despising blessing and retaining his curse,
refused to amend their perverseness,—if, I say, I
should attempt to do this, I should not be able, even
in many books, to set forth all that would need to
be written.   Yet out of the vast number it will not
be without use to mention a few by way of example,
seeing that, in order to console the faithful and
instruct the weak, it has pleased the Divine Majesty
thus evidently to exercise against the perverse the
strictness of just punishment, that the words of the
Psalmist might be fulfilled, 'The righteous shall
rejoice when he seeth the vengeance, he shall wash
his footsteps in the blood of the ungodly ; so that a
man shall say, Verily there is a reward for the
righteous ; doubtless there is a God which judgeth
the earth.'"[1]   The first instance brought forward in
illustration introduces us to a story, the "curious
facts of which are fully confirmed by various entries
in the public records of the time."[2]   There was one
Thomas de Saleby, a Lincolnshire knight of advanced age, married to a wife who was younger than
himself, but was without children.   The next heir to
the property, should no child be born, was a brother
of the knight, by name William de Hardredeshill,
between whom and the dame de Saleby there was no
kindly feeling.   The lady determined, therefore, to

---

[1] *Magna Vita*, p. 169.
[2] Mr. Dimock's note to *Magna Vita*, p. 170.

pretend that she was about to give birth to a child, and, in due time, pretended that a child was born ; and having obtained, by bribing its mother, a young female child, she presented it as her own. The brother—who was convinced that deception had been practised, but was unable to prove it—betook himself to the Bishop of Lincoln and laid the case before him. Hugh sent for the knight, who, in terror of his wife, feared to acknowledge the fraud, though by his hesitation he evidently showed that the charge was true. The bishop then solemnly excommunicated the guilty parties. The next day Thomas de Saleby was found dead in his bed ; but the wife, unmoved by this fearful judgment, still persisted in her wicked fraud. She had the advantage on her side that the young child, if confirmed as heiress, would be a valuable present for the king to make to one of his courtiers, and in fact she was given, when only four years old, as a bride to a brother of Hugh de Neville, the chief forester. The bishop forbade the marriage, and threatened with excommunication any priest who should perform the ceremony. They were nevertheless married, and the bishop's excommunication followed. Shortly afterwards the attendant of the lady confessed her share in the crime, and then the lady herself made her confession to the bishop with much expression of penitence. But the rightful heir still did not come by his own. Adam de Neville, the child's husband, having friends in high places, was able to maintain that by the law of

R

England every child was legitimate who was acknowledged to be such by the husband during his life.
Presently, however, Adam de Neville also died
suddenly.   But the child-widow was given to
another husband ; and again at his death to a
third, Brian de Insula, who paid King John 300
marks for the gift of the heiress, and enjoyed the
property during her life-time.   At her death it at
last reverted to the son of William de Hardredeshill.
It would seem, therefore, that in this case the intervention of St. Hugh (though the sudden deaths of
Thomas de Saleby and Adam de Neville were doubtless attributed to it) did not, nevertheless, succeed in
reaching the most guilty person,[1] nor in abating the
injustice done to the rightful heir.   It has been
already said that Hugh was especially opposed to
the tyrannical forest laws of the Plantagenet kings,
and one of the first acts of his episcopate had been
to excommunicate the king's chief forester.   This
man submitted himself to the bishop, underwent the
penance prescribed, and became afterwards the
bishop's firm friend.   Another forester, however, who
had incurred his sentence for some acts of oppression, did not fare so well.   A few days after the
bishop's excommunication, which he proudly despised, he perished by a fearful end.   Some of the
people in his district, whom he had treated with

---

[1] Dame de Saleby is said to have been a long sufferer from illness,
and to have died at length painfully, but nothing beyond natural causes
is attributed.

cruelty, revenged themselves upon him by murdering him, and cutting his body in pieces, exposed the pieces in different parts of the neighbourhood as a warning to all ill-doers.   How far there was any connection between the crime of the oppressed peasants and the bishop of Lincoln's anathema may, however, be a question.   A similar doubt may also be raised as to the termination of the next instance brought forward by Hugh's biographer. One Richard de Waure, a deacon of the diocese of Lincoln, had accused a knight, by name Reginald de Argentun, of treason.   The bishop, having good reason to believe that the charge was a false one, inhibited the deacon from proceeding in the secular courts in a matter of life and death.   On the contrary, Archbishop Hubert, then acting as the grand justiciary of the kingdom, encouraged him to proceed.   Hugh, who was greatly offended by the exercise of the secular power by the archbishop, disregarding his opinion, suspended the deacon.   The archbishop, by virtue of his ordinary legatine power, relaxed the suspension.   Upon this the deacon repaired to the bishop and took a high tone with him.   Hugh, instead of being abashed, proceeded to the further step of excommunicating him.   The archbishop, being appealed to, absolved him, and furnished him with a letter to the bishop signifying this.   But this only served to make the Bishop of Lincoln more wrathful.   " Know," he said, " if the lord archbishop should absolve you a hundred times,

I would as often re-excommunicate you, so long as you remain obstinate in your presumption." The deacon, confounded by this persistence, and awed by the terrible threats of the bishop, said he would take time to consider the matter. While, however, he was deliberating, and (as it would seem) likely to yield, he was murdered by one of his servants. The next story told to illustrate the terrible power which Hugh is said to have wielded, is of a young bride at Oxford who left her lawful husband, and, going through the form of marriage to another, went to live with him. The bishop commanded her to return to her husband, but she, being supported by her mother, violently refused. Hugh then commanded the husband to offer her the kiss of peace, declaring that if she did not accept it a terrible chastisement should follow. The husband offering her the salute, her reply was to spit in his face. The bishop immediately excommunicated her, and in a few days, still remaining obstinate, she was cut off by a sudden death. In the next instance, as it took place within the diocese of York, Hugh must have been acting under papal commission. A clerk named William had been unjustly thrust out of his benefice by a knight who was the possessor of the property, and who had intruded his brother into it by force. He was supported in this by both the secular and ecclesiastical authorities, and the oppressed clerk was left to a tedious appeal to Rome, which produced no result. He then betook himself

to Hugh as the great champion of the oppressed, and
the bishop "(being supported by the apostolic
authority), anathematised the intruder and his aiders
and abettors.   Straightway vengeance lighted upon
them.   Some of them went mad, some of them died
suddenly, the eyes of some fell out of their heads
with fearful torments, and the rightful possessor
quickly obtained possession of his own."[1]   We have
given these stories not only as illustrating the
manners, but as representing the sentiments of the
time.   They are, in fact, a sample of thousands of
similar mediæval stories.   But how far the good
Bishop of Lincoln himself shared in the stern ferocity
which could contemplate with calmness, and even
with satisfaction, the utter destruction of a fellow-
creature, it is not easy to say.   Judging from other
parts of his character, it would seem probable that
the exercise of his anathema, said to be so powerful,
must have been very painful to him.[2]   But we gladly

---

[1] We get an inkling from the narration in the *Magna Vita* as to
how this story was made up.   "It became known to me," says the
writer, "from the accounts of many religions."   This was a case of
collision between the authorities of the country and the papal court.
The monks, who were strongly bent to support the latter as against
the bishops, who were their proper visitors, would not scruple to make
out a tragical history as to the fate of those who ventured to oppose
the papal orders.

[2] Among Hugh's disciplinary proceedings ought, I suppose, to be
mentioned his causing the corpse of Fair Rosamond to be removed out
of the church of Godstow, as related by *Benedictus, s. a.* 1191.   This
is not mentioned in the *Magna Vita*.   Collier, in relating it, says :
"This was done like a man of conscience and courage.   This was
like a primitive bishop, who was not afraid to censure vice, though under

turn from such narratives to contemplate him in milder mood, to look at him at the times of all others most happy and enjoyable to him, when, throwing aside the cares of his diocese, and "taking his holiday" in the fullest sense, he retreated to Witham, his old Carthusian home, and was again the genuine simple monk among his brethren.   These visits to Witham were paid every year, and sometimes twice in the year, so that with the time required for travelling so long a distance, and the two or three months given to the visit, a large portion of St. Hugh's time was taken up in what might be called relaxation. But the time thus given to devotion Hugh doubtless held to be most effectually applied to the discharge of his office, and as he was unable to preach to the people through ignorance of their language, and was utterly averse to anything like secular work, which he held to be unbecoming a bishop, he may have been able to find, legitimately, sufficient time for what he so much rejoiced in.   It is the fashion in mediæval writers to speak of the two lives, the active and contemplative, as represented metaphorically by Leah and Rachel in the Old Testament, and by Martha and Mary in the New.   Hugh, says his biographer, delighted far more in the embraces of his well-beloved Rachel, and was glad to fly from the

royal protection" (*Ch. Hist.*, ii. 375).   It was doubtless right in Hugh to stop the honours which were paid to the tomb by the nuns, but the body of the poor erring woman might have been left in peace.   Did Hugh object to Henry or Richard being buried within the sacred walls of Fontevrault ?

society of the blear-eyed Leah. He sought the happy company of Elias and Enoch, and gladly exchanged the troubles of the world for the tranquillity of paradise. In that vineyard which he had himself planted, his soul was "joyful in the Lord, and he rejoiced in the God of his salvation." A cell was ever kept vacant for him in the monastery, and into this he used to retreat, conforming in all things to the rule of the order, taking his food separately,[1] and devoting much time to solitary prayer and meditation. But when he came forth from his cell at the fixed periods to salute those who desired speech with him, then his face would shine with heavenly rays (says his biographer), and he would seem to be surrounded with a halo of glory, which he would render less awful to the beholders by the suavity and sprightliness of his conversation, and the sallies of his wit. But out of the abundance of the heart the mouth would speak, and his words would come forth like new wine, fiery and sweet, tempered with the honey of heavenly wisdom. To the laity, and to secular persons unable to practise the more perfect life, he would speak in this wise: "Not alone monks and hermits shall obtain the kingdom of God. God will

[1] The Carthusian rule was framed on what may be called "The separate system." Each monk passed almost the whole of his time alone in his cell. The monks of most of the other orders were always in company. The Cistercians worked together in the fields, ate together in the hall, worshipped together in the chapel, and slept in a common dormitory. This was the popular order from the time of St. Bernard downwards. The harsh solitariness of the Carthusians prevented them from ever becoming popular.

not require of any man to have been a monk or
hermit, but to have been truly a Christian. That
which is truly indispensable in all is that they shall
have had love in their hearts, truth in their mouths,
purity in their lives." Upon this teaching he would
constantly dwell. He would tell the married that if
they lived virtuously, they were to be held no way
inferior to virgins. He sought to give short and
pithy rules to all, that they might easily remember
them and be able to teach others also. He did not,
like some rigid ascetics, shrink from the society of
women, but encouraged them to come to him, and
would place his hands on their heads to give them
benediction, and treat them with the utmost tender-
ness ; and he was ever wont to say to devout women
that " the privilege of their sex was the highest, inasmuch as the Omnipotent did not disdain to be born
of a woman. To no man was allowed the dignity of
being called Father of God, but to a woman was permitted the title of Mother of God." Immediately on
the bishop's arrival at the monastery he would lay
aside the large brown cloak which he was wont to
wear ordinarily and assume a dress of sheepskin
which agreed with the white garments of the monks.
Under this was worn the hair shirt which was his
constant companion. A blanket, a pillow, and some
skins sufficed for his bedding. On rising he was
wont so far to transgress the strictness of the order
as to wash his hands, but he would use no towel to
dry them with. Having risen, his first care was to

say mass, in doing which he was contented with two
attendants, the sacrist of the monastery, and his own
chaplain.   He would take his week of service in the
monastery as the other monks, singing the services of
the hours, distinguished only by his pontifical ring
from the brethren, and wearing no other vestments
at the mass than those which the Carthusians used.[1]
On Sundays, after supper he would go with the rest
of the monks in silence and gravity to the door of
the refectory and receive his single loaf, which was to
suffice for the food of the whole week.[2]   Sometimes,
however, instead of the new loaf, he would ask the
prior's leave to take the dry crusts and fragments
which were put together in a box after being collected
from the various cells ; for these, he said, tasted to
him more sweet than the loaf.   So great a pleasure
did he take in everything connected with the monastery that he delighted to clean to a marvellous
brightness not only his own porringer, but any others
which he could discover which had not been properly
polished.   On the Saturday, according to the Carthusian rule, he would ever go to confession.   Sometimes indeed he would confess oftener, ever showing
at this exercise a most overwhelming sense of sin and a
most profound humility.   In coming among the monks
the bishop was wont to say that he desired not only

[1] These were the Alb, the Amice, the Stole, and the Chasuble, of
white stuff and plain, without any ornament of silk, gold fringe, and
jewels.—*Magna Vita*, p. 199.
[2] Besides the bread, porridge and vegetables were served each day
to the monks.

to receive from them but also to impart to them
some spiritual gift, and, indeed, by his presence and
conversation he gave joy to the strong, strength to
the weak, firmness to the wavering, and higher
advance to those who were already firm.   One
Adam de Dryburgh, who had left the abbey over
which he had presided, and become a Carthusian
monk at Witham, was an especial friend and companion of the bishop.   This good man affected
great plainness of speech, and used to tell Hugh with
much freedom that he was but a poor sort of bishop,
and not worthy to compare with the great men of
past generations.   Another favourite companion of
Hugh's was a very aged lay brother of the order,
called Einard, who had been employed by the great
Chartreuse Monastery in various affairs in their
service in all the lands of Europe.   He had come to
Witham when nearly a hundred years old, and in
spite of the remonstrances of his friends and especially of the bishop, set out again to drag his aged
limbs into Burgundy, that he might die there.   In
order to avoid the kindly opposition shown to his
departure, the aged monk had stolen away secretly,
but Hugh quickly discovered his departure, and
hastening after him overtook him as he was entering
a large wood.   " How unkind !" exclaimed the bishop,
" art thou, Einard, to go away to the dear home and
leave your friend and pupil behind you.   Behold, I
am desirous to accompany you."   Then taking his
episcopal ring from his finger and giving it to one

of those who were with him, the bishop said, "Go at
once to my clerks at Lincoln, tell them that I have
resigned the see in order that I may return to the
Great Chartreuse in company with brother Einard."
At which a huge outcry was instantly raised, and
brother Einard was assailed with reproaches, for
taking away from them the light of their eyes. At
this the poor old monk, frightened and abashed, fell
down at the bishop's feet, and besought him with tears
not to carry out his purpose. "I will give it up,"
said the bishop, "if you will abandon yours and
return to Witham." To this Einard agreed, and they
returned joyfully together, each of them thinking
that he had triumphed over the other. The bishop's
yearly visits to Witham were usually paid in the
autumn, when his servants and the people of his
diocese generally were most employed in gathering
in the harvest. Then, as he would say, he
would gather in his spiritual harvest and store up
good things in the barn of his soul. After about
two months passed in retreat he would prepare himself again with many sighs for his public duties, but
before taking leave of the brethren he would visit
each cell separately, and earnestly commend himself
and his work to the prayers of each individual inmate
of the house ; then, when they met in the common
hall, he would demand leave of the prior, and solemnly
give them his benediction, generally using the words,
"Now, brethren, I commend you to God and to the
word of His grace." After this it was his custom to

retire for the night before his departure to the house
of the lay brethren, which was separate from that of
the clerical monks.   It was here that on the occasion
of his last visit to Witham a fire broke out in the
temporary kitchen which had been erected to cook
for the bishop's attendants and for those who came
to visit him at the monastery.   This building was
made of twigs, and the cells of the lay brethren all
around were of wood, so that it was greatly feared
that the fire would spread and destroy the church.
The bishop, however, resorted to his powerful weapon
of prayer, and though the kitchen was utterly consumed, the church was saved, and it was held by all
that the progress of the fire had been stayed by the
intercession of the saint.[1]   Such was Hugh in his
Carthusian home at Witham.   We must now contemplate him among other scenes and different
companions, where to many he will seem even more
to be admired than when occupied in the monotonous
routine of the monastery and with the amiable but
somewhat childish amenities of monkish friendships.

[1] *Magna Vita*, B. IV. chap. ix.-xiv.

CHAPTER VII.

THE writer of the long and elaborate life of St.
Hugh known as the *Magna Vita*, treats the subject
of his memoir altogether from the point of view of
the saint, and scarce gives us any information as to
his connection with the public events of his day.
Unfortunately also the *Chronicles* furnish but very
meagre assistance towards supplying this defect.
Hugh was not a statesman.   He shrank altogether
from secular affairs, and loved better to be cleaning
the scuttles at Witham, than to be taking his
place in the Curia Regis.   There is, therefore, much
more to say of his inner life than of his outer.   But
some sort of connection with the politics of the day
he must have had, and from his position must have
taken some part in public affairs.   The next year
after his elevation to the Episcopate came the
terrible news of the capture of Jerusalem by Saladin,
and the complete overthrow of the exotic Christian
power which had been established in the Holy Land.

The excitement that this caused was intense ; King Henry held a solemn meeting of the bishops and barons at Chartres.   A tenth of all goods was agreed to be levied, under the anathema of the Church against those who resisted.   Prince Richard solemnly assumed the cross, free remission of sins was promised to all who would join in the expedition, and a scheme of morality was set forth for the expedition.   None were to swear enormously, none were to play at dice or tables, none were to use bright colours or costly furs in their dress, nor to require more than two dishes at a meal.   No women, save a few washer-women, were to accompany the expedition, and strange fashions in clothes were to be altogether eschewed.   The rights of creditors were to be in abeyance against those who should contribute to the work, and clerks were to have the power of pledging their benefices for three years.   The Archbishop of Canterbury went throughout his province to preach the Crusade,[1] and must consequently have advocated it in the diocese of Lincoln.   What amount of support he received from Bishop Hugh, or what the latter's views as to Crusades were, we have no means of judging ; but it seems not improbable from various indications of his opinions, that he would not be inclined to advocate the use of the arm of flesh, but would rather look for the recovery of the holy places by the spiritual weapons of faith and prayer.   Cer- tainly, as will appear presently, he was not disposed

---

[1] *Gervas. Dorobern.* p. 1528 (Ed. Twysden).

to sanction and uphold, to gratify the royal whims,
those terrible exactions by which England, in the days
of Richard, was reduced almost to a desert.   The
first commencement of the Crusade was not propitious,
for, before their preparations for the East could be
made, a fierce war broke out between the kings of
France and England.   Henry, it would seem, was
really desirous of peace, and despatched to the King
of France his two most saintly prelates, Baldwin,
Archbishop of Canterbury, and Hugh, Bishop of
Lincoln, " that at least they might mitigate by their
words and exhortations the fierce anger which he had
conceived in his mind against the King of England."[1]
The prelates, however, were not able to accomplish
their pacific object, and probably Hugh returned to
his diocese soon afterwards.   The next year, however
(1189), when after Henry's melancholy death at
Chinon, Richard was solemnly invested at Rouen
with the Dukedom of Normandy, it is probable
that Hugh was present.   Benedictus speaks of " all
the bishops " of Richard's dominions being there, and
shortly after he records that Baldwin, Archbishop of
Canterbury, and Hugh, Bishop of Lincoln, had license
to return into England.[2]   On the great solemnity of
the coronation of Richard at Westminster (September 3, 1189) Hugh was present,[3] as he was also at
the council held by the new king soon afterwards at

---

[1] *Benedictus, s. a.* 1188.

[2] *Benedictus, s. a.* 1189.   *Roger de Hoveden,* p. 373 b (Ed. Savile).

[3] *Benedictus, u. s.*

Pipewell Abbey in Northamptonshire, at which Richard filled up the sees and abbeys which were then vacant. Whatever Richard's exactions were, he does not seem to have imitated his father in the evil pratice of keeping bishoprics and abbeys vacant in order to seize upon their revenues.

This council at Pipewell must have possessed especial interest for the Bishop of Lincoln, for two of that magnificent chapter, whose names as candidates for the bishopric had been presented to the king before his own, and who had despised his meanness, were now promoted to the episcopal rank. Richard, Dean of Lincoln, the king's treasurer, was made Bishop of London, and Godfrey de Luci, one of the canons who had previously declined the bishopric of Exeter as not sufficient for his expenses, was now fortunate enough to obtain the wealthy see of Winchester. It is not unlikely that Bishop Hugh was not ill-pleased to be well quit of these courtier-canons, whose ways were not his ways. During King Richard's absence in the Crusade, William Longchamp, Bishop of Ely, acted as his justiciary, and for a time controlled all things at his will. If we are to believe the testimony of Hugh Nonant, Bishop of Coventry, and that of the monkish historians, nothing could exceed the luxury, pride, injustice, and oppression of this prelate. But there is good reason to believe that their accounts of him are unfairly exaggerated. He had bitterly offended the monks by expelling them from the chapter of

Coventry, and placing prebendaries in their room ;[1] and though this was done at the desire of the Bishop of Coventry, yet this prelate afterwards turned against the Bishop of Ely, and joining the intrigues of the opposite faction, headed by Prince John, lent himself to blacken the character of his former friend with the utmost malice.[2]   That the Bishop of Lincoln did not set himself against Longchamp there is clear evidence.   It was to him as to a friend that after his fall and banishment the Bishop of Ely addressed the bull of Pope Cœlestine granted in his favour, and excommunicating John and his supporters. He addresses Bishop Hugh as his "dearest friend," and says that he has "the greatest confidence in his love, and had found him ever constant in his support," and exhorts him boldly to carry out and publish the Pope's anathemas.[3]   But though by no means favouring John's intrigues, and willing to give a loyal support to the king's legal representative, the Bishop of Lincoln was not disposed to act in this submissive manner as the Pope's agent to invade the liberties of his country.   He declined to take

---

[1] The monks were afterwards restored by Hugh and other commissioners under the pope's order.   "Hubertus Cantuarensis archiepiscopus et Hugo Lincolniensis episcopus ex præcepto papæ Cœlestini tertii amotis clericis monachos Coventrenses restituerunt."—*Ann de Osenia*, s. a. 1197.   See Palgrave's Preface to *Rotuli Curiæ Regis*.

[2] See Collier's *Ch. Hist.* ii. 372.   Peter of Blois published a strong vindication of Longchamp.   See also the letter of the Rouen clergy. *Hoveden*, 409.   Mr. Stubbs appears to be in error in stating that the monkish party upheld Longchamp.—(Preface to *Epp. Cantuar.*)

[3] *Benedictus*, s. a. 1191.

any steps to execute the Pope's bull, and the Bishop of Ely's cause fell to the ground. Hugh, with the other bishops (with the exception of the Bishop of Coventry), was faithful to the cause of Richard ; and when, on Richard's return being imminent, John more openly showed his traitorous designs, Hugh joined with the other bishops in excommunicating him solemnly at Westminster.[1] At Richard's first council at Nottingham Hugh was present, and in the ceremony of his second coronation at Winchester he took a part.[2] There can be no more complete proof of the estimation in which the Bishop of Lincoln was held by all parties than the way in which all constantly refer to him in matters of importance, having evidently entire faith both in his impartiality and his capacity. Thus, as has been already stated, in the dispute between Archbishop Baldwin and the monks of Christ Church both sides looked to him and appealed to his judgment. William Longchamp selected him as the most competent person to act in his behalf, and now, through the high opinion entertained of him by Pope Cœlestine, Hugh is involved in the very troublesome and scandalous quarrel between Geoffrey, Archbishop of York, and some members of his chapter. The archbishop does not seem to have acquired that meetness for the episcopal character which he had modestly disclaimed when he resigned his pretensions to the diocese of Lincoln. His time had been passed

1 *Hoveden*, f. 418 (Ed. Savile). 2 *Hoveden*, *ibid*.

since his elevation to the archiepiscopate in leading
armies in the field and fiercely contending with
domestic enemies.   He had exasperated his chapter
by various acts of high-handed oppression, and having also in many ways shown his contempt for the
power of Rome, his enemies were able to present a
good case against him to the Pope, who ordered the
cause to be inquired into at York, and the evidence,
attested by the seals of the commissioners, to be
sent to him at Rome.   The Bishop of Lincoln was
the chief commissioner, and with him the Archdeacon of Nottingham and the Prior de Ponte Sancto
were associated.   They held their inquisition in the
cathedral church of York, and having called together
"the abbots, priors, and ecclesiastical persons of the
diocese of York, they proceeded according to the
tenor of the apostolical mandate," to inquire diligently into the charges made ; and having found an
abundance of testimony forthcoming against the
archbishop, they sent it under their seals to the
Roman court.   Archbishop Geoffrey was accused of
vilipending the sacraments of the Church, of spend-
ing his time in hunting, hawking, or military affairs.
He was charged with never consecrating a church,
never holding a synod, never giving the benediction
to an abbot, although at malediction and excommunication they declared him to be very ready.
He was utterly careless, they said, about the liberties
and customs of his Church ; and if any were rash
enough to appeal to Rome, he would strip them of

their goods, and throw them into prison.   He would break down the doors of churches when they were closed against him, force men to perjure themselves, seize on preferment as he pleased, and either take the profits for himself, or appoint some unworthy persons to important posts.[1]   Such were the charges presented to Bishop Hugh against the archbishop by divers leading Churchmen in the diocese of York. Having formally recorded them and sealed them, the commissioners despatched them to the Pope, and gave notice to the archbishop that he must present himself at Rome within four months and two weeks, to make his defence against these grave accusations, and meet his accusers there.   But the prince-bishop appears to have treated the whole thing with great indifference.   The clerks of his diocese duly appeared, but the archbishop sent a message to the Pope that the time fixed was inconvenient to him, and the season unhealthy, and he declined to come.   The Pope then fixed another time, but neither then did the archbishop appear nor send a competent representative, and in consequence he was suspended from his office.[2]   Soon afterwards, also, he so far angered the king, his brother, that he ordered him to be stripped of all his revenues.[3]   But neither of these sentences appears to have taken effect.   As regards the first, the Bishop of Lincoln, though often and greatly solicited by the canons of York to declare

---

[1] *Hoveden*, f. 425 (Ed. Savile).   [2] *Hoveden*, u. s.

[3] *Hoveden*, f. 428.

and execute the Pope's sentence of suspension, flatly refused to do so.   He would rather, he declared, be suspended himself than suspend the archbishop.[1] Either, therefore, Hugh believed the charges to be greatly exaggerated, or else in this, as in the former instance, he refused to be the minister of the Pope to interfere with the discipline of the Anglican Church.   There was not, indeed, in spite of his monastic training, much of the spirit of subordination in the Bishop of Lincoln.   Whether it were pope, king, or archbishop who laid their commands upon him, he did not scruple to disobey them if he saw good reason why he should do so.

We have already had occasion to speak of his bold opposition to Henry II.   That talented and impetuous monarch, who ever loved and respected him, bore the utmost plain speaking and plain dealing at his hands, giving thereby a strong testimony to the genuineness and sincerity of the bishop's character. We shall now see him in opposition to Henry's still more impetuous son, Richard the Lion-hearted, and perceive how calmly and resolutely ·he faced and overcame the violent tempers of that unbridled nature.   This is perhaps the strongest evidence of Hugh's perfect moral courage, and the ascendency of his great qualities.[2]   And it was not with Richard as with Henry, who from the first had taken a

---

[1] *Hoveden*, f. 431.

[2] Roger de Wendover says of him, " Potestatis sæcularis in rebus ecclesiæ sævientis impetus adeo constanter elidere consuevit ut et rerum et corporis sui periculum contemnere videretur."—*Flor. Hist.*, iii. 157.

decided personal liking to St. Hugh. Richard knew
but little of him. His trusted minister was Hubert,
Archbishop of Canterbury, a man between whom and
Hugh there was but little love. These two prelates
were indeed of altogether different types of character,
and entirely opposed in their views of duty. Hubert
was a good specimen of a secular prelate, and his
influence over Richard was salutary, but Hugh, who
held the most romantic notions as to the subordination and inferiority of the secular power, was indignant at seeing a bishop administering civil affairs and
using temporal weapons, and constantly upbraided
Hubert with this, and openly opposed him. The archbishop, on his part, was desirous to reduce this proud
and defiant spirit, which gave him no little trouble
by encouraging the resistance of Churchmen to his
difficult task of collecting money for Richard's foreign
wars ; and so Hugh would be represented by him
to the king as an impracticable and turbulent man,
who needed to be sternly dealt with, and to be
brought to due obedience. The king, no doubt,
signified his readiness to exert his authority when
occasion required, and the malice of the evil one (as
Hugh's biographer puts it) soon discovered an occasion. There existed a custom for the bishop of
Lincoln to pay to the king a tax or tribute of a
costly mantle, which had been commuted into a
yearly payment of one hundred marks, or (according
to some) one hundred pounds.[1] This tribute appears

[1] See page 67.

to have been paid more or less regularly down to the death of Bishop Robert de Chesney. After his death had occurred that long vacancy of the see, when its revenues were alienated to the rapaciousness of the Crown, or absorbed by a titular bishop. Walter de Coutances, who only occupied the see for one year, made no payment, so that there was a long arrear which might be claimed, and this, on the suggestion of Archbishop Hubert, was now (1195) demanded of the Bishop of Lincoln by the Crown. The injustice of the demand was palpable. During the vacancy of the see and the seizure of its revenues, a far larger amount must have gone into the king's coffers than was represented by this payment, and yet Hugh was now to be made pay not only for the arrears of his own episcopate, but for this time also. But the injustice of the thing did not represent the whole grievance in the view of Bishop Hugh. To him it seemed "that nothing could be more unworthy, nothing more intolerable than that the spouse of the King of Heaven, or he himself, her guardian, should be put under tax and made tributary by mortal man." Hence he determined not only to discharge this grievous burden, but to remove it for all time to come from the church, and by a composition made not without great difficulty with the king, he covenanted that for a payment of 3000 marks, the church of Lincoln should be released from this claim for ever. But how was this large sum of money to be raised? Hugh, as has been already said, was liberal in the extreme,[1] and no saver of money. His proposition was that he should retire to the monastery of Witham and devote the whole revenues of the see to pay the charge until it should be satisfied. It was not without a secret joy that he found himself, as he thought, constrained to the necessity of a long retreat in his beloved retirement. But his clergy stoutly resisted his proposal. They would not consent to be so long deprived of their head, and to have the whole government of the diocese again completely paralysed. Much to their honour they undertook to raise the sum among themselves, and inasmuch as this tribute had been formerly held by the bishops an occasion for levying a tax, which, it was thought, far exceeded the amount remitted to the Crown, it was indeed only fair that the clergy who had been long spared this, should be the contributors of the arrears. Hugh agreed to the proposal, only on the distinct understanding that the contributions were to be voluntary and that no one was to be constrained to help, and that there were to be no commutations of penances for money fines—a thing, says Hugh's biographer, that he always stoutly refused, though St. Thomas of Canterbury was of another mind.[2] This matter could scarcely have

---

[1] Two instances are given in the *Metrical Life* of his remitting the mortuaries or death-fines which accrued to him as lord upon the death of any of his tenants in fee. If the bishop was in the habit of thus dealing with his *reditus*, his stewards must often have been hard put to it.—See *Life* by *Giraldus Camb.*, vii. 96.

[2] *Magna Vita*, p. 184 *seq.*

tended to smooth the relations between King Richard and the Bishop of Lincoln, and it was followed almost immediately by another in which they again came into collision.   The patronage of the Abbey of Eynsham had from the time of the Conquest been in the bishops of Lincoln, Remigius having refounded or greatly benefited the abbey, and Bishop Bloet having much augmented it.   In the tenth year of Hugh's episcopate, the aged Geoffrey, Abbot of Eynsham, who had governed the monastery for forty-four years, died.   The bishop, as was usual, sent his clerks to the abbey to receive the custody of it into their hands, and to arrange with the monks for the due election of his successor.   Their claims were disputed by the king's officers, Richard himself being at that time absent in his French war.   The bishop's friends counselled him not to press his claim.   They said that the king's father, Henry II., had enacted a constitution that the patronage of all the abbeys should be in his hands,[1] and that it was not likely that the son, who was more obstinate than the father, would yield in this matter.   It would be, they said, a difficult and laborious task to press his rights against those of the Crown, and there was little to be gained even if he were successful.   But Hugh did not take this view of the case.   He regarded it as a solemn duty to guard ecclesiastical rights from civil usurpation.   His predecessors, he said, had been no

---

[1] This is probably the 12th Constitution of the Constitutions of Clarendon, and afterwards abandoned by Henry II.

parties to this constitution, and it should never be by
his act that the church should be deprived of her
just rights out of fear of the great and powerful.
He accordingly commenced a suit, and after a long
and laborious struggle, by the verdict of twenty-four
men worthy of credit, clerks and laymen, to whom
the decision was referred, his rights were established,
and he went personally to Eynsham to receive and
confirm the new abbot.[1]   This successful opposition
to the king's claims was soon followed by a more
bold and important and still more exasperating act
of resistance, on the part of the bishop against the
royal will.   In his fierce struggle against Philip
Augustus, King of France, King Richard, sorely
pressed for money, sent to Archbishop Hubert, his
zealous representative in England, bidding him con-
trive by some means or other to furnish supplies.
The archbishop summoned all the barons to meet
at Oxford (December 1197), and putting before them
the king's needs, besought their counsel and aid.
The barons agreed that they would furnish 300
knights a year to the king for his wars, and that
they would tax themselves for this purpose.   The
bishops, by virtue of their baronies, were bound to
take a part in this contribution.   The Archbishop
of Canterbury and the Bishop of London expressed

---

[1] *Magna Vita*, p. 188 *seq*.   The abbot afterwards accompanied the
bishop to Lincoln for benediction, at which ceremony there was great
feasting, and the abbot was solemnly presented by Hugh with a pastoral
staff of silver and ivory, and a goblet huge and splendid.

themselves most ready to bear their share, when Hugh, Bishop of Lincoln, rose and said: "I must appeal to your indulgence, my lords, as you are aware that I am a stranger in these parts and was promoted to the office of bishop from being a simple recluse. I have, however, diligently laboured to make myself acquainted with the customs and privileges of the church of St. Mary at Lincoln, since the time that I became bishop there, and though I find that that church is bound to do military service to the king within the bounds of England, I do not find that any such thing is due from it for parts outside England ; I cannot, therefore, agree to this.   Indeed, I would rather find my way on foot back to my native soil and to the solitude where I was wont to dwell, than be a bishop here on the condition of sacrificing any of the ancient privileges of the church which I have undertaken to uphold."[1]   At this bold and decided answer the archbishop could scarcely contain himself for wrath.   With a voice broken by passion he demanded of Herbert, Bishop of Salisbury, what was his determination about helping the king.   Herbert, encouraged by Hugh's boldness, said, "It seems to me that without enormous mischief to my church I cannot say or do anything except what I gather from the answer of the Bishop of Lincoln that he intends to do."   At this Archbishop Hubert could no longer contain himself.   He broke out against Bishop Hugh with furious words, dissolved the council,

[1] *Magna Vita*, p. 249.

and sent an express messenger to the king to tell
him that it was through the Bishop of Lincoln's resistance that no aid could be sent to him.   Richard,
in no mild mood, we may be sure, ordered that all
the goods of the bishops of Lincoln and Salisbury
should be confiscated.   Salisbury at once submitted,
and after much exaction and heavy payments
redeemed his episcopal revenues.   But it was otherwise with the Bishop of Lincoln.   He utterly
refused to yield, and patiently awaited the worst that
his enemies could inflict on him.   Orders were issued
for the king's officers to enter and seize upon his
property, but no one could be found hardy enough
to attempt to execute the order.   Each believed
that it would be equivalent to rushing upon certain
destruction, for " they dreaded his anathema as though
it were·capital punishment."   Thus, for nine months
the bishop remained unaffected by the royal proscription, while the unhappy officials were constantly
urged on and threatened for their slackness.   At
length these men, who were exposed to destruction
on either side, earnestly besought the bishop to settle
matters with the king, if only for their sakes.   And
no doubt, though his biographer may disguise it,
Bishop Hugh must have been subjected to very great
inconvenience and trouble by thus being put outside
the pale of the law, even if it were the case that no
one was bold enough to take possession of his goods
in the name of the king.   To remove this, therefore,
and to put affairs on a better footing, Hugh deter-

mined to cross the sea and have a personal interview
with Richard.   Under the circumstances, this was a
sufficiently bold undertaking.   All that the king
knew of the bishop as yet was likely to exasperate
him against him.   He was in the very midst of
what might easily be construed to be an act of treason
and rebellion against the royal authority.   Richard's
violent temper and impetuous ways were well known.
It was therefore an act of very great courage for
Hugh to go at all.   But, when we read the way in
which the interview was carried out, we are still more
astonished at the irrepressible boldness and unquailing
spirit of the man.   On his way, when at Rouen, he
had been met by William, Earl Marshall, and the
Earl of Albemarle, and these distinguished noblemen
had most earnestly pressed him to forego his purpose
of visiting the king.   They told him that Richard had
treated the Bishop of Salisbury with great contumely,
and had threatened terrible things against the Bishop
of Lincoln ; and they feared, as they said, not so
much for the bishop as for the king himself, knowing
what terrible vengeance always overtook those who
set themselves against the Bishop of Lincoln.   They
therefore desired that he would put his cause in their
hands, promising to do their utmost, even to braving
the king's extreme wrath for him.   The bishop, however, would by no means consent that they should
run any risk for him.   He merely desired them to
acquaint the king that he was coming, and to ask
him to appoint an interview.   This having been

arranged, the bishop proceeded on his way. He found Richard, according to his appointment at Roche d' Andeli, and at the moment of his arrival occupied in hearing mass in the chapel of the château, it being St. Augustine's Day. Richard's royal seat stood near the door, raised a step or two, and under it sat the Bishops of Durham and Ely in attendance on him. The Bishop of Lincoln entered the chapel, and seeing the king, saluted him, but received no recognition or salutation in reply. The king glared upon him with a fierce look, such as the Moslems had learned to tremble at. But there was no trembling in the bosom of the intrepid Bishop of Lincoln. He stepped up to the side of the king and exclaimed, "Give me the kiss, my lord king." Richard turned away his face from him with an angry gesture, without deigning to reply. Then Hugh, who doubtless knew his man, and that he, like his father, did not object to a little rough play or a somewhat biting jest, took hold of the king's robe on the breast and gave it a hearty shake,[1] exclaiming, " I demand the kiss ; you owe it to me, for I have come from far to see you." Then the king at length spoke, but in surly tones—" You don't deserve the kiss." Whereupon the bold bishop gave him a stronger shake than before, and drawing the king's cape out as far as it would reach, sent his voice along it in a familiar tone,[2] " Nay, but I do ; give me the

---

[1] *" Fortiter constringens hanc vehementius concussit."*—*Magna Vita.*
[2] *" Per capam quam strictâ tenebat manu confidenter ait."*—*Ibid.*

kiss." At this Richard, secretly pleased at witnessing such perfect coolness and boldness, and unable to repress a smile at the absurdity of the scene, gave him the kiss. It may well be supposed that during this strange contest the service was suspended, but Hugh had no sooner obtained his demand than he left the king, and the service again proceeded. There had been many eyes within the chapel watching the event with the deepest interest. Between the king's throne and the altar no less than two archbishops and five bishops were sitting, all of whom would be intensely concerned to see how this struggle between the bold Churchman and the bold monarch would terminate. Had the bishop been forced to succumb, had he offered humble apologies and been ignominiously repulsed, it is probable that his brethren would not have been very ready to smile upon him, but anxious, perhaps, openly to separate their cause from his. But as it was, by his strength of will and unfailing boldness he had been completely successful, and the great prelates anxiously vied with one another to pay him respect and honour. They eagerly offered him a seat among them. But Hugh, perhaps not without some knowledge of their quality, passed by them all, and reverently approaching the altar, remained there in an attitude of deep devotion while the mysteries proceeded, the king meanwhile keeping his gaze intensely fixed on him. At the threefold invocation of the Agnus Dei, the priest kissed the Pax and handed it to one of the arch-

bishops, who conveyed it with deep reverence to the
king for him to receive the blessing thus transmitted
from the altar.   Richard advanced several paces to
receive the sacred instrument, but instead of taking
the kiss from it as he was wont, he himself carried
it with a deep reverence to the Bishop of Lincoln,
who was absorbed in his devotions and not the least
expecting so high an honour.   The reception which
he had thus won for himself, and the complete
removal of the king's bitter feeling against him which
was thus made evident, would enable Hugh to treat at
ease on the matters which had brought him to the royal
presence.   He was able to prove clearly that he had not
in any way opposed any legal right of the Crown, but
had only stood in defence of the acknowledged and
undeniable privileges of his own church.   The king
admitted the truth of this, but said that he had been
constantly receiving letters full of accusation against
him from the Archbishop of Canterbury.   "By the
honour of God, and by the salvation of our souls,"
exclaimed the bishop, "I have never, even in the
smallest particular, opposed your interests."[1]   Then
the king declared himself quite satisfied, and, to show
his good will, offered the bishop presents, and begged
him to take up his lodging for a time at a new castle
which he had lately built on an island near, and to
return to him again on the morrow, that he might
have the pleasure of another interview with him.

---

[1] This must be taken with a salvo of "*legal* interests."   The actual
interests of the king he had very vigorously opposed.

But the bishop, before he left the king, thought it right to avail himself of the opportunity of giving him some spiritual instruction. Drawing him, therefore, to a spot near to the altar, he reminded him that he was one of his parishioners,[1] and inquired after the state of his soul, as it was now a year since he had seen him. Richard replied that he had nothing on his conscience save a rather strong hatred of his enemies, who were so bitterly hostile to him. " If you serve God," said the bishop, " He will make your enemies peaceably disposed towards you, or He will overthrow them. But beware lest you commit some sin either against God or your neighbour. It is currently reported of you that you are unfaithful to your marriage bed, and that you receive bribes for appointments to spiritual offices. If this be true, you cannot have peace from the Lord." With this admonition the bishop left the king. Richard, who was greatly impressed by his whole interview with him, is reported to have said, " If the rest of the bishops were such as he, no king or prince would dare to lift up his neck against them." But the king was yet to have some further revelations of the bishop's character. His courtiers, who were above all things anxious for the raising money in England, suggested to Richard that though the bishop might refuse to contribute himself, he might not be averse to carrying the king's letters into England, urging

[1] Richard was born in the diocese of Lincoln, at Oxford, A.D. 1157. —Mr. Dimock's note *ad loc.*

T

his subjects there to send supplies ; and that if
he would do this, immense weight would be given
to the king's request, coming by the hands of such
a messenger.   At the same time his fellow-church-
men pressed upon Hugh the desirableness of using
this opportunity of altogether reinstating himself
in the king's favour.   But the bishop was not to be
thus cajoled.   " It is not my business," he exclaimed,
" nor does it comport with my office, to be the king's
messenger.   I do not desire in any way to be mixed
up with these exactions.   They may be . called
voluntary, but they are really compulsory, and have
in them many elements of injustice."   These scruples
of Hugh's soon came to the king's ears.   Richard
was no doubt greatly angered by what he considered
this impracticable scrupulousness.   But he knew
the man well enough now not to attempt to argue
with him.   He simply ordered him off at once to his
home, paying him, however, the compliment of asking for his prayers.   Whether, indeed, Richard cared
or thought much about the efficacy of these prayers
when he spoke of them may be doubted, but circumstances soon led him to attach a high value to
them.   Shortly after the bishop's departure he was
engaged in a sharp skirmish with the King of France
at Gisors, and was completely successful, capturing a
great number of prisoners, the Count de Nevers, a
powerful enemy, having been drowned in the castle
moat, and King Philip himself having been in danger
of the same fate.   All this the king announced in a

letter to the bishop, desiring the continuance of his powerful intercession.[1]   But his feelings towards the bishop were soon again changed.   It was doubtless not altogether agreeable to King Richard, sorely pressed for want of funds, that the rich church of Lincoln should, by the boldness and dexterity of its head, have thus escaped the hands of the spoiler. Revolving this in his mind, he bethought him that if the bishop was too dangerous a person to meddle with, at any rate the canons of his church had not either his boldness or his sanctity.   These canons were represented to him as " enriched with innumerable revenues, with gold and silver furnished beyond measure, and able, without any harm to themselves, to contribute a handsome sum of money to his coffers."   It was suggested to the king that he should desire the Archbishop of Canterbury to send twelve of them over to him to be employed in diplomatic service for him in various countries, at their own cost.   The archbishop, thinking that, now, at length, he had the desired opportunity of humbling his impracticable suffragan, sent twelve letters under his seal to the bishop, desiring him to fill in the names and to serve them upon the persons who should thus be cited.   When the message arrived Hugh was at his manor of Bugden.   His clerks, who surrounded him, hearing its purport, trembled for themselves, and were especially fearful lest the bishop, returning a sharp answer to the messenger,

[1] *Magna Vita*, Lib. v. cap. 5, 6.

should make things worse for them. The bishop, however, who was just about to dine, took no notice of the message, but went tranquilly to his dinner, while the terrified clerks kept whispering among themselves as to their apprehensions. Dinner over, the bishop summoned the archbishop's messenger, and told him that "this was a new and unheard of sort of business. He had never made it his employment to carry other people's letters, and he did not intend to do so. As to his clerks, he had often prohibited them from intermeddling in secular things, and he certainly was not going to encourage such a thing now. It was quite enough to have archbishops thus forgetting their sacred calling. However, if he should compel the canons to come to him, he must count on having the bishop also. If they shall be sent to the king, the bishop would go too." The messenger, a haughty clerk of the court, began to threaten. Hugh bade him go about his business instantly. He then sent some of his clerks to expostulate with the archbishop for having grievously infringed the privileges of the Church. Archbishop Hubert made an evasive reply ; but he soon showed his true feeling in the matter by an edict ordering all the possessions of the Bishop of Lincoln to be taken by the royal receivers. Again the officers trembled at the duty entrusted to them, and remonstrated with the king as to the certain destruction upon which they were sent. "If you are afraid," said Richard, "we will send Marchadæus, our captain

of Roturiers, he will know how to play with that
Burgundian." "Marchadæus cannot be spared from
your wars, sire," answered the courtiers, "and if the
bishop's anathema is as deadly as they say it is, we
should certainly lose a very useful bravo." "Then
let Stephen de Turnham undertake the office," said
the king, "and as he values his life and limbs let
him perform it efficiently." Stephen de Turnham,
a good man, and one that loved the bishop well, had
then this unpleasant office thrust upon him. Constrained to act, he set out for Sleaford, one of the
bishop's manors in Lincolnshire, with the intention
of taking possession. But the party on their road,
not very far from Peterborough, met the cortége of
the bishop himself. Terrified beyond measure, they
fled from the highway ; and then, sending for some
of the bishop's clerks, they explained to them how
unwillingly they were acting, and how earnestly they
desired that the bishop would come to some understanding with the king, promising that they would
keep his property safe meanwhile. "What have they
to do with keeping my property safe ?" exclaimed
Hugh ; "let them go on and lay their hands upon
all that we have, yea, and on that which belongs to
the holy Mother of God as well." He then, taking
out his stole, which he always wore when travelling,
under his cloak, shook the fringe of it. "This fringe,"
he said, "will restore to us, even to the last penny,
whatever they shall have thought fit to carry off."
The bishop then proceeded to Bugden, and immedi-

ately despatched his letter to his archdeacons and
rural deans, bidding them that whenever these officers
should come to take possession of anything belonging to the see, they should straightway excommunicate them, with bell, book, and candle, as unjust
spoilers of the Church.   At this decisive step all
around the bishop were in fear and trembling.   He,
however, calmly went to bed and to sleep, being only
heard to murmur in his sleep Amen somewhat more
frequently and distinctly than usual.[1]   It is evident,
however, that how bold a line soever the bishop
might take, he was no more able, even with the
dread weapon of his curse, to resist the power of the
Crown on this occasion than before.   He saw at once
that he would have again to go to the king's presence, and with this view had taken solemn leave of
the chapter of Lincoln, even before that journey to
Bugden in which the events just recorded happened.
After a short stay at Bugden he went onwards to
London to consult with the archbishop and the other
magnates of the land, to see if they could suggest
any course which might haply save his journey to
the king.

An incident occurred on the way, which well
illustrates that ready tact and presence of mind
which the bishop possessed in such an eminent
degree, and which will go far to account for many
of the miracles attributed to him.   In one of the
Hunts villages there was a "wise woman," famous

[1] *Magna Vita*, Lib. v. cap. 7.

for her powers of detecting crimes and telling any secret transaction. These powers being held to be unorthodox, she had been frequently delated before the priest, but so great was her power of tongue and volubility, that her accusers were always talked out of countenance and silenced. The case seemed one for the intervention of the bishop, and at the request of the rural dean, he ordered the woman to be brought before him. Hugh, probably divining without much difficulty the nature of the case, addressed her, "What, my poor woman, are you a diviner? Come now, if this be so, you will be able to tell me what I have in my hand" (which was some of the fringe of his stole). The poor woman, frightened to death at being brought before so great a man, and one who had such a reputation for holiness and power, at once humbly disclaimed all supernatural gifts, and sought the bishop's pardon and blessing. Hugh was obliged, in his ignorance of the language, to use the rural dean as interpreter, but through him he gave the poor woman some salutary counsel, and having prayed for her and recommended her to the care of the Prior of Huntingdon, who was penitentiary of the district, he went on his way. Arriving the next day in the neighbourhood of St. Alban's, he was met by a body of officials who were leading a condemned thief to execution. The officers could not pass the saintly bishop without going to seek his blessing, and the criminal, left for a moment free, rushed

eagerly to him also, and falling before the feet of
his horse, earnestly besought his mercy and help.
Hugh reined in his horse and asked who the man
was, and what was about to be done to him, and
having had it explained to him, he told the officers
that they had no longer power over him. "It is the
undoubted right of the holy mother Church to give
sanctuary to all," he said, "and where there is a
bishop and his clergy, there is the Church ; so that
the poor man has found shelter just as much as if
he had taken sanctuary in a cathedral." This
somewhat startling explanation of the right of
sanctuary the officers are said to have at once
admitted, only desiring the bishop to bear them
harmless with the king, which he readily undertook
to do. The joyful thief was admitted into the
bishop's train and taken to London with him, where
he was set at liberty to go where he pleased.[1]
Having reached London, the bishop went to meet
Archbishop Hubert and the chief men of the land,
with whom he desired to take counsel. They all
advised him to exact a good round sum from his
clergy, and to appease the king's mind therewith.
"Know you not, my lord," said the archbishop,
"that like a dropsical man thirsts for water, so does
our lord the king thirst for money?" "If he is
thus thirsty," answered Hugh, "I will not be the
water to quench his thirst." There was therefore

[1] The same action is recorded of Baldwin, Archbishop of Canterbury, when he was Bishop of Worcester.

nothing for it but either he must yield and submit to the king's exactions, and thus expose the church, which he was called upon to defend, to unjust oppressions, or else he must once more go and visit the king himself, and again try the effect of his personal influence in bringing him to a better mind. This latter he determined to do. Richard should once more hear the plain truth from his lips. After taking this resolve it was necessary that the bishop should return to his diocese to make the final preparations. It would appear to have been on his return at this time, as he passed through Cheshunt, that the incident of the mad sailor, who was said to have been cured by the bishop, occurred. A poor wretch was found by him tied in a most inhuman manner in his house, raging in furious delirium. The bishop, with the calm courage which never deserted him, went to him, and loosing his bonds, made over him the sign of the cross, at the same time reciting the opening verses of the Gospel of St. John, and afterwards sprinkling him with holy water. The strange form, the religious garb, the calm and gentle voice, the words of divine power, so different from all that had before surrounded the poor sufferer, worked an instantaneous effect upon him. He became calm and subdued, and when the bishop left him, gave good promise of being completely cured of his troubles, which the writer of the *Magna Vita* informs us was afterwards the result. Very soon after this the bishop was again

in London on his way to carry out his purpose of
visiting the king.   As a precautionary measure he
paid a visit before he went to the Barons of the
Exchequer, to request them not to allow the privileges of his church to be infringed in his absence.
This they readily agreed to do, paying him the
greatest deference, and entreating him to be seated
awhile.   Hugh, accepting their courtesy, sat down
with them, and then one of them exclaimed, " We
have gained a great triumph to-day, for we have the
Bishop of Lincoln sitting at the King's Exchequer."
Hugh sprang up hastily and gave to these lords the
kiss of peace, exclaiming as he did so, " Now,
indeed, I have my triumph over you, for after the
kiss you must needs show kindness to my church."[1]
He then at once departed for Normandy ; but it was
not fated that he should ever again meet with King
Richard alive.

[1] *Magna Vita,* Lib. v. cap. 9.

CHAPTER VIII.

BISHOP HUGH AND KING JOHN.

WHEN the bishop arrived in Normandy (1199), a truce had been established between Richard and King Philip. But the restless King of England was not enjoying the repose of peace. One of his vassals, Vidomar, Viscount of Limoges, had incurred his displeasure by not sending to him the whole of a treasure which had been discovered on his estate, and Richard had gone to besiege and destroy the Castle of Chalus,[1] declaring that he would accept no quarter, but would hang every man in it. Could Bishop Hugh have been by his side at that moment instead of the vile ruffian Marchadæus, the Brabançon bravo, gentler counsels might have prevailed, the king's life might have been saved, and the massacre of all those in the castle prevented. But the violent man was struck down in the midst of his fury by the arrow of Bertram de Gurdon, and the wound quickly becoming mortal, Bishop Hugh never saw his

---

[1] This is the account generally accepted as to the circumstances of Richard's death. The writer of the *Magna Vita* says that Richard had gone against the Count of Engoulême, agreeing in this with Gervase of Canterbury.

"parishioner" again. During the time that he was waiting for the king's return from his expedition, Hugh took the opportunity of paying a visit to Angers, where he was lodged in the Abbey of St. Nicholas, and where he celebrated Orders.[1] We find, incidentally, that the famous satirical writer, Walter Map, or Mapes, who had been Precentor of Lincoln and was now Archdeacon of Oxford, was present at Angers at that time, and was anxious that the bishop should ordain one of his servants a subdeacon. Hugh, however, steadily refused, without giving any reason for his refusal.[2] When, a few days afterwards, the unfortunate youth who had been offered for orders was seized with leprosy, it was thought that the bishop, by his saintly power, had been able to discern what was coming upon him, and had refused him orders in consequence. Hugh's stay at Angers was full of grievous troubles and annoyances to him. The canons of Lincoln were there, trembling lest the iron grasp of King Richard should enclose them, anxious to escape under the powerful shield of the bishop, but fearing lest that shield should not avail to protect them—desirous therefore,

---

[1] It is not said that he had the permission of the bishop of the diocese to do this, but it may be presumed that this was so. The bishop was absent at Rome. See p. 287.

[2] Probably the satirical and very unclerical archdeacon was no very great favourite with his bishop. He was a bitter hater of monks, as his poems testify, and Hugh was a great lover of them. He was, or had been, one of the king's itinerant justices, and the bishop thought all secular employments for the clergy utterly to be reprobated.

as weak timid men, of a compromise, and ready to
buy off their attendance, by paying a handsome fine.
There, too, was a deputation of the canons of Hereford, who were on their way to the king to seek his
confirmation of their election of a bishop.   They
desired to have Walter Mapes, who was a canon of
Hereford, for their bishop, but Walter was an archdeacon in the diocese of Lincoln, and they feared
that this fact would be sufficient to make the king
exasperated against him, in so violent a temper and
so full of threats was Richard represented to be
against everything in any way connected with the
Bishop of Lincoln.   The Lincoln and Hereford
canons determined, therefore, to make common cause,
and to try with all their might to procure Hugh's
submission to the king, and a declaration of his
readiness to contribute something to the Royal
Exchequer.   In order to add further weight to their
deputation, they induced the dean and canons of
Angers to accompany them, and the three cathedral
bodies together assailed the bishop, pressing him with
every argument that they could devise to induce him
to yield, to contribute something for the king's needs,
and thus to gain his favour for himself and all Churchmen connected with him, and to be set free to return to
his diocese without more trouble.   They urged upon
the bishop that the country in which they were was
full of danger to them, that wars were all around
them, that the highways were not safe, and that soon
it would be neither secure to stay there, nor easy to

depart. But though from morning till night these three bands (like Job's friends of old, as the author of the *Magna Vita* puts it) assailed the bishop, their arguments were utterly unable to move him. He stood firm as a rock on this one point, that to subject the dignity and liberty of the Church to a base slavery to the lay power was both sacrilegious and also impolitic, seeing that to lay exactions once begun there would be no end.[1] The remonstrants, however, would not take a refusal, but insisted again and again. The bishop, wearied with their importunities, at length said, "Enough, brethren, for to-day. To-morrow perhaps we may be of one mind. The night often brings counsel." Having thus freed himself from them, he sat sad and meditative, feeling, doubtless, that he had no man on whom he could rely, and that all were taking sordid and cowardly views. When almost inclined to despair, from weariness he fell asleep, and seemed to hear a voice repeating to him words out of the Psalms, "God is to be admired in His saints, even the God of Israel. He will give strength and power unto His people : blessed be God." He awoke thoroughly comforted and strengthened, and only penitent for the desponding thoughts of yesterday. The next day he was secretly informed by the Abbess of Fontevrault of the king's wound, and how he was lying hovering between life and death. The tidings of Richard's

---

[1] This was a prediction which the author of the *Magna Vita*, writing in the time of John, had good reason to confirm in its truthfulness.

danger soon reached the other churchmen also, for
no more requests came to the bishop to sacrifice his
principles and propitiate the king.   During the
period in which Richard lingered after his wound
the timid canons were doubtless in a continual state
of excitement, but we may easily imagine that
Bishop Hugh's principal feeling would be one of
sorrow at not being able to be present at Richard's
side during such a critical time.   Hugh was asked
to preach and celebrate mass at Angers Cathedral
on Palm Sunday (April 11), the Bishop of Angers
being absent at Rome, and consented to do so.   As
he was on his way to the cathedral from the monastery where he was staying, on the Saturday
before Palm Sunday, he was met by a clerk
named Gilbert de Lacy, who told him of the king's
death, and that he was to be buried the next day
at Fontevrault.   The bishop, groaning aloud, determined to go at once to Fontevrault to watch and
pray.   He had now the opportunity of witnessing
the disturbed state of the country and the breaking
up of all law consequent upon the death of the king.
He heard at Angers how persons were openly and
violently attacked on the roads and plundered.   The
bishop's own servants had been thus treated, and
robbed of forty marks.   Hugh's timid friends represented how great danger he incurred by moving
about in the midst of this anarchy, and would fain
persuade him to remain at Angers until the new king
should have repressed the prevailing lawlessness.

Hugh, however, was by no means to be deterred by considerations of danger from doing what he held to be right.   He determined to attend Richard's funeral and pay him all the honour in his power.   " For myself, I say," said the bishop, " that he who is gone ever received me with honour, and never refused to hear me.   If he was indignant with me when absent, that was more the fault of the bad men who were around him than his own.   If I am robbed of my horse on my journey, I must needs go afoot, at any rate as far as my feet will carry me."   Accordingly he continued his journey to Fontevrault with only two attendants, but finding that Queen Berengaria, the widow of Richard, was at Beaufort, he turned out of his way to pay her a consolatory visit, with which she was much comforted.   The bishop arrived at Saumur on the Saturday evening, and there was very hospitably entertained and highly honoured.   The next morning, being Palm Sunday, he went early to Fontevrault, meeting the funeral procession just at the abbey gates.   After the funeral had been performed with great magnificence, the bishop retired to the abbey, where he remained for three days saying masses for the repose of the soul of the king.   Having thus carefully performed what he held to be his duty towards the dead monarch, Hugh was now to become acquainted with his successor, a man in every way different from his brother, and by no means so much to the bishop's mind as the bold king who was gone, and who, in spite of his money exactions and violence, it is easy to see was yet loved by the bishop. The Castle of Chinon, standing on its bold cliff above the Loire, is at no great distance from Fontevrault. It was here that Henry II. had died, and hence had been conveyed to Fontevrault for burial; and here John Lackland, on the fourth day after his brother's funeral, was received and acknowledged as king by the chief men who had been in attendance upon Richard. John had been in Brittany with his nephew Arthur, when he heard of Richard's death, on which he immediately hastened to Chinon. His first act after his arrival was to send an express messenger for the Bishop of Lincoln, whose presence and support, he felt, would be in the highest degree valuable to him. His title to the crown was bad.[1] His character was contemptible; and he had but a short time before been stripped of all his possessions by the king who was gone, as a punishment for his open and manifest treasonable practices in conjunction with the King of France. But now he had taken a solemn oath that he would execute the will of his brother, and that he would inviolably preserve the rights and liberties of his subjects. If, in addition, he could secure the support of one whose character gave him so great a weight as Bishop Hugh, all, he thought, would go well. The

---

[1] "It is clear," says Mr. Dimock, "that Hugh had no notion that John was usurping the sovereignty in prejudice to any prior rights of inheritance in Arthur. He at once considered him Richard's rightful successor after his recognition as such in Chinon."—*Introd. to Magna Vita*, p. lxii.

U

bishop came in answer to the summons. It is probable that he had not altogether made up his mind how to act, and he went to ascertain the opinions of the magnates who were assembled at Chinon. John met him on his way with the greatest professions of joy and devotion, and humbly besought him to remain with him and to accompany him into England when he should go thither. But this Hugh excused himself from doing. He consented, however, to go with him back to Fontevrault, where John paid a visit of respect to the tombs of his father and brother. Arrived at Fontevrault, and desiring to enter the choir of the church where the tombs were, John was refused admittance by the nuns, it being against their rules that any should enter there, without the presence of the abbess, who was then absent. Being now on his good behaviour, John dutifully submitted to this rebuff, meekly desiring the Bishop of Lincoln to beg the nuns for their prayers, and to make them acquainted with the magnificent gifts which he purposed to bestow upon them. To this Hugh, who knew John's character well, answered, " You know that I cannot endure anything that is false ; do not, therefore, make me promise anything with my lips that you do not most certainly intend to perform." John of course swore solemnly that he would perform everything, and the bishop then informed the nuns of his intentions, and entreating their prayers for him, and giving them his blessing, went away with the king. He gave him many good counsels as to piety,

mercy, and justice, and John declared that he would'
obey him in all things, and desired ever to have him
as his instructor.   Presently he showed the bishop
with great glee an amulet which he wore, and which
he declared was certain to confer power upon its
possessor.   Hugh, taking his text from this bauble,
exclaimed : " Put not your trust upon a senseless
stone, but upon the living and heavenly stone, our
Lord Jesus Christ.   Make Him the foundation stone
of your life and the anchor of your hope.   He is the
solid and living stone, who dashes to pieces those
who resist Him, and supports those who lean upon
Him, raising them up ever more and more towards
heavenly things."   Then pointing to a sculpture of
the future judgment over the porch of the church, the
bishop showed his companion the representation of
wicked kings being dragged down to torments, and
said, " Think on the woes which these are enduring,
and be wise in time."   To this John replied by
pointing to the good kings receiving the crown of
heavenly glory.   "These, my lord bishop," he exclaimed, " you ought rather to show me, for these, by
God's help, I mean to imitate."   For the next three
days nothing could exceed the humility and devotion
exhibited by this unbelieving profligate.   He humbly
bent himself before wretched beggars, desiring their
prayers, and laid himself out in every way to gain
the good opinion of the Churchmen around him.
But this hypocrisy could not last long.   The bishop
and the court had spent the remaining part of passion

week at Saumur, and here, on Easter Sunday, the king attended divine service. At the offertory, the king was accustomed to come forward to the altar to make his oblation, and the celebrating bishop to hold out his hand to receive it, and at the same time to be kissed by the offerer. John, attended by a large number of nobles, stood before the altar, and his chamberlain brought him the accustomed royal offering, viz. twelve golden crowns. These were placed in the king's hand, and Bishop Hugh, who was acting as celebrant, stretched forth his hand to receive them. But John, looking tenderly at the unfamiliar coins, began to chink them one against another and to play with them. Bishop Hugh, scandalised at having to wait so long, at length exclaimed, "Why do you look thus upon the money?" "Ah!" replied the king, "a few days since, if I had had those shining pieces in my hand, it would not have been to you that I would have given them, but to my own pocket. However, now you may take them." The bishop, struck with indignation and disgust, drew back his outstretched hand, and turning from him with contempt, pointed to the alms-dish. "Throw," he said, "what you have got into that, and be off." The bishop then ascended the pulpit and commenced his discourse upon the duties of kings, and upon the strict judgment which they would have to undergo. John was not very well pleased with the subject chosen, but he was still more exasperated by the length to which the bishop protracted his homily,

eager as he was to get to the feast, a part of the
day's ceremonial which he could fully appreciate.
Three times he sent a messenger to Hugh in the
pulpit requesting him to bring his sermon to an end, as
he was fainting from hunger. But Hugh utterly
disregarded these imperative hints. He went on
warming with his subject and rising up to such
eloquence, that all who heard him, with the exception
of the hardened prince himself, were greatly affected.
No sooner was the sermon completed than John
hastily departed to his banquet. He waited not for
the reception of the sacramental elements, for this
Christian privilege he habitually neglected, never, as
it is said, having received the holy communion since
he came to years of discretion. His life certainly
disqualified him from rightly receiving it, but bitter
indeed must have been the reflections of the good
bishop when, after all his exhortations, and after the
hopes excited by John's first days of power, he
witnessed his irreverence, and saw him carelessly turn
his back upon the altar and hasten away to his
unhallowed banquet. The bishop was glad, doubtless,
when he was relieved of the company of this man, in
whose doings he could find so little pleasure. The
royal cavalcade went on to Rouen, where, on the
octave of Easter, John was invested with the duchy,
displaying the same levity and irreverence in the
cathedral there, as he had shown at Saumur.[1] About a

---

[1] The lance, with the banner of the duchy, which conveyed the
investiture, was handed to him in the midst of the service by the arch-

year after these events, Hugh again met John in
France, when, at his request, he went to be present
at the ratification of peace between him and the King
of France.   Nor was this his last interview with him.
When the bishop, on the return from that journey to
the great Chartreuse, which is presently to be recorded,
lay sick almost to death in London, the king, who
probably respected him as much as he could respect
any one, paid a visit of condolence and sympathy to
the dying bishop.   On this occasion Hugh, who had
seen and known enough of John to be utterly hopeless
as to any amendment in him, showed but scant
respect for the royal presence, and gave but little
heed to the words which John addressed to him.
He gave him no more exhortations, feeling vividly
that it was but the casting of pearls before swine ; he
merely expressed a hope that the king would see
that justice was done in the settlement of his affairs,
and that he would not oppress or injure the church
of Lincoln.   That John was not irritated by this
want of deference, knowing, perhaps, how well it was
deserved, may be inferred from the fact that he afterwards took a personal part in Hugh's obsequies,
helping to bear his coffin upon his shoulders to its
resting-place in Hugh's noble pile at Lincoln.

bishop.   John, hearing the suppressed tittering of some of his wild
companions behind him, turned round to them and, with a broad grin,
shook the lance at them, as in sport.   The lance accidentally fell from
his hand, an omen, says the chronicler, of his speedy loss of the duchy,
and soon after of Aquitaine.—*Magna Vita*, B. v. chap. xi.

CHAPTER IX.

BISHOP HUGH'S VISIT TO THE GREAT CHARTREUSE.

THE bishop quitted King John immediately after the famous scene at Saumur on Easter Sunday (April 18, 1199) and set out on his homeward journey. On arriving at the town of La Flèche he went, as was his wont, into the church to say mass. He was accompanied by the Bishop of Rochester and by a large number of clergy, who were, no doubt, glad to travel with one who had shown himself so well able to cope with the great ones of the earth. Mass had not begun, the bishop was still occupied in vesting himself in the sacred garments, when breathless messengers arrived at the church, telling him that his horses and carriages had been seized by the town authorities, and that some of the pack-horses had been carried away by robbers. The terrified clerks who were Hugh's companions thought that under these circumstances the religious service might well be dispensed with, and that it was highly expedient that they should leave the church and go to look after their property. But Hugh was by no means of this opinion. Impressed as he was in so remarkable a manner with

the power of faith to protect and deliver in any and
every circumstance, it appeared to him that the
occasion required not the shortening of the religious
service, but the celebrating it with more devotion and
earnestness than usual.   No part of the ceremonies
ever used at the mass would he omit, and after having
fully completed his work, and while he was putting
off his vestments, the authorities of the town came
hastily to the church to apologise for the ill treatment
to which his retinue had been exposed, and to offer all
the amends in their power.   Hugh answered them
in his merry way, and accepting the safe conduct
which they offered, went forward with his companions
to Le Mans, where they were lodged in the Abbey
of St. Peter, outside the city.   Their adventures were,
however, by no means over.   The Countess of Brittany,
the mother of Prince Arthur, the direct heir to the
crown of England, though John had been permitted
by the magnates of the realm to step over his head,
was anxious by a bold *coup-de-main* to secure the
person of him whom she regarded as a usurper, and
thus obtain the succession for her son.   John had
arrived the night before at Le Mans, and the followers
of the countess, well informed of his movements,
made a sudden attack upon the town in the early
morning, thinking themselves safe of their prey.   But
the new king had perceived, immediately on his
arrival at Le Mans, that all was not right, and that
some plot against him was intended, and taking the
alarm, had slipped away from the town without being

perceived, so that when the retainers of the countess
rushed to the attack, they discovered that their opportunity was gone.   Their armed attack was sufficient,
however, to cause great terror in the place.   Brother
Gerard, one of the Bishop of Lincoln's clerks, rushed
frantically to the monastery to give the alarm.   The
bishop was saying matins, and Gerard would have
had him use at least short lections, and omit the
hymns, that he might haste away after his people
who had already fled.   But Hugh was not a man
who could be easily hurried in the face of danger.
Being absolutely without fear, and perfectly confident
in the divine protection, it was beyond the power of
the timid souls around him to cause him trepidation,
or to make him neglect any part of his usual work.
He tranquilly finished matins, sang the accustomed
hymns to the Most High, and then condescended to
inquire the cause of all this terror and perturbation.
Explanations and entreaties for him to fly were given,
but the bishop declined.   Presently the wisdom of
his hesitation appeared.   The Abbot of St. Peter's
arrived, and offered to be his guide by secure paths.
Hugh, accepting the offer, was safely conveyed to the
next town, while many of those who had fled away
in terror at the first alarm were seized and ill treated
by the followers of the countess.   The bishop left
behind him at the abbey part of his equipage, but
this was immediately sent after him by the orders of
the countess, who, like all others of that day, was
impressed with the holiness of the bishop, and desired

that she and her son might have a place in his
prayers. Meantime the bishop arrived safely at Sees,
and here, in spite of the restless eagerness of his companions to get safe out of the dangers of this
disturbed country, he would insist on turning out of
his way, and expending considerable time and toil in
paying a visit to an abbot in the neighbourhood, who
had a great reputation for sanctity.   We cannot
avoid thinking that Hugh, who was himself so
superior to the alarms and nervousness of his followers, must have felt somewhat of a malicious pleasure
in inflicting a little torture upon them.   Certainly
he must have been rather a trying person for a
nervous man to travel with.   The bishop appears to
have reached his diocese without further adventures,
only everywhere, both in Normandy and England, he
was greeted by the partisans of the clerical party
with congratulations and triumphal orations, having
boldly held his own against the violence and threats
of Richard, and saved his canons from the exactions
with which they were threatened.   But to get back
from the dangers and intrigues of courts to his own
diocese was no rest or holiday for the Bishop of
Lincoln.   Various and constant labours vexed him.
Innumerable suits demanded his decision.   The vast
needs of many thousands of souls waiting for the bread
of life pressed heavily upon him.   " The only difference," he used to exclaim bitterly, " between a bishop
and a temporal judge is this, that the latter has to
hear causes on certain fixed days, the former con-

tinuously.   The latter has time occasionally to look
after the affairs of his family.   The former has scarce
a moment to attend to the concerns of his own soul."
It was Hugh's misfortune to stand so high in the
estimation of both great and small, on account of the
acuteness of his discrimination, the perfect fairness of
judgment, and the fearlessness of his character,[1] that
everybody wished to get their cause heard by him.
A succession of popes found him most valuable to
them as a commissioner, and much as he might desire
rest, he was far too useful a personage to be allowed
to take it.   A request which he preferred to the pope
to be permitted to resign his see and again to enter
his beloved Carthusian retirement, was sternly and
even angrily refused.   He was condemned, like many
another good man, to forego the cherished wish of
his heart, and to work on to the end.   Chafe though
he might at these unwelcome duties, considering them
no work fitted for a bishop, and as not productive of
any spiritual profit, he yet could not avoid them.

After nearly a year spent in the hard and trying duties of his judicial and diocesan work,[2] Hugh

---

[1] His fearlessness as a judge is illustrated by a story related in the
Magna Vita of one Jordan de Turri, a very powerful citizen of London,
who had seized upon the property of some orphans, and when the
cause came on for hearing before the bishop, endeavoured to intimidate
him by coming with a huge retinue of armed men, and backed up by
the solicitations of numerous great people.   The bishop vanquished
him by threatening to report him to the Pope, and did justice to the
orphans.—*Magna Vita*, p. 300.

[2] "Portabat vero, sed in angaria, crucem hujusmodi actionum ; de
solius merito obedientiæ, excusationis potius suffragium, quam præmium
rei commendabilis expectans."—*Magna Vita*, p. 301.

was again summoned across the sea to attend on
the king.   His reputation for sanctity made him an
important personage in political combinations, and
especially in such a matter as the ratification of a
treaty of peace between the kings of France and
England, which now took place at Paris.   Finding
himself again in France, and somewhat advanced towards that which was the great object of his longing
desire, the bishop could no longer repress his eager
wish to visit again the scene of his early struggles
and triumphs, the Grande Chartreuse.   He had long
looked forward to the day when it might be permitted
to him to make this visit, not as a bishop still in
charge of a large diocese, but as one who had laid
aside the responsibilities and anxieties of the episcopal office, and sought again to become the simple
monk.   Such a complete deliverance was not to be
allowed him, but yet he would gladly welcome the
opportunity even for a short visit.   " It was no im-
pulse," says his biographer, " of flesh and blood, but
truly the prompting of the blessed Spirit, which
moved the bishop, at the beginning of the hot season,
to undertake so great a journey, proposing also, as he
did, to visit all the holy places and relics of the saints
near which he should pass on his way." [1]   There was
doubtless a vast difference between the bold spirit of
the bishop, and the feeble and somewhat querulous
nature of his biographer and chaplain.   The journey
across France, in early June, for a native of the land,

[1] *Magna Vita*, p. 302.

and one held in honour everywhere, when the object, also, was one which was specially dear to him, was nothing but a delight to the bishop, and we may be sure he did not indulge in complaints of its hardships. Abbot Adam has probably given his own colour to the bishop's feelings as to undertaking the journey. We wish we could think that it was of himself that he was writing, rather than of Hugh, when he gives us so many and such disagreeable stories as to the bishop's hunting after relics, his eagerness to possess the teeth or some bone of dead saints—an eagerness which occasionally led him into acts of positive dishonesty,[1] as though any means were justifiable for one to obtain possession of these coveted but somewhat nauseous treasures.   The caring for such things seems to exhibit the bishop to us in a point of view which contradicts some of the most prominent and admirable parts of his character.   He who could despise reputed miracles, could rise superior to the superstition of the necessity of receiving the holy communion

---

[1] As for instance, when at Meulan the sole part of the head of St. Nicasius, and at Fescamp of a bone of St. Mary Magdalen.   This relic was enclosed reverentially in silken coverings, and none of the monks had ever seen it bare, but Hugh, getting it into his hands, borrowed a knife of one of the attendants and cut off the covering. While the monks were in amazement at this proceeding, they were still further horrified at seeing the bishop put the bone into his mouth and bite off a piece of it, which he slipped into the hand of his attendant chaplain, bidding him carefully preserve it.   To the monks, who were greatly scandalised, he made a plausible excuse, but he kept the relics, which, even in a mercantile point of view, were most valuable property. At Peterborough, also, he contrived to cut off and secure for himself a tendon of the arm of St. Oswald.   What would have been done to a layman who ventured to do these things?

fasting, who showed in so many ways his superiority
to the opinions of his age, is yet represented as running with puerile eagerness, from one shrine to
another, and striving by every possible means to add
to his collection of the bones of the saints.   We
gladly turn from such matters to record some more
agreeable incidents.   At Paris, before his departure,
Hugh received an ovation from the scholars of the
University, and was honourably entertained by one of
them named Reimund, who was a kinsman of his own,
and who was afterwards promoted to be Canon of
Lincoln and Archdeacon of Leicester.   Here too the
bishop was also visited by Prince Louis of France,
who had just been betrothed, under the recent treaty,
to Blanche of Castille, the niece of King John, and
with the French prince there came also to greet the
bishop Prince Arthur, now in his 14th year, and who
boldly aspired to the throne which he considered to
be unjustly occupied by his uncle John.   Hugh's
counsels as to humility and dutiful submission to his
uncle were by no means agreeable to the proud-
spirited boy.   He received them with much contempt,
and showed a very different demeanour towards the
the bishop from that which was exhibited by the
French prince.   Louis listened with devout attention
to the bishop's words, and begged him to be kind
enough to visit the Princess Blanche, who was suffering
from some trouble, and to cheer her by his judicious
counsel.   This the bishop readily undertook to do.
Early in June (A.D. 1200) Hugh quitted Paris to

make his way to his beloved Burgundy.   At Troyes
he had a remarkable meeting.   A man approached
him in humble guise with piteous voice, demanding
mercy.   On being asked for an explanation, he
confessed that he had been once excommunicated by
the bishop, and was living in constant dread of the
fate which awaited him in the next world if the
dread sentence could not be done away with.   The
cause of his having incurred the bishop's displeasure
was as follows :—He had been a bailiff of the Earl of
Leicester at Brackley, and being in pursuit of a thief
who had made some depredations on his farm, he
had found himself baffled by the criminal having
taken sanctuary in the church at Brackley.   Pre-
suming, however, upon the station and importance of
his master, the bailiff had not scrupled to decoy the
malefactor from his asylum and to hang him.   The
summary process of hanging a man without trial,
and under the feudal power of a lord of the manor,
was not held to be a crime.   It was, in fact, the
ordinary proceeding of the day.   But to decoy a
man from sanctuary was held to be a very great
crime, and when Bishop Hugh heard of this, he
inflicted a very severe punishment.   He commenced
by excommunicating the whole party.   The rest
submitted and professed themselves ready to do
penance.   The bailiff escaped to his lord in Normandy,
and while his accomplices were stripped and scourged,
and compelled to disinter the body of the thief and
bury it in the churchyard with their own hands, the

bailiff, no doubt, thought himself secure under the protection of his powerful patron. He had probably indeed calculated that he would be specially acceptable to the Earl of Leicester from the fact of his lying under the censure of the Bishop of Lincoln, for there had been a notable quarrel between these two formerly as to the title to a farm near Leicester, in which the bishop had got the better. But misfortune had pursued the unhappy bailiff. His lord's favour had been turned from him and he had been dismissed, and tormented by remorse, he now determined to seek out the bishop and sue for his pardon. It was granted, but not on easy terms. A seven years' severe penance was prescribed, which the unfortunate bailiff gladly undertook to perform. From Troyes the bishop proceeded on his way, but thought it worth while to go three days' journey out of the direct road that he might visit St. Anthony's, near Vienne, where the relics of the famous hermit-saint, after many migrations, reposed, and where innumerable cures of the terrible scrofulous complaint, known as St. Anthony's fire, were said to be worked. Arrived at length at Grenoble, Hugh was received with the highest marks of respect and honour. Accompanied by the venerable bishop of the see, he went in solemn pomp through the streets of the city, which were decorated with flowers and silken banners, to the Cathedral of St. John Baptist, who was at once the patron saint of Grenoble and of the Carthusian order, and towards whom the Bishop of

Lincoln had a special devotion. Here he celebrated high mass with the greatest reverence, and preached to the people who crowded to hear their countryman, now become so famous for his saintly virtues. His words were so touching that tears were drawn from the eyes of all. Hugh spoke of the humble beginning from which he had sprung among themselves, and of the perilous height of responsibility which he had now reached, and he earnestly besought their prayers. To the joy and satisfaction which the bishop must have experienced from celebrating this service in the midst of the associations of his youth, there was added a special family pleasure. William de Avalon, Hugh's elder brother, brought to the bishop his son, seven years old, to receive from his saintly uncle the sacrament of baptism ; another brother of Hugh's, named Peter, was also present, and was particularly urgent that the boy should be called by his name. It was suggested, however, by the bishop's chaplain, the writer of his Life, who was present, that on the fête-day of St. John it was fitting that the young noble should be baptized by that name.[1] This suggestion was adopted, and the chaplain had afterwards the satisfaction of teaching the young John his letters, both which and the baptism seem to have been rather inordinately delayed. The happy day was concluded by a splendid

---

[1] Hugh's love for the name of John, his patron saint, is illustrated by a story told in the Metrical Life, which represents the bishop very indignant with a rustic who had brought to him a boy named John, desiring to have his name changed.

X

banquet given by the Bishop of Grenoble to Hugh,
his brothers, and the chief persons of the place; a
banquet which was so magnificent that, says the
writer of the *Magna Vita*, "you would say that the
elegance of the Burgundians surpassed even the
lavish luxury of the English."[1]   The next morning,
at break of day, the party started for the Great
Chartreuse.   The rough and mountainous road compelled them to go on foot the most part of the way,
and the bishop, spite of his sixty-five years and
portly size, set an example of activity to his retinue.
Arrived at length at the familiar solitude, he was
welcomed with the greatest respect and devotion by
the brethren.   They were desirous of treating one of
their order who had reached so great distinction
with special marks of deference, but Hugh was by no
means prepared to admit anything of the sort.   His
pleasure was to fall into the ranks once more, a
simple monk ; to put himself under the orders of the
prior ; to take a part in all the ordinary discipline of
the house ; to have his place in the choir at the
hours of service both by day and night, and to sleep
in his solitary cell without any attendant to wait
upon him.   Meantime the fame of his arrival spread
abroad, and visitors flocked from all parts to greet
one endeared to them both by old recollections and
the fame which he had since won.   Bishops, clerks,
and distinguished laymen came to salute him.   But
the visitors whom Hugh himself most delighted to

[1] *Magna Vita*, p. 312.

welcome were the poor inhabitants of the neighbouring villages, who remembered him when he had
acted as procurator of the monastery, and had often
experienced kindly aid at his hands.   These he
welcomed with affectionate embraces, nor did his
ever liberal hand forget to add more substantial gifts.
There was another class to whom the bishop gave
special attention.   These were the lay brethren
(conversi) who lived apart from the monks proper,
and many of whom were men who had filled high
positions in life, but who, to prepare themselves
for their end, had left their worldly callings to
practise the austerities of the strict rule of the
Carthusians.   With these Hugh remained part of
the time which he spent at the monastery, giving
them many exhortations, admitting also the neighbouring poor to the expositions and sermons which
he gave among them.   Among other good works
which the bishop performed when at the monastery,
he was able to bring about a reconciliation between
the Count of Geneva and the bishop of the see, who had
been carrying on a bitter quarrel for some fifteen
years.   At length, however, the time came when, in
the midst of these religious delights the bishop bethought him of his vast diocese in a foreign land, and
of the urgent want that it must needs be experiencing
of the presence of its head.   Before his departure he
made to the monastery a gift most precious in his
own eyes and in those of the monks—his reliquary—
containing a large collection of various sacred frag-

ments of departed saints; and having solemnly
invoked God's blessing on all in the Great Chartreuse
he "departed from them in body, though still present
with them in heart and in mind." After leaving one
beloved home of his earlier monkish days, Hugh prepared to visit the spot where he had commenced the
monastic life, and from whence he had migrated in so
questionable a manner to the Chartreuse. But first
he visited his natural home, the Castle of Avalon,
which lay in his way, and where his two brothers
William and Peter resided. Here he was welcomed
with joy, and these strenuous knights, says his biographer, stirred him up to contend more vigorously
for the faith and the privileges of Holy Church
against all traitors and opponents, however highly
placed. This exhortation, however, if it were given,
was certainly not needed. There was a great muster
at Avalon of all the neighbours, both high and low,
to greet the saintly bishop, who spent two days among
them. On the third day he went to Villarbenoit,
where was the canons' house in which he had first
professed. He made to the brethren the valuable
present of a Bible, which had cost him ten marks.
From thence he visited St. Maximin, where he had
formerly occupied a "cell" or detached station, when
he acted as pastor of the parish. The people
naturally flocked around him, and the aged declared
that they had always predicted the advancement of
their young pastor, from the wonderful gifts which he
had displayed when among them. Once more to

Avalon for a day, and then bidding adieu for ever to his beloved Burgundy, the bishop hastened on his journey back to England.   The record of his homeward way is most interesting, and illustrates very well the comfort and ease with which great ecclesiastics could travel in those days.   The abundance of monasteries scattered throughout the land, the universal hospitality with which they welcomed clerical guests, and especially such a guest as Hugh, far more than compensated for the badness of roads and the absence of convenient hostelries.   At Arveria, a Carthusian house, Hugh met the Bishop of Bellay, who had actually carried out the plan which Hugh himself had desired to put in practice, and had retired from his see to the convent from whence he had been taken, to spend the latter part of his days in the cloister.[1]   At Clugni, the famous monastery of Peter the Venerable, the opponent of St. Bernard, the most magnificent and polished establishment of the (so-called) reformed Benedictines,[2] Hugh was hospitably

---

[1] It appears that the good man had only been bishop for six years, and that he lived sixteen after retiring (Mr. Dimock's note to *Magna Vita*, p. 321).   The bishop at the meeting with Hugh showed rather a tendency to gossip, and was rebuked by Hugh for asking for the news *before the monks*.

[2] The magnificent monastery of Clugni, which ruled over 10,000 monks scattered in various daughter establishments throughout Europe, had greatly modified the strictness of the Benedictine rule.   The notion of the abbots of Clugni was that the monk was called to the life of Mary, not to that of Martha,—that every comfort and convenience was to be provided, that religious men might give themselves wholly to religious services and studies.   The wealth, the revenues, and the luxury of Clugni were something extreme.

entertained. Here he had the opportunity of seeing, perhaps for the first time, a type of monasticism altogether different from that to which he had been accustomed among the ascetic Carthusians, but so delighted was he with the order of the house, the splendour of the services, and the perfection of all the arrangements, that he declared that had he known Clugni before he knew the Chartreuse, he would have become a Clugniac.[1] One of the rules observed at Clugni was that at the first reception of a guest he should be taken into the hall and a portion of a devout book read to him, and that then he should be treated with all hospitality. Hugh was welcomed by the reading of a chapter from the works of St. Gregory, and then, having given all present his benediction, the prior and monks were free to devote themselves to their office of hosts. From the splendid abode of the black monks of Clugni Hugh went to the ascetic home of the white Cistercians at Citeaux. This order had not then been in existence for a very long period, and

---

[1] Hugh, though himself inured to the hard fare of the Carthusians, yet, as a matter of principle, strongly objected to the senseless self-murder of the ascetic, which was a thing which found no countenance at Clugni. Thus, he used to scold religious persons who practised these austerities, telling them that they were only exchanging one form of self-pleasing for another ; that, by the rejection of proper nourishment, first sleeplessness, then mental torpor, lastly, utter prostration and complete uselessness would be produced. He himself, he said, did not take meat, simply because the rule of his order forbade it. But no one was wise to make for himself such a rule. In his last illness the bishop did attempt to eat meat, but with very poor success.—*Magna Vita*, p. 343.

the first fervour of its discipline and rigour had not
passed away ; so that Hugh might here find something akin to his own Carthusians.   Whether the
peculiarity of this order, the manual field-work done
by the monks, pleased the bishop or not, we are not
told.   In fact, the writer of the *Magna Vita* being a
Benedictine, could scarcely be expected to say anything
to the credit of the Cistercians.   He informs us that
the reason of Hugh's visit was that he might celebrate
the feast of the Assumption, France being then
under an interdict.[1]   From Citeaux the party
went to Clairvaux,[2] the monastery of St. Bernard,
the place where, not long before, he had died in all
the odour of sanctity.   But not a word of St. Bernard,
though by far the greatest saint of that era, have
we in the *Magna Vita*, for was not St. Bernard a
Cistercian, and had he not read the Clugniacs and
Benedictines some rather severe lectures ?   At Clairvaux he met John, retired Archbishop of Lyons,
who had been anxiously desirous to see him.   He
was a man of great age and had left his see, retaining,
by permission of the Pope, all his archiepiscopal

[1] The Cistercians had the special privilege of exemption from an
interdict, and while other churches were shut, theirs were permitted to
be open.   This, during the interdict which prevailed so long in England
in the reign of King John, specially exasperated the king against them,
and brought grievous oppressions and troubles upon them.

[2] Clairvaux, which became the most famous monastery in Europe
from being presided over by St. Bernard, was founded from Citeaux,
but had numberless daughter churches of its own.   At one time all
these meditated adopting the name of Bernardines and founding a new
order, but this was given up, and they still remained Cistercian.

insignia.   Now, at Clairvaux, he occupied his time,
as he told Hugh, in meditations on the Psalms, from
which he found a constant supply of spiritual food.
From Clairvaux the bishop passed on to Rheims,
where, in the abbey of St. Remigius, he stayed two days.
Here was a fine collection of ancient manuscripts, and
the bishop, in examining them, reflected severely on
the moderns who were so far behind the ancients in
the labour they bestowed in copying, and who cared
not to read and learn from the manuscripts which had
been written for them with so much care and pains,
in days gone by.   Here too the bishop also saw
and reverenced the holy vessel said to have been
brought from heaven to St. Remigius by a dove, in
which the holy oil used at the coronation of the kings
of France was contained.   Journeying onwards towards the sea, Hugh reached St. Omers on September
5, intending to rest there awhile before venturing on
the Channel.   Here he determined to keep the feast
of the Nativity of the Blessed Virgin, as there was a
Cistercian abbey near, in which privileged institution
sacred rites might be had while the rest of the land
suffered the spiritual famine of an interdict.   To prepare himself physically as well as spiritually for his
sea voyage, the bishop caused himself to be bled,
having felt for some time a heaviness and weakness.
Immediately after his bleeding he found himself, as
might be expected, very much worse.   He was
obliged to take to his bed, and was bathed in profuse
perspirations, experiencing also complete loss of

appetite.   The bishop was no doubt suffering from a
low intermittent fever, which needed rest and nourishment to meet it, and to which the weakness produced
by bleeding would be the most valuable ally.   Yet
he roused himself to go on the eve of the festival
to Clermaretz, the place of the Cistercian abbey.
Dismissing his retinue back to St. Omers and
entering the infirmary of the abbey as any ordinary
stranger, Hugh trusted himself, though sick and
suffering, to the care of these good monks.   They
tended him with pious solicitude, and in the morning
he was able to perform mass, and then, without taking
any corporal refreshment, he returned back again to
St. Omers.   In spite of the fatigue, Hugh felt considerably better on his return, and the next day the
party proceeded to the port of Wissan, embarking for
England on the day following (Sep. 10).   The Blessed
Virgin was invoked for a good course and St. Anne,
her mother, for a favourable breeze, and under these
combined good influences the bishop made a rapid
passage, and landed at Dover with all good success.
Here his first care was to celebrate in the church
the mass of the Blessed Virgin, a part of his duty in
which he ever greatly delighted.[1]   His return was
welcomed by a crowd which craved his blessing.
Arrived at Canterbury, the bishop made his devotions
in the Cathedral Church, praying the longest and

---

[1] See *Magna Vita*, p. 235.   "Erat vero Sabbatum ; quo semper
die, si vacaret de beatâ Dei Genitrice Mariâ tam diurnum quam noc-
turnum officium solebat celebrare."

most devoutly at the shrine of St. Thomas, which had already thrown all the others in the church into the shade. The king's justices and many great men who were at Canterbury holding an assize, paid their respects to him, and expressed their hopes for the recovery of his health. He replied that he welcomed the chastisement of his Heavenly Father, and was ready to submit to His will. At Canterbury he rapidly grew worse. His eyesight almost entirely failed, and it was with great difficulty and suffering that partly on horseback and partly by water-carriage the bishop at length[1] reached his house at the Old Temple near London, where he felt that his earthly pilgrimage was rapidly drawing to a close.

[1] Sept. 18.

CHAPTER X.

ST. HUGH'S DEATH AND BURIAL.

ON arriving at the house belonging to the see of Lincoln
at the Old Temple,[1] the bishop at once took to his bed,
and while his friends were weeping around him and
offering up prayers that so great a pillar of the Church
might be spared to them, Hugh answered with his
wonted calmness : " Dear children in Christ, even if
absent in the body, I shall be present with you in
spirit : with regard to my health and my whole state,
may the will of my heavenly Father be done."   The
next day he said to the writer of his Life who was
attending upon him, " Those who love me after the
flesh, and those, too, who have a spiritual love
towards me, would desire my bodily life, of which,
truly, I have long been wearied, to be prolonged.
My thoughts are very different ; I see clearly to what
a lamentable state the English Church will soon be
brought.   It is better for me to die than to live and
see the realisation of the evils which are imminent.
Without doubt that must be fulfilled on the descendants of Henry II. which the Scripture has predicted,
viz.—' The multiplying brood of the ungodly shall

[1] See page 116.

not thrive,'[1] and 'The seed of an unrighteous bed
shall be rooted out.'[2]   The King of the French that
now is, shall take vengeance for his holy father
Louis on the seed of the evil-doer (Eleanor), who
left his chaste bed, and shamelessly united herself to
his rival the King of the English.   Wherefore that
Gallic Philip shall destroy the royal family of the
English, as an ox is wont to pluck grass down to its
root.   Three sons of his have been already cut off
by the French, two who were kings, one who was a
noble.   The fourth, who survives, will have but short
peace from them.   In two days will be the fête-day of
my master, the evangelist and apostle St. Matthew.[3]
That day was also the birthday of my episcopate ;
on it, as you know, I received episcopal unction.   I
have often been ill, but I have never received that
unction which we call the unction of the sick.   This
is the only one of the unctions in which I am
deficient, and this, if God will, to-morrow, on the vigil
of St. Matthew, I hope to obtain.   It is fitting that
I should prepare myself for it by a sincere and full
confession, that the venerable sacrament may be
worthily received and may have a blessed effect."[4]
Accordingly the bishop entered into a full and minute
confession of every error, neglect, and shortcoming
of his whole life, taxing his memory to recall them,
and astonishing those who heard him by the acuteness,

---

[1] Wisdom iv. 3.   [2] Wisdom iii. 16.
[3] Hugh was consecrated on St. Matthew's Day, September 21.
[4] *Magna Vita*, p. 332.

severity, and force, with which he denounced the most venial transgressions of which he had been guilty. The monk Adam who compiled the account was present, as were also Richard de Rolleston, the Dean of Lincoln, the Precentor, William de Blois, who was afterwards bishop, and Richard of Kent, the Archdeacon of Northampton. In his confession he constantly repeated, " My sins are simply sins without admixture of good ; my good deeds, if there be any, are not simply good, but mingled with many imperfections and much evil." Having finished his confession, which lasted the greater part of two days, and received absolution, the holy sacrament was brought to him. The bishop rose from his bed and went to meet it with bare feet, in his hair shirt, cloak, and hood, and falling before it with profound devotion, poured forth a long and earnest prayer. He commemorated the infinite benefits conferred by the Saviour of mankind on the human race, and devoutly offered thanksgiving for them all ; he commended himself, a miserable sinner, to His mercy; he besought His constant presence and continual help, even to the end, and that He would never leave him nor forsake him. Then, being refreshed with the divine banquet, and having received also the rite of extreme unction, he poured forth his thanks to God. " Now," he said, " let the doctors and the diseases settle it between them as they please ; I have not much anxiety about either of them. I have given myself to Him, I have received Him, and I will hold closely to Him, in

whom to abide is good, whom to hold is nothing less
than happiness, and with whom he who hath committed himself to His care is strong and safe for
ever."[1]   The bishop was now admonished to make
his will and settle his temporal affairs, an employment which was very irksome to him.   "The custom
of will-making," he said, "now prevalent in the
Church pleases me not.   I don't consider that I
have or ever had anything specially my own ; all
belongs to the church of which I was the governor.
But, in order to prevent Treasury exactions, I here
solemnly bequeath all my goods to Christ's poor."
He then ordered his stole to be brought, and having
put it on he anathematised all and each who should
oppose this bequest and rob the poor of that which he
left to them.[2]   The bishop had thus prepared himself
for that change which he thought imminent.   But it
did not come immediately.   For two months he lay
in his bed vexed by the fever, but resisting its attacks
by the strength of his constitution.   Every day, and
sometimes more than once in a day, he repeated his
confession, taxing himself with every little impatient
word or movement wrung from him by his malady.
His mind was wholly taken up with serious
subjects.   Matins and vespers were said daily by
his bed, and any neglect or hastening in the recita-
tions drew from him most severe reproofs.   He

---

[1] *Magna Vita*, p. 334.

[2] *Ibid.*   The bishop certainly carried this carelessness as to money
matters to an excess.   Thus he would never sit at his own exchequer,
nor look into his accounts.—*Magna Vita*, p. 301.

would even endeavour, as long as he was able, to preserve the accustomed posture, standing, sitting, or kneeling at the prescribed times ; thus preserving to the last that which had been the habit of his life; no business, however important, having been able ever to make him neglect the stated hours of service. Feeling himself already beyond the world, the bishop was careless about observing the ordinary conventionalities of life, and the great ones of earth were, in his view, nothing more than ordinary mortals. Thus, when King John came to visit him, he did not attempt to rise, or even sit up, to do him honour. The king spoke kindly to him and offered his services, but the bishop scarcely replied. He merely requested him to see to the performance of his will, and to have regard to the church of Lincoln, and then he bade him farewell. " He had," says his biographer, " long ago despaired of working any amendment in him, and he did not wish to spend his words in vain." Another visitor to his sick-bed was Archbishop Hubert. Something has already been said as to the way in which Bishop Hugh thought fit to carry himself towards his ecclesiastical superior, a prelate too much absorbed, indeed, in secular affairs, but still in many ways worthy of honour and respect. Their last interviews differed in no way from former ones, except that the Bishop of Lincoln showed a still more decided antipathy to the archbishop than before. The archbishop suggested that there were some sharp passages in the bishop's behaviour towards him which seemed to need pardon, and intimated that he was ready to give it if it were asked for. This roused the dying bishop to make an answer, which proves that the discipline of a sick bed had in no way changed his ancient character. "Yes," he exclaimed, "I have often angered you, I know, but I am by no means sorry for it ; rather I repent that I have not angered you much more. Should I be spared to converse with you again, be assured this shall be mended. I have often refrained, having more respect for you than for my heavenly Father, and in this I have not only sinned myself, but perhaps caused you also to sin."[1] It is probable that this rebuff brought the visits of Archbishop Hubert to a close. To Geoffrey de Noiers, the architect of the cathedral church which Hugh had been long rebuilding at Lincoln, he gave especial charge that, with a view to the congress which was about to be held in Lincoln, he should hasten the completion of the altar of St. John Baptist, which he desired should at that time be dedicated by the Bishop of Rochester. "I shall be present at the congress myself," said the bishop. "I had wished to perform the ceremony, but God has otherwise willed it ; I desire, therefore, that it may be performed before I come." He then expressed his wish that all those connected with the church of Lincoln should be zealous in their hospitable duties to the great people who were shortly to meet there. The attacks of the fever and dysentery now grew more violent,

[1] *Magna Vita*, p. 336.

and it was evident that the wasted form could not long hold out. A few days before his death he gave directions about his obsequies. " Prepare," said he, " some ashes which have been fittingly blessed, and spread them in the shape of a cross upon the bare ground ; upon this I desire that you place me when you perceive my last moments near. It is not the custom of our order, as of some, to put the hair shirt under the dying, who had previously been without it. We are content to keep that when dying, which we before used in life and health."[1] Marvellous, indeed, was the constancy of the man, and the complete triumph which his ascetic training and his iron will had given him over the body. During all his illness, amidst the heat and irritation of the fever, he had never suffered his hair shirt to be taken from him. Once or twice it had been changed when it had become saturated with perspiration and hard and twisted like a rope. It was found that the harsh and rough texture of the garment had caused cruel abrasions of the skin, but nothing would induce Hugh to be without the hair shirt. It was urged upon him that the rules of his order allowed this indulgence to the sick. " God forbid," he exclaimed ; " this garment does not hurt but soothes me, instead of wounds it gives me joy." With perfect calmness and composure the bishop gave the most minute directions as to the funeral rites. His chaplains were to send to Westminster for seven or eight monks

[1] *Magna Vita*, p. 338.

Y

to join with them in the office of commendation at the time of death, and also to apply to the Dean of St. Paul's for a strong body of the clergy of his church. After the service had been performed as solemnly as possible, the body was to be very carefully washed, which was to be done by the Monk Adam and one other regular whom he might select to help him, and they were to be waited upon by Peter, a lay-brother. Having been duly washed, the body was to be vested in the episcopal robes and to be placed in a coffin, to be conveyed to Lincoln. Arrived there, those who had the charge of the funeral were to be careful to see that all the vestments which the bishop wore at his consecration were placed upon him. He was to have on his finger the ring he had constantly used when a bishop, and as though he foresaw the translation of his body which would afterwards take place, and the inspection of his remains which would be made, and desired to guard against them, he ordered that he should be enclosed in two coffins, one of lead and one of stone, and most carefully sealed and closed. Before the altar of his patron saint, the forerunner of the Lord, he desired to rest, but yet not so as to occupy too prominent a place, but rather to be placed on one side near the wall.[1] These minute instructions had not been given without interruptions from paroxysms of terrible

---

[1] The Chapel of St. John Baptist, where St. Hugh was buried, is on the north part of the eastern side of the north-eastern transept of the cathedral, close to the entrance to the cloisters. A musical mass was afterwards celebrated here every day *primâ horâ*.

pain and suffering. Often the bishop would breathe forth an earnest prayer for rest. " O blessed are they," he would exclaim, "to whom the day of judgment shall give an unbroken rest." His attendants answered to this: " Such a day of judgment will be yours when you put off the burden of this flesh." " Not so," he exclaimed ; " this will be to me not a day of judgment, but of grace and mercy." The wonderful spirit, composure, and vigour of the man seemed, as the medical attendants said, to prevent his dying. It was remarked that his voice remained strong and vigorous to the last. He bade his attendants break off the reading of the passage of St. John's Gospel, which they were reciting, at the place where the Gospel to be used in the mass for the dead would commence.[1] At length, on Thursday, November 16, the end came. All his instructions were punctually carried out. The monks were fetched from Westminster and the clerks from St. Paul's. The cross of consecrated ashes was prepared. Compline was begun, and in the midst of it he gave the sign that he was to be laid upon the ashes. Just as the voices of the choir began to chant the Nunc Dimittis, the good bishop entered into the rest which he had so ardently desired.

After his death his directions as to his obsequies were carefully followed out. The office of commendation was sung, the body was washed and arrayed in

---

[1] St. Hugh's devotion to Scripture was so great that he never omitted his daily readings, even when riding. The four Gospels were always read through by him four times a year.

the pontifical vestments, and then taken to St. Mary's
Church, where, during the whole night, psalms and
hymns were chanted. On Friday morning (November
17) mass was celebrated, and then, on the recommendation of the physicians, the body was disembowelled, in order to fit it for so long a journey, the
bowels being buried in the Church of St. Mary at
the Old Temple. The body was then embalmed, and
without more delay the procession in charge of it set
out on its way to Lincoln. The bishop's reputation
as a saint had already become universal. Crowds of
people flocked around the procession, each striving to
obtain the privilege of touching the bier. Four
youths carrying lighted torches led the way, and it
was said that though the torches were unprotected,
and the wind sometimes high, and the rain heavy,
yet, nevertheless, the torches never went out. The
procession started on Saturday and reached Hertford
that evening. On the evening of Sunday, November
19, they reached Biggleswade, where a mighty crowd
of the inhabitants met them with every mark of
grief, one of whom having suffered from the press a
fracture of the arm, is said to have been miraculously
healed. On Monday they rested at the episcopal
manor of Bugden. On Tuesday they reached
Stamford. Here the crowd was so great that they
were long delayed, and it was dark before they could
arrive at the church, where the body was deposited.
Here horn lanterns were procured for carrying candles
in place of the waxen torches which had caused much

trouble. On Wednesday they arrived at Ancaster, a village on the old Roman road of Ermine Street, and about eighteen miles in a straight line from Lincoln. On Thursday, November 23, the sixth day, they arrived at Lincoln. The road descends by a steep hill from the high ground traversed by Ermine Street about a mile from the city, and here the cortège was met by a great and distinguished company. At their head was King John,[1] then holding his council at that city, and with him archbishop, bishops, abbots, and nobles in great numbers. The king and some of his chief nobles took the bier containing the sacred body on their shoulders and carried it for some distance. Before entering the city, however, they gave up the task to others, and here a scene of wild confusion ensued, all the great men striving and contending furiously with one another for the honour of taking part in the conveyance of the body. No sooner had any by dint of strength and activity reached it, than he was thrust away by others, and the whole way through the city and up the steep hill on the top of which Hugh's noble cathedral stands, the same violent struggles continued. The streets were almost knee deep in mud, in the midst of which the crowd jostled and fought, the Jews even, of whom Lincoln was always

[1] The writer of the *Magna Vita* says that William, King of Scotland, was there, and that he was remarkable for the grief which he displayed. It is certain, however, that the King of Scotland was not present, as he had left Lincoln early that morning.—See *Hoveden, Burton Annals*, etc.

a great resort, making themselves conspicuous by
their demonstrations of grief. Those who could not
succeed in reaching the bier threw money on it,[1] to
signify their respect, while others held up their hands
in the attitude of prayer, desiring the saint to inter-
cede for them. In all the churches of the city the
bells were tolled and psalms and hymns chanted, and
thus, in the midst of these violent demonstrations,
the bishop's body was conveyed to the door of his
cathedral church, then partially constructed. On
arriving there, it was taken on the shoulders of
archbishops and bishops,[2] and conveyed into the
choir of the church. Here, according to his directions, the body was arrayed in the vestments he had
worn at his consecration, and which he had always
preserved for this purpose. The ring, gloves, and
pastoral staff were placed on him; the face, after being
anointed with balsam, was exposed to the reverential
gaze of the crowd, which, with torches in hand, pressed
to do honour to the saint, and already began to
make costly offerings of gold and jewels. During
the night the lections for the vigils of obsequies were
read by the archbishop and bishops.[3]   On the next
day (Friday, November 24), the much-honoured body
was interred near the altar of St. John Baptist, on the
north side of the church, King John and his nobles,

---

[1] Copiosissima oblatio et magna donaria ei oblata sunt quamdiu
intumulatus super terram jacuit.—*Coggeshall, Martene,* v. 867.

[2] This is mentioned by *Hoveden* and the *Burton Annals;* the writer
of the *Magna Vita* does not mention it.

[3] *Coggeshall* in *Martene Coll.,* v. 867.

the Prince of Galloway, the Archbishop of Canterbury, the Archbishop of Dublin, the Archbishop of
Ragusa, and thirteen other bishops being present at
the ceremony.[1] The service for the dead had been
already sung in the church by the assembled bishops
when they first heard of Hugh's death. It was now
more solemnly repeated, the archbishops and bishops
reading the lections and singing the versicles and
responses. It was the remark of every one that he
who had been so zealous to do honour to the dead,
and had so often officiated at funerals, had himself
more honour done to him in his burial than any
other, having kings for mourners and archbishops as
ministering priests. King John is said to have
testified great compunction at the funeral, and to
have been moved by this bright example of monastic
virtue to be gracious to the abbots of the Cistercian
order, who, to the number of more than fifty, had
come to Lincoln to protest against his exactions.
This clemency, however, is, by some annalists attributed to another cause,[2] and it certainly was not of

---

[1] *Hoveden, Giraldus Cambrensis*, vii. 114, says nine. Before the
corpse was laid in the tomb, the vestments were grievously torn by the
excited crowd struggling to obtain a relic.—*Magna Vita*, p. 377.

[2] One of John's first acts on reaching England after his coronation
was to demand money from the Cistercian abbots in the North, which,
on the strength of their exemptions, they refused. Furious at this, the
king at once declared himself the bitter enemy of their order. The
chief abbots of the Cistercians accordingly came, by the advice of
Archbishop Hubert, to the king at Lincoln. John bade his attendants
tread them under the feet of their horses. This they did not venture
to do, and the night following the king had a terrible dream. He
seemed to be summoned before a stern judge, while the abbots stood

long duration. Thus, with every circumstance of honour, the good Bishop of Lincoln was buried, November 24, 1200. In the year 1220 he was, after due inquiry, declared a canonised saint by the Romish Church,[1] and in the same year his body was translated[2] from the chapel of St. John Baptist where it was first buried, to a place in the church more suited for the crowds of worshippers who pressed to his shrine. The worship of St. Hugh, indeed, in the north rapidly grew into almost as vast proportions as that of St. Thomas in the south, but the details of this, and of the miracles said to have been worked at his tomb seem to accord but badly with the simple and truthful character of the bishop. They will be found specified at length in another place.[3] Sixty years later his remains were again translated. At that time a magnificent presbytery had been built on to the east end of the choir of Lincoln cathedral, and in this gorgeous Gothic tabernacle, known as the angel-choir, a grand shrine, said to

round and accused him. Then the judge commanded that punishment should be inflicted on the king, and the shrinking culprit seemed to himself to be fearfully scourged. On awaking in the morning, he declared he could still feel the smarting of the blows. The terror of the dream at once led the king to seek pardon of the insulted abbots, and further induced him to propitiate the order by the founding of Faringdon and Beaulieu Monasteries.—*Coggeshall, Chron. Anglic.* in *Martene,* v. 861. *Dugdale, Monast.,* v. 682. *Annales de Melsa.*

[1] *Legenda of St. Hugh, Girald. Camb.,* vii. 187. *Annales de Waverleid. Ann. Monast.,* ii. 292. *Matt. Paris,* p. 309.

[2] *Chronicon Thomæ Wykes, Ann. Monast.,* iv. 61. There is somewhat of a doubt whether this translation did actually take place. See Appendix A.

[3] See Appendices A and E.

have been of pure gold, was prepared for the reception of the famous Lincoln saint. On the day of St. Faith, October 6, 1280, in the presence of King Edward I. and his queen, the remains of St. Hugh reached their last resting-place.[1] So died and was buried the famous Carthusian bishop of Lincoln, nor is he without a monument. The shrine where worship was once paid to him has indeed been dismantled and destroyed,[2] but the whole cathedral church of Lincoln is properly and specially his monument, inasmuch as it is in great part the work of his hands, the creation of his munificence, zeal, and taste. The church, rebuilt or restored by Bishop Alexander, had been very unfortunate. The latter part of the twelfth century was marked in England by several severe earthquakes. Roger de

---

[1] *Annales Monastici*, iii. 283, iv. 285, 286. A contemporary account of the translation is printed in *Girald. Camb., Op.*, vii. 220. It was done at the expense of Bishop Thomas Bek. There were present—King Edward and his queen, Edmund, brother of the king, the Queen of Navarre, his wife, the Earl of Gloucester, the Earl and Countess of Lincoln, the Earl of Warwick, the Archbishop of Canterbury, the Archbishop of Edessa, the Bishops of Lincoln, Bath, Ely, Norwich, Worcester, Llandaff, St. Asaph, Bangor, and the elect of Exeter. There were present also 230 knights. Two conduits were made to run with wine from nine o'clock till curfew time.

[2] In the reign of Charles II. a slab was placed by Bishop Fuller over the place where St. Hugh's shrine was supposed to have stood, which bears the following inscription :—

> Texerat hos cineres aurum non marmora, præda
>   Altera sacrilegis ni metuenda foret.
> Quod fuit argenti nunc marmoris esse dolemus
>   Degeneri ætati convenit iste lapis.
> Ingenium pietatis hoc est frugalis Hugonis.
>   Qui condit tumulum, condit et ipse suum.

Hoveden tells us that in the year 1179 the ground near Darlington was raised up to a great height, so that it had the appearance of a tower, and continued in this fashion the whole day, falling towards evening with a terrible crash and sinking into a pit of great depth; and under the year 1185 the same respectable chronicler informs us, that a "huge movement of the earth was heard almost through the whole of England, such as from the beginning of the world had not been heard in that land. Rocks were rent, stone houses fell. The mother church of Lincoln was split from top to bottom. This earthquake happened on the Monday after Palm Sunday, that is to say, on the 15th of April 1185.[1]" Hugh, therefore, when he succeeded the next year to the see of Lincoln, succeeded, in fact, to a dilapidated cathedral, which was, perhaps, in imminent danger of falling. Indeed, it is not at all impossible that the preparation for the restoration had begun before Hugh was made bishop, for the Dean and Canons of Lincoln were then a wealthy and energetic body. But if this were so, the Burgundian monk, who ever desired to be foremost in every good work, threw himself heartily into the vast undertaking, and under him a considerable portion of the structure, as it now stands, was brought to completion. The plan which he took to raise funds for the building of the cathedral was very judicious, and proved most valuable in operation. He instituted a fraternity or guild in his diocese, the

---

[1] *Hoveden*, pp. 332, 359 (Ed. Savile).

members of which bound themselves to raise funds
for the building of the church, and by their means
about 1000 marks a year were collected.[1] The most
detailed account which we have of the actual building
is to be found in the Metrical Life of St. Hugh; and here
the chronicler begins by telling us that the church was
lying in ruins when he was appointed to it, and was far
too small, but that Hugh applied himself to raising it
up from its ruin and giving it much greater size,
beauty, and grandeur. It is probable that the first
step was to pull down the injured fabric almost
entirely, except the western front. Then a considerable time would be required for the preparation
of materials and plans, so that the rebuilding did
not begin till about 1190, or perhaps two years later.[2]
When the work was commenced, the greatest energy
was displayed. The bishop himself worked with his
own hands at it, carrying cut stones in a basket, or
sometimes a hod of mortar on his head.[3] The part

[1] *Coggeshall*, in *Martene Collect*, v. 867. A testimony to the successful efforts of this fraternity will be found in the letters patent issued
in 1206 to William de Blois, the next bishop. See Appendix B.

[2] In two valuable papers on Lincoln Cathedral by Mr. Sharpe and
Mr. Dimock, the former puts St. Hugh's commencement at 1190, the
latter at 1192.—*Lincoln Architect. Soc. Transactions, s. a.* 1868.
Coggeshall says : "Novam quandam ecclesiam in honore Dei genetricis
elegante schemate in urbe illâ inchoavit, quæ omnes alias basilicas in
Angliâ quâdam structuræ excellentiâ superexcellere videtur, quam se
vivo sive mortuo consummandam esse prædixit."—*Martene Coll.*,
v. 867.

[3] In connection with St. Hugh's hod a supposed miraculous occurrence is related in the Legenda and the Metrical Life. A cripple supported on two sticks took the hod which had been used by the bishop

first commenced was the choir and eastern transepts.
The idea was to build the church in the shape of a
simple cross.   The rhyming Chronicler dwells on the
three main parts of the building, the foundation, the
walls, and the roof, and he tells us that the foundation
was buried in the very womb of the earth, the wall
with proud daring springs aloft to the clouds, the
roof reaches to the stars.   The shafts were so deftly
cut and joined that they seemed all one piece.   Some
were of white stone, some of the more precious
material of Purbeck, prepared for the tool, like
Hannibal's rocks, by the application of vinegar.
The spectator gazed uncertain whether it were jasper
or marble.   Around the solid column the pilasters
clustered as though in the dance.   Brightly polished,
they reflected every ray of light, and the veining
which they displayed from their natural formation
was far beyond anything that art could do.   Beau-
teously did these thousand columns adorn the choir,
and up above them the windows exhibited gorgeous
puzzles—the citizens of the heavenly city subduing the
tyrant of Styx.   Two circular ones, like to the sun
and moon, graced the transepts.[1]   Every part of the
building was a symbolism of some great truth and
holy doctrine.[2]   The worker of all these wonders was
the bishop, full of zeal and love for the House of God,

to carry mortar, and immediately his legs recovered their strength, his
sticks were thrown away, and he was a sound man again.

[1] Both these circular windows are later than St. Hugh's time, whose
work was arrested in the south-west transept.

[2] *Metrical Life*, Lines 833-965.   See Appendix C.

but the actual designer and executor of them was
Geoffry de Noiers, principal architect, a man, who,
spite of the French sound of his name, was a true
Englishman, and who produced work, altogether
different in character from the foreign work of
the period. Glorious indeed was the result of his
skill. "The dignified simplicity of the whole of
this work, and the vigorous boldness which marks
the design of all its details; its simply clustered
piers, the single vaulting shaft descending in their
front in an unbroken line from the clerestory to
the floor, their spreading capitals and projecting
foliage; the bold sweep of their overhanging bands
and circular bases; the deeply moulded pier arches
and vaulted ribs, and the tall single lancet windows;
above all, the largeness of treatment, and the vigorous
originality of conception, with which the entire design
has been conceived and executed, demand our highest
admiration, and place this grand work clearly at the
head, as well in point of time as in excellence, of the
works of the Lancet Period."[1] The choir and eastern
transepts were finished before St. Hugh's death,
and witnessed the grand ceremony of his funeral.

---

[1] Mr. E. Sharpe (*Transactions of the Lincoln Architectural Society*,
1868). Mr. Freeman, whose learned and artistic touch of all subjects
connected with history is truly admirable, says: "Before the twelfth
century had run its course, the fully developed pointed architecture had
reached its perfection, not at the hands of a Frenchman, at St. Denis,
but at the hands of the saint whom imperial Burgundy gave to England.
What Diocletian did at Spalato for the round arch, Saint Hugh did at
Lincoln for the pointed arch."—*Norman Conquest*, v. 641.

But the part of the church erected in his lifetime did
not represent the whole of the work done by St. Hugh
for the cathedral of Lincoln.   The entire church, as
it now stands, with the exception of the presbytery,
was conceived in the mind of Hugh's architect,
and gradually perfected under his successors.   The
" second " Hugh, who followed after a short interval
his more famous namesake, was a munificent con-
tributor to the work.[1]   Under him the nave was
nearly if not quite finished.   In the time of Grosseteste
the central tower was rebuilt, after having fallen, up
to a great portion of its height, and about 1256 the
eastern extension of the church by the angel-choir
was commenced.   Into this, on its completion, in
1280, as has been already said, the shrine of St.
Hugh was translated, and thus the good Burgundian monk, chosen in a happy hour to preside over the diocese of Lincoln, was the cause,
directly or indirectly, of the erection of the whole
cathedral church of Lincoln as it now stands, presiding in its magnificent proportions over the city beneath
it.   The monument is worthy of the man.   The
pure and fearless character of the bishop—his life
above the world—seem symbolised and expressed in
those faultless combinations of arch and buttress
which raise aloft and lift up to heaven the un-
equalled central tower of his church.   The strong
and solid mass speaks of the firm and unchanging
resolution of its founder's nature.   The beauty of

---

[1] See Appendix B.

the details suggests the amiable and pleasing graces
which adorned it.

> Go, stand beneath some minster tall,
> Stretching in aisles majestical,
> In branchings of embowering length,
> And avenues of pillared strength,
> Mid arch and pile aloft arrayed,
> And clustering reach of vaulted shade.
> Far stooping from the deeps of night,
> Truth stands reveal'd to mortal sight,
> Like the broad Heaven's o'er-arching span,
> Divinity encircling man.[1]

[1] Williams. "The Cathedral."

APPENDIX A.

WILLIAM DE BLOIS, 1203-1206—HUGH DE WELLS, 1209-1235.

To illustrate the progress of St. Hugh's great work in the rebuilding of the cathedral church of Lincoln, and at the same time to exhibit the causes which retarded it, it may be well to append a sketch of the lives of his two immediate successors. The first of these was William of Blois, who had been precentor of the church under Hugh, and one of those who had been with him in his last illness, and listened to his searching confessions. King John imitated the evil practice of his father, and kept the see vacant for upwards of two years after Hugh's death. He would indeed have consented to an election sooner had the chapter been willing to receive a nominee of his own, but they boldly stood out for the right of free election,[1] and at length, in the summer of 1203, were allowed to elect William de Blois. He was consecrated at Canterbury, August 24, by William, Bishop of London, and Gilbert, Bishop of Rochester, the primate then lying dangerously ill.[2] William was just such a successor as St. Hugh would have desired. The first act which is recorded of him is the establishment of a vicarage in accordance with the provisions of the Council

[1] *Roger de Hoveden*, p. 464 (Ed. Savile).
[2] *Ann. de Waverleia* (*Ann. Monast.* ii. 205) *Ann. Thomæ Wykes.* (*Ann. Monast.* iv. 51).

of Lateran (1179), which had been accepted as the law for
the English Church at a synod held at Westminster
(September 1200). This was probably the first vicarage
established in England. It was in the church of Pulloke-
shulle held by the canons of Dunstable.[1] Its effect was
to oblige the monastery to appoint a clerk to serve the
church regularly, and to secure to him a fixed payment out
of the revenues of the church. This arrangement was
vigorously followed up by the succeeding bishops of Lincoln.
During the episcopate of William de Blois happened that
strange and terrible scene in the cathedral of Lincoln
which is recorded in the *Waverley Annals.* On 24th
September 1205 William de Bramford, sub-dean, was slain
in the cathedral church before the altar of St. Peter by a
clerk who had been vicar of the church. The murderer
was instantly assailed by the servants of the sub-dean and
others, and torn limb from limb (*membratim discerptus*), his
remains being afterwards hanged up outside the city.[2] In
pleasing contrast to this savage business is another fact
which is recorded about this period, and which we may fairly
ascribe to the influence of Bishop William, who would be mind-
ful of St. Hugh's tender care for the leper. A royal letter
was issued to the justices, sheriffs, and bailiffs of Lincoln,
to let them know that the king had taken into his custody,
protection, and defence the house of the lepers in Lincoln,
and all their lands, tenants, and possessions; they are bid
" to guard, protect, and defend the said lepers of Lincoln
and all their property, as though it were his own, and not
to do them, or permit to be done, any molestation or injury,
and if anything has been abstracted from them to cause it
at once to be made good, and to prevent any one hindering
the friars or any clerks who preach for them and collect

---

[1] *Ann. Monast.* iii. 28.
[2] *Ann. Waverl. Ann. Monast.* ii. 257. *Rot. Lit. Claus.* p. 54.

alms for their use."[1] Equally zealous was Bishop William to carry on Hugh's great structural work. The cathedral church had advanced to about the east wall of the central transept at Hugh's death. By establishing the Guild of St. Mary, and thus making a provision for raising the funds for its continuance, Hugh had left a comparatively easy task to his successor. It was William's business to confirm and perpetuate this arrangement, and accordingly, he procured from the king letters patent, which recite as follows:—" The king, to all in the diocese of Lincoln, greeting. We give you manifold thanks for all the good deeds and alms which you have contributed to the church of Lincoln for the construction of the new work. How bountifully and how liberally you have given is shown by the noble structure of that building. But how incongruous would it be that such a noble work should be left unfinished! And inasmuch as it has not yet reached completion, and for its perfectness still needs your help and aid, we beg of all of you, we admonish and exhort you in the Lord, that, desirous to finish that which you have well begun, ye would, under the divine guidance, and for the honour of the glorious Virgin, patroness of the same church, and also for the love of us and at our request, allow an assessment to be made among yourselves of a contribution for the work of the said building, and would form a society to last at the least five years to further that purpose.[2] So that on account of the contribution of aids and alms for building upon earth an abode for so excellent a patroness, which you have lovingly given, ye may be received by her Son our Lord into the everlasting abodes."[3] Soon after the issue of these letters, Bishop William

[1] *Rot. Lit. Pat.* p. 54.

[2] St. Hugh's *fraternitas* had produced about 1000 marks a year. Probably the time for which it had been formed was about to expire. (*See Coggeshall, Martene,* v. 867.)

[3] *Rot. Lit. Pat.* p. 57 (Ed. Hardy).

died (May 1206) and once more there was a three years'
interregnum in the episcopate, during which time it is
hardly to be supposed that the building advanced rapidly.
The Rolls of Letters Patent supply numerous instances of
the exercise of patronage by the king in the diocese of Lincoln during this interval,[1] and the Close Rolls exhibit to us
the king taking advantage of the episcopal rights for his
own profit; e.g., the king writes to the guardians of the
bishopric of Lincoln to receive his huntsmen with twelve
couple of hounds, and to accommodate them at Sleaford.
The said custodians are credited for divers outlays, as for
£54 paid for 39 horses at Stow Fair, money spent upon the
king's pavilions, purchase of scarlet and blue cloth for the
wrappers of the horses, and £25 for 300 pigs.[2] At the
time of the interdict the king issued the letters patent following to provide for seizing on the revenues of the see :—
"The king to all his clerks and laymen of the diocese of
Lincoln, greeting.   Know ye that from Monday next before
the Feast of Easter,[3] we have committed to William de
Cornhull, Archdeacon of Huntingdon, and to Gerard de
Caville all the lands and property of the abbots and priors
and of all religious, and also of all clerks in the diocese of
Lincoln, who shall refuse from that date to celebrate the
divine offices, and we command you from that time forward to be obedient unto them as our bailiffs, and to give
credit to them in those matters in which they shall adver-
tise you in the meanwhile, as to our proper selves."[4] These
writs for the diocese of Lincoln were committed to the
charge of a clerk in the service of the chancellor,
whose name was Hugh Troteman. He was brother to
Joceline, Bishop of Wells, and himself archdeacon in that

---

[1] *Rot. Lit. Pat.* pp. 84, 85, 86, 99, 124.
[2] *Rot. Lit. Claus.* pp. 94 100.
[3] The interdict was published on Passion Sunday.
[4] *Rot. Lit. Pat.* p. 80. *Rymer's Fœdera*, i. 100.

diocese. The readiness of Archdeacon Hugh to perform the king's orders was probably interpreted by John to imply that he would take the side of the king as against the Pope in the great quarrel then proceeding, and as it was now of the utmost importance for the king to have some prelates on his side, John procured the election of Hugh to the see of Lincoln.[1] As the pressure of the interdict made it almost impossible to obtain Hugh's consecration in England, he was sent to Rouen for the purpose. In France the bishop-elect was speedily carried away from the side of the king to that of the Pope and the prelates, then in banishment. In utter disregard of the king, he made the oath of canonical obedience to Archbishop Stephen Langton, and was consecrated by him, December 20, 1209. Of course the king upon this immediately seized upon all the revenues of the see once more. It was not till July 16, 1213, that Bishop Hugh was able, in company with the primate and the other bishops, to come to England. During all these years, and amidst the troubles of the interdict and the exactions of the king, the Lincoln work must have stood still. John, however, now appears to be inclined to shower favours on Bishop Hugh. A large sum of money was assessed on the royal revenue as a compensation to the Diocese of Lincoln, of which 15,000 marks were paid.[2] The rent of eight pounds for the Stow Fair was remitted ; the manor of Wilsthorpe was given to the church for the annual payment of twenty pounds. The bishops had given to them the right of holding courts in all their manors, and of treating their woods as being under the forest laws. The king writes to Roger de Neville

---

[1] *Roger de Wendover, Flor. Hist.* iii. 231. *Matt. Paris, Hist. Maj.* p. 228. In the very first year of his episcopate an order from the Crown was issued for the canons of Lincoln to have the timber and the lead which they had purchased for the use of the church (*Rot. Lit. Pat.*)   [2] *Rot. Lit. Pat.* p. 106.

to restore to the bishop the money received from the abbey of Eynsham. He bids Brian de Insulâ furnish him with three hundred stags for Stow Park. He writes to the Sheriff of Nottingham to eject all trespassers on the bishop's lands.[1] But the advent of happier days for the see was not yet to be realised. The terrible troubles of the next few years, the struggle of the barons against the king, the French invasion, the manifold horrors of the latter days of John (probably the most troublous time ever known in England [2]), fell with peculiar intensity on the diocese and county of Lincoln. Gilbert de Gaunt and Robert de Roppel *subjugated* Lincolnshire, which implies that they pretty effectually despoiled it, and not much could have been left for the Guild of St. Mary. Then, after the momentary relief of John's death, followed the horrors of the battle of Lincoln Fair and the sack of the town. The clergy of the cathedral and the bishop (who was absent) being regarded as partisans of the barons, the cathedral church was spoiled, and the precentor, Geoffrey of Deeping, was robbed of eleven thousand marks of silver, probably the fund destined to be employed in the building.[3] When the bishop returned to his diocese, he was compelled to pay a fine of 1000 marks to the Pope and 100 to the legate before he could occupy his see. His vigorous administration, however, soon began to produce an amendment. In 1219 he was acting as itinerant justice or judge of assize.[4] His discipline was very severe. He reduced the unhappy Jews to such straits that the king was obliged to interfere to help them.[5] On other occasions, also, the

---

[1] *Ann. de Dunstapliâ, Ann. de Waverleiâ. Rot. Lit. Claus.* 138, 154, 179b, 180, 217, 399, 580, 581.

[2] Roger de Wendover says :—" Nundinæ cum mercimoniis cessabant, res venales in cæmeteriis agebantur, agricultura quievit, nec quisquam ecclesiarum limites egredi ausus est."—*Flor. Hist.* iii. 351.

[3] *Roger de Wendover, Flor. Hist.* iv. 25; *Matt. Paris, Hist. Maj.* 297. [4] *Rot. Lit. Claus.* pp. 387, 403, 405.

[5] *Rot. Lit. Claus.* p. 567.

royal clemency was exerted to persons in the bishop's prisons.[1] No doubt the gross disorders prevalent needed a strong hand to repress them ; and while the bishop exercised a vigorous discipline, especially over the monasteries, enforcing everywhere the settlement of vicarages, he also carried on building and restoration with zeal. The cathedral church again began to rise in the beauty conceived for it by the first Hugh. An episcopal house was built at Bugden ;[2] the hall of the Lincoln bishop's-house, begun by St. Hugh, was carried to completion.[3] Another hall was built at Thame.[4] The bishop's parks were stocked with deer.[5] A thoroughly energetic man was at the helm of the diocese. The monkish historian raises a wail, calling him "the persecutor of monks, the violent destroyer of canons and all religious men."[6] To Bishop Hugh of Wells we owe the earliest, probably, of those papers of inquiries which afterwards figure so frequently in the lives of mediæval bishops. As they curiously illustrate the state of the Church at this period, the questions are subjoined *in extenso* :—

Inquiries to be made by the Archdeacons in each of the Archdeaconries in the Diocese of Lincoln.

1. Are there any rectors or vicars of churches enormously illiterate ?

2. Is the Sacrament of the Eucharist carried to the sick with due reverence, and kept carefully protected, as is fitting?

---

[1] *Rot. Lit. Claus.* pp. 541, 563.   [2] *Rot. Lit. Claus.* 612, 638.

[3] The king gives to the bishop, " quadraginta fusta in forestâ nostrâ de Sirewood ab aulam suam Lincolniæ faciendam."—*Rot. Lit. Claus.* p. 606. John de Schalby says, "Hic aulam episcopalem a sancto Hugone inchoatam et coquinam sumptuoso opere consummavit."

[4] *Rot. Lit. Claus.* p. 399.   [5] *Rot. Lit. Claus.* pp. 505, 554, 616.

[6] *Matt. Paris Hist. Maj.* p. 409.

3. Are any in holy orders incontinent?

4. Are incontinent persons corrected by the archdeacon, and how often has each been corrected, and how?

5. Have any persons convicted and confessing incontinency bound themselves to resign their benefices, or to any canonical penalty, if they shall relapse, and has any of them relapsed after being so bound?

6. Are any beneficed persons in orders married?

7. Do any clerks frequent the churches of the nuns without reasonable cause?

8. Does any clerk in holy orders keep in his house a woman who is his relation, or any other of whom there is evil suspicion?

9. Are any given to drink, or frequenters of taverns, or usurers, or traders, or fighters, or remarkable for any vice?

10. Are any of them farmers, giving or taking in farm churches without the licence of the bishop?

11. Are any employed as sheriffs, or secular justices, or bailiffs to lay persons, to whom they are obliged to render account?

12. Do any rectors make agreement with their curates [1] that besides the pay they receive from the rector they shall receive annuals and tricennials? [2]

13. Do any parish priests not receive from the rector a sufficient sustentation?

14. Is any free land of any church given to laymen in farm?

15. Are the revenues assigned for lights or for any specified uses in a church, used for these specified purposes, or are they given to the uses of the rectors or vicars?

16. Are the parishioners in any place compelled both to communicate and make their offerings on Easter-day?

[1] Sacerdotes annui.

[2] The pay for celebrating a mass for the dead either yearly or tricennially.

17. Do any clerks frequent the performances of actors, or play at dice or bones ?[1]

18. Do any carry arms, or decline the tonsure and the dress which belongs to them ?

19. Have any more cures of souls than one without dispensation ?

20. Is any rector or vicar of a church the son of the last incumbent ?

21. Does any priest extort money for penance or the other sacraments, or enjoin penances which bring him gain ?

22. Do deacons ever minister the sacraments which belong to priests alone, or hear confessions ?

23. Is any rector or vicar not in the orders which his cure requires ?

24. Is any church not supplied with a clerk or clerks according to the means which the church possesses ?

25. Are markets, or plays, or secular law proceedings, held anywhere in consecrated places ?

26. Are graveyards everywhere enclosed, and churches decently built and adorned, and the vessels for use in them rightly provided and kept ?

27. Does any priest use vinegar in the celebration of Holy Communion ?

28. Do any beneficed men attend or give lectures on the secular laws ?

29. Is the canon of the mass properly corrected ?

30. Is there any custom of using tournaments with battering rams,[2] accompanied with Scot-ales, or of contending

---

[1] Taxillos.

[2] It would appear that propelling one against another large wooden rams raised on wheels was a common sport among the people, in imitation, no doubt, of the knights' tournaments, and was probably attended with considerable danger ; also that in the processions of the parishes made at Whitsuntide to carry their dues to the mother church (of which mention will be found in the *Life of Bishop Robert de Chesney*),

for precedence with the banner of the mother church in the procession?

31. Have these things been publicly forbidden in the different churches, according to the bishop's command?

32. Does any clerk or layman keep in his house a clerk's concubine, and where are the dwelling-places of these concubines?

33. Is any priest negligent in visiting the sick?

34. Are the vessels for containing the holy oil used for ordinary purposes?

35. Have any religious persons appropriated to themselves any tithes or churches without the license of the bishop, or some license of a similar character?

36. Are any churches now or at any time kept [by them] without a priest?

37. Do any vicars constitute themselves rectors or the contrary?

38. Do any illegitimate persons hold, without a dispensation, ecclesiastical benefices, or take holy orders?

39. Do any carry themselves as rectors or vicars who have not been instituted by the bishop?

40. Are the super-altars comely, and not used for grinding colours on them.[1] And what churches have not been consecrated?

it was the custom to have serious fights for the right of precedence. The Scot-ales were meetings of the clubs or guilds, partly convivial, partly also for organised social action. The bishops always very strictly forbade them.

[1] The super-altar was a small piece of metal or stone let into the wooden altar, which had been specially blessed, and on which the consecration took place. We find from various episcopal inquiries about this time that they were often detached and taken out for unseemly uses. The word sometimes signifies the ciborium or pyx.—*V. Ducange, s. v.*

41. Has any church been thrown down since the Oxford Council without the bishops' license?[1]

42. Are there any Jews living where they have not been accustomed to live?

43. Are adulteries and open crimes of the lay people properly corrected by the archdeacon, and are there any which have not been corrected?

44. Are there sufficient penitentiaries of the bishop in each archdeaconry?

45. Do any laymen persist in standing in the chancel with the clerks, and what priests have been ordained not in the diocese, and by whom have they been licensed for officiating?

46. Does any priest celebrate twice in the day except in the allowed cases, and does he celebrate in his proper character, and in his own church?[2]

47. Has any retreat for anchorites been made without the consent of the bishop?

48. Does celebration take place in any chapel without the consent of the bishop?

49. Do any monks or other religious dwell in granges or other possessions of theirs, and how do they carry themselves, and of what character are they?[3]

The zeal of the second Hugh in the building of the cathedral is attested in the Metrical Life of St. Hugh (see Appendix B), and further appears in his will, dated at Stow, 1233, in which he gives one hundred marks to the fabric of the church in Lincoln, and all the timber throughout his

---

[1] The Oxford Council had strictly ordered that no churches should be used without being consecrated.

[2] This seems to inquire whether a priest celebrates as the parson of the parish which he holds, or as a vicar or chaplain of some other parish or religious house.

[3] *Wilkin's Concil.* v. i. pp. 627-8.

episcopal estates of which he might die possessed, reserving
to his successor the right of redeeming this for 50 marks.[1]
Hugh had the pleasure of witnessing the canonisation of
his famous namesake in 1220, and his first translation,[2] and
also of seeing one of his canons, Richard the Chancellor,
elevated to the primacy.   He died Feb. 7, 1235, and was
buried in the cathedral, Feb. 10.   He was succeeded by
the famous Grosseteste, whose constant patron he had been.

APPENDIX B.

THE ACCOUNT OF THE BUILDING OF THE CATHEDRAL.
FROM THE METRICAL LIFE OF ST. HUGH.[3]

Pontificis vero pontem facit ad Paradisum
Provida religio, provisio religiosa ;
Ædificare Sion in simplicitate laborans
Non in sanguinibus.   Et mirâ construit arte
Ecclesiæ cathedralis opus ; quod in ædificando
Non solum concedit opes operamque suorum,
Sed proprii sudoris opem ; lapidesque frequenter
Excisos fert in calatho, calcemque tenacem.
Debilitas claudi, baculis suffulta duobus,
Illius officium calathi sortitur, inesse
Omen ei credens ; successivèque duorum
Indignatur opem baculorum.   Rectificatque
Curvum, quæ rectos solet incurvare diæta.[4]

---

[1] See Will of Hugh de Wells in Appendix to *Girald. Camb.* vol. vii.

[2] *Chronicon Thomæ Wykes, Ann. Monast.* iv. 61.

[3] Edited by Mr. Dimock from British Museum and Bodleian MSS.
in 1860.   (Lines 833-963.)

[4] This story of the cripple being cured by carrying St. Hugh's hod
is also told in the *Legenda of St. Hugh.*

O gregis egregius ; non mercenarius iuimo
Pastor ! Ut ecclesiæ perhibet structura novella.
Mater nempe Sion dejecta jacebat et ærcta,
Errans, ignara, languens, anus, acris, egena,
Vilis, turpis : Hugo dejectam sublevat, arctam
Ampliat, errantem regit, ignaram docet, ægram
Sanat, anum renovat, acrem dulcorat, egenam
Fecundat, vilem decorat, turpemque decorat.
Funditus obruitur moles vetus, et nova surgit ;
Surgentisque status formam crucis exprimit aptam.
Tres integrales partes labor arduus unit :
Nam fundamenti moles solidissima surgit
A centro, paries supportat in aera tectum :
Sic fundamentum terræ sepelitur in alvo,
Sed paries tectumque patent, ausuque superbo
Evolat ad nubes paries, ad sidera tectum.
Materiæ pretio studium bene competit artis—
Nam quasi pennatis avibus testudo locuta
Latas expandens alas, similisque volanti,
Nubes offendit, solidis innisa columnis,
Viscosusque liquor lapides conglutinat albos,
Quos manus artificis omnes excidit ad unguem.
Et paries ex congerie constructus eorum,
Hoc quasi dedignans, mentitur continuare
Contiguas partes ; non esse videtur ab arte,
Quin a naturâ ; non res unita sed una.
Altera fulcit opus lapidum pretiosa nigrorum
Materies, non sic uno contenta colore,
Non tot laxa poris, sed crelro sidere fulgens,
Et rigido compacta situ ; nulloque domari
Dignatur ferro, nisi quando domatur ab arte ;
Quando superficies nimiis laxatur arenæ
Pulsibus, et solidum ferri penetratur aceto.
Inspectus lapis ipse potest suspendere mentes

Ambiguas utrum jaspis marmorve sit ; at si
Jaspis, hebes jaspis, si marmor, nobile marmor.
Inde columnellæ, quæ sic cinxere columnas,
Ut videantur ibi quamdam celebrare choream,
Exterior facies, nascente politior ungue,
Clara repercussis opponit visibus astra :
Nam tot ibi pinxit varias fortuna figuras,
Ut si picturam similem simulare laboret
Ars conata diu, naturam vix imitetur.
Sic junctura decens serie disponit honestâ
Mille columnellas ibi : quæ rigidæ, pretiosæ,
Fulgentes, opus ecclesiæ totale rigore
Perpetuant, pretio ditant, fulgore serenant.
Ipsarum siquidem status est procerus et altus,
Cultus sincerus et splendidus, ordo venustus
Et geometricus, decor aptus et utilis, usus
Gratus et eximius, rigor inconsumptus et acer.
   Splendida prætendit oculis ænigmata duplex
Pompa fenestrarum ; cives inscripta supernæ
Urbis, et arma quibus stygium domuere tyrannum.
Majoresque duæ, tanquam duo lumina ; quorum
Orbiculare jubar fines aquilonis et austri
Respiciens, geminâ premit omnes luce fenestras.
Illæ conferri possunt vulgaribus astris ;
Hæc duo sunt unum quasi sol, aliud quasi luna.
Sic caput ecclesiæ duo candelabra serenant,
Vivis et variis imitata coloribus irim ;
Non imitata quidem sed præcellentia ; nam sol
Quando repercutitur in nubibus, efficit irim ;
Illa duo sine sole micant sine nube coruscant.
Hæc descripta quasi pueriliter, allegoriæ
Pondus habent.   Foris apparet quasi testa, sed intus
Consistit nucleus : foris est quasi cera, sed intus
Est favus ; et lucet jucundior ignis in umbrâ.

Nam fundamentum, paries, tectum, lapis albus
Excisus, marmor planum, spectabile, nigrum,
Ordo fenestrarum duplex, geminæque fenestræ,
Quæ quasi despiciunt fines aquilonis et austri,
In se magna quidem sunt sed majora figurant.
    Est fundamentum corpus, paries homo, tectum
Spiritus ; ecclesiæ triplex divisio.   Corpus
Terram sortitur, homo nubes, spiritus astra.
    Albus et excisus castos lapis et sapientes
Exprimit ; albedo pudor est, excisio dogma.
    Marmoris effigie, planâ, splendente, nigellâ,
Sponsa figuratur, simplex, morosa, laborans.
Recte nimirum designat simplicitatem
Planities, splendor mores, nigredo laborem.
    Illustrans mundum divino lumine, cleri
Est præclara cohors, claris expressa fenestris.
Ordo subalternus utrobique potestque notari ;
Ordine canonicus extante, vicarius imo.
Et quia, canonico tractante negotia mundi,
Jugis et assiduus divina vicarius implet,
Summa fenestrarum series nitet inclita florum
Involucro, mundi varium signante decorem ;
Inferior perhibet sanctorum nomina patrum.
    Præbentes geminæ jubar orbiculare fenestræ,
Ecclesiæ duo sunt oculi ; rectèque videtur
Major in his esse præsul, minor esse decanus.
Est aquilo zabulus, est Sanctus Spiritus auster ;
Quos oculi duo respiciunt.   Nam respicit austrum
Præsul, ut invitet ; aquilonem vero decanus,
Ut vitet ; videt hic ut salvetur, videt ille
Ne pereat.   Frons ecclesiæ candelabra cæli,
Et tenebras Lethes oculis circumspicit istis.
    Sic insensibiles lapides mysteria claudunt
Vivorum lapidum, manualis spiritualem

Fabrica designat fabricam ; duplexque refulget
Ecclesiæ facies, duplici decorata paratu.
Introitumque chori majestas aurea pingit :
Et propriè propriâ crucifixus imagine Christus
Exprimitur, vitæque suæ progressus ad unguem
Insinuatur ibi. Nec solum crux vel imago,
Immo columnarum sex lignorumque duorum
Ampla superficies, obrizo fulgurat auro.
Astant ecclesiæ capitolia, qualia nunquam
Romanus possedit apex ; spectabile quorum
Vix opus inciperet nummosa pecunia Cræsi.
Scilicet introitus ipsorum sunt quasi quadra
Porticus ; interius spatium patet orbiculare, ·
Materiâ tentans templum Salamonis et arte.
Si quorum vero perfectio restat, Hugonis
Perficietur opus primi sub Hugone secundo."

APPENDIX C.

Letters of St. Hugh to the Archdeacons of his Diocese and the Dean and Chapter.[1]

I. Hugo, Dei gratiâ Lincolniensis episcopus, omnibus
archidiaconis et eorum officialibus per diœcesim Lincolniensem constitutis, salutem et Dei benedictionem. Cum
cura et solicitudo Lincolniensis ecclesiæ, quam Deo authore

---

[1] These letters, of which several MS. copies exist, are transcribed
from the *Lives of the Bishops of Lincoln*, by John de Schalby (*Girald.
Camb.* vii. 200). They are merely formal documents, and were re-
issued verbatim by the next bishop, but as they are the only complete
letters remaining of St. Hugh, it has been thought best to print them
entire. For the occasion of their issue see page 205. For a notice of
the Whitsuntide Processions, see *Life of Robert de Chesney.*

regendam suscepimus nos admodum invitent ea quæ hactenus minus bene fuerint ordinata in meliorem statum redigere, canonicorum ibidem Deo jugiter famulantium commodo imposterum profuturo invigilare tenemur. Movemur siquidem, nec illud clausis oculis de ætero præterire possumus, quod etiam vos movere deberet et non movemini, ad quos specialius pertinet cura et solicitudo ecclesiæ Lincolniensis, quod cum tantam habeat filiorum multitudinem, ipsi eam contemnunt, ut saltem eam semel in anno secundum consuetudinem ecclesiæ nostræ, quæ in aliis ecclesiis episcopalibus celebris habetur, eam in propriâ personâ vel de suis facultatibus condignas oblationes mittendo, negligant visitare. Quod quidem ex negligentiâ clericorum, potius quam laicorum simplicitate, novimus accidisse. Quocirca universitati vestue authoritate quâ fungimur præcipimus, quatenus decanis, personis, presbiteris per nostram diæcesim constitutis, in virtute obedientiæ injungatis, ut in singulis parochiis singuli capellani fideles sibi commissos ad hoc sufficienter authoritate nostrâ inducant, quod de singulis domibus aliqui in festo Pentecostes ad locum consuetum et processionibus destinatum singulis annis satagant convenire, oblationes condignas in remissionem peccatorum suorum, et in signum obedientiæ et recordationis matris suæ Lincolniensis ecclesiæ afferentes. Jubeatis etiam ut singuli decani personis presbiteris sibi commissis auctoritate nostrâ præcipiant quatinus universi attentâ solicitudine provideant, ut, nominibus parochianorum suorum seorsim notatis decanis cum clericis nostris in Penthecoste ad hoc destinandis sciant per nominum adnotationes fideliter respondere qui secundum mandatum nostrum ut filii obedientes vel venerint vel miserint, et qui mandatum nostrum transgredientes venire vel mittere neglexerint.

II. Hugo, Dei gratiâ Lincolniensis Episcopus dilectis in Christo filiis decano et capitulo Lincolniensis ecclesiæ, salutem et Dei benedictionem. Quia fervens habemus desiderium ut ad honorem Dei et beatæ virginis genetricis ejus Mariæ, in ecclesiâ Lincolniensi debitâ celebritate singulis quibusque temporibus prout decet, devina celebrentur; ad id competenter et commodè prosequendum, canonicorum et vicariorum ibi residentium utilitati prospicere cupientes, tibi decano et canonicis residentiam facientibus, et si decanus fuerit absens, tibi subdecano et canonicis residentiam facientibus, hanc potestatem indulgemus; ut nostrâ authoritate licitum sit vobis coercere omnes canonicos qui non faciunt residentiam, per detentionem præbendæ suæ, ut idoneos vicarios loco suo constituant, et de communi consilio canonicorum residentium eis honestam et sufficientem sustentationem provideant. Præter ea vobis etiam hanc facimus indulgentiam ut omnes injustos detentores communæ vestræ et omnes qui vel hominibus vel possessionibus ad eandem communam pertinentibus, injuriam molestiam vel gravamen intulerint, liberum sit vobis ecclesiasticâ censura coercere et in eos usque ad condignam satisfactionem canonicam justitiam exercere. Salvo in omnibus jure episcopï et ejus potestate. Nec liceat archidiaconis, decanis, vel aliis officialibus Lincolniensis episcopatûs, excommunicutos aut interdictos a vobis absolvere citra mandatum episcopi vel vestri. Præcipimus autem ut sententia, quæ a vobis lata fuerit, per archidiaconos vel decanos, seu alios episcopatûs officiales executioni mandetur.

These letters are said, in John de Schalby's *History*, to be *granted* (concedi) to the chapter, and like letters were also *granted* by Hugh's successor, William de Blois. They are perhaps not the composition of the bishop, but of the chapter, having a direct bearing upon the revenues of the cathedral church.

APPENDIX D.

THE following account of the *Cultus* and art representation of St. Hugh has been kindly contributed by the Rev. Christopher Wordsworth, M.A., rector of Glaston.

It may be thought interesting by some who have found pleasure in reading the life of St. Hugh of Lincoln to know something of the way in which his memory has been observed. Some notes are accordingly appended to show how it has been treated (I.) in the services and calendars of the Church, and (II.) in works of art.

I. The numerous miracles which were reported to have occurred at the tomb of St. Hugh show at once that his memory was not forgotten after the remarkable interest of his funeral. He became indeed a saint by common consent, as one Archbishop (Thomas Becket) had already done, and another (Edmund Rich) was about to do.

The prerogative of enrolling the names of the dead in the catalogue of saints was now monopolised by the see of Rome, which demanded the allegation of miracles, attested by authority in the case of each holy person departed, for whom the title of saint was claimed.

Although St. Hugh had shown great devotion for sacred relics, he had discouraged the popular craving after miracles. Nevertheless, after his death, the proceedings for his canonisation took what had then become the usual course.

Upon a request of the Archbishops of Canterbury and York, with others, Honorius III. sent (27th April 1219), a commission to the former, and to John, Abbot of Fountains (afterwards Bishop of Ely), to inquire and report upon miracles which were alleged to have been wrought at St. Hugh's tomb.[1]

The result appears to have been that the pope sent two bulls, dated 17th February 1220, the one to the bishop, chapter, clergy, and people of Lincoln, to the effect, that their petition for Hugh's canonisation having been long deliberated on, he was duly enrolled among the saints (on the satisfactory report of the commissioners upon the miracles which were too numerous to enumerate); and notice was thereby given to them to keep the anniversaries of his death, or depositio, on the 17th November. The second bull was addressed to the faithful generally. It ordered the translation of his remains, and granted a relaxation of forty days of penance to all who should visit his tomb within the octave of his actual removal, or on an anniversary of that his translation.[2]

In the same year (1220) another bull was addressed to the Bishop of Lincoln, specially ordering the translation of his remains. It is probable that a translation took place then, but there is no certain record of it. The great and famous translation of St. Hugh took place on October 6, 1280, after the building of the beautiful angels' choir, in which the new shrine for his body was constructed, and on the day of the consecration of Bishop Thomas Bek to the See of St. David's. It was attended by King Edward I., his Queen, his brother Edmund, and his wife, the Queen of Navarre, ten bishops, 230 knights. The body of the saint was placed[3] in a rich shrine supported on marble, and his head was put back in the chapel of St. John the Baptist

[1] *Bullarium Romanum*, iii. 208 (ex Registr. Vatic.)

[2] Both of these bulls were printed by Mr. Dimock in an appendix to *Giraldus Cambrensis* (Master of the Rolls Series), vol. vii. pp. 243-4, 245-6. The latter is also in *Bullar. Rom.*, iii. 213.

[3] See Appendix F, *Girald. Camb.* vol. vii.

(the northernmost of the two chapels on the east side of the north transept of the choir), where he had been laid at first.   A marble slab with a Latin inscription, erected by Bishop Fuller in the reign of Charles II., marks the place where the shrine probably stood.

His head was stolen about the year 1364, for the sake of the jewels and precious things with which it had been adorned, but being found in a field (watched by a raven), it was again enriched by John de Welburn, treasurer of Lincoln.   There is preserved in the chapter muniment room at Lincoln a volume (entitled *Apertura capitis et feretri St. Hugonis*) containing the audit of offerings made at St. Hugh's shrines twice a year, for about two centuries.

A narrative was drawn up of the life of St. Hugh, with the authorised account of miracles done by him, and those performed at his tomb.   Several MS. editions of this narrative have been collected by Mr. Dimock, and are given in appendix D to his 7th vol. of *Giraldus Cambrensis* (Master of the Rolls Series).   These were, no doubt, read in part in the service, and in part in the refectory of the convents of St. Hugh's order, the Carthusian.

The lessons read at matins on St. Hugh's Day were such as he would perhaps have most approved.   They correspond generally with chapters i.-xi. inclusive of the Legenda in Mr. Dimock's appendix, though certain passages are transposed in a way different from the arrangement both of the text and of the notes of the Rolls edition. The passages thus read in choir relate no miracles after his *burial ;* though certain signs after his death are recorded. The 12th to the 16th, and the greater part of the 17th chapter of the Legenda, as printed by Mr. Dimock, appear never to have been read in church.

The feast of St. Hugh of Lincoln, 17th of November (which is retained in the reformed calendar, and was held memorable by Protestants as the accession-day of Queen Bess, and as the occasion of a great "no popery" demonstration in 1679),[1] was especially regarded by his own order. St. Hugh is the only saint, beside scriptural saints and the four doctors, whose commemoration was made for the Carthusians a *festum capituli quoad monachos* (*hoc est, cum collatione in capitulo monachorum*), according to their *Antiqua Statuta de Sacris Ritibus*.[2] In these Statutes his name occurs more than once as follows :—

§ 27. Conceditur domui Carthusiæ, ut possit facere festum capituli de domno Ugone Lincolniensi episcopo, qui fuit monachus Carthusiæ.

§ 42. Ordinamus quod festum B. Hugonis episcopi Lincolniensis, quondam monachi Carthusiæ et prioris de Vitam [Witham] cum candelis et capitulo per totum ordinem celebretur. Conversi ab operibus non cessent, nec habeant capitulum. In primis vesperis super psalmos dici debet antiphona prima de laudibus, *Ecce Sacerdos magnus*, et ii. responsorium, et missa sine symbolo.

Probably the earliest existing *office* for the commemoration of St. Hugh is to be seen in the latter (though in *date* the earlier) of two imperfect MS. missals which are bound in one volume in the Lincoln chapter library.[3] This missal or sacramentary seems to have been written about the date of St. Hugh's death.[4] It appears to be a unique variety

---

[1] Scott's *Dryden*, vi. 222 ; Hone's *Every Day Book*, i. 1488-1490.

[2] Migne *Patrol.* cliii. 1132, 1134. (*Cf.* Du Cange, *Glossar.* s. v. *Festa Capituli* et *Festa seu Solemnitates Candelarum*.) The *Hugo* or *Ugo* mentioned in § 28 of these ancient Carthusian Statutes, and in 1102 from those dated A.D. 1261 (*Patrolog.* cliii. column 1140), was probably St. Hugh of Grenoble, whose feast was on the 1st of April.

[3] Classed in the MS. catalogue, A. 5.5.

[4] It is difficult, judging from the writing, to date it later than his canonisation (1220), or St. William's (1226).

of the Gregorian liturgy, corrected (when it was a new book) for the use of some English convent, perhaps Carthusian. An appendix contains, after the votive masses, the subjoined office for St. Hugh (followed by others, *de S. Wilhelmo Confessore; pro defunctis; de S. Luca evangelista,* differing from that in the Sanctorale ; *pro benefactoribus,* etc).

The words in square brackets are supplied from the mass of St. Hugh as it was printed *in extenso* in the Sarum Missal of 1531, etc.

De S. Hugone [Ep. et Conf.]

[*Officium.* Statuit ei Dominus. } *de Communi unius*
Psalmus. Misericordias Domini. } *Confessoris et Pontificis.*]

Coll. ["*Oratio.*"] Deus qui beatum Hugonem confessorem tuum atque pontificem eminentia meritorum et claritate signorum excellenter ornasti : concede propicius : ut ejus exempla provocent et virtutes illustrent, Per.[1]

[*Epistola.* Dilectus Deo. ⎫
Gradale. Domine praevenisti. ⎪
V. Vitam petiit. ⎪ [*haec Omnia de Com-*
Alleluya, V. Justus germinabit. ⎬ *muni.*]
Sequentia. Alma cohors. ⎪
Evangelium. Videte, vigilate. ⎪
Offertorium. Veritas mea.] ⎭

Secreta. Oblata tibi munera quaesumus Domine beatus Hugo confessor tuus et pontifex prosequatur : et meritis ejus adjuti per ea gratiam et gloriam consequamur, Per Dominum.

[*Communio.* Beatus servus quem (*de Communi*).]

Postcommunio. Nostrae servitutis obsequia quaesumus

---

[1] Here followed "memories" (or commemorations) of S. Anianus, bishop, and of the Martinmas octave. From the fact that the *Crede Mihi* contains a special caution, prescribing the commemoration of St. Anianus "in die S. Hugonis," we may perhaps be right in inferring that St. Hugh engrossed at least his share of the attention of the Sarum clergy on his day at the close of the fifteenth century.

Domine Deus beatus Hugo confessor tuus et pontifex tibi
reddat accepta : ne sacramenti caelestis effectum reatus
noster a nobis excludat, Per etc.

From the Arbuthnott missal, which was written in 1491,
we gather that this mass for St. Hugh's Day had penetrated,
with other Sarum customs, to the diocese of St. Andrews,
in Scotland. In the calendar of this Scottish missal the
respect shown to the Lincoln saint is, that six out of nine
lessons at matins were devoted to his history, and three
to the commemoration of St. Anianus. *Proper* lessons
being thus provided for the three nocturns, there was no
recourse had to the *common* "exposition" of the Gospel.
Moreover, we may observe that no account was taken in
our insular uses of Gregory Thaumaturgus, the saint
who occupies this day in the Roman calendar. In the
calendars at present in use among Roman Catholics in
England and Ireland, this saint's day has been transferred
to make way for St. Hugh's.

St. Hugh had no place in either the Parisian or the
continental Roman service books.

A few remarks must be added regarding the breviary
office for St. Hugh's Day, according to Sarum use.

The principal collect for the day was the one given
above from the missal; then were added commemorations
of St. Edmund the Confessor, St. Anianus, and St. Martin.
The lessons of the second nocturn referred to St. Anianus
of Orleans : but those of the first and third nocturns were,
according to the great breviary of 1531, the long extracts
from the Legenda, as has been already indicated. However, according to the shorter lectionary of the portuary of
1518, the three first lessons *de proprietate*, consisted of an
abbreviated edition of the longer lessons, 1-3, with a bit
from the commencement of the 7th, and three tiny lessons
for the third nocturn are extracted from what were the long

7th and 9th lessons in 1531. Thus the Sarum lessons of 1518 recorded no miracles of St. Hugh. It may be added that the three proper lessons in the modern Roman breviary in use in England, are extracted *ex Adamo auctore coætanco*, and are almost severely historical.

In the Aberdeen breviary (1510) the festival is of St. Anianus, with only a commemoration of St. Hugh, and the three middle lessons corresponding with the lessons 1-3 of the Sarum portuary of 1518.

No regard was paid to St. Hugh in the York or Hereford Use.

The Pie of Sarum Use provided specially for the observance of the day as a double feast, with vespers *in the diocese of Lincoln*, even when it fell on Saturday, so that the first vespers of the Sunday gave way to it.[1]

Mr. Dimock, when he wrote, was unable to find that the order for keeping the anniversary of St. Hugh's translation was observed. There is, however, evidence that it was kept *in some places*, probably at Lincoln and throughout the diocese, if not at St. Quethiock in Cornwall, or if there were any other churches dedicated to the honour of St. Hugh of Lincoln.

The Directorium Sacerdotum of 1495 has indeed only " de S. Fide, Invitatorium simplex, tres lectiones " as the rule

---

[1] The two following extracts will show liturgical students what was the Sarum order for St. Hugh's day when it fell (1) on a common week day, and (2) on a Saturday, according to the pie or directorium as it was printed by Wynkyn de Worde in 1496-9.

" *Sextum B.* Feria quinta, de S. Hugone, ix. lectiones. Mediæ lectiones de S. Aniano, memoria de Octavis [S. Edmundi Conf.]

" Ubi festum S. Hugonis est duplex, tunc memoriæ de S. Aniano et de Octavis erunt sub silentio."

" *Sextum G.* Sabbatto de S. Hugone, ix. lectiones. Mediæ lectiones de S. Aniano et memoria de Octavis. Vesperæ erunt de Dominica et memoria de S. Hugone, et de Octava Trinitatis et processio fiat."

for the 6th of October ; but in the pie in the breviary of
1531 provision is made for the Translation of St. Hugh on
October 6th *ubi celebratur*, with nine lessons, none of which
are taken from his legends.

II. While the memory of St. Hugh was thus preserved
in the services of the mediæval Church of England, it would
not be unreasonable to suppose that he must have become
a favourite subject for the painter.

Yet so general had been the destruction of glass, frescoes,
and other pictures, that Mr. Dimock, writing in 1860, was
unable to refer to more than two pictures of St. Hugh
beside the glass in the rose window of the north transept
of Lincoln Cathedral.[1]　The pictures mentioned are these :
one by L. Van Leyden in the Boisserée Gallery, a woodcut
of which is given in Mrs. Jameson's *Legends of the Monastic
Orders* (p. 136, 2d ed.)　The other, by J. W. Van Assen—
a wood-engraving, I presume—is in the Munich Gallery.
Both of these must date about 1520 or 1530.　(Dimock's
Introd. to *Metrical Life* of St. Hugh, p. xxiii.)

There is, however, another picture (a small panel painting in the possession of the present Bishop of Lincoln),
which represents the saint walking by a brick wall in his
white Carthusian dress, a red and gold mitre on his head,
and a light pastoral staff reclining on his shoulder.　The
portrait is not idealised.　The character of the staff, and
the carriage of the body, which is somewhat more slender
than the sturdy saint is said to have worn, have suggested
the observation that the painter may have had a bronze
effigy before him, like Caius Gabriel Cibber's William of
Wykeham in later times.

In this picture not only is the faithful swan represented

[1] *i.e.* A representation of his funeral.　There is a copy of this by
Messrs. Clayton and Bell, in the Gilbert Memorial window in the
chapter-house.

(as it is in the aforementioned pictures), but the saint holds in his right hand the chalice with the miraculous manifestation which is alleged to have been seen by a monk when the bishop was celebrating mass. It may remind us of the characteristic rebuke which he on one occasion administered to one whose carnal mind relied on " such a sign of his unbelief." [1]

Across the picture are printed the words S · HVGO · LINCOLNIE · EP. It was purchased in Cologne, in which place it was said to have been painted about 1550 by Ant. Woensan Von Worms.

In the catalogue of the small but choice gallery at Antwerp the two following pictures are contained :—

No. 278. Miracle de St. Hugues de Lincoln. Par Quellin (Érasme) le jeune, 1607-1678.

No. 292. Miracle de St. Hugues, évêque de Lincoln. Par Quellin (Joan-Érasme), 1634 (?).

These pictures were perhaps painted for the Chartreuse de la Sainte Catherine au faubourg du Kiel près d'Anvers, the miraculous preservation of whose founder, Duncard or Gratian Molenaer, the younger Quellin painted (No. 279), as the elder did St. Bernard receiving the religious dress (No. 288).

Of late years St. Hugh has been represented in the chapels of the two great colleges of Cambridge, in a window at Trinity, and on the painted roof at St. John's; in the former he and Grosseteste are represented in contiguous lights, supporting Lincoln Cathedral by the parts which they severally built; at St. John's College Hugh is repre-

---

[1] *Magna Vita*, v. iii. of v. iv. See also the abbreviated *Life* reprinted in Migne's *Patrol.*, cliii. 1036 (where Pez remarks, "Inde data occasio S. Hugonis cum parvulo supra calicem repraesentandi.") See also *Patrol.*, cliii. 1041. *Bene* (*inquit*) *in nomine Domini habeant sibi signa infidelitatis suæ.*

resented in pontificals, attended by the swan. There has been a window, also, in his memory, executed by the present vicar of St. Quethiock, in Cornwall, for the church of that parish, which was dedicated to St. Hugh.

———

In the church of Clee, Lincolnshire, lately restored, there is an inscription, testifying to the fact of its dedication by St. Hugh, as follows :—

h′ ECCL′IA : DEDICATA : ECT :
IN : hONORE : SCĒ : T′NITA
TIC : ET SCĒ : MARIE :
VIIī . Ñ ſDARTII
A : DÑO : hUGONE . LINCOLN
ĒSI : EP̃O : ANNO : AB :
ĬCARNACI
ONE : DÑI : M : C : XCII +
TĒPORE : RICARDI : REGIS

The inscription on the restored church is as follows :—

+ Hæc Ecclesia a Domino Hugone Lincolniensi,
  Episcopo dedicata A.D. MCXCII. tempore Ricardi Regis
  Instaurata est ab Alexandro Gulielmo Thorold Grant Thorold
  Armigero et inaugurata est a Domino Christophoro
  Lincolniensi Episcopo Die XX Mensis Julii
  Anno ab Incarnatione MDCCCLXXVIII. tempore
      Victoriæ Reginæ —— Laus Deo.

APPENDIX E.

APPENDIX E.

MIRACLES ATTRIBUTED TO ST. HUGH.

*From Giraldus Cambrensis, the Metrical Life, and the
Legenda Sancti Hugonis.*

IN writing the life of St. Hugh, and endeavouring as far as
possible to make it an historical biography, but little notice
has been taken of the miracles attributed to him. These,
however, are of themselves interesting, as illustrative of the
times, if for no other reason. A short summary of them is,
therefore, here appended. Those mentioned in the *Legenda*
were investigated and accepted by the Papal commissioners,
Archbishop Langton, and the Abbot of Fountains.

Very few miracles are recorded of St. Hugh in his life-
time, probably because of his own strong objection to statements of this kind and his attributing the craving after
miracles to a want of faith.

THE MIRACULOUS CHALICE.

The first probably is the miracle of the chalice at Bugden. A certain clerk had been warned by visions three
times repeated to go to the Bishop of Lincoln and denounce
to him the miserably corrupt state of the clergy, that he
might strive to amend it. He does so, and finding the
bishop about to celebrate the Mass of the Blessed Virgin,
enters the church and attends the service. At the elevation
of the chalice by the bishop, he beholds with amazement the
appearance of a young child rising out of and above the

chalice, surrounded by a divine radiance. This he sees also at the second elevation of the chalice [1] (*Magna Vita*).

THE ALCONBURY CHILD.

When the bishop was once at Alconbury, near Huntingdon, a man brought a young child of a year old to him, praying him to deliver him from a terrible affliction. A fortnight previously he had given to the child for a plaything a splinter of a broken ploughshare. The child had endeavoured to swallow it and it had stuck in its throat. The bishop compressed the child's throat with his hand, and signed it with the cross and gave his blessing. This was on the Friday. On the following Sunday the child disgorged the iron (*Legenda and Metrical Life*).

THE MAD SAILOR OF CHESHUNT.

Hugh, one Sunday about the end of the year 1198, passing through Cheshunt in Hertfordshire, was requested to visit a sailor who for three weeks had been in a state of raging madness. Hugh, descending from his horse and entering the house, found the poor wretch with his head fastened to a post and his hands and feet to stakes fixed in the ground. Having made over him the sign of the cross, and holding his right hand open near his mouth, Hugh repeated the beginning of St. John's Gospel, " In principio erat verbum." This having no effect, Hugh consecrated some holy water, and having sprinkled the sufferer, gave his blessing to all and went away. The man fell asleep, and waking the same day free from madness, lived sane for years afterwards (*Magna Vita, Legenda, Metrical Life*).

---

[1] This is related in *Magna Vita* alone (p. 235). With regard to the chalice, it is said that it had been brought by some monks to the bishop to be consecrated by him ; and the bishop had admired its beauty, and had read a severe lecture to certain rich clerks, who were then present, as to their neglect of their churches and their own luxurious expenditure.

THE DELIRIOUS CITIZEN OF LINCOLN.

A man affected by a fever became suddenly delirious, so that he could scarcely be held by eight men. His friends, thinking him mad, get him into a carriage and take him to the cathedral to the bishop. Hugh sprinkles him with holy water. He lies as one dead. He is again sprinkled, and gradually recovers his health and senses (*Legenda, Metrical Life*).

THE CRIPPLE WHO USES HUGH'S HOD.

The bishop had personally worked at the building of the cathedral, carrying a hod of mortar on his head. A cripple, supported on two sticks, takes up this hod and uses it. Upon which his lameness is instantly cured (*Legenda, Metrical Life*).

THE LINCOLN BOY WITH THE TUMOUR.

A certain matron of Lincoln, named Lauretta, had two sons, of whom one had from his infancy a huge tumour on his side. Fearing for his life, his mother brought him to St. Hugh. The bishop placed his hands on the tumour and sent her away. The child was soon afterwards completely cured (*Legenda*).

THE BOY WITH THE JAUNDICE.

The other son of the same mother soon afterwards had the jaundice. He was brought to the bishop, and in like manner cured (*Legenda*).

THE MIRACULOUS TORCHES.

On the way, when the bishop's body was being conveyed to Lincoln, though it was tempestuous and very wet, the torches were never extinguished. If one were blown out, the others immediately rekindled it (*Metrical Life, Legenda*).

THE KNIGHT OF LINDSEY WITH A CANCER.

A knight of Lindsey had been for three years afflicted with a cancer in his arm. When Hugh's body was brought to Lincoln, he went to it and laid the diseased arm upon the corpse. It was immediately healed (*Giraldus, Legenda, Metrical Life*).

THE RURAL DEAN OF MARNHAM.

The rural dean of Marnham was afflicted with a terrible abscess in the face, and thought his end near. In the night he had a vision which bade him mould an image of St. Hugh, which would restore him to health. He proceeded to do this, and before the head of the figure was finished his disease was healed. His son was in a dying state, and the father besought for his restoration through the merits of St. Hugh. This was immediately granted (*Giraldus*).

THE WICKED WOMAN OF KEAL.

At Keal there was a woman who, in spite of the exhortations of the Abbot of Flaye for the strict observance of Sunday, would needs work on Saturday evenings; upon which her hands both became contracted. She goes to the tomb of St. Hugh, but the penitentiary will not believe her story and sends her away. She then visits the shrine of St. Thomas, and is warned in a vision to go back to Lincoln. Visiting again the tomb of St. Hugh, she recovers the use of her hands (*Giraldus*).

THE DROPSICAL WOMAN OF BEVERLEY.

A woman of Beverley had been afflicted with the dropsy for three years. She visits the tomb of St. Hugh, and remains there for a month praying in vain. Then she determines to visit the shrine of St. Thomas. But before departure she again visits St. Hugh, and is immediately healed [1] (*Giraldus*).

THE BLIND MAN OF LINCOLN.

A blind man, who was a pensioner of the chapter of Lincoln, came to the tomb of St. Hugh, and prayed earnestly on the vigil of Pentecost. On Whitsunday his sight was completely restored (*Giraldus*).

THE MADMAN OF ANCASTER.

A madman of Ancaster was brought to the tomb of St. Hugh bound with chains. For seven days he was kept there, prayer being continually offered for him. He is restored to sanity and returns to his home (*Giraldus*).

THE BLIND MAN OF STUBTRE.

A blind man of Stubtre was brought to the tomb of St. Hugh, and after passing the night there in devotion, on the morrow received his sight (*Giraldus*).

THE CRIPPLED GIRL OF WIGFORD.

A girl called Alice, of Wigford, saw in the night a vision, in which she seemed to be carried up into the air and then to be plunged into deep water. In the morning she was found to be absolutely paralysed and unable to stand. Carried by her friends to the tomb of St. Hugh, she was healed.

THE DUMB BOY OF WIGFORD.

A boy of Wigford, who was the pensioner of Adam the Mayor, had his tongue firmly fastened to his palate, so that he could not eat or speak ; was carried to the tomb of St.

---

[1] In these two miracles the rivalry between the great saints of the south and the north is plainly perceptible.

Hugh. Passing the night there in devotion, he saw in a vision the bishop, accompanied by a lady of incomparable beauty, to whom the bishop made request that she would heal the afflicted youth. Upon this she touched his tongue with her finger, and the boy waking, found himself healed (*Giraldus*).

THE DUMB BOY OF POTTERGATE.

A dumb boy of Pottergate, having heard of this miracle, goes to the tomb and passes the night in prayer. At matins, being thrust aside by the crowd of people pressing to the tomb, he exclaims aloud, "Thank God and St. Hugh, my speech is restored" (*Giraldus*).

THE MAD GIRL OF WIGFORD.

A girl of Wigford fell into madness about Michaelmas. On the feast of St. Simon and St. Jude she was taken to the tomb of St. Hugh. She remained there till All Saints' Day. During the whole night preceding the festival she disturbed the church by her loud cries. At dawn, when a crowd of worshippers came to the tomb, she was found to be perfectly healed. She was afterwards placed by the dean as a nurse at the hospital (*Giraldus*).

SIR JOHN BURDET.

John Burdet, a knight of Lindsey, was struck with paralysis in his right arm at the assault of Montauban. After a year he returns to Lincoln, and offers a waxen image of the diseased arm at the tomb of St. Hugh. Gradually he recovers his health (*Giraldus*).

THE BLIND SEMPSTRESS.

A needle-woman of Lindsey was struck blind in a storm, and obliged to turn beggar. She remains about the cathedral for a year. At Whitsuntide she keeps vigil at St. Hugh's tomb, and falls asleep with her head in one of the circular apertures of the tomb. She sees a vision of St. Hugh celebrating Mass at the adjoining altar of St. John Baptist, and on waking finds she has recovered her sight (*Giraldus*).

JOHN DE PLUMGARD.

A man named John of Plumgard, suffering from a cancer in his thigh, was healed by applying mortar from the tomb to his sores (*Giraldus*).

THE KNIGHT MILO.

A knight named Milo incautiously using his arm after blood-letting, an inflammation and swelling set in, and he was given up by the doctors. He prays to God and St. Hugh, and is healed. Upon which he offers a waxen effigy of the arm at St. Hugh's tomb (*Giraldus*).

THE YOUNG PARALYTIC MAN.

A young man struck with paralysis was unable to move any of his lower limbs, and lay for four years and a half bedridden in the hospital. He then became a beggar in the Minster-yard. On the vigil of the Assumption, at the tomb of St. Hugh, he sees a vision of the bishop and two clerks celebrating Mass at the altar of St. John Baptist. The bishop bids him rise, and he finds himself restored to his power of motion (*Giraldus, Legenda*). [The *Legenda* mentions five other cases of the cure of paralysis, which it seems unnecessary to specify.]

THE BEDRIDDEN MAN OF LYNN.

A man confined to his bed at Lynn sees a vision of St. Hugh, who bids him go to the cell of a certain recluse called Margaret Graves, at Worksop Abbey. He is to mention a certain secret to the prior, who will procure his restoration to health. He goes in a cart and does as he is commanded. He is immediately healed (*Giraldus*).

THE INSENSIBLE BOY.

A boy was lying apparently dead. His mother, believing him dead, said, "Even if my son were buried, God could restore him to me by the merits of St. Hugh." Upon this the boy began to show signs of life, and quickly recovered (*Legenda*).

———

Giraldus says at the end of his account of these miracles that there were present at the recitation of them in the chapter Geoffrey the precentor, Reimund, archdeacon of Leicester, William, archdeacon of the West Riding, and many canons and clerks of the church, as also many laymen, who all publicly gave thanks to God for thus glorifying His saints (*Girald. Camb.* vol. vii. p. 147).

THE END.

Printed by R. & R. CLARK, *Edinburgh.*

50A, ALBEMARLE STREET, LONDON,
January, 1878.

MR. MURRAY'S
GENERAL LIST OF WORKS.

ABINGER'S (LORD Chief Baron of the Exchequer) Life. By the
Hon. P. CAMPBELL SCARLETT. Portrait. 8vo. 15s.

ALBERT MEMORIAL. A Descriptive and Illustrated Account
of the National Monument erected to the PRINCE CONSORT at
Kensington. Illustrated by Engravings of its Architecture, Decora-
tions, Sculptured Groups, Statues, Mosaics, Metalwork, &c. With
Descriptive Text. By DOYNE C. BELL. With 24 Plates. Folio. 12l. 12s.

———— HANDBOOK TO, 1s.; or Illustrated Edition, 2s. 6d.

———— (PRINCE) SPEECHES AND ADDRESSES, with an Introduction, giving some outline of his Character. With Portrait. 8vo.
10s. 6d.; or Popular Edition, fcap. 8vo. 1s.

ALBERT DÜRER; his Life, with a History of his Art. By DR.
THAUSING, Keeper of Archduke Albert's Art Collection at Vienna.
Translated from the German. With Portrait and Illustrations 2 vols.
8vo. [In the Press.

ABBOTT (REV. J.). Memoirs of a Church of England Missionary
in the North American Colonies. Post 8vo. 2s.

ABERCROMBIE (JOHN). Enquiries concerning the Intellectual
Powers and the Investigation of Truth. Fcap. 8vo. 3s. 6d.

———————————— Philosophy of the Moral Feelings. Fcap. 8vo.
2s. 6d.

ACLAND (REV. CHARLES). Popular Account of the Manners and
Customs of India. Post 8vo. 2s.

ÆSOP'S FABLES. A New Version. With Historical Preface.
By Rev. THOMAS JAMES. With 100 Woodcuts, by TENNIEL and WOLF.
Post 8vo. 2s. 6d.

AGRICULTURAL (ROYAL) JOURNAL. (Published half-yearly.)

AIDS TO FAITH: a Series of Theological Essays. By various
Authors. 8vo. 9s.
Contents:—Miracles; Evidences of Christianity; Prophecy & Mosaic
Record of Creation; Ideology and Subscription; The Pentateuch; In-
spiration; Death of Christ; Scripture and its Interpretation.

AMBER-WITCH (THE). A most interesting Trial for Witchcraft. Translated by LADY DUFF GORDON. Post 8vo. 2s.

ARMY LIST (THE). Published Monthly by Authority.

ARTHUR'S (LITTLE) History of England. By LADY CALLCOTT.
New Edition, continued to 1872. With 36 Woodcuts. Fcap. 8vo. 1s. 6d.

AUSTIN (JOHN). LECTURES ON GENERAL JURISPRUDENCE; or, the
Philosophy of Positive Law. Edited by ROBERT CAMPBELL. 2 Vols.
8vo. 32s.

———————— STUDENT'S EDITION, by ROBERT CAMPBELL, compiled
from the above work. Post 8vo. 12s.

———————— Analysis of. By GORDON CAMPBELL, M.A. Post 8vo. 6s.

ARNOLD (THOS.). Ecclesiastical and Secular Architecture of
Scotland: The Abbeys, Churches, Castles, and Mansions. With Illustrations. Medium 8vo. [In Preparation.

B

ATKINSON (Dr. R.) Vie de Saint Auban. A Poem in Norman-
French. Ascribed to MATTHEW PARIS. With Concordance, Glossary
and Notes. Small 4to, 10s. 6d.

ADMIRALTY PUBLICATIONS; Issued by direction of the Lords
Commissioners of the Admiralty:—

A MANUAL OF SCIENTIFIC ENQUIRY, for the Use of Travellers.
Fourth Edition. Edited by ROBERT MAIN, M.A. Woodcuts. Post
8vo. 3s 6d.

GREENWICH ASTRONOMICAL OBSERVATIONS 1841 to 1846,
and 1847 to 1871. Royal 4to. 20s. each.

MAGNETICAL AND METEOROLOGICAL OBSERVATIONS. 1840
to 1847. Royal 4to. 20s. each.

APPENDICES TO OBSERVATIONS.

1837. Logarithms of Sines and Cosines in Time. 3s.
1842. Catalogue of 1439 Stars, from Observations made in 1836 to
1841. 4s.
1845. Longitude of Valentia (Chronometrical). 3s.
1847. Description of Altazimuth. 3s.
Twelve Years' Catalogue of Stars, from Observations made
in 1836 to 1847. 4s.
Description of Photographic Apparatus. 2s.
1851. Maskelyne's Ledger of Stars. 3s.
1852. I. Description of the Transit Circle. 3s.
1853. Refraction Tables. 3s.
1854. Description of the Zenith Tube. 3s.
Six Years' Catalogue of Stars, from Observations. 1848 to
1853. 4s.
1862. Seven Years' Catalogue of Stars, from Observations. 1854 to
1860. 10s.
Plan of Ground Buildings. 3s.
Longitude of Valentia (Galvanic). 2s.
1864. Moon's Semid. from Occultations. 2s.
Planetary Observations, 1831 to 1835. 2s.
1868. Corrections of Elements of Jupiter and Saturn. 2s.
Second Seven Years' Catalogue of 2760 Stars for 1861 to
1867. 4s.
Description of the Great Equatorial. 3s.
1856. Descriptive Chronograph. 3s.
1860. Reduction of Deep Thermometer Observations. 2s.
1871. History and Description of Water Telescope. 3s.

Cape of Good Hope Observations (Star Ledgers: 1856 to 1863. 2s.
——————— ——————— 1856. 5s.
——————— Astronomical Results. 1857 to 1858. 5s.
Report on Teneriffe Astronomical Experiment. 1856. 5s.
Paramatta Catalogue of 7385 Stars. 1822 to 1826. 4s.

ASTRONOMICAL RESULTS. 1847 to 1871. 4to. 3s. each.

MAGNETICAL AND METEOROLOGICAL RESULTS. 1847 to
1871. 4to. 3s. each.

REDUCTION OF THE OBSERVATIONS OF PLANETS. 1750 to
1830. Royal 4to. 20s. each.

——————— LUNAR OBSERVATIONS. 1750
to 1830. 2 Vols. Royal 4to. 20s. each.
——————— 1831 to 1851. 4to. 10s. each.

BERNOULLI'S SEXCENTENARY TABLE. 1779. 4to. 5s.

BESSEL'S AUXILIARY TABLES FOR HIS METHOD OF CLEAR-
ING LUNAR DISTANCES. 8vo. 2s.

ENCKE'S BERLINER JAHRBUCH, for 830. *Berlin*, 1828. 8vo. 9s.

HANSEN'S TABLES DE LA LUNE. 4to. 20s.

LAX'S TABLES FOR FINDING THE LATITUDE AND LONGI-
TUDE. 1821. 8vo. 10s.

LUNAR OBSERVATIONS at GREENWICH. 1783 to 1819. Compared
with the Tables. 1821. 4to. 7s. 6d.

MACLEAR ON LACAILLE'S ARC OF MERIDIAN. 2 Vols. 20s. each

ADMIRALTY PUBLICATIONS—*continued.*
MAYER'S DISTANCES of the MOON'S CENTRE from the
PLANETS. 1822, 3s.; 1823, 4s. 6d. 1824 to 1835. 8vo. 4s. each.
———— TABULÆ MOTUUM SOLIS ET LUNÆ. 1770. 5s.
———— ASTRONOMICAL OBSERVATIONS MADE AT GOT-
TINGEN, from 1756 to 1761. 1826. Folio. 7s. 6d.
NAUTICAL ALMANACS, from 1767 to 1877, 60s. 2s. 6d. each.
———————————— SELECTIONS FROM, up to 1812. 8vo. 5s.
1834-54. 5s.
———————————— SUPPLEMENTS, 1828 to 1833, 1837 and 1838.
2s. each.
———————————— TABLE requisite to be used with the N.A.
1781. 8vo. 5s.
SABINE'S PENDULUM EXPERIMENTS to DETERMINE THE FIGURE
OF THE EARTH. 1825. 4to. 40s.
SHEPHERD'S TABLES for CORRECTING LUNAR DISTANCES. 1772.
Royal 4to. 21s.
———————— TABLES, GENERAL, of the MOON'S DISTANCE
from the SUN, and 10 STARS. 1787. Folio. 5s. 6d.
TAYLOR'S SEXAGESIMAL TABLE. 1780. 4to. 15s.
———————— TABLES OF LOGARITHMS. 4to. 60s.
TIARK'S ASTRONOMICAL OBSERVATIONS for the LONGITUDE
of MADEIRA. 1822. 4to. 5s.
———————— CHRONOMETRICAL OBSERVATIONS for DIFFERENCES
of LONGITUDE between DOVER, PORTSMOUTH, and FALMOUTH. 1823.
4to. 5s.
VENUS and JUPITER: OBSERVATIONS of, compared with the TABLES.
London, 1822. 4to. 2s.
WALES AND BAYLY'S ASTRONOMICAL OBSERVATIONS.
1777. 4to. 21s.
———————— REDUCTION OF ASTRONOMICAL OBSERVATIONS
MADE IN THE SOUTHERN HEMISPHERE. 1764—1771. 1788. 4to.
10s. 6d.

BARBAULD (MRS.). Hymns in Prose for Children. With
Illustrations. Crown 8vo.

BARCLAY (JOSEPH). The Talmud : Selected Extracts,
chiefly illustrating the Teaching of the Bible. With an Introduction.
8vo. 14s.

BARKLEY (H. C.). Five Years among the Bulgarians and Turks
between the Danube and the Black Sea. Post 8vo. 10s 6d.

———————— Bulgaria North of the Balkans before the
War, derived from a Seven Years' Experience of European Turkey and
Its Inhabitants. Post 8vo. 10s. 6d.

———————— My Boyhood : a Story Book for Boys. With
Illustrations. Post 8vo. 6s.

BARROW (SIR JOHN). Autobiographical Memoir, from Early
Life to Advanced Age. Portrait. 8vo. 16s.

———————— (JOHN) Life, Exploits, and Voyages of Sir Francis
Drake. Post 8vo. 2s.

BARRY (SIR CHARLES). Life and Works. By CANON BARRY.
With Portrait and Illustrations. Medium 8vo. 15s.

BATES' (H. W.) Records of a Naturalist on the River Amazon
during eleven years of Adventure and Travel. Illustrations. Post 8vo.
7s. 6d.

BAX (CAPT. R.N.). Russian Tartary, Eastern Siberia, China, Japan,
and Formosa. A Narrative of a Cruise in the Eastern Seas. With
Map and Illustrations. Crown 8vo. 12s.

BELCHER (LADY). Account of the Mutineers of the ' Bounty,'
and their Descendants; with their Settlements in Pitcairn and Norfolk
Islands. With Illustrations. Post 8vo. 12s.

BELL'S (Sir Chas.) Familiar Letters. Portrait. Post 8vo. 12s.

BELL'S (Doyne C.) Notices of the Historic Interments in the Chapel in the Tower of London, with an account of the discovery of the remains of Queen Anne Boleyn. With Illustrations. Crown 8vo. 14s.

BELT'S (Thos.) Naturalist in Nicaragua, including a Residence at the Gold Mines of Chontales; with Journeys in the Savannahs and Forests; and Observations on Animals and Plants. Illustrations. Post 8vo. 12s.

BERTRAM'S (Jas. G.) Harvest of the Sea: an Account of British Food Fishes, including sketches of Fisheries and Fisher Folk. With 50 Illustrations. 8vo. 9s.

BIBLE COMMENTARY. Explanatory and Critical. With a Revision of the Translation. By BISHOPS and CLERGY of the ANGLICAN CHURCH. Edited by F. C. Cook, M.A., Canon of Exeter. Vols. I. to VI. (The Old Testament). Medium 8vo. 6l. 15s.

| Vol. I. 30s. | Genesis. Exodus. Leviticus. Numbers. Deuteronomy. | Vol. IV. 24s. | Job. Psalms. Proverbs. Ecclesiastes Song of Solomon. |
| Vols. II. 20s. and III. 16s. | Joshua, Judges, Ruth, Samuel, Kings, Chronicles, Ezra, Nehemiah, Esther. | Vol. V. 20s. Vol. VI. 25s. | Isaiah. Jeremiah. Ezekiel. Daniel. Minor Prophets. |

BIGG-WITHER (T. P.). Pioneering in S. Brazil; three years of forest and prairie life in the province of Parana. Map and Illustrations. 8vo.

BIRCH (Samuel). A History of Ancient Pottery and Porcelain: Egyptian, Assyrian, Greek, Roman, and Etruscan. With Coloured Plates and 200 Illustrations. Medium 8vo. 42s.

BIRD (Isabella). Hawaiian Archipelago; or Six Months among the Palm Groves, Coral Reefs, and Volcanoes of the Sandwich Islands. With Illustrations. Crown 8vo. 7s. 6d.

BISSET (General). Sport and War in South Africa from 1834 to 1867, with a Narrative of the Duke of Edinburgh's Visit. With Map and Illustrations. Crown 8vo. 14s.

BLACKSTONE'S COMMENTARIES; adapted to the Present State of the Law. By R. Malcolm Kerr, LL.D. Revised Edition, Incorporating all the Recent Changes in the Law. 4 vols. 8vo. 60s.

BLUNT (Rev. J. J.). Undesigned Coincidences in the Writings of the Old and New Testaments, an Argument of their Veracity: containing the Books of Moses, Historical and Prophetical Scriptures, and the Gospels and Acts. Post 8vo. 6s.

————— History of the Church in the First Three Centuries. Post 8vo. 6s.

————— Parish Priest; His Duties, Acquirements and Obligations. Post 8vo. 6s.

————— Lectures on the Right Use of the Early Fathers. 8vo. 9s.

————— University Sermons. Post 8vo. 6s.

————— Plain Sermons. 2 vols. Post 8vo. 12s.

BLOMFIELD'S (Bishop) Memoir, with Selections from his Correspondence. By his Son. Portrait, post 8vo. 12s.

BOSWELL'S Life of Samuel Johnson, LL.D. Including the
Tour to the Hebrides. Edited by Mr. CROKER. *Seventh Edition.*
Portraits. 1 vol. Medium 8vo. 12*s.*

BRACE (C. L.). Manual of Ethnology; or the Races of the Old
World. Post 8vo. 6*s.*

BOOK OF COMMON PRAYER. Illustrated with Coloured
Borders, Initial Letters, and Woodcuts. 8vo. 18*s.*

BORROW (GEORGE). Bible in Spain; or the Journeys, Adventures,
and Imprisonments of an Englishman in au Attempt to circulate the
Scriptures in the Peninsula. Post 8vo. 5*s.*

———— Gypsies of Spain; their Manners, Customs, Religion, and Language. With Portrait. Post 8vo. 5*s.*

———— Lavengro; The Scholar—The Gypsy—and the Priest.
Post 8vo. 5*s.*

———— Romany Rye—a Sequel to "Lavengro." Post 8vo. 5*s.*

———— WILD WALES: its People, Language, and Scenery.
Post 8vo. 5*s.*

———— Romano Lavo-lil; Word·Book of the Romany, or
English Gypsy Language; with Specimens of their Poetry, and an
account of certain Gypsyries. Post 8vo. 10*s.* 6*d.*

BRAY (MRS.). Life of Thomas Stothard, R.A. With Portrait
and 60 Woodcuts. 4to. 21*s.*

BRITISH ASSOCIATION REPORTS. 8vo.

York and Oxford, 1831-32, 13*s.* 6*d.*
Cambridge, 1833, 12*s.*
Edinburgh, 1834, 15*s.*
Dublin, 1835, 13*s.* 6*d.*
Bristol, 1836, 12*s.*
Liverpool, 1837, 16*s.* 6*d.*
Newcastle, 1838, 15*s.*
Birmingham, 1839, 13*s.* 6*d.*
Glasgow, 1840, 15*s.*
Plymouth, 1841, 13*s.* 6*d.*
Manchester, 1842, 10*s.* 6*d.*
Cork, 1843, 12*s.*
York, 1844, 20*s.*
Cambridge, 1845, 12*s.*
Southampton, 1846, 15*s.*
Oxford, 1847, 18*s.*
Swansea, 1848, 9*s.*
Birmingham, 1849, 10*s.*
Edinburgh, 1850, 15*s.*
Ipswich, 1851, 16*s.* 6*d.*
Belfast, 1852, 15*s.*
Hull, 1853, 10*s.* 6*d.*
Liverpool, 1854, 18*s.*

Glasgow, 1855, 15*s.*
Cheltenham, 1856, 18*s.*
Dublin, 1857, 15*s.*
Leeds, 1858, 20*s.*
Aberdeen, 1859, 15*s.*
Oxford, 1860, 25*s.*
Manchester, 1861, 15*s.*
Cambridge, 1862, 20*s.*
Newcastle, 1863, 25*s.*
Bath, 1864, 18*s.*
Birmingham, 1865, 25*s.*
Nottingham, 1866, 24*s.*
Dundee, 1867, 26*s.*
Norwich, 1868, 25*s.*
Exeter, 1869, 22*s.*
Liverpool, 1870, 18*s.*
Edinburgh, 1871, 16*s.*
Brighton, 1872, 24*s.*
Bradford, 1873, 25*s.*
Belfast, 1874. 25*s.*
Bristol, 1875, 25*s.*
Glasgow, 1876, 25*s.*

BROUGHTON (LORD). A Journey through Albania, Turkey in
Europe and Asia, to Constantinople. Illustrations. 2 Vols. 8vo. 30*s.*

———————— Visits to Italy. 2 Vols. Post 8vo. 18*s.*

BRUGSCH (PROFESSOR). A History of Egypt, from the earliest
period. Derived from Monuments and Inscriptions. *New Edition.* Translated by H. DANBY SEYMOUR. 2 vols. 8vo. [*In Preparation.*

BUCKLEY (ARABELLA B.). A Short History of Natural Science,
and the Progress of Discovery from the time of the Greeks to the
present day, for Schools and young Persons. Illustrations. Post
8vo. 9*s.*

BURGON (REV. J. W.). Christian Gentleman; or, Memoir of
Patrick Fraser Tytler. Post 8vo. 9*s.*

———————— Letters from Rome. Post 8vo. 12*s.*

BURN (Col.). Dictionary of Naval and Military Technical Terms, English and French—French and English. Crown 8vo. 15s.

BUXTON'S (Charles) Memoirs of Sir Thomas Fowell Buxton, Bart. With Selections from his Correspondence. Portrait. 8vo. 16s. *Popular Edition.* Fcap. 8vo. 5s.

———— Ideas of the Day. 8vo. 5s.

BURCKHARDT'S (Dr. Jacob) Cicerone ; or Art Guide to Painting in Italy. Edited by Rev. Dr. A. Von Zahn, and Translated from the German by Mrs. A. Clough. Post 8vo. 6s.

BYLES (Sir John). Foundations of Religion in the Mind and Heart of Man. Post 8vo. 6s.

BYRON'S (Lord) Life, Letters, and Journals. By Thomas Moore. *Cabinet Edition.* Plates. 6 Vols. Fcap. 8vo. 18s.; or One Volume, Portraits. Royal 8vo., 7s. 6d.

———————— and Poetical Works. *Popular Edition.* Portraits. 2 vols. Royal 8vo. 15s.

—— Poetical Works. *Library Edition.* Portrait. 6 Vols. 8vo. 45s.

———————— *Cabinet Edition.* Plates. 10 Vols. 12mo. 30s.

———————— *Pocket Edition.* 8 Vols. 24mo. 21s. *In a case.*

———————— *Popular Edition.* Plates. Royal 8vo. 7s. 6d.

———————— *Pearl Edition.* Crown 8vo. 2s. 6d.

———————— Childe Harold. With 80 Engravings. Crown 8vo. 12s.

———————— 16mo. 2s. 6d.

———————— Vignettes. 16mo. 1s.

———————— Portrait. 16mo. 6d.

———— Tales and Poems. 24mo. 2s. 6d.

———— Miscellaneous. 2 Vols. 24mo. 5s.

———— Dramas and Plays. 2 Vols. 24mo. 5s.

———— Don Juan and Beppo. 2 Vols. 24mo. 5s.

———— Beauties. Poetry and Prose. Portrait. Fcap. 8vo. 3s. 6d.

BUTTMANN'S Lexilogus ; a Critical Examination of the Meaning of numerous Greek Words, chiefly in Homer and Hesiod. By Rev. J. R. Fishlake. 8vo. 12s.

———————— Irregular Greek Verbs. With all the Tenses extant—their Formation, Meaning, and Usage, with Notes, by Rev. J. R. Fishlake. Post 8vo. 6s.

CALLCOTT (Lady). Little Arthur's History of England. *New Edition, brought down to* 1872. With Woodcuts. Fcap. 8vo. 1s. 6d.

CARNARVON (Lord). Portugal, Gallicia, and the Basque Provinces. Post 8vo. 3s. 6d.

CARTWRIGHT (W. C.). The Jesuits: their Constitution and Teaching. An Historical Sketch. 8vo. 9s.

CASTLEREAGH DESPATCHES, from the commencement of the official career of Viscount Castlereagh to the close of his life. 12 Vols. 8vo. 14s. each.

CAMPBELL (Lord). Lord Chancellors and Keepers of the Great Seal of England. From the Earliest Times to the Death of Lord Eldon in 1838. 10 Vols. Crown 8vo. 6s. each.

———————— Chief Justices of England. From the Norman Conquest to the Death of Lord Tenterden. 4 Vols. Crown 8vo. 6s. each.

CAMPBELL (Lord). Lives of Lyndhurst and Brougham. 8vo. 16s.
————— Shakspeare's Legal Acquirements. 8vo. 5s. 6d.
————— Lord Bacon. Fcap. 8vo. 2s. 6d.
————— (Sir George) India as it may be: an Outline of a proposed Government and Policy. 8vo. 12s.
————————————— Handy-Book on the Eastern Question; being a Very Recent View of Turkey. With Map. Post 8vo. 9s.
————— (Thos.) Essay on English Poetry. With Short Lives of the British Poets. Post 8vo. 3s. 6d.

CAVALCASELLE and CROWE'S History of Painting in North Italy, from the 14th to the 16th Century. With Illustrations. 2 Vols. 8vo. 42s.

————— Early Flemish Painters, their Lives and Works. Illustrations. Post 8vo. 10s. 6d.; or Large Paper, 8vo. 15s.

————— Life and Times of Titian, with some Account of his Family. With Portrait and Illustrations. 2 vols. 8vo. 42s.

CESNOLA (Gen. L. P. di). Cyprus; its Ancient Cities, Tombs, and Temples. A Narrative of Researches and Excavations during Ten Years' Residence in that Island. With Maps and 400 Illustrations. Medium 8vo. 50s.

CHILD (G. Chaplin, M.D.). Benedicite; or, Song of the Three Children; being Illustrations of the Power, Beneficence, and Design manifested by the Creator in his works. Post 8vo. 6s.

CHISHOLM (Mrs.). Perils of the Polar Seas; True Stories of Arctic Discovery and Adventure. Illustrations. Post 8vo. 6s.

CHURTON (Archdeacon). Poetical Remains, Translations and Imitations. Portrait. Post 8vo. 7s. 6d.

————— New Testament. Edited with a Plain Practical Commentary for Families and General Readers. With 100 Panoramic and other Views, from Sketches made on the Spot. 2 vols. 8vo. 21s.

CICERO'S Life and Times. His Character as a Statesman, Orator, and Friend, with a Selection from his Correspondence and Orations. By William Forsyth. With Illustrations. Crown 8vo.

CLARK (Sir James). Memoir of Dr. John Conolly. Comprising a Sketch of the Treatment of the Insane in Europe and America. With Portrait. Post 8vo. 10s. 6d.

CLASSIC PREACHERS OF THE ENGLISH CHURCH. The St. James' Lectures in 1877. By Canon Lightfoot, Prof. Wace, Dean of Durham, Prcby. Clark, Cannon Farrar, and Dean of Norwich. With Introduction by Rev. J. E. Kempe. Post 8vo. 7s. 6d.

CLIVE'S (Lord) Life. By Rev. G. R. Gleig. Post 8vo. 3s. 6d.

CLODE (C. M.). Military Forces of the Crown; their Administration and Government. 2 Vols. 8vo. 21s. each.

————— Administration of Justice under Military and Martial Law, as applicable to the Army, Navy, Marine, and Auxiliary Forces. 8vo. 12s.

CHURCH & THE AGE. Essays on the Principles and Present Position of the Anglican Church. By various Authors. 2 vols. 8vo. 20s.

COLCHESTER PAPERS. The Diary and Correspondence of Charles Abbott, Lord Colchester, Speaker of the House of Commons. 1802-1817. Portrait. 3 Vols. 8vo. 42s.

COLERIDGE'S (Samuel Taylor) Table-Talk. Portrait. 12mo. 3s. 6d.

COLLINGWOOD (CUTHBERT). Rambles of a Naturalist on the Shores and Waters of the China Sea. With Illustrations. 8vo. 16s.

COLONIAL LIBRARY. [See Home and Colonial Library.]

COMPANIONS FOR THE DEVOUT LIFE. The St. James' Lectures, 1875 and 1876. New Edition. Post 8vo. 6s.

COOK (Canon). Sermons Preached at Lincoln's Inn. 8vo. 9s.

COOKE (E. W.). Leaves from my Sketch-Book. A selection from sketches made during many tours. 25 Plates. Small folio. 31s. 6d.

———— Second Series. Consisting chiefly of Views in Egypt and the East. With Descriptive Text. Small folio. 31s. 6d.

COOKERY (MODERN DOMESTIC). Founded on Principles of Economy and Practical Knowledge. By a Lady. Woodcuts. Fcap. 8vo. 5s.

COOPER (T. T.). Travels of a Pioneer of Commerce on an Overland Journey from China towards India. Illustrations. 8vo. 16s.

CORNWALLIS Papers and Correspondence during the American War.—Administrations in India,—Union with Ireland, and Peace of Amiens. 3 Vols. 8vo. 63s.

COWPER'S (COUNTESS) Diary while Lady of the Bedchamber to Caroline, Princess of Wales, 1714–20. Portrait. 8vo. 10s. 6d.

CRABBE (REV. GEORGE). Life and Poetical Works. With Illustrations. Royal 8vo. 7s.

CRAWFORD & BALCARRES (Earl of). Etruscan Inscriptions. Analyzed, Translated, and Commented upon. 8vo. 12s.

CRIPPS (WILFRED). Old English Plate : Ecclesiastical, Decorative, and Domestic, its makers and marks. Illustrations. Medium 8vo.
[In the Press.

CROKER (J. W.). Progressive Geography for Children. 18mo. 1s. 6d.

———— Stories for Children, Selected from the History of England. Woodcuts. 16mo. 2s. 6d.

———— Boswell's Life of Johnson. Including the Tour to the Hebrides. Seventh Edition. Portraits. 8vo. 12s.

———— Early Period of the French Revolution. 8vo. 15s.

———— Historical Essay on the Guillotine. Fcap. 8vo. 1s.

CROWE AND **CAVALCASELLE.** Lives of the Early Flemish Painters. Woodcuts. Post 8vo, 10s. 6d.; or Large Paper, 8vo, 15s.

———— History of Painting in North Italy, from 14th to 16th Century. Derived from Researches into the Works of Art in that Country. With Illustrations. 2 Vols. 8vo. 42s.

———— Life and Times of Titian, with some Account of his Family, chiefly from new and unpublished records. With Portrait and Illustrations. 2 vols. 8vo. 42s.

CUMMING (R. GORDON). Five Years of a Hunter's Life in the Far Interior of South Africa. Woodcuts. Post 8vo. 6s.

CUNYNGHAME (SIR ARTHUR). Travels in the Eastern Caucasus, on the Caspian and Black Seas, in Daghestan and the Frontiers of Persia and Turkey. With Map and Illustrations. 8vo. 18s.

CURTIUS' (PROFESSOR) Student's Greek Grammar, for the Upper Forms. Edited by DR. WM. SMITH. Post 8vo. 6s.

———— Elucidations of the above Grammar. Translated by EVELYN ABBOT. Post 8vo. 7s. 6d.

———— Smaller Greek Grammar for the Middle and Lower Forms. Abridged from the larger work. 12mo. 3s. 6d.

CURTIUS' (PROFESSOR) Accidence of the Greek Language. Extracted from the above work. 12mo. 2s. 6d.
———— Principles of Greek Etymology. Translated by A. S. WILKINS, M.A., and E. B. ENGLAND, B.A. 2 vols. 8vo. 15s. each.

CURZON (HON. ROBERT). Visits to the Monasteries of the Levant. Illustrations. Post 8vo. 7s. 6d.

CUST (GENERAL). Warriors of the 17th Century—The Thirty Years' War. 2 Vols. 16s. Civil Wars of France and England. 2 Vols. 16s. Commanders of Fleets and Armies. 2 Vols. 18s.
———— Annals of the Wars—18th & 19th Century, 1700—1815. With Maps. 9 Vols. Post 8vo. 5s. each.

DAVIS (NATHAN). Ruined Cities of Numidia and Carthaginia. Illustrations. 8vo. 16s.

DAVY (SIR HUMPHRY). Consolations in Travel; or, Last Days of a Philosopher. Woodcuts. Fcap. 8vo. 3s. 6d.
———— Salmonia; or, Days of Fly Fishing. Woodcuts. Fcap. 8vo. 3s. 6d.

DARWIN (CHARLES). Journal of a Naturalist during a Voyage round the World. Crown 8vo. 9s.
———— ———— Origin of Species by Means of Natural Selection; or, the Preservation of Favoured Races in the Struggle for Life. Crown 8vo. 7s. 6d.
———— Variation of Animals and Plants under Domestication. With Illustrations. 2 Vols. Crown 8vo. 18s.
———— Descent of Man, and Selection in Relation to Sex. With Illustrations. Crown 8vo. 9s.
———— ———— Expressions of the Emotions in Man and Animals. With Illustrations. Crown 8vo. 12s.
———— ———— Various Contrivances by which Orchids are Fertilized by Insects. Woodcuts. Crown 8vo. 9s.
———— Movements and Habits of Climbing Plants. Woodcuts. Crown 8vo. 6s.
———— Insectivorous Plants. Woodcuts. Crown 8vo. 14s.
———— Effects of Cross and Self-Fertilization in the Vegetable Kingdom. Crown 8vo. 12s.
———— Different Forms of Flowers on Plants of the same Species. Crown 8vo. 10s. 6d.
———— Facts and Argument for Darwin. By FRITZ MÜLLER. Translated by W. S. DALLAS. Woodcuts. Post 8vo. 6s.

DE COSSON (E. A.). The Cradle of the Blue Nile; a Journey through Abyssinia and Scudan, and a residence at the Court of King John of Ethiopia. Map and Illustrations. 2 vols. Post 8vo. 21s.

DELEPIERRE (OCTAVE). History of Flemish Literature. 8vo. 9s.

DENNIS (GEORGE). The Cities and Cemeteries of Etruria. A new Edition, revised, recording all the latest Discoveries. With 20 Plans and 150 Illustrations. 2 vols. 8vo. 42s.

DENT (EMMA). Annals of Winchcombe and Sudeley. With 120 Portraits, Plates and Woodcuts. 4to. 42s.

DERBY (EARL OF). Iliad of Homer rendered into English Blank Verse. 10th Edition. With Portrait. 2 Vols. Post 8vo. 10s.

DERRY (BISHOP OF). Witness of the Psalms to Christ and Christianity. The Bampton Lectures for 1876. 8vo. 10s. 6d.

DEUTSCH (EMANUEL). Talmud, Islam, The Targums and other Literary Remains. 8vo. 12s.

DILKE (Sir C. W.). Papers of a Critic. Selected from the
Writings of the late Chas. Wentworth Dilke. With a Biographical Sketch. 2 Vols. 8vo. 24s.

DOG-BREAKING, with Odds and Ends for those who love the
Dog and Gun. By Gen. Hutchinson. With 40 Illustrations.
Crown 8vo. 7s. 6d.

DOMESTIC MODERN COOKERY. Founded on Principles of
Economy and Practical Knowledge, and adapted for Private Families.
Woodcuts. Feap. 8vo. 5s.

DOUGLAS'S (Sir Howard) Life and Adventures. Portrait. 8vo. 15s.

———— Theory and Practice of Gunnery. Plates. 8vo. 21s.

———— Construction of Bridges and the Passage of Rivers
in Military Operations. Plates. 8vo. 21s.

———— (Wm.) Horse-Shoeing; As it Is, and As it Should be.
Illustrations. Post 8vo. 7s. 6d.

DRAKE'S (Sir Francis) Life, Voyages, and Exploits, by Sea and
Land. By John Barrow. Post 8vo. 2s.

DRINKWATER (John). History of the Siege of Gibraltar,
1779-1783. With a Description and Account of that Garrison from the
Earliest Periods. Post 8vo. 2s.

DUCANGE'S Mediæval Latin-English Dictionary. Translated
and Edited by Rev. E. A. Dayman and J. H. Hessels. Small 4to.
[In preparation.

DU CHAILLU (Paul B.). Equatorial Africa, with Accounts
of the Gorilla, the Nest-building Ape, Chimpanzee, Crocodile, &c.
Illustrations. 8vo. 21s.

———— Journey to Ashango Land; and Further Pene-
tration into Equatorial Africa. Illustrations. 8vo. 21s.

DUFFERIN (Lord). Letters from High Latitudes; a Yacht
Voyage to Iceland, Jan Mayen, and Spitzbergen. Woodcuts. Post
8vo. 7s. 6d.

DUNCAN (Major). History of the Royal Artillery. Compiled from the Original Records. With Portraits. 2 Vols. 8vo. 30s.

———— The English in Spain; or, The Story of the War of
Succession, 1834 and 1840. Compiled from the Letters, Journals, and
Reports of the British Commissioners with Queen Isabella's Armies.
With Illustrations. 8vo. 16s.

EASTLAKE (Sir Charles). Contributions to the Literature of
the Fine Arts. With Memoir of the Author, and Selections from his
Correspondence. By Lady Eastlake. 2 Vols. 8vo. 24s.

EDWARDS (W. H.). Voyage up the River Amazons, including a
Visit to Para. Post 8vo. 2s.

EIGHT MONTHS AT ROME, during the Vatican Council, with
a Daily Account of the Proceedings. By Pomponio Leto. Translated from the Original. 8vo. 12s.

ELDON'S (Lord) Public and Private Life, with Selections from
his Correspondence and Diaries. By Horace Twiss. Portrait. 2
Vols. Post 8vo. 21s.

ELGIN (Lord). Letters and Journals. Edited by Theodore
Walrond. With Preface by Dean Stanley. 8vo. 14s.

ELLESMERE (Lord). Two Sieges of Vienna by the Turks.
Translated from the German. Post 8vo. 2s.

ELLIS (W.). Madagascar Revisited. Setting forth the Perse-
cutions and Heroic Sufferings of the Native Christians. Illustrations.
8vo. 16s.

ELLIS (W,) Memoir. By His Son. With his Character and Work. By Rev. Henry Allon, D.D. Portrait. 8vo. 10s. 6d.

———— (Robinson) Poems and Fragments of Catullus. 16mo. 5s.

ELPHINSTONE (Hon. Mountstuart). History of India—the Hindoo and Mahomedan Periods. Edited by Professor Cowell. Map. 8vo. 18s.

———————— (H. W.) Patterns for Turning; Comprising Elliptical and other Figures cut on the Lathe without the use of any Ornamental Chuck. With 70 Illustrations. Small 4to. 15s.

ENGLAND. See Callcott, Croker, Hume, Markham, Smith, and Stanhope.

ESSAYS ON CATHEDRALS. With an Introduction. By Dean Howson. 8vo. 12s.

ELZE (Karl). Life of Lord Byron. With a Critical Essay on his Place in Literature. Translated from the German. With Portrait. 8vo. 16s.

FERGUSSON (James). History of Architecture in all Countries from the Earliest Times. With 1,600 Illustrations. 4 Vols. Medium 8vo.
Vol. I. & II. Ancient and Mediæval. 63s.
Vol. III. Indian and Eastern. 42s.
Vol. IV. Modern. 31s. 6d.

———————— Rude Stone Monuments in all Countries; their Age and Uses. With 230 Illustrations. Medium 8vo. 24s.

———————— Holy Sepulchre and the Temple at Jerusalem. Woodcuts. 8vo. 7s. 6d.

———————— The Temple at Jerusalem, and the other buildings in the Haram Area, from Solomon to Saladin, with numerous Illustrations. 4to.

FLEMING (Professor). Student's Manual of Moral Philosophy. With Quotations and References. Post 8vo. 7s. 6d.

FLOWER GARDEN. By Rev. Thos. James. Fcap. 8vo. 1s.

FORD (Richard). Gatherings from Spain. Post 8vo. 3s. 6d.

FORSYTH (William). Life and Times of Cicero. With Selections from his Correspondence and Orations. Illustrations. Crown 8vo.

———— Hortensius; an Historical Essay on the Office and Duties of an Advocate. Illustrations. 8vo. 12s.

———————— History of Ancient Manuscripts. Post 8vo. 2s. 6d.

———————— Novels and Novelists of the 18th Century, in Illustration of the Manners and Morals of the Age. Post 8vo. 10s. 6d.

FORTUNE (Robert). Narrative of Two Visits to the Tea Countries of China, 1843-52. Woodcuts. 2 Vols. Post 8vo. 18s.

FORSTER (John). The Early Life of Jonathan Swift. 1667-1711. With Portrait. 8vo. 15s.

FOSS (Edward). Biographia Juridica, or Biographical Dictionary of the Judges of England, from the Conquest to the Present Time, 1066-1870. Medium 8vo. 21s.

FRANCE (History of). See Markham—Smith—Student's.

FRENCH IN ALGIERS; The Soldier of the Foreign Legion—and the Prisoners of Abd-el-Kadir. Translated by Lady Duff Gordon. Post 8vo. 2s.

FRERE (Sir Bartle). Indian Missions. Small 8vo. 2s. 6d.

———— Eastern Africa as a field for Missionary Labour. With Map. Crown 8vo. 5s.

FRERE (Sir Bartle). Bengal Famine. How it will be Met and How to Prevent Future Famines in India. With Maps. Crown 8vo. 5s.

GALTON (Francis). Art of Travel; or, Hints on the Shifts and Contrivances available in Wild Countries. Woodcuts. Post 8vo. 7s. 6d.

GEOGRAPHICAL SOCIETY'S JOURNAL. (*Published Yearly.*)

GEORGE (Ernest). The Mosel; a Series of Twenty Etchings, with Descriptive Letterpress. Imperial 4to. 42s.

———— Loire and South of France; a Series of Twenty Etchings, with Descriptive Text. Folio. 42s.

GERMANY (History of). See Markham.

GIBBON (Edward). History of the Decline and Fall of the Roman Empire. Edited by Milman and Guizot. Edited, with Notes by Dr. Wm. Smith. Maps. 8 Vols. 8vo. 60s.

———— The Student's Edition; an Epitome of the above work, incorporating the Researches of Recent Commentators. By Dr. Wm. Smith. Woodcuts. Post 8vo. 7s. 6d.

GIFFARD (Edward). Deeds of Naval Daring; or, Anecdotes of the British Navy. Fcap. 8vo. 3s. 6d.

GLADSTONE (W. E.). Financial Statements of 1853, 1860, 63-65. 8vo. 12s.

———— Rome and the Newest Fashions in Religion. Three Tracts. 8vo. 7s. 6d.

GLEIG (G. R.). Campaigns of the British Army at Washington and New Orleans. Post 8vo. 2s.

———— Story of the Battle of Waterloo. Post 8vo. 3s. 6d.

———— Narrative of Sale's Brigade in Affghanistan. Post 8vo. 2s.

———— Life of Lord Clive. Post 8vo. 3s. 6d.

———— Sir Thomas Munro. Post 8vo. 3s. 6d.

GLYNNE (Sir Stephen). Notes on the Churches of Kent. With Illustrations. 8vo. 12s.

GOLDSMITH'S (Oliver) Works. Edited with Notes by Peter Cunningham. Vignettes. 4 Vols. 8vo. 30s.

GORDON (Sir Alex.). Sketches of German Life, and Scenes from the War of Liberation. Post 8vo. 3s. 6d.

———— (Lady Duff) Amber-Witch: A Trial for Witchcraft. Post 8vo. 2s.

———— French in Algiers. 1. The Soldier of the Foreign Legion. 2. The Prisoners of Abd-el-Kadir. Post 8vo. 2s.

GRAMMARS. See Curtius; Hall; Hutton; King Edward; Matthiæ; Maetzner; Smith.

GREECE (History of). See Grote—Smith—Student.

GREY (Earl). Parliamentary Government and Reform; with Suggestions for the Improvement of our Representative System. *Second Edition.* 8vo. 9s.

GUIZOT (M.). Meditations on Christianity. 3 Vols. Post 8vo. 30s.

GROTE (George). History of Greece. From the Earliest Times to the close of the generation contemporary with the death of Alexander the Great. *Library Edition.* Portrait, Maps, and Plans. 10 Vols. 8vo. 120s. *Cabinet Edition.* Portrait and Plans. 12 Vols. Post 8vo. 6s. each.

———— Plato, and other Companions of Socrates. 3 Vols. 8vo. 45s.

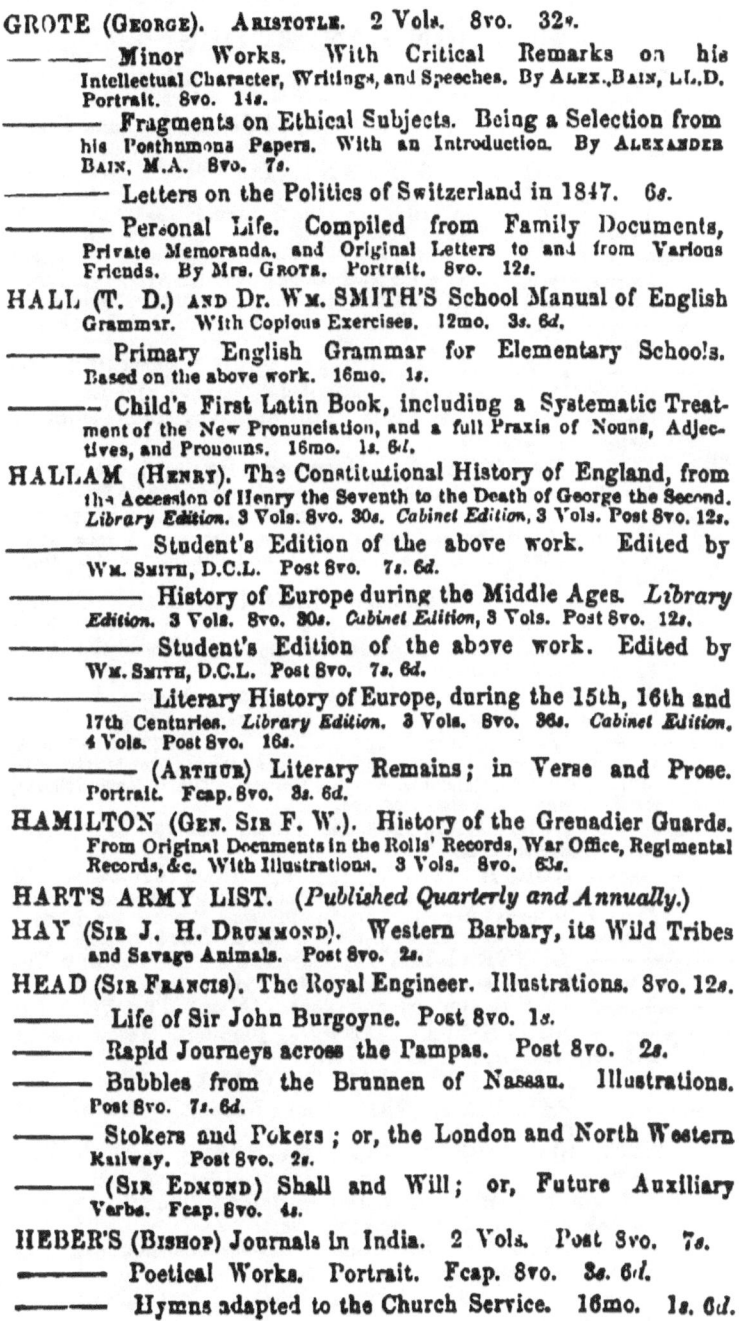

GROTE (GEORGE). ARISTOTLE. 2 Vols. 8vo. 32s.

———— —— Minor Works. With Critical Remarks on his Intellectual Character, Writings, and Speeches. By ALEX.,BAIN, LL.D. Portrait. 8vo. 14s.

———— Fragments on Ethical Subjects. Being a Selection from his Posthumous Papers. With an Introduction. By ALEXANDER BAIN, M.A. 8vo. 7s.

———— Letters on the Politics of Switzerland in 1847. 6s.

———— Personal Life. Compiled from Family Documents, Private Memoranda, and Original Letters to and from Various Friends. By Mrs. GROTE. Portrait. 8vo. 12s.

HALL (T. D.) AND Dr. WM. SMITH'S School Manual of English Grammar. With Copious Exercises. 12mo. 3s. 6d.

———— Primary English Grammar for Elementary Schools. Based on the above work. 16mo. 1s.

———— Child's First Latin Book, including a Systematic Treatment of the New Pronunciation, and a full Praxis of Nouns, Adjectives, and Pronouns. 16mo. 1s. 6d.

HALLAM (HENRY). The Constitutional History of England, from the Accession of Henry the Seventh to the Death of George the Second. Library Edition. 3 Vols. 8vo. 30s. Cabinet Edition, 3 Vols. Post 8vo. 12s.

———— Student's Edition of the above work. Edited by WM. SMITH, D.C.L. Post 8vo. 7s. 6d.

———— History of Europe during the Middle Ages. Library Edition. 3 Vols. 8vo. 30s. Cabinet Edition, 3 Vols. Post 8vo. 12s.

———— Student's Edition of the above work. Edited by WM. SMITH, D.C.L. Post 8vo. 7s. 6d.

———— Literary History of Europe, during the 15th, 16th and 17th Centuries. Library Edition. 3 Vols. 8vo. 36s. Cabinet Edition, 4 Vols. Post 8vo. 16s.

———— (ARTHUR) Literary Remains; in Verse and Prose. Portrait. Fcap. 8vo. 3s. 6d.

HAMILTON (GEN. SIR F. W.). History of the Grenadier Guards. From Original Documents in the Rolls' Records, War Office, Regimental Records, &c. With Illustrations. 3 Vols. 8vo. 63s.

HART'S ARMY LIST. (Published Quarterly and Annually.)

HAY (SIR J. H. DRUMMOND). Western Barbary, its Wild Tribes and Savage Animals. Post 8vo. 2s.

HEAD (SIR FRANCIS). The Royal Engineer. Illustrations. 8vo. 12s.

———— Life of Sir John Burgoyne. Post 8vo. 1s.

———— Rapid Journeys across the Pampas. Post 8vo. 2s.

———— Bubbles from the Brunnen of Nassau. Illustrations. Post 8vo. 7s. 6d.

———— Stokers and Pokers; or, the London and North Western Railway. Post 8vo. 2s.

———— (SIR EDMUND) Shall and Will; or, Future Auxiliary Verbs. Fcap. 8vo. 4s.

HEBER'S (BISHOP) Journals in India. 2 Vols. Post 8vo. 7s.

———— Poetical Works. Portrait. Fcap. 8vo. 3s. 6d.

———— Hymns adapted to the Church Service. 16mo. 1s. 6d.

FOREIGN HANDBOOKS.

HAND-BOOK—TRAVEL-TALK. English, French, German, and Italian. 18mo. 3s. 6d.

—————— - HOLLAND AND BELGIUM. Map and Plans. Post 8vo. 6s.

—————— NORTH GERMANY and THE RHINE,— The Black Forest, the Hartz, Thüringerwald, Saxon Switzerland, Rügen the Giant Mountains, Taunus. Odenwald, Elass, and Lothringen. Map and Plans. Post 8vo. 10s.

—————— SOUTH GERMANY, — Wurtemburg, Bavaria, Austria, Styria, Salzburg, the Austrian and Bavarian Alps, Tyrol, Hungary, and the Danube, from Ulm to the Black Sea. Map. Post 8vo. 10s

—————— PAINTING. German, Flemish, and Dutch Schools. Illustrations. 2 Vols. Post 8vo. 24s.

—————— LIVES OF EARLY FLEMISH PAINTERS. By CROWE and CAVALCASELLE. Illustrations. Post 8vo. 10s. 6d.

—————— SWITZERLAND, Alps of Savoy, and Piedmont. Maps. Post 8vo. 9s.

—————— FRANCE, Part I. Normandy, Brittany, the French Alps, the Loire, the Seine, the Garonne, and Pyrenees. Post 8vo. 7s. 6d.

—————— Part II. Central France, Auvergne, the Cevennes, Burgundy, the Rhone and Saone, Provence, Nimes, Arles, Marseilles, the French Alps, Alsace, Lorraine, Champagne, &c. Maps. Post 8vo. 7s. 6d.

—————— MEDITERRANEAN ISLANDS—Malta, Corsica, Sardinia, and Sicily. Maps. Post 8vo.   [In the Press.

—————— ALGERIA. Algiers, Constantine, Oran, the Atlas Range. Map. Post 8vo 9s.

—————— PARIS, and its Environs. Map. 16mo. 3s. 6d. *.* MURRAY'S PLAN OF PARIS, mounted on canvas. 3s. 6d.

—————— SPAIN, Madrid, The Castiles, The Basque Provinces, Leon, The Asturias, Galicia, Estremadura, Andalusia, Ronda, Granada, Murcia, Valencia, Catalonia, Aragon, Navarre, The Balearic Islands, &c. &c. Maps. 2 Vols. Post 8vo.

—————— PORTUGAL, LISBON, Porto, Cintra, Mafra, &c. Map. Post 8vo. 12s.

—————— NORTH ITALY, Turin, Milan, Cremona, the Italian Lakes, Bergamo, Brescia, Verona, Mantua, Vicenza, Padua, Ferrara, Bologna, Ravenna, Rimini, Piacenza, Genoa, the Riviera, Venice, Parma, Modena, and Romagna. Map. Post 8vo. 10s.

—————— CENTRAL ITALY, Florence, Lucca, Tuscany, The Marches, Umbria, and late Patrimony of St. Peter's. Map. Post 8vo. 10s.

—————— ROME AND ITS ENVIRONS. Map. Post 8vo. 10s.

—————— SOUTH ITALY, Naples, Pompeii, Herculaneum, and Vesuvius. Map. Post 8vo. 10s.

—————— KNAPSACK GUIDE TO ITALY. 16mo.

—————— PAINTING. The Italian Schools. Illustrations. 2 Vols. Post 8vo. 30s.

—————— LIVES OF ITALIAN PAINTERS, FROM CIMABUE to BASSANO. By Mrs. JAMESON. Portraits. Post 8vo. 12s.

—————— n NORWAY, Christiania, Bergen, Trondhjem. The Fjelds a d Fjords. Map. Post 8vo. 9s.

—————— SWEDEN, Stockholm, Upsala, Gothenburg, the Shores of the Baltic, &c. Post 8vo. 6s.

—————— DENMARK, Sleswig, Holstein, Copenhagen, Jutland, Iceland Map. Post 8vo. 6s.

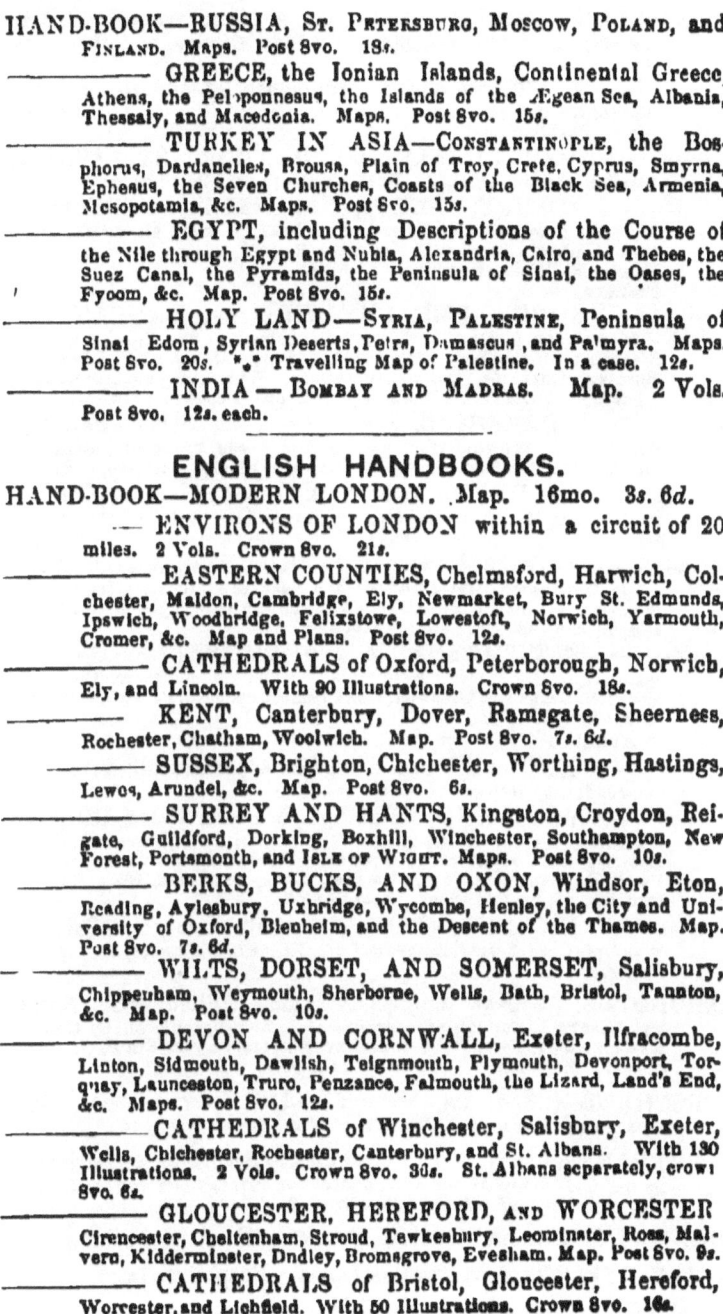

HAND-BOOK—RUSSIA, St. Petersburg, Moscow, Poland, and Finland. Maps. Post 8vo. 18s.

———— GREECE, the Ionian Islands, Continental Greece, Athens, the Peloponnesus, the Islands of the Ægean Sea, Albania, Thessaly, and Macedonia. Maps. Post 8vo. 15s.

———— TURKEY IN ASIA—Constantinople, the Bosphorus, Dardanelles, Brousa, Plain of Troy, Crete, Cyprus, Smyrna, Ephesus, the Seven Churches, Coasts of the Black Sea, Armenia, Mesopotamia, &c. Maps. Post 8vo. 15s.

———— EGYPT, including Descriptions of the Course of the Nile through Egypt and Nubia, Alexandria, Cairo, and Thebes, the Suez Canal, the Pyramids, the Peninsula of Sinai, the Oases, the Fyoom, &c. Map. Post 8vo. 15s.

———— HOLY LAND—Syria, Palestine, Peninsula of Sinai Edom, Syrian Deserts, Petra, Damascus, and Palmyra. Maps. Post 8vo. 20s. *.* Travelling Map of Palestine. In a case. 12s.

———— INDIA — Bombay and Madras. Map. 2 Vols. Post 8vo. 12s. each.

ENGLISH HANDBOOKS.

HAND-BOOK—MODERN LONDON. Map. 16mo. 3s. 6d.

—— ENVIRONS OF LONDON within a circuit of 20 miles. 2 Vols. Crown 8vo. 21s.

———— EASTERN COUNTIES, Chelmsford, Harwich, Colchester, Maldon, Cambridge, Ely, Newmarket, Bury St. Edmunds, Ipswich, Woodbridge, Felixstowe, Lowestoft, Norwich, Yarmouth, Cromer, &c. Map and Plans. Post 8vo. 12s.

———— CATHEDRALS of Oxford, Peterborough, Norwich, Ely, and Lincoln. With 90 Illustrations. Crown 8vo. 18s.

———— KENT, Canterbury, Dover, Ramsgate, Sheerness, Rochester, Chatham, Woolwich. Map. Post 8vo. 7s. 6d.

———— SUSSEX, Brighton, Chichester, Worthing, Hastings, Lewes, Arundel, &c. Map. Post 8vo. 6s.

———— SURREY AND HANTS, Kingston, Croydon, Reigate, Guildford, Dorking, Boxhill, Winchester, Southampton, New Forest, Portsmouth, and Isle of Wight. Maps. Post 8vo. 10s.

———— BERKS, BUCKS, AND OXON, Windsor, Eton, Reading, Aylesbury, Uxbridge, Wycombe, Henley, the City and University of Oxford, Blenheim, and the Descent of the Thames. Map. Post 8vo. 7s. 6d.

———— WILTS, DORSET, AND SOMERSET, Salisbury, Chippenham, Weymouth, Sherborne, Wells, Bath, Bristol, Taunton, &c. Map. Post 8vo. 10s.

———— DEVON AND CORNWALL, Exeter, Ilfracombe, Linton, Sidmouth, Dawlish, Teignmouth, Plymouth, Devonport, Torquay, Launceston, Truro, Penzance, Falmouth, the Lizard, Land's End, &c. Maps. Post 8vo. 12s.

———— CATHEDRALS of Winchester, Salisbury, Exeter, Wells, Chichester, Rochester, Canterbury, and St. Albans. With 130 Illustrations. 2 Vols. Crown 8vo. 30s. St. Albans separately, crown 8vo. 6s.

———— GLOUCESTER, HEREFORD, and WORCESTER, Cirencester, Cheltenham, Stroud, Tewkesbury, Leominster, Ross, Malvern, Kidderminster, Dudley, Bromsgrove, Evesham. Map. Post 8vo. 9s.

———— CATHEDRALS of Bristol, Gloucester, Hereford, Worcester, and Lichfield. With 50 Illustrations. Crown 8vo. 16s.

HAND-BOOK—NORTH WALES, Bangor, Carnarvon, Beaumaris, Snowdon, Llanberis, Dolgelly, Cader Idris, Conway, &c. Map. Post 8vo. 7s

———————— **SOUTH WALES**, Monmouth, Llandaff, Merthyr, Vale of Neath, Pembroke, Carmarthen, Tenby, Swansea, The Wye, &c. Map. Post 8vo. 7s.

———————— **CATHEDRALS OF BANGOR, ST. ASAPH**, Llandaff, and St. David's. With Illustrations. Post 8vo. 15s.

———————— **DERBY, NOTTS, LEICESTER, STAFFORD**, Matlock, Bakewell, Chatsworth, The Peak, Buxton, Hardwick, Dove Dale, Ashborne. Southwell, Mansfield, Retford, Burton, Belvoir, Melto Mowbray, Wolverhampton, Lichfield, Walsall, Tamworth. Map. Post 8vo. 9s.

———————— **SHROPSHIRE, CHESHIRE AND LANCASHIRE** —Shrewsbury, Ludlow, Bridgnorth, Oswestry, Chester, Crewe, Alderley, Stockport, Birkenhead, Warrington, Bury, Manchester, Liverpool, Burnley, Clitheroe, Bolton, Blackburn, Wigan, Preston, Rochdale, Lancaster, Southport, Blackpool, &c. Map. Post 8vo. 10s.

———————— **YORKSHIRE**, Doncaster, Hull, Selby, Beverley, Scarborough, Whitby, Harrogate, Ripon, Leeds, Wakefield, Bradford, Halifax, Huddersfield, Sheffield. Map and Plans. Post 8vo. 12s.

———————— **CATHEDRALS** of York, Ripon, Durham, Carlisle, Chester, and Manchester. With 60 Illustrations. 2 Vols. Crown 8vo. 21s.

———————— **DURHAM AND NORTHUMBERLAND**, Newcastle, Darlington, Gateshead, Bishop Auckland, Stockton, Hartlepool, Sunderland, Shields, Berwick-on-Tweed, Morpeth, Tynemouth, Coldstream, Alnwick, &c. Map. Post 8vo. 9s.

———————— **WESTMORLAND AND CUMBERLAND**—Lancaster, Furness Abbey, Ambleside, Kendal, Windermere, Coniston, Keswick, Grasmere, Ulswater, Carlisle, Cockermouth, Penrith, Appleby. Map. Post 8vo. 6s.
⸋ MURRAY'S MAP OF THE LAKE DISTRICT, on canvas. 3s. 6d.

———————— **ENGLAND AND WALES**. Alphabetically arranged and condensed into one volume. Post 8vo [In the Press.

———————— **SCOTLAND**, Edinburgh, Melrose, Kelso, Glasgow, Dumfries, Ayr, Stirling, Arran, The Clyde, Oban, Inverary, Loch Lomond, Loch Katrine and Trossachs, Caledonian Canal, Inverness, Perth, Dundee, Aberdeen, Braemar, Skye, Caithness, Ross, Sutherland, &c. Maps and Plans. Post 8vo. 9s.

———————— **IRELAND**, Dublin, Belfast, Donegal, Galway, Wexford, Cork, Limerick, Waterford, Killarney, Munster, &c. Maps. Post 8vo. 12s.

HERODOTUS. A New English Version. Edited, with Notes and Essays, historical, ethnographical, and geographical, by CANON RAWLINSON, assisted by SIR HENRY RAWLINSON and SIR J. G. WILKINSON. Maps and Woodcuts. 4 Vols. 8vo. 48s.

HERSCHEL'S (CAROLINE) Memoir and Correspondence. By MRS. JOHN HERSCHEL. With Portraits. Crown 8vo 12s.

HATHERLEY (LORD). The Continuity of Scripture, as Declared by the Testimony of our Lord and of the Evangelists and Apostles. 8vo. 6s. *Popular Edition.* Post 8vo. 2s. 6d.

HOLLWAY (J. G.). A Month in Norway. Fcap. 8vo. 2s.

HONEY BEE. By REV. THOMAS JAMES. Fcap. 8vo. 1s.

HOOK (DEAN). Church Dictionary. 8vo. 16s.

HOME AND COLONIAL LIBRARY. A Series of Works adapted for all circles and classes of Readers, having been selected for their acknowledged interest, and ability of the Authors. Post 8vo. Published at 2s. and 3s. 6d. each, and arranged under two distinctive heads as follows:—

CLASS A.

HISTORY, BIOGRAPHY, AND HISTORIC TALES.

1. SIEGE OF GIBRALTAR. By John Drinkwater. 2s.
2. THE AMBER-WITCH. By Lady Duff Gordon. 2s.
3. CROMWELL AND BUNYAN. By Robert Southey. 2s.
4. LIFE of Sir FRANCIS DRAKE. By John Barrow. 2s.
5. CAMPAIGNS AT WASHINGTON. By Rev. G. R. Gleig. 2s.
6. THE FRENCH IN ALGIERS. By Lady Duff Gordon. 2s.
7. THE FALL OF THE JESUITS. 2s.
8. LIVONIAN TALES. 2s.
9. LIFE OF CONDÉ. By Lord Mahon. 3s. 6d.
10. SALE'S BRIGADE. By Rev. G. R. Gleig. 2s.
11. THE SIEGES OF VIENNA. By Lord Ellesmere. 2s.
12. THE WAYSIDE CROSS. By Capt. Milman. 2s.
13. SKETCHES of GERMAN LIFE. By Sir A. Gordon. 3s. 6d.
14. THE BATTLE of WATERLOO. By Rev. G. R. Gleig. 3s. 6d.
15. AUTOBIOGRAPHY OF STEFFENS. 2s.
16. THE BRITISH POETS. By Thomas Campbell. 3s. 6d.
17. HISTORICAL ESSAYS. By Lord Mahon. 8s. 6d.
18. LIFE OF LORD CLIVE. By Rev. G. R. Gleig. 3s. 6d.
19. NORTH-WESTERN RAILWAY. By Sir F. B. Head. 2s.
20. LIFE OF MUNRO. By Rev. G. R. Gleig. 3s. 6d.

CLASS B.

VOYAGES, TRAVELS, AND ADVENTURES.

1. BIBLE IN SPAIN. By George Borrow. 3s. 6d.
2. GYPSIES of SPAIN. By George Borrow. 3s. 6d.
3 & 4. JOURNALS IN INDIA. By Bishop Heber. 2 Vols. 7s.
5. TRAVELS in the HOLY LAND. By Irby and Mangles. 2s.
6. MOROCCO AND THE MOORS. By J. Drummond Hay. 2s.
7. LETTERS FROM the BALTIC. By a Lady.
8. NEW SOUTH WALES. By Mrs. Meredith. 2s.
9. THE WEST INDIES. By M. G. Lewis. 2s.
10. SKETCHES OF PERSIA. By Sir John Malcolm. 3s. 6d.
11. MEMOIRS OF FATHER RIPA. 2s.
12 & 13. TYPEE AND OMOO. By Hermann Melville. 2 Vols. 7s.
14. MISSIONARY LIFE IN CANADA. By Rev. J. Abbott. 2s.
15. LETTERS FROM MADRAS. By a Lady. 2s.
16. HIGHLAND SPORTS. By Charles St. John. 3s. 6d.
17. PAMPAS JOURNEYS. By F. B. Head. 2s.
18. GATHERINGS FROM SPAIN. By Richard Ford. 3s. 6d.
19. THE RIVER AMAZON. By W. H. Edwards. 2s.
20. MANNERS & CUSTOMS OF INDIA. By Rev. C. Acland. 2s.
21. ADVENTURES IN MEXICO. By G. F. Ruxton. 3s. 6d.
22. PORTUGAL AND GALICIA. By Lord Carnarvon. 3s. 6d.
23. BUSH LIFE IN AUSTRALIA. By Rev. H. W. Haygarth. 2s.
24. THE LIBYAN DESERT. By Bayle St. John. 2s.
25. SIERRA LEONE. By A Lady. 3s. 6d.

₊ Each work may be had separately.

C

HOOK'S (THEODORE) Life. By J. G. LOCKHART. Fcap. 8vo. 1s.

HOPE (T. C.). ARCHITECTURE OF AHMEDABAD, with Historical
Sketch and Architectural Notes. With Maps, Photographs, and
Woodcuts. 4to. 5l. 5s.

———— (A. J. BERESFORD) Worship in the Church of England.
8vo. 9s., or, Popular Selections from. 8vo. 2s. 6d.

HORACE; a New Edition of the Text. Edited by DEAN MILMAN.
With 100 Woodcuts. Crown 8vo. 7s. 6d.

———— Life of. By DEAN MILMAN. Illustrations. 8vo. 9s.

HOUGHTON'S (LORD) Monographs, Personal and Social. With
Portraits. Crown 8vo. 10s. 6d.

———— POETICAL WORKS. Collected Edition. With Portrait. 2 Vols. Fcap. 8vo. 12s.

HUME (The Student's). A History of England, from the Invasion of Julius Cæsar to the Revolution of 1688. Corrected and continued to 1868 Woodcuts. Post 8vo. 7s. 6d.

HUTCHINSON (GEN.) Dog Breaking, with Odds and Ends for
those who love the Dog and the Gun. With 40 Illustrations. 6th
edition. 7s. 6d.

HUTTON (H. E.). Principia Græca; an Introduction to the Study
of Greek. Comprehending Grammar, Delectus, and Exercise-book,
with Vocabularies. Sixth Edition. 12mo. 3s. 6d.

IRBY AND MANGLES' Travels in Egypt, Nubia, Syria, and
the Holy Land. Post 8vo. 2s.

JACOBSON (BISHOP). Fragmentary Illustrations of the History
of the Book of Common Prayer; from Manuscript Sources (Bishop
SANDERSON and Bishop WREN). 8vo. 5s.

JAMES' (REV. THOMAS) Fables of Æsop. A New Translation, with
Historical Preface. With 100 Woodcuts by TENNIEL and WOLF.
Post 8vo. 2s. 6d.

JAMESON (MRS.). Lives of the Early Italian Painters—
and the Progress of Painting in Italy—Cimabue to Bassano. With
50 Portraits. Post 8vo. 12s.

JENNINGS (LOUIS J.). Field Paths and Green Lanes. Being
Country Walks, chiefly in Surrey and Sussex. With Illustrations.
Post 8vo. 10s. 6d.

JERVIS (REV. W. H.). The Gallican Church, from the Con-
cordat of Bologna, 1516, to the Revolution. With an Introduction.
Portraits. 2 Vols. 8vo. 28s.

JESSE (EDWARD). Gleanings in Natural History. Fcp. 8vo. 3s. 6d.

JEX-BLAKE (REV. T. W.). Life in Faith: Sermons Preached
at Cheltenham and Rugby. Fcap. 8vo. 3s. 6d.

JOHNS (REV. B. G.). Blind People; their Works and Ways. With
Sketches of the Lives of some famous Blind Men. With Illustrations.
Post 8vo. 7s. 6d.

JOHNSON'S (DR. SAMUEL) Life. By James Boswell. Including
the Tour to the Hebrides. Edited by MR. CROKER. 1 vol. Royal
8vo. 12s New Edition. Portraits. 4 Vols. 8vo. [In Preparation.

———— Lives of the most eminent English Poets, with
Critical Observations on their Works. Edited with Notes, Corrective
and Explanatory, by PETER CUNNINGHAM. 3 vols. 8vo. 22s. 6d.

JUNIUS' HANDWRITING Professionally investigated. By Mr. CHABOT,
Expert. With Preface and Collateral Evidence, by the Hon. EDWARD
TWISLETON. With Facsimiles, Woodcuts, &c. 4to. £3 3s.

KEN'S (Bishop) Life. By a Layman. Portrait. 2 Vols. 8vo. 18*s.*
———— Exposition of the Apostles' Creed. 16mo. 1*s.* 6*d.*

KERR (Robert). Gentleman's House; or, How to Plan Eng-
lish Residences from the Parsonage to the Palace. With
Views and Plans. 8vo. 24*s.*
———— Small Country House. A Brief Practical Discourse on
the Planning of a Residence from 20*0l.* to 500*0l.* With Supple-
mentary Estimates to 700*ul.* Post 8vo. 3*s.*
———— Ancient Lights; a Book for Architects, Surveyors,
Lawyers, and Landlords. 8vo. 5*s.* 6*d.*
———— (R. Malcolm) Student's Blackstone. A Systematic
Abridgment of the entire Commentaries, adapted to the present state
of the law. Post 8vo. 7s. 6*d.*

KING EDWARD VITH's Latin Grammar. 12mo. 3*s.* 6*d.*
———— First Latin Book. 12mo. 2*s.* 6*d.*

KING GEORGE IIIrd's Correspondence with Lord North,
1769-82. Edited, with Notes and Introduction, by W. Bodham Donne.
2 vols. 8vo. 32*s.*

KING (R. J.). Archæology, Travel and Art; being Sketches and
Studies, Historical and Descriptive. 8vo. 12*s.*

KIRK (J. Foster). History of Charles the Bold, Duke of Burgundy. Portrait. 3 Vols. 8vo. 45*s.*

KIRKES' Handbook of Physiology. Edited by W. Morrant
Baker, F.R.C.S. 10*th Edition.* With 400 Illustrations. Post 8vo. 14*s.*

KUGLER'S Handbook of Painting.—The Italian Schools. Re-
vised and Remodelled from the most recent Researches. By Lady
Eastlake. With 140 Illustrations. 2 Vols. Crown 8vo. 30*s.*
———— Handbook of Painting.—The German, Flemish, and
Dutch Schools. Revised and in part re-written. By J. A. Crowe.
With 60 Illustrations. 2 Vols. Crown 8vo. 24*s.*

LANE (E. W.). Account of the Manners and Customs of Modern
Egyptians. With Illustrations. 2 Vols. Post 8vo. 12*s*

LAWRENCE (Sir Geo.). Reminiscences of Forty-three Years'
Service in India; including Captivities in Cabul among the Affghans
and among the Sikhs, and a Narrative of the Mutiny in Rajputana.
Crown 8vo. 10*s.* 6*d.*

LAYARD (A. H.). Nineveh and its Remains. Being a Nar-
rative of Researches and Discoveries amidst the Ruins of Assyria.
With an Account of the Chaldean Christians of Kurdistan; the Yezedis,
or Devil-worshippers; and an Enquiry into the Manners and Arts of
the Ancient Assyrians. Plates and Woodcuts. 2 Vols. 8vo. 36*s.*
*** A Popular Edition of the above work. With Illustrations.
Post 8vo. 7*s.* 6*d.*
———— Nineveh and Babylon; being the Narrative of Dis-
coveries in the Ruins, with Travels in Armenia, Kurdistan and the
Desert, during a Second Expedition to Assyria. With Map and
Plates. 8vo. 21*s.*
*** A Popular Edition of the above work. With Illustrations.
Post 8vo. 7*s.* 6*d.*

LEATHES' (Stanley) Practical Hebrew Grammar. With the
Hebrew Text of Genesis I.—vi., and Psalms I.—vi. Grammatical
Analysis and Vocabulary. Post 8vo. 7*s.* 6*d.*

LENNEP (Rev. H. J. Van). Missionary Travels in Asia Minor.
With Illustrations of Biblical History and Archæology. With Map
and Woodcuts. 2 Vols. Post 8vo. 24*s.*
———— Modern Customs and Manners of Bible Lands in
Illustration of Scripture. With Coloured Maps and 300 Illustrations.
2 Vols. 8vo. 21*s.*

c 2

LESLIE (C. R.). Handbook for Young Painters. With Illustrations. Post 8vo. 7s. 6d.
———— Life and Works of Sir Joshua Reynolds. Portraits and Illustrations. 2 Vols. 8vo. 42s.

LETO (Pomponio). Eight Months at Rome during the Vatican Council. With a daily account of the proceedings. Translated from the original. 8vo. 12s.

LETTERS From the Baltic. By a Lady. Post 8vo. 2s.
———— Madras. By a Lady. Post 8vo. 2s.
———— Sierra Leone. By a Lady. Post 8vo. 3s. 6d.

LEVI (Leone). History of British Commerce; and of the Economic Progress of the Nation, from 1763 to 1870. 8vo. 16s.

LIDDELL (Dean). Student's History of Rome, from the earliest Times to the establishment of the Empire. Woodcuts. Post 8vo. 7s. 6d.

LLOYD (W. Watkiss). History of Sicily to the Athenian War; with Elucidations of the Sicilian Odes of Pindar. With Map. 8vo. 14s.

LISPINGS from LOW LATITUDES; or, the Journal of the Hon. Impulsia Gushington. Edited by Lord Dufferin. With 24 Plates. 4to. 21s.

LITTLE ARTHUR'S History of England. By Lady Callcott. New Edition, continued to 1872. With Woodcuts. Fcap. 8vo. 1s. 6d.

LIVINGSTONE (Dr.). Popular Account of his First Expedition to Africa, 1840-56. Illustrations. Post 8vo. 7s. 6d.
———— Popular Account of his Second Expedition to Africa, 1858-64. Map and Illustrations. Post 8vo. 7s. 6d.
———— Last Journals in Central Africa, from 1865 to his Death. Continued by a Narrative of his last moments and sufferings. By Rev Horace Waller. Maps and Illustrations. 2 Vols. 8vo. 28s.

LIVINGSTONIA. Journal of Adventures in Exploring Lake Nyassa, and Establishing a Missionary Settlement there. By E. D. Young, R.N. Revised by Rev. Horace Waller. Maps. Post 8vo. 7s. 6d.

LIVONIAN TALES. By the Author of "Letters from the Baltic." Post 8vo. 2s.

LOCH (H. B.). Personal Narrative of Events during Lord Elgin's Second Embassy to China. With Illustrations. Post 8vo. 9s.

LOCKHART (J. G.). Ancient Spanish Ballads. Historical and Romantic. Translated, with Notes. With Portrait and Illustrations. Crown 8vo. 5s.
———— Life of Theodore Hook. Fcap. 8vo. 1s.

LOUDON (Mrs.) Gardening for Ladies. With Directions and Calendar of Operations for Every Month. Woodcuts. Fcap. 8vo. 3s. 6d.

LYELL (Sir Charles). Principles of Geology; or, the Modern Changes of the Earth and its Inhabitants considered as illustrative of Geology. With Illustrations. 2 Vols. 8vo. 32s.
———— Student's Elements of Geology. With Table of British Fossils and 600 Illustrations. Post 8vo. 9s.
———— Geological Evidences of the Antiquity of Man, including an Outline of Glacial Post-Tertiary Geology, and Remarks on the Origin of Species. Illustrations. 8vo. 14s.
———— (K. M.). Geographical Handbook of Ferns. With Tables to show their Distribution. Post 8vo. 7s. 6d.

LYTTON (Lord). A Memoir of Julian Fane. With Portrait. Post 8vo. 5s

McCLINTOCK (Sir L.). Narrative of the Discovery of the Fate of Sir John Franklin and his Companions in the Arctic Seas. With Illustrations. Post 8vo. 7s. 6d.

MACDOUGALL (Col.). Modern Warfare as Influenced by Modern Artillery. With Plans. Post 8vo. 12s.

MACGREGOR (J.). Rob Roy on the Jordan, Nile, Red Sea, Gennesareth, &c. A Canoe Cruise in Palestine and Egypt and the Waters of Damascus. With Map and 70 Illustrations. Crown 8vo. 7s. 6d.

MAETZNER'S ENGLISH GRAMMAR. A Methodical, Analytical, and Historical Treatise on the Orthography, Prosody, Inflections, and Syntax of the English Tongue. Translated from the German. By CLAIR J. GRECE, LL.D. 3 Vols. 8vo. 36s.

MAHON (LORD), see STANHOPE.

MAINE (SIR H. SUMNER). Ancient Law: its Connection with the Early History of Society, and its Relation to Modern Ideas. 8vo. 12s.

———— Village Communities in the East and West. With additional Essays. 8vo. 12s.

———— Early History of Institutions. 8vo. 12s.

MALCOLM (SIR JOHN). Sketches of Persia. Post 8vo. 3s. 6d.

MANSEL (DEAN). Limits of Religious Thought Examined. Post 8vo. 8s. 6d.

———— Letters, Lectures, and Papers, including the Phrontisterion, or Oxford in the XIXth Century. Edited by H. W. CHANDLER, M.A. 8vo. 12s.

———— Gnostic Heresies of the First and Second Centuries. With a sketch of his life and character. By Lord CARNARVON. Edited by Canon LIGHTFOOT. 8vo. 10s. 6d.

MANUAL OF SCIENTIFIC ENQUIRY. For the Use of Travellers. Edited by REV. R. MAIN. Post 8vo. 3s. 6d. (Published by order of the Lords of the Admiralty.)

MARCO POLO. The Book of Ser Marco Polo, the Venetian. Concerning the Kingdoms and Marvels of the East. A new English Version. Illustrated by the light of Oriental Writers and Modern Travels. By COL. HENRY YULE. Maps and Illustrations. 2 Vols. Medium 8vo. 63s.

MARKHAM'S (MRS.) History of England. From the First Invasion by the Romans to 1867. Woodcuts. 12mo. 3s. 6d.

———— History of France. From the Conquest by the Gauls to 1861. Woodcuts. 12mo. 3s. 6d.

———— History of Germany. From the Invasion by Marius to 1867. Woodcuts. 12mo. 3s. 6d.

MARLBOROUGH'S (SARAH, DUCHESS OF) Letters. Now first published from the Original MSS. at Madresfield Court. With an Introduction. 8vo. 10s. 6d.

MARRYAT (JOSEPH). History of Modern and Mediæval Pottery and Porcelain. With a Description of the Manufacture. Plates and Woodcuts. 8vo. 42s. [Post 8vo. 7s. 6d.

MARSH (G. P.). Student's Manual of the English Language.

MASTERS in English Theology. The King's College Lectures, 1877. By Canon Barry, Dean of S'. Paul's; Prof. Plumptre, Canon Westcott, Canon Farrar, and Prof. Cheetham. With an Historical Introduction by Canon Barry. Post 8vo. 7s 6d.

MATTHIÆ'S GREEK GRAMMAR. Abridged by BLOMFIELD. Revised by E. S. CROOKE. 12mo. 4s.

MAUREL'S Character, Actions, and Writings of Wellington. Fcap. 8vo. 1s. 6d.

MAYNE (CAPT.). Four Years in British Columbia and Vancouver Island. Illustrations. 8vo. 16s.

MAYO (LORD). Sport in Abyssinia; or, the Mareb and Tackazzee. With Illustrations. Crown 8vo. 12s.

MEADE (HON. HERBERT). Ride through the Disturbed Districts of New Zealand, with a Cruise among the South Sea Islands. With Illustrations. Medium 8vo. 12s.

MELVILLE (Herman). Marquesas and South Sea Islands.
2 Vols. Post 8vo. 7s.

MEREDITH (Mrs. Charles). Notes and Sketches of New South Wales. Post 8vo. 2s.

MESSIAH (THE): The Life, Travels, Death, Resurrection, and Ascension of our Blessed Lord. By A Layman. Map. 8vo. 18s.

MICHELANGELO, Sculptor, Painter, and Architect. His Life and Works. By C. Heath Wilson. Illustrations. Royal 8vo. 26s.

MILLINGTON (Rev. T. S.). Signs and Wonders in the Land of Ham, or the Ten Plagues of Egypt. with Ancient and Modern Illustrations. Woodcuts. Post 8vo. 7s. 6d.

MILMAN (Dean). History of the Jews, from the earliest Period down to Modern Times. 3 Vols. Post 8vo. 18s.

———— Early Christianity, from the Birth of Christ to the Abolition of Paganism in the Roman Empire. 3 Vols. Post 8vo. 18s.

———— Latin Christianity, including that of the Popes to the Pontificate of Nicholas V. 9 Vols. Post 8vo. 54s.

———— Annals of St. Paul's Cathedral, from the Romans to the funeral of Wellington. Portrait and Illustrations. 8vo. 18s.

———— Character and Conduct of the Apostles considered as an Evidence of Christianity. 8vo. 10s. 6d.

———— Quinti Horatii Flacci Opera. With 100 Woodcuts. Small 8vo. 7s. 6d.

———— Life of Quintus Horatius Flaccus. With Illustrations. 8vo. 9s.

———— Poetical Works. The Fall of Jerusalem—Martyr of Antioch—Balshazzar—Tamor—Anne Boleyn—Fazio, &c. With Portrait and Illustrations. 3 Vols. Fcap. 8vo. 18s.

———— Fall of Jerusalem. Fcap. 8vo. 1s.

———— (Capt. E. A.) Wayside Cross. Post 8vo. 2s.

MIVART (St. George). Lessons from Nature; as manifested in Mind and Matter. 8vo. 15s.

MODERN DOMESTIC COOKERY. Founded on Principles of Economy and Practical Knowledge. *New Edition.* Woodcuts. Fcap. 8vo. 5s.

MONGREDIEN (Augustus). Trees and Shrubs for English Plantation. A Selection and Description of the most Ornamental which will flourish in the open air in our climate. With Classified Lists. With 30 Illustrations. 8vo. 16s.

MOORE (Thomas). Life and Letters of Lord Byron. *Cabinet Edition.* With Plates. 6 Vols. Fcap. 8vo. 18s.; *Popular Edition*, with Portraits. Royal 8vo. 7s. 6d.

MORESBY (Capt.), R.N. Discoveries in New Guinea, Polynesia, Torres Straits, &c., during the cruise of H.M.S. Basilisk. Map and Illustrations. 8vo. 15s.

MOTLEY (J. L.). History of the United Netherlands: from the Death of William the Silent to the Twelve Years' Truce, 1609. *Library Edition.* Portraits. 4 Vols. 8vo. 60s. *Cabinet Edition.* 4 Vols. Post 8vo. 6s. each.

———— Life and Death of John of Barneveld, Advocate of Holland. With a View of the Primary Causes and Movements of the Thirty Years' War. *Library Edition.* Illustrations. 2 Vols. 8vo. 28s. *Cabinet Edition.* 2 vols Post 8vo. 12s.

MOSSMAN (Samuel). New Japan; the Land of the Rising Sun; its Annals and Progress during the past Twenty Years, recording the remarkable Progress of the Japanese in Western Civilisation. With Map. 8vo. 15s.

MOUHOT (Henri). Siam, Cambojia, and Lao ; a Narrative
Travels and Discoveries. Illustrations. 2 Vols. 8vo.

MOZLEY (Canon). Treatise on Predestination. 8vo. 14s.

———— Primitive Doctrine of Baptismal Regeneration. Post 8vo.

MUIRHEAD (Jas.). The Vaux-de-Vire of Maistre Jean Le Houx
Advocate of Vire. Translated and Edited. With Portrait and Illustrations. 8vo. 21s.

MUNRO'S (General) Life and Letters. By Rev. G. R. Gleig.
Post 8vo. 3s. 6d.

MURCHISON (Sir Roderick). Siluria ; or, a History of the
Oldest rocks containing Organic Remains. Map and Plates. 8vo. 18s.

———————— Memoirs. With Notices of his Contemporaries,
and Rise and Progress of Palæozoic Geology. By Archibald Geikie.
Portraits. 2 Vols. 8vo. 30s.

MURRAY'S RAILWAY READING. Containing:—

Wellington. By Lord Ellesmere. 6d.	Mahon's Joan of Arc. 1s.
Nimrod on the Chase. 1s.	Head's Emigrant. 2s. 6d.
Music and Dress. 1s.	Nimrod on the Road. 1s.
Milman's Fall of Jerusalem. 1s.	Croker on the Guillotine. 1s.
Mahon's "Forty-Five." 3s.	Hollway's Norway. 2s.
Life of Theodore Hook. 1s.	Mausel's Wellington. 1s. 6d.
Deeds of Naval Daring. 3s. 6d.	Campbell's Life of Bacon. 2s. 6d.
The Honey Bee. 1s.	The Flower Garden. 1s.
Æsop's Fables. 2s. 6d.	Taylor's Notes from Life. 2s.
Nimrod on the Turf. 1s. 6d.	Rejected Addresses. 1s.
Art of Dining. 1s. 6d.	Penn's Hints on Angling. 1s.

MUSTERS' (Capt.) Patagonians ; a Year's Wanderings over
Untrodden Ground from the Straits of Magellan to the Rio Negro.
Illustrations. Post 8vo. 7s. 6d.

NAPIER (Sir Wm.). English Battles and Sieges of the Peninsular
War. Portrait. Post 8vo. 9s.

NAPOLEON at Fontainebleau and Elba. A Journal of
Occurrences and Notes of Conversations. By Sir Neil Campbell,
C.B. With a Memoir. By Rev. A. N. C. Maclachlan, M.A. Portrait.
8vo. 15s.

NARES (Sir George), R.N. Official Report to the Admiralty of
the recent Arctic Expedition. Map. 8vo. 2s. 6d.

NASMYTH and **CARPENTER**. The Moon. Considered as a
Planet, a World, and a Satellite. With Illustrations from Drawings
made with the aid of Powerful Telescopes, Woodcuts, &c. 4to. 30s.

NAUTICAL ALMANAC (The). (By Authority.) 2s. 6d.

NAVY LIST. (Monthly and Quarterly.) Post 8vo.

NEW TESTAMENT. With Short Explanatory Commentary.
By Archdeacon Churton, M.A., and Archdeacon Basil Jones, M.A.
With 110 authentic Views, &c. 2 Vols. Crown 8vo 21s. bound.

NEWTH (Samuel). First Book of Natural Philosophy ; an Introduction to the Study of Statics, Dynamics, Hydrostatics, Optics, and
Acoustics, with numerous Examples. Small 8vo. 3s. 6d.

———————— Elements of Mechanics, including Hydrostatics,
with numerous Examples. Small 8vo. 8s. 6d.

———————— Mathematical Examinations. A Graduated
Series of Elementary Examples in Arithmetic, Algebra, Logarithms,
Trigonometry, and Mechanics. Small 8vo. 8s. 6d.

NICHOLS' (J. G.) Pilgrimages to Walsingham and Canterbury.
By Erasmus. Translated, with Notes. With Illustrations. Post 8vo. 6s.

———— (Sir George) History of the English Poor Laws.
2 Vols. 8vo.

NICOLAS' (Sir Harris) Historic Peerage of England. Exhibiting the Origin, Descent, and Present State of every Title of Peerage which has existed in this Country since the Conquest. By
William Courthope. 8vo. 30s.

NIMROD, On the Chace—Turf—and Road. With Portrait and
Plates. Crown 8vo. 5s. Or with Coloured Plates, 7s. 6d.

NORDHOFF (Chas.). Communistic Societies of the United
States; including Detailed Accounts of the Shakers, The Amana,
Oneida, Bethell, Aurora, Icarian and other existing Societies; with
Particulars of their Religious Creeds, Industries, and Present Condi-
tion. With 40 Illustrations. 8vo. 15s.

NORTHCOTE'S (Sir John) Notebook in the Long Parliament.
Containing Proceedings during its First Session, 1640. From the
Original MS. in the possession of Sir Stafford Northcote, Bart. Edited,
with a Memoir. By A. H. A. Hamilton. Crown 8vo. 9s.

OWEN (Lieut.-Col.). Principles and Practice of Modern Artillery,
including Artillery Material, Gunnery, and Organisation and Use of
Artillery in Warfare. With Illustrations. 8vo. 15s.

OXENHAM (Rev. W.). English Notes for Latin Elegiacs; designed
for early Proficients in the Art of Latin Versification, with Prefatory
Rules of Composition in Elegiac Metre. 12mo. 3s. 6d.

PALGRAVE (R. H. I.). Local Taxation of Great Britain and
Ireland. 8vo. 5s.

———————— Notes on Banking in Great Britain and Ireland, Sweden, Denmark. and Hamburg, with some Remarks on
the amount of Bills in circulation, both Inland and Foreign. 8vo. 6s.

PALLISER (Mrs.). Brittany and its Byeways, its Inhabitants,
and Antiquities. With Illustrations. Post 8vo. 12s.

———————— Mottoes for Monuments, or Epitaphs selected for
General Use and Study. With Illustrations. Crown 8vo. 7s. 6d.

PARIS' (Dr.) Philosophy in Sport made Science in Earnest;
or, the First Principles of Natural Philosophy inculcated by aid of the
Toys and Sports of Youth. Woodcuts. Post 8vo. 7s. 6d.

PARKMAN (Francis). Discovery of the Great West; or, The
Valleys of the Mississippi and the Lakes of North America. An
Historical Narrative. Map. 8vo. 10s. 6d.

PARKYNS' (Mansfield) Three Years' Residence in Abyssinia:
with Travels in that Country. With Illustrations. Post 8vo. 7s. 6d.

PEEK PRIZE ESSAYS. The Maintenance of the Church of
England as an Established Church. By Rev. Charles Hole—Rev.
R. Watson Dixon—and Rev. Julius Lloyd. 8vo. 10s. 6d.

PEEL'S (Sir Robert) Memoirs. 2 Vols. Post 8vo. 15s.

PENN (Richard). Maxims and Hints for an Angler and Chess-
player. Woodcuts. Fcap. 8vo. 1s.

PERCY (John, M.D.). Metallurgy. 1st Division.— Fuel,
Wood, Peat, Coal, Charcoal, Coke. Fire-Clays. *New Edition.* With
Illustrations. 8vo. 30s

———————— 2nd Division.—Copper, Zinc, and Brass. *New Edition.*
With Illustrations. [*In the Press.*

———————— 3rd Division.—Iron and Steel. *New Edition.* With
Illustrations. [*In Preparation.*

———————— 4th Division.—Lead, including part of Silver. With
Illustrations. 30s. [*Ready.*

———————— 5th Division. — Silver. With Illustrations.
[*Nearly Ready.*

———————— 6th Division.—Gold, Mercury, Platinum, Tin, Nickel,
Cobalt, Antimony, Bismuth, Arsenic, and other Metals. With Illustrations. [*In Preparation.*

PHILLIPS' (John) Memoirs of William Smith. 8vo. 7s. 6d.

———————— (John) Geology of Yorkshire, The Coast, and
Limestone District. Plates. 2 Vols. 4to.

———————— Rivers, Mountains, and Sea Coast of Yorkshire.
With Essays on the Climate, Scenery, and Ancient Inhabitants.
Plates. 8vo. 15s.

PHILLIPS (SAMUEL). Literary Essays from "The Times." With Portrait. Fcap. 8vo. 7s.

POPE'S (ALEXANDER) Works. With Introductions and Notes, by REV. WHITWELL ELWIN. Vols. I., II., VI., VII., VIII. With Portraits. 8vo. 10s. 6d. each.

PORTER (REV. J. L.). Damascus, Palmyra, and Lebanon. With Travels among the Giant Cities of Bashan and the Hauran. Map and Woodcuts. Post 8vo. 7s. 6d.

PRAYER-BOOK (ILLUSTRATED), with Borders, Initials, Vignettes, &c. Edited, with Notes, by REV. THOS. JAMES. Medium 8vo. 18s. cloth; 31s. 6d. calf; 36s. morocco.

PRINCESS CHARLOTTE OF WALES. A Brief Memoir. With Selections from her Correspondence and other unpublished Papers. By LADY ROSE WEIGALL. With Portrait. 8vo. 8s. 6d.

PUSS IN BOOTS. With 12 Illustrations. By OTTO SPECKTER. 16mo. 1s. 6d. Or coloured, 2s. 6d.

PRIVY COUNCIL JUDGMENTS in Ecclesiastical Cases relating to Doctrine and Discipline. With Historical Introduction, by G. C. BRODRICK and W. H. FREMANTLE. 8vo. 10s. 6d.

QUARTERLY REVIEW (THE). 8vo. 6s.

RAE (EDWARD). Land of the North Wind; or Travels among the Laplanders and Samoyedes, and along the Shores of the White Sea. With Map and Woodcuts. Post 8vo. 10s. 6d.

—— The Country of the Moors. A Journey from Tripoli in Barbary to the City of Kairwan. With Illustrations. Crown 8vo. 12s.

RAMBLES in the Syrian Deserts. Post 8vo. 10s. 6d.

RANKE (LEOPOLD). A History of the Popes of Rome during the 16th and 17th Centuries. Translated from the German by SARAH AUSTIN. 3 Vols. 8vo. 30s.

RASSAM (HORMUZD). Narrative of the British Mission to Abyssinia. With Notices of the Countries Traversed from Massowah to Magdala. Illustrations. 2 Vols. 8vo. 28s.

RAWLINSON'S (CANON) Herodotus. A New English Version. Edited with Notes and Essays. Maps and Woodcut. 4 Vols 8vo. 48s.

—————— Five Great Monarchies of Chaldæa, Assyria, Media, Babylonia, and Persia. With Maps and Illustrations. 3 Vols. 8vo. 42s.

—————— (SIR HENRY) England and Russia in the East; a Series of Papers on the Political and Geographical Condition of Central Asia. Map. 8vo. 12s.

REED (E. J.). Shipbuilding in Iron and Steel; a Practical Treatise, giving full details of Construction, Processes of Manufacture, and Building Arrangements. With 5 Plans and 250 Woodcuts. 8vo.

—— Iron-Clad Ships; their Qualities, Performances, and Cost. With Chapters on Turret Ships, Iron-Clad Rams, &c. With Illustrations. 8vo. 12s.

—— Letters from Russia in 1875. 8vo. 5s.

REJECTED ADDRESSES (THE). By JAMES AND HORACE SMITH. Woodcuts. Post 8vo. 3s. 6d.; or Popular Edition, Fcap. 8vo. 1s.

REYNOLDS' (SIR JOSHUA) Life and Times. By C. R. LESLIE, R.A. and TOM TAYLOR. Portraits. 2 Vols. 8vo.

RICARDO'S (DAVID) Political Works. With a Notice of his Life and Writings. By J. R. M'CULLOCH. 8vo. 16s.

RIPA (FATHER). Thirteen Years' Residence at the Court of Peking. Post 8vo. 2s.

ROBERTSON (CANON). History of the Christian Church, from the Apostolic Age to the Reformation, 1517. Library Edition. 4 Vols. 8vo. Cabinet Edition. 8 Vols. Post 8vo. 6s. each.

ROBINSON (Rev. Dr.). Biblical Researches in Palestine and the Adjacent Regions, 1838—52. Maps. 3 Vols. 8vo. 42s.

———————— Physical Geography of the Holy Land. Post 8vo. 10s. 6d.

———————— (Wm.) Alpine Flowers for English Gardens. With 70 Illustrations. Crown 8vo. 12s.

———————— Wild Gardens; or, our Groves and Shrubberies made beautiful by the Naturalization of Hardy Exotic Plants. With Frontispiece. Small 8vo. 6s.

———————— Sub-Tropical Gardens ; or, Beauty of Form in the Flower Garden. With Illustrations. Small 8vo. 7s. 6d.

ROBSON (E. R.). School Architecture. Being Practical Remarks on the Planning, Designing, Building, and Furnishing of School-houses. With 300 Illustrations. Medium 8vo. 18s.

ROME (History of). *See* Liddell and Smith.

ROWLAND (David). Manual of the English Constitution. Its Rise, Growth, and Present State. Post 8vo. 10s. 6d.

———————— Laws of Nature the Foundation of Morals. Post 8vo. 6s.

RUNDELL (Mrs.). Modern Domestic Cookery. Fcap. 8vo. 5s.

RUXTON (George F.). Travels in Mexico ; with Adventures among the Wild Tribes and Animals of the Prairies and Rocky Mountains. Post 8vo. 3s. 6d.

SALE'S (Sir Robert) Brigade in Affghanistan. With an Account of the Defence of Jellalabad. By Rev. G. R. Gleig. Post 8vo. 2s.

SCEPTICISM IN GEOLOGY; and the Reasons for It. By Verifier. Crown 8vo. 6s.

SCHLIEMANN (Dr. Henry). Troy and Its Remains. A Narrative of Researches and Discoveries made on the Site of Ilium, and in the Trojan Plain. With Maps, Views, and 500 Illustrations. Medium 8vo. 42s.

———————— Discoveries on the Sites of Ancient Mycenæ and Tiryns. With 500 Illustrations, Plans, &c. Medium 8vo. 50s.

SCOTT (Sir G. G.). Secular and Domestic Architecture, Present and Future. 8vo. 9s.

——— (Dean) University Sermons. Post 8vo. 8s. 6d.

SCROPE (G. P.). Geology and Extinct Volcanoes of Central France. Illustrations. Medium 8vo. 30s.

SHADOWS OF A SICK ROOM. With a Preface by Canon Liddon 16mo. 2s. 6d.

SHAH OF PERSIA'S Diary during his Tour through Europe in 1873. Translated from the Original. By J. W. Redhouse. With Portrait and Coloured Title. Crown 8vo. 12s.

SMILES (Samuel). British Engineers; from the Earliest Period to the death of the Stephensons. With Illustrations. 5 Vols. Crown 8vo. 7s. 6d. each.

——— George and Robert Stephenson. Illustrations. Medium 8vo. 21s.

——— Boulton and Watt. Illustrations. Medium 8vo. 21s.

——— Life of a Scotch Naturalist (Thomas Edward). With Portrait and Illustrations. Crown 8vo. 10s. 6d.

——— Huguenots in England and Ireland. Crown 8vo. 7s. 6d.

——— Self-Help. With Illustrations of Conduct and Perseverance. Post 8vo. 6s. Or in French, 5s.

——— Character. A Sequel to "Self-Help." Post 8vo. 6s.

——— Thrift. A Book of Domestic Counsel. Post 8vo. 6s.

——— Industrial Biography; or, Iron Workers and Tool Makers. Post 8vo. 6s.

SMILES (Samuel). 'Boy's Voyage round the World. With Illustrations. Post 8vo. 6s.

SMITH (Dr. Wm.). A Dictionary of the Bible; its Antiquities, Biography, Geography, and Natural History. Illustrations. 3 Vols. 8vo. 105s.

———— Concise Bible Dictionary. With 300 Illustrations. Medium 8vo. 21s.

———— Smaller Bible Dictionary. With Illustrations. Post 8vo. 7s. 6d.

———— Christian Antiquities. Comprising the History, Institutions, and Antiquities of the Christian Church. With Illustrations. Vol. I. 8vo. 31s. 6d.

———— Biography, Literature, Sects, and Doctrines; from the Times of the Apostles to the Age of Charlemagne. Vol. I. 8vo 31s. 6d.

———— Atlas of Ancient Geography—Biblical and Classical. Folio. 6l. 6s.

———— Greek and Roman Antiquities. With 500 Illustrations. Medium 8vo. 28s.

———— Biography and Mythology. With 60) Illustrations. 3 Vols. Medium 8vo. 4l. 4s.

———— Geography. 2 Vols. With 500 Illustrations. Medium 8vo. 56s.

———— Classical Dictionary of Mythology, Biography, and Geography. 1 Vol. With 750 Woodcuts. 8vo. 18s.

———— Smaller Classical Dictionary. With 200 Woodcuts. Crown 8vo. 7s. 6d.

———— Smaller Greek and Roman Antiquities. With 200 Woodcuts. Crown 8vo. 7s. 6d.

———— Complete Latin-English Dictionary. With Tables of the Roman Calendar, Measures, Weights, and Money. 8vo. 21s.

———— Smaller Latin-English Dictionary. 12mo. 7s. 6d.

———— Copious and Critical English-Latin Dictionary. 8vo. 21s.

———— Smaller English-Latin Dictionary. 12mo. 7s. 6d.

———— School Manual of English Grammar, with Copious Exercises. Post 8vo. 3s. 6d.

———— Modern Geography, Physical and Political. Post 8vo. 5s.

———— Primary English Grammar. 16mo. 1s.

———— History of Britain. 12mo. 2s. 6d.

———— French Principia. Part I. A First Course, containing a Grammar, Delectus, Exercises, and Vocabularies. 12mo. 3s. 6d.

———— Part II. A Reading Book, containing Fables, Stories, and Anecdotes, Natural History, and Scenes from the History of France. With Grammatical Questions, Notes and copious Etymological Dictionary. 12mo. 4s. 6d.

———— Part III. Prose Composition, containing a Systematic Course of Exercises on the Syntax, with the Principal Rules of Syntax. 12mo. [In the Press.

———— Student's French Grammar. By C. Heron-Wall. With Introduction by M. Littré. Post 8vo 7s. 6d.

———— Smaller Grammar of the French Language. Abridged from the above. 12mo. 3s. 6d.

———— German Principia, Part I. A First German Course, containing a Grammar, Delectus, Exercise Book, and Vocabularies. 12mo. 3s. 6d.

SMITH'S (DR. WM.) German Principia, Part II. A Reading
Book; containing Fables, Stories, and Anecdotes, Natural History, and
Scenes from the History of Germany. With Grammatical Questions,
Notes, and Dictionary. 12mo. 3s. 6d.

—————————————— Part III. An Introduction to
German Prose Composition; containing a Systematic Course of Exer-
cises on the Syntax, with the Principal Rules of Syntax. 12mo.
[*In the Press.*

————— Practical German Grammar. Post 8vo. 3s. 6d.

————— Principia Latina—Part I. First Latin Course, containing a Grammar, Delectus, and Exercise Book, with Vocabularies.
12mo. 3s. 6d.
₊ In this Edition the Cases of the Nouns, Adjectives, and Pronouns
are arranged both as in the ORDINARY GRAMMARS and as in the PUBLIC
SCHOOL PRIMER, together with the corresponding Exercises.

—————————————— Part II. A Reading-book of Mythology, Geography, Roman Antiquities, and History. With Notes and
Dictionary. 12mo. 3s. 6d.

—————————————— Part III. A Poetry Book. Hex-
ameters and Pentameters; Eclog. Ovidianæ; Latin Prosody. 12mo.
3s. 6d.

—————————————— Part IV. Prose Composition. Rules of
Syntax with Examples, Explanations of Synonyms, and Exercises
on the Syntax. 12mo. 3s. 6d.

————— Principia Latina—Part V. Short Tales and Anecdotes
for Translation into Latin. 12mo. 3s.

————— Latin-English Vocabulary and First Latin-English
Dictionary for Phædrus, Cornelius Nepos, and Cæsar. 12mo. 3s. 6d.

————— Student's Latin Grammar. Post 8vo. 6s.

————— Smaller Latin Grammar. 12mo. 3s. 6d.

————— Tacitus, Germania, Agricola, &c. With English Notes.
12mo. 3s. 6d.

————— Initia Græca, Part I. A First Greek Course, containing a Grammar, Delectus, and Exercise-book. With Vocabularies. 12mo. 3s. 6d.

—————————————— Part II. A Reading Book. Containing
Short Tales, Anecdotes, Fables, Mythology, and Grecian History.
12mo. 3s. 6d.

—————————————— Part III. Prose Composition. Containing
the Rules of Syntax, with copious Examples and Exercises. 12mo.
3s. 6d.

————— Student's Greek Grammar. By CURTIUS. Post 8vo. 6s.

————— Smaller Greek Grammar. 12mo. 3s. 6d.

————— Greek Accidence. 12mo. 2s. 6d.

————— Plato, Apology of Socrates, &c., with Notes. 12mo.
3s. 6d.

————— Smaller Scripture History. Woodcuts. 16mo. 3s. 6d.

————— Ancient History. Woodcuts. 16mo. 3s. 6d.

————— Geography. Woodcuts. 16mo. 3s. 6d.

————— Rome. Woodcuts. 16mo. 3s. 6d.

————— Greece. Woodcuts. 16mo. 3s. 6d.

————— Classical Mythology. Woodcuts. 16mo. 3s. 6d.

————— History of England. Woodcuts. 16mo. 3s. 6d.

————— English Literature. 16mo. 3s. 6d.

————— Specimens of English Literature. 16mo. 3s. 6d.

SHAW (T. B.). Student's Manual of English Literature. Post 8vo.
7*. 6d.
———— Specimens of English Literature. Selected from the
Chief Writers. Post 8vo. 7*. 6d.
———— (ROBERT). Visit to High Tartary, Yarkand, and Kashgar
(formerly Chinese Tartary), and Return Journey over the Karakorum
Pass. With Map and Illustrations. 8vo. 16*.

SHIRLEY (EVELYN P.). Deer and Deer Parks; or some Account
of English Parks, with Notes on the Management of Deer. Illustrations. 4to. 21*.

SIERRA LEONE; Described in Letters to Friends at Home. By
A LADY. Post 8vo. 3*. 6d.

SIMMONS (CAPT.). Constitution and Practice of Courts-Mar-
tial. Seventh Edition. 8vo. 15*.

SMITH (PHILIP). A History of the Ancient World, from the
Creation to the Fall of the Roman Empire, A.D. 476. Fourth Edition.
3 Vols. 8vo. 31*. 6d.

SPALDING (CAPTAIN). The Tale of Frithiof. Translated from the
Swedish of ESIAS TEGNER. Post 8vo. 7*. 6d.

STANLEY (DEAN). Sinai and Palestine, in connexion with their
History. Map. 8vo. 14*.
———————— Bible in the Holy Land; Extracted from the above
Work. Woodcuts. Fcap. 8vo. 2*. 6d.
———————— Eastern Church. Plans. 8vo. 12s.
———————— Jewish Church. 1st & 2nd Series. From the Earliest
Times to the Captivity. 2 Vols. 8vo. 24*.
———————— Third Series. From the Captivity to the
Christian Era. 8vo. 14*.
———————— Epistles of St. Paul to the Corinthians. 8vo. 18s.
———————— Life of Dr. Arnold, of Rugby. With selections from
his Correspondence. With portrait. 2 vols. Crown 8vo. 12*.
———————— Church of Scotland. 8vo. 7*. 6d.
———————— Memorials of Canterbury Cathedral. Woodcuts.
Post 8vo. 7*. 6d.
———————— Westminster Abbey. With Illustra-
tions. 8vo. 15*.
———————— Sermons during a Tour in the East. 8vo. 9*.
———————— ADDRESSES AND CHARGES OF THE LATE BISHOP STANLEY.
With Memoir. 8vo. 10*. 6d.

STEPHEN (REV. W. R.). Life and Times of St. Chrysostom.
With Portrait. 8vo. 15*.

ST. JAMES' LECTURES, 1875—6. Companions for the Devout
Life. New Edition. Crown 8vo. 6*.

IMITATION OF CHRIST. CANON FARRAR.   THEOLOGIA GERMANICA. CANON
PENSÉES OF BLAISE PASCAL. DEAN   ASHWELL.
CHURCH.   FÉNELON'S ŒUVRES SPIRITUELLES.
S. FRANÇOIS DE SALES. DEAN   REV. T. T CARTER.
GOULBURN.   ANDREWES' DEVOTIONS. BISHOP OF
BAXTER'S SAINTS' REST. ARCHBISHOP   ELY.
TRENCH.   CHRISTIAN YEAR. CANON BARRY.
S. AUGUSTINE'S CONFESSIONS. BISHOP   PARADISE LOST. REV. E. H. BICKER-
ALEXANDER.   STETH.
JEREMY TAYLOR'S HOLY LIVING AND   PILGRIM'S PROGRESS. DEAN HOWSON.
DYING. REV. DR. HUMPHRY.   PRAYER BOOK. DEAN BURGON.

ST. JOHN (CHARLES). Wild Sports and Natural History of the
Highlands. Post 8vo. 3*. 6d.
———————— (BAYLE) Adventures in the Libyan Desert. Post 8vo. 2*

STUDENT'S OLD TESTAMENT HISTORY ; from the Creation to the Return of the Jews from Captivity. Maps and Woodcuts. Post 8vo. 7s. 6d.

———— NEW TESTAMENT HISTORY. With an Introduction connecting the History of the Old and New Testaments. Maps and Woodcuts. Post 8vo. 7s. 6d.

———— ECCLESIASTICAL HISTORY. A History of the Christian Church from its Foundation to the Eve of the Reformation. By PHILIP SMITH, B.A. Post 8vo. 7s. 6d.

———— MANUAL OF ENGLISH CHURCH HISTORY, from the Reformation to the Present Time. By Rev. G. G. PERRY, Prebendary of Lincoln and Rector of Waddington. Post 8vo. 7s. 6d.

———— ANCIENT HISTORY OF THE EAST ; Egypt, Assyria, Babylonia, Media, Persia, Asia Minor, and Phœnicia. Woodcuts. Post 8vo. 7s. 6d.

———— GEOGRAPHY. By REV. W. L. BEVAN. Woodcuts. Post 8vo. 7s. 6d.

———— HISTORY OF GREECE ; from the Earliest Times to the Roman Conquest. By WM. SMITH, D.C.L. Woodcuts. Crown 8vo. 7s. 6d.
  ₊ Questions on the above Work, 12mo. 2s.

———— HISTORY OF ROME ; from the Earliest Times to the Establishment of the Empire. By DEAN LIDDELL. Woodcuts. Crown 8vo. 7s. 6d.

———— GIBBON'S Decline and Fall of the Roman Empire. Woodcuts. Post 8vo. 7s. 6d.

———— HALLAM'S HISTORY OF EUROPE during the Middle Ages. Post 8vo. 7s. 6d.

———— HALLAM'S HISTORY OF ENGLAND ; from the Accession of Henry VII. to the Death of George II. Post 8vo. 7s. 6d.

———— HUME'S History of England from the Invasion of Julius Cæsar to the Revolution in 1688. Continued down to 1868. Woodcuts. Post 8vo. 7s. 6d.
  ₊ Questions on the above Work, 12mo. 2s.

———— HISTORY OF FRANCE ; from the Earliest Times to the Establishment of the Second Empire, 1852. By REV. H. W. JERVIS. Woodcuts. Post 8vo. 7s. 6d.

———— ENGLISH LANGUAGE. By GEO. P. MARSH. Post 8vo. 7s. 6d.

———— LITERATURE. By T. B. SHAW, M.A. Post 8vo. 7s. 6d.

———— SPECIMENS of English Literature from the Chief Writers. By T. B. SHAW. Post 8vo. 7s. 6d.

———— MODERN GEOGRAPHY ; Mathematical, Physical, and Descriptive. By REV. W. L. BEVAN. Woodcuts. Post 8vo. 7s. 6d.

———— MORAL PHILOSOPHY. By WILLIAM FLEMING, D.D. Post 8vo. 7s. 6d.

———— BLACKSTONE'S Commentaries on the Laws of England. By R. MALCOLM KERR, LL.D. Post 8vo. 7s. 6d.

SUMNER'S (BISHOP) Life and Episcopate during 40 Years. By Rev. G. H. SUMNER. Portrait. 8vo. 14s.

STREET (G. E.) Gothic Architecture in Spain. From Personal Observations made during several Journeys. With Illustrations. Royal 8vo. 30s.

———— Italy, chiefly in Brick and Marble. With Notes of Tours in the North of Italy. With 60 Illustrations. Royal 8vo. 26s.

STANHOPE (EARL) England from the Reign of Queen Anne to the Peace of Versailles, 1701-83. *Library Edition.* 8 vols. 8vo. *Cabinet Edition*, 9 vols. Post 8vo. 5s. each.

————— British India, from its Origin to 1783. 8vo. 3s. 6d.

————— History of " Forty-Five." Post 8vo. 3s.

————— Historical and Critical Essays. Post 8vo. 3s. 6d.

————— French Retreat from Moscow, and other Essays. Post 8vo. 7s. 6d.

————— Life of Belisarius. Post 8vo. 10s. 6d.

————————— Condé. Post 8vo. 3s. 6d.

—————————William Pitt. Portraits. 4 Vols. 8vo. 24s. '

————— Miscellanies. 2 Vols. Post 8vo. 13s.

————— Story of Joan of Arc. Fcap. 8vo. 1s.

————— Addresses on Various Occasions. 16mo. 1s.

STYFFE (KNUTT). Strength of Iron and Steel. Plates. 8vo. 12s.

SOMERVILLE (MARY). Personal Recollections from Early Life to Old Age. With her Correspondence. Portrait. Crown 8vo. 12s.

————— Physical Geography. Portrait. Post 8vo. 9s.

————— Connexion of the Physical Sciences. Portrait. Post 8vo. 9s.

————— Molecular and Microscopic Science. Illustrations. 2 Vols. Post 8vo. 21s.

SOUTHEY (ROBERT). Lives of Bunyan and Cromwell. Post 8vo. 2s.

SWAINSON (CANON). Nicene and Apostles' Creeds; Their Literary History; together with some Account of " The Creed of St. Athanasius." 8vo. 16s.

SYBEL (VON) History of Europe during the French Revolution, 1789—1795. 4 Vols. 8vo. 48s.

SYMONDS' (REV. W.) Records of the Rocks; or Notes on the Geology, Natural History, and Antiquities of North and South Wales, Siluria, Devon, and Cornwall. With Illustrations. Crown 8vo. 12s.

THIBAUT'S (ANTOINE) Purity in Musical Art. Translated from the German. With a prefatory Memoir by W, H. Gladstone, M.P. Post 8vo. 7s. 6d.

THIELMANN (BARON) Journey through the Caucasus to Tabreez, Kurdistan, down the Tigris and Euphrates to Nineveh and Babylon, and across the Desert to Palmyra. Translated by CHAS. HENEAGE. Illustrations. 2 Vols. Post 8vo. 18s.

THOMS (W. J.). Longevity of Man; its Facts and its Fiction. Including Observations on the more Remarkable Instances. Post 8vo. 10s. 6d.

THOMSON (ARCHBISHOP). Lincoln's Inn Sermons. 8vo. 10s. 6d.

————— Life in the Light of God's Word. Post 8vo. 5s.

TITIAN'S LIFE AND TIMES. With some account of his Family, chiefly from new and unpublished Records. By CROWE and CAVALCASELLE. With Portrait and Illustrations. 2 Vols. 8vo. 42s.

TOCQUEVILLE'S State of Society in France before the Revolution, 1789, and on the Causes which led to that Event. Translated by HENRY REEVE. 8vo. 14s.

TOMLINSON (CHARLES); The Sonnet; Its Origin, Structure, and Place in Poetry. With translations from Dante, Petrarch &c. Post 8vo. 9s.

TOZER (Rev. H. F.) Highlands of Turkey, with Visits to Mounts
Ida, Athos, Olympus, and Pelion. 2 Vols. Crown 8vo. 24s.
———— Lectures on the Geography of Greece. Map. Post
8vo. 9s.

TRISTRAM (Canon) Great Sahara. Illustrations. Crown 8vo. 15s.
———————— Land of Moab; Travels and Discoveries on the East
Side of the Dead Sea and the Jordan. Illustrations. Crown 8vo. 15s.

TWISLETON (Edward). The Tongue not Essential to Speech,
with Illustrations of the Power of Speech in the case of the African
Confessors. Post 8vo. 6s.

TWISS' (Horace) Life of Lord Eldon. 2 Vols. Post 8vo. 21s.

TYLOR (E. B.) Early History of Mankind, and Development
of Civilization. 8vo. 12s.
———————— Primitive Culture; the Development of Mythology,
Philosophy, Religion, Art, and Custom. 2 Vols. 8vo. 24s.

VAMBERY (Arminius) Travels from Teheran across the Turko-
man Desert on the Eastern Shore of the Caspian. Illustrations. 8vo. 21s.

VAN LENNEP (Henry J.) Travels in Asia Minor. With
Illustrations of Biblical Literature, and Archæology. With Woodcuts.
2 Vols. Post 8vo. 24s.
———————— Modern Customs and Manners of Bible Lands,
In Illustration of Scripture. With Maps and 300 Illustrations.
2 Vols. 8vo. 21s.

WELLINGTON'S Despatches during his Campaigns in India,
Denmark, Portugal, Spain, the Low Countries, and France. Edited
by Colonel Gurwood. 8 Vols. 8vo. 20s. each.
———————— Supplementary Despatches, relating to India,
Ireland, Denmark, Spanish America, Spain, Portugal, France, Congress of Vienna, Waterloo and Paris. Edited by his Son. 14 Vols.
8vo. 20s. each. *₊* An Index. 8vo. 20s.
———————— Civil and Political Correspondence. Edited by
his Son. Vols. I. to V. 8vo. 20s. each.
———————— Vol. VI., relating to the Eastern Question of
1829. Russian Intrigues, Turkish Affairs, Treaty of Adrianople, &c.
8vo.
———————— Speeches in Parliament. 2 Vols. 8vo. 42s.

WHEELER (G.). Choice of a Dwelling; a Practical Handbook of
Useful Information on Building a House. Plans. Post 8vo. 7s. 6d.

WHITE (W. H.). Manual of Naval Architecture, for the use of
Officers of the R. N. and Mercantile Service, Yachtsmen, Shipowners,
and Shipbuilders. Illustrations. 8vo. 24s.

WILBERFORCE'S (Bishop) Life of William Wilberforce. Portrait.
Crown 8vo. 6s.

WILKINSON (Sir J. G.). Manners and Customs of the
Ancient Egyptians, their Private Life, Government, Laws, Arts, Manu-
factures, Religion, &c. A new edition, with additions by the late
Author. Edited by Samuel Birch, LL.D. Illustrations. 3 Vols. 8vo.
———————— Popular Account of the Ancient Egyptians. With
500 Woodcuts. 2 Vols. Post 8vo. 12s.

WOOD'S (Captain) Source of the Oxus. With the Geography
of the Valley of the Oxus. By Col. Yule. Map. 8vo. 12s.

WORDS OF HUMAN WISDOM. Collected and Arranged by
E. S. With a Preface by Canon Liddon. Fcap. 8vo. 3s. 6d

WORDSWORTH'S (Bishop) Athens and Attica. Plates. 8vo. 5s.

YULE'S (Colonel) Book of Marco Polo. Illustrated by the Light
of Oriental Writers and Modern Travels. With Maps and 80 Plates.
2 Vols. Medium 8vo. 63s.

BRADBURY, AGNEW & CO. PRINTERS, WHITEFRIARS